ICE

Stephon Stewart

ICE TM & © 2025 Stephon Stewart & Markosia Enterprises, Ltd. All Rights Reserved. Reproduction of any part of this work by any means without the written permission of the publisher is expressly forbidden. All names, characters and events in this publication are entirely fictional. Any resemblance to actual persons, living or dead is purely coincidental. Published by Markosia Enterprises, PO BOX 3477, Barnet, Hertfordshire, EN5 9HN.

FIRST PRINTING, February 2025.
Harry Markos, Director.

Paperback: ISBN 978-1-917459-47-1
eBook: ISBN 978-1-917459-48-8

Editor: Alexia Markos
Book design by: Ian Sharman
Cover illustration by: David Cousens

www.markosia.com

First Edition

For Civilization

ICE

The key to immortality is first living a life worth remembering.
Bruce Lee

ICE

SUBZERO

In the infinite universe, they navigate into the interstellar medium, drifting toward the troubled orbit of Earth. A world parched and plundered. Oil wars rage like hellfire across the scorched plains. Earth had surrendered its black gold, sparking conflicts that knew no bounds. The greed of nations, like a fevered madness, consumed all reason. As the wells ran dry and the last drops of natural resources were wrung from the Earth's veins, desperation spread its long shadow over humanity. Diplomacy withered in the heat of conflict. Seeds of destruction were distributed in the fertile soil of resentment.

Then came the cataclysm, born of man's foolishness and the uncontrollable hunger for power. Nuclear warheads, unleashed in a final gambit for dominion, blaze forth with a ferocity that defied the gods themselves. Mushroom clouds—handmaiden harbingers of the apocalypse—rise high into the heavens. Clouds of darkness eclipse the Sun's rays. In the aftermath of the ashen twilight, dense and suffocating clouds obscure the daylight. Earth entered an eternal darkness. The bitter winds, born of a *Nuclear Winter*'s icy breath, sweep across the decimated land, freezing all in their path. And so, in the wake of the *nuclear holocaust*, Earth descends into a modern-day Ice Age. Ice—soundless watchers of mortality—creep ever onward like a plague, devouring civilizations. An impact winter rages, draping the planet in frozen webs, extending across the globe, be it land or sea. Humanity fades into phantoms.

The world submits to the numbing grasp of a surreal frost. A *snowball Earth* emerged from the cosmic stage, an echo of Enceladus, that distant moon of Saturn; a subzero sphere entering the frozen grip of nature. The tales of these glacial epochs weave a narrative of primordial upheaval. In the hallowed halls of geological memory, ice ages stand as testament to the capricious whims of *Mother Nature*, a dance of elemental forces that shaped and reshaped the face of the Earth. From the frozen past of time, they emerge, each a chapter in the cyclical saga of planetary evolution. A celestial pause in the everlasting ballet of genesis and annihilation.

A feminine voice, soft yet weighted with her unease, speaks of the cataclysm that overthrew humanity. "It wasn't fire that destroyed us, but *ice*, sealing our fate in a tomb of frost," the voice declares. "In the frozen depths lies both the birthplace and graveyard of existence," it continues, a solemn reminder of nature's duality.

The notion of a cosmic architect, a divine force to shepherd us through the apocalypse, was a dying hope against Earth's frigid fury. Divine silence prevailed. Divine aid never came. All that remained was God witnessing our demise.

From the distant perch of a celestial onlooker, they witness the metamorphosis of our world. The ocean lay imprisoned, its waves frozen in time—a gargantuan range of crystalline stillness stretching to the horizon. The chilling truth of the Ice Age consumes the planet. Earth appears as a ghost of its former self. Where once the seas shimmered in hues of cerulean, now lies a frozen wasteland. Snowstorms rage, swirling and dancing amidst the sublime rocky landscape, pulverizing all in their path. A phantasmagorical dreamscape, where twilight skies merge effortlessly with auroras, creating an otherworldly radiance upon the frozen Earth.

The fossil fuel, oil, persists as a coveted treasure, a precious natural asset in a world depleted of its resources. Oil, once feared for its ability to poison Earth and corrupt the souls of mankind, had now become our messiah. Gazing out across the horizon, one could see the flickering lights of countless oil rigs with pumps churning, extracting the lifeblood of Earth from its subterranean underground. Black gold gushes forth against icy metal tubes, oozing into cylinders with a sluggish determination. Each drop a haunting reminder of a world long lost.

The woman's voice comes out soft with a hint of resignation as she speaks, her words carrying the truth long denied. "The substance that was destined to destroy us is now our savior," she says. "Oil has become the god of Earth."

"I've never seen daylight before." Wonder fills her voice. The Sun was whispered about in hushed tones among the remnants of humanity. It was a miracle from ages long past, something ancient civilizations would pray to. The star couldn't be seen through the dark cloud. A polar eclipse. Following the *Nuclear War*, our Sun unleashed a turbulent magnetic storm, ejecting a surging influx of coronal mass rays. This massive release of plasma and magnetic energy from the Sun's corona induced perturbations in solar wind, subsequently affecting Earth's magnetosphere and triggering geomagnetic storms. These disturbances wreaked havoc on satellite and radio communications, destabilized power grids, and rendered technology communication systems inert on a global scale. The celestial ghosts of auroras submerged the entire world. Haunted, phantasmagorical, and surreal green skylines.

In the subzero wastelands of a world plunged into perpetual winter, humanity waits, holding its breath for a miracle. As each day unfolds, the chilling event of the apocalypse increases, pushing humanity toward a mass extinction-level event. On the edge of entering the ranks of the Ordovician, Devonian, Permian, Triassic, and Cretaceous. In history, this event would be dubbed the Anthropocene.

* * *

ICE

A chilling scene unfolds as the coastline of a beach remains trapped in ice. Frost and sand meld into one, while the ocean freezes over under the subzero conditions. A realm where the essence of life is choked by the bitterness of cold. Empty barrels of oil scatter like discarded husks upon the snow-covered beach. Worldwide currency drifts aimlessly, a trifling echo of the bustling commerce that formerly defined the world's bustling markets. In today's reality, paper holds little value, and the abstract concept of money resembles nothing more than a game of Monopoly. Instead, the driving force is the pursuit of oil to maintain warmth.

Snow cascades from the heavens, blanketing the shoreline in a pristine cloud of white. Underneath this icy veil, the remnants of World War III are displayed across the battlefield. A violent tribute to the carnage that has unfolded. Millions of frozen soldiers—former champions of nations forgotten—lie entombed in the icy tomb of death. Immersed in the frozen hell, a lone figure moves. They experience a ceremonious purpose. It was a *monk*, wandering into a sea of desolation. He navigates the field of annihilation, his prayers a whispered plea for the souls lost to World War III. Despite the grimness of the task, he presses on, his dedication fueled by a mixture of patriotism and spirituality amidst despair. Silent blessings over the bodies—the only semblance of communion in a world devoid of life.

"Why must we fall into darkness that disaster brings?" the woman's voice echoes across the frozen warzone. Beneath the unearthly spectacle of bodies, a *woman* emerges, covered in the masquerade of a *welder's mask*, scarf, and winter trench coat. Her long hair billows in the biting wind, a wild tangle of strands blowing in the frigid gusts.

Omega was the woman's name—a hybrid of an interloper and warrior. She embodied the beginning and end of everything within humanity's consciousness.

SUBZERO

As Omega traverses the dystopian beach, her eyes fall upon an *hourglass* half-buried in the sand. After World War III, time lost all significance—once a fundamental aspect of civilization. Humans had always been preoccupied with the fear of wasting time. However, after the nuclear devastation, time became sluggish, creeping along like a snail in an increasingly inhospitable environment.

The sand moves in a peculiar manner, oscillating back and forth instead of following a singular direction. Mesmerized, Omega watches as sand defies the laws of physics, swirling in a paradoxical dance of ebbs and flows. A reflection of the chaotic world surrounding her. Eerie silence envelops Omega as her intense eyes fall upon a surreal sight. A *child shadow* appears as a ghostly spirit, haunting the shoreline, their presence a dream of lives once lived. The child shadow wanders along the coast until it notices Omega watching.

The child shadow then vanishes into the ether, leaving behind only the chill of their absence. Omega's fingers tremble, and she releases her grip on the hourglass. Realization crashes down as the hourglass falls. Her soul sinks; the disappearance of the child shadow brought her sadness. The sands of time continue to flow erratically, moving both up and down, the vessel submerged in the snow.

The monk continues his duty, bestowing blessings upon the fallen. Twilight looms and auroras crest the horizon, the vivid lights beaming on the snowy coast. Shaken from the odd anomaly, Omega ventures forward, undeterred by the arctic conditions and eerie vision of the child shadow. She trudges toward the frozen expanse of the ocean, her steps swallowed by the deep snow.

From the serene skyline, a cataclysm unfurls its dark wings. Violence from Hell unleashes, a *nuclear bomb* erupting across the horizon, rending the sky asunder under its infernal might. A colossal mushroom cloud rises, a titan's breath exhaled in fury—a testament to the arrogance of mankind and the curse of his creations. It hangs in the firmament like a god's wrath, an ominous cloud upon the land, blocking out the aurora's glow. The dark cloud looms, swallowing all light whole. This polar eclipse was the darkness of death, akin to a black hole engulfing light. It created a void in the sky where nothing shined bright.

A sonic boom follows thunderous shock waves. The Earth convulses beneath the weight of the detonation, its foundation shaken by violent tremors. Ice fractures atop the ocean's surface. Then, as if nature herself rebels against such hubris, a *gravitational* event takes hold, twisting the laws of the cosmos. Repulsion and attraction forces collide in a bombardment of power. Caught in the maelstrom, Omega becomes a pawn in this cosmic struggle. Lifted and thrusted by forces beyond comprehension, she is but a mere vessel tossed into the tempestuous currents. Tossed through the sky by a brutal force, Omega had lost all control. Gravity pulls her over the ocean. She is dropped and hurled into the freezing ocean, her body swallowed.

The impact reverberates through her being as she succumbs to the subzero temperatures. She sinks, descending into the icy abyss. Lost and forgotten. Above, the world fades into the inferno's fury. That day marked a permanent change in the world. *Nuclear War* dominated without rival. Snowflakes swirl faster and faster, the world disappearing into the pristine white.

* * *

Inside the sterile confines of the interrogation chamber, an orange glow emanates from the harsh lights above. The snow world had disappeared, replaced by an inferno-like room, equally confining as another form of purgatory. Palls of orange light loom over the room. Empty oxygen tanks litter the floor. A vestige of what humanity needed during the nuclear fallout due to radiation. Oddly, books were disregarded and scattered, their pages fluttering in the stale air. Canned food items piled haphazardly. It was a room that felt like a bunker from the aftermath of a world war.

Omega sits bound to a cold steel chair, her hands and feet shackled and her weathered trench coat bearing the scars of countless trials endured. A cyclical cycle. The room exuded an aura of endured journeys. A black mask obscures her features, veiling her identity as she teeters on the edge of consciousness. Omega was trapped in limbo between wakefulness and sleep. Suddenly, a violent tremor shakes the room to its core, sending cans clattering and books tumbling. An oxygen canister careens across the floor, its path erratic as it crashes against the walls. As swiftly as it began, the tremor subsides, leaving behind silent tension. Omega jolts awake from her dreams, her concerns heightened.

A voice breaks through the silence, its words a chilling echo of the horrors that lurk beyond. "The world has fallen into a haunting silence, gripped by the democide against its own citizens... The magnitude of the casualties is unfathomable... billions of lives lost."

Her urgency hardens, and she sheds her black mask, revealing a face hardened by determination. An EEG cap adorns her head, its intricate sensors poised to unlock secrets buried in her mind. Something or someone seemed to be observing her dream state. Seduced into a trance-like state, her thoughts continue to drift amidst the currents of uncertainty. Omega's eyes fixate on a bizarre sight before her: the hourglass from her dream was perched upon the table. With each passing moment, grains of sand cascade through the narrow passage, their descent accompanied by a gentle, rhythmic whisper.

Omega pondered the whimsical nature of time. It was a principle one could never get ahead of—the foundation upon which all species relied. Humans, animals, and creatures alike. In reality, it was an absolute, governed by the laws of physics. In this fantastical world, Omega possessed the key to unlocking the truth. It was buried in her psyche, hidden from herself. The other world held the answer, and Omega was consumed, having a burning desire to return. She closed her eyes and drifted off into a state of unconsciousness, slipping away into her dream state.

* * *

In an alternate dreamscape, ash flakes now replace the snowflakes. The aftermath of the nuclear bomb was evident. Humanity had pressed the button. Reversing the flow of time remained a fantasy beyond even the abilities of magicians to conjure. Each delicate ash flake descending was burdened by sadness. The snowy beach was blanketed in ash, as if a global cremation event had taken place. Nature, indifferent to civilization or humanity, continued to play out its symphony. The rhythmic cadence of waves crashing upon the shore persisted. Earth had witnessed it all, and this time was no exception. Species came and went across epochs, as they had since the dawn of time.

From the veils of swirling ash, an *adult Shadow* emerges—a figure taller and more imposing than its childlike predecessor. Its inky form strides toward a rowboat, nestled upon the snowy coastline. An entity embarking on a serious mission. The Shadow moved urgently, as though a ticking time bomb were about to explode. The wood of the rowboat displayed the marks of countless voyages, not the sturdiest but reliable enough to endure. Reality and imagination, the tangible and ethereal, blend into obscurity. Snowflakes and ash flakes obscure perception, blotting out the Shadow as it begins pushing the rowboat into the ocean.

* * *

Majestic ice-covered ancient mountains loom across the horizon, their peaks adorned with icy caps—an enduring subzero environment of nature; their rocky brown slopes overwhelmed by the Arctic tundra. Immersed in this winter wonderland, an isolated *cabin* stands defiantly. Wisps of chimney smoke curl into the frigid air, a faint beacon of warmth in the ice world. Icicles dangle like crystalline daggers outside the frost-encrusted window and logs. The cabin was insulated against freezing temperatures.

A crackling fireplace bathes the room in an apricot light. Shadows fluidly dance across the worn wooden floor from the strong flames. Omega stirs from a slumber on the couch, her makeshift bed. Sitting upright, her eyes become ensnared by the dance of flames, their hungry tongues licking at the logs. Her soulful eyes watch a glowing jar of oil, its ebony contents pulsating. A mystical radiance. A glass container, slender and transparent, held the dark and viscous substance, shimmering an ethereal sheen. Oil swirls languidly, as if possessed by a hypnotic spell. Its earthy aroma remained lingering in the air like a whispered promise of vitality. Her subconscious contained a respect for truthfulness. She would always delve into the words of her mind. Isolation became Omega's constant companion, driving her to converse with herself more frequently than any other soul. In these frigid, apocalyptic times, she found peace in the company of her own thoughts, becoming her own confidante.

In the recesses of her mind, a whispered mantra echoes, barely audible against the crackle of flames and the howl of wind outside. "I've seen the depths humans will sink to in the game of survival," she mutters, her voice carrying the weight of years spent traversing the wasteland of the human soul. "A human's desperation knows no bounds when faced with the ghost of their own mortality." Her eyes, like wayward wanderers, lose themselves in the dazzling dance of the flames.

* * *

Omega, a child of eight, navigates the eerie labyrinth of snow-laden trees, her small form swallowed by the oppressive darkness of the night. Peering cautiously over the edge of a cliff, she beholds a gang of roughnecks toiling tirelessly upon an oil derrick, their labor illuminated by the glow of torches. Beyond them, a river of oil flows ominously, a liquid serpent winding its way through the freezing landscape.

Overwhelmed by curiosity, she takes hesitant steps forward. Omega edges nearer to the precipice, her steps unsure on the icy, perilous ground. In an instant, the slick ground gives way beneath her, and she slips and stumbles uncontrollably down the steep incline. The little girl glides like a sled, gathering momentum down the icy slope.

Roughnecks, alerted by the commotion, reach out in vain as Omega hurtles toward the inky abyss below, where the oily river awaits. She is swept into the current of oil.

Engulfed by the viscous blackness, Omega struggles against the powerful current, desperately seeking escape from the slick surface. The thick, molasses-like fossil fuel was a formidable obstacle for any mortal to escape—nothing but darkness flowing. Omega bobs up and down like a buoy in the river, until she manages to cling to the last vestiges of hope, her tiny hands grasping for anything to anchor her to life. Then, like a miracle rising from the heavens, a welder's mask emerges from the swirling oil, a messenger of salvation in the chaos. Omega seizes upon it, her gloved fingers clutching the cold metal as she is swept away by the unforgiving current; her journey through the nightmarish river only just beginning.

* * *

On the cliff of the ice-crowned peak, Omega sways in a weathered rocking chair, her silhouette etched against the stark backdrop of the Arctic expanse—an image of superlunary magnificence. Veiny auroras beeline across the sky, yet amidst this tranquil panorama, the horizon unleashes a harrowing spectacle: Atomic bombs erupt in violent bursts over the frozen ocean, cracking the ice. Thunderous concussions. Radiation permeates every corner. Molecules of toxicity from atomic weapons contaminate the atmosphere. As the radioactive fallout descends, its insidious grasp spread, taking lives from the devastation brought on by the nuclear bomb. Omega gazes upon the chaos with a stoic expression, obscured behind the cold steel of the welder's mask—her shield amidst World War III. An oxygen tank clings to her back, and the precious air from the tank combats the radiation, enabling Omega to breathe.

Omega swings an axe. Her movements carry extreme intensity, each strike echoing through the subzero woods. The blade meets the asteroid embedded in the ground, shattering it with a resounding crack from the impact. A dark, thick substance oozes from the fractured surface, pooling at Omega's feet. She stares hypnotically at the oil, recognizing it as her creator, the substance that sculpted her into the woman she had become. Memories of her oil encounter flood her psyche, a harrowing moment etched into her soul, forever altering her. Omega blinks hard, refocusing herself.

She gathers broken pieces of the asteroid, tossing them into a wheelbarrow. Labor was grueling, but Omega was resilient. A warrior gifted having formidable strength, possessing a power that even the ancient gods would admire. The interloper presses on through the snow, regulating her breathing, endeavoring to conserve every precious ounce of oxygen from her tank in the frigid air. She pushes the wheelbarrow carrying the asteroid fragments toward her cabin.

Inside the log cabin, Omega empties the jar of oil onto the firewood, the syrupy liquid seeping into the cracks and crevices. Oil had become the new gold, the new water, the new currency in this frozen world. To ward off the subzero temperatures, this fossil fuel held unparalleled significance. In these times, its importance remained akin to the legendary holy grail of immortality. Without oil, there was no life. She strikes a match, igniting the oil-soaked logs. A burst of flames grows in magnitude.

Omega warms her hands by the hearth's glow. "That's the last of you," she murmurs, her voice barely audible over the crackling fire. Exhaling a sigh, she tosses the empty jar into the flames, watching as it disappeared amidst the hungry blaze.

Her moment of serenity was short-lived. Distant sounds of gunfire began to echo through the stillness of the arctic world. Omega's heart quickens as she recognizes the unmistakable sound, a grim reminder of the dangers that lurk beyond the safety of her refuge. Instinctively, Omega finds cover behind a nearby couch as bullets tear through the walls of the cabin, sending splinters of wood flying through the air. Through the window, she catches sight of soldiers moving through the snow.

Her cabin remained trapped in battleground territory of the last great war of them all—the war for oil. In this part of the world, every inch of land was fiercely contested, making the conflicts of the past world wars pale in comparison. Omega retrieves a key and unlocks a hatch concealed beneath a trapdoor, leading underground. She swiftly unlatches the trapdoor and down descends a ladder. Before her lies an escape passageway, where an underground tunnel awaits. The front door shudders under the assault from above, bullets punctuating throughout the cabin with their echoes relentlessly striking the wooden walls. Omega slams the hatch shut, sealing herself in the safety of the underground.

In the subterranean labyrinth, Omega quickly picks up her pace. Urgency floods her being as the stone corridor guides her away from the ambush. She puts on her *welder mask*, its face a heroic silhouette against the candlelight. She plunges into the labyrinthine. The wrath above ground swells through the world with an ominous intensity, like a harbinger of death that awaited on the surface. War had become the sole familiarity in the soul of humankind, a commodity that had surfaced since the days of hunter-gatherers and would persist until the end of time.

Omega reaches the end of the corridor and grapples with another hatch, a gateway between the subterranean shadows and the frigid surface. As she breaches the surface into the twilight, an abrupt disruption shatters her flight; a Russian soldier's hand grabs her ankle, seeking to drag her back into the subterranean world from whence she came. Quickly, Omega's boot meets the Russian soldier's jaw. With a brief moment of defiance, he tumbles back into the abyss below. But even as she breaks free, her eyes catch sight of her cabin breached—her home under siege in the distance. Time was of the essence, and she could not afford to waste a single moment.

Across the snow clearing, a figure emerges. An Iraqi soldier charges straight for Omega, rifle aimed directly at her as he runs like a madman. She races toward the shelter of a majestic *forest*, attempting to escape the storm of conflict. A bullet pierces the frozen air, shattering an ice-covered evergreen tree into crystalline shards. Omega, startled, instinctively ducks and hides behind a tree. She watches as the Iraqi soldier's boots slip on the treacherous ice, sending him crashing hard to the ground. She seizes the fallen rifle and unleashes a single bullet upon her assailant, his life then extinguished in a haze. Danger continues to permeate the area as the crack of another gunshot pierces the frostbitten air, grazing perilously close to Omega's head. Adversaries close in rapidly and she flees into the forest. Omega moves, resembling the cautious grace of a shadow, slipping between the gnarled trunks and twisted branches, a ghost in the wintry landscape. A specimen of athletic endurance—vibrant, a pinnacle of physical prowess. She skirts the edges of visibility in the monstrous sea of white.

Emerging into a twilight clearing, surreal auroras illuminate the sky. Omega's gaze falls upon the glowing lights of a distant village. The picturesque region resembled a scene from Van Gogh's infamous painting *Starry Night*, showcasing its dreamy landscape and ethereal beauty. Yet even as she approaches this semblance of civilization, an uneasy tension hangs in the air, the quietness broken by the distant howl of the wind and the whispered secrets of the arctic forest.

Inside the village, rows of igloos and their icy forms embrace the frozen wasteland. A solitary *oil derrick* pumps tirelessly. Bundled in layers of clothing and equipped with oxygen tanks to brave the freezing weather, Inuit stand in line, each clutching a bucket in hand. The Inuit were indigenous peoples inhabiting the Arctic regions. Renowned for their unique culture and survival skills in extreme conditions, they rely on hunting, fishing, and gathering for food whilst embodying a connection and a rich heritage of oral traditions. Each bucket was brimmed, containing a plentiful amount of oil, marking a jackpot discovery for them. This was their land, and they knew exactly how to live off of it.

Omega observes the tranquil surroundings. Despite the chaos of the world war, this group seems unaffected, maintaining a serene existence. Impressed by their resilience, Omega finds solace in watching their simple way of life, if only for a moment, until her eyes falls upon the horizon, where the ominous silhouette of Chinese soldiers advance, their body language displaying ruthless intent.

A shrill wail of sirens pierces the air; the clash erupts in a frenzy of violence. Inuit armed with flamethrowers charge forth to meet the onslaught. Flames begin to lick at the frost as bullets tear through flesh and bone, leaving a trail of carnage. Inuit and Chinese soldiers battle head-on for the capture of the oil derrick. A ferocious battle ensues, reminiscent of the Civil War in America from years past. Despite facing supremely technologically advanced Chinese soldiers, the Inuit prove themselves formidable warriors, refusing to yield without putting up a fierce fight.

Omega finds herself entangled in the brutal dance of survival. She makes a desperate dash, fleeing from both sides of the conflict. Surrounded from all angles, Omega must navigate her way through the battleground, weaving between combatants in order to escape unscathed. The cacophony of battle reaches its crescendo, and Omega's world narrows to a singular point of focus. Immersed in the gauntlet of war, she dodges and weaves through predicaments. The interloper has the agility of a wild animal evading its predators. Humanity's darkest instincts reign supreme. Violence ultimately remains entrenched in the psyche of human consciousness, with an enduring battle persisting across epochs and among all species.

The Chinese soldiers advance, a relentless force of conquest as they seize control of the oil derrick. The surviving Inuit, their spirits battered but not broken, clutch buckets of precious oil in a desperate bid for escape. However, before they can vanish into the safety of the forest, gunfire rattles off, a cruel reminder of the ever-present specter of death. They fall, their bodies crumpling to the frozen tundra, their own blood and spilled oil intermixing to create a nightmare portrait. Oil and blood intermingle in the pristine purity of the snow. Red and black, a blend of crimson and darkness—the oil wars have once more spilled blood.

Omega observes the chaos around her as she continues sprinting away from the action, flanked by numerous Inuit. Periodically, members of their group are gunned down from above. Omega looks skyward and notices a military drone hovering ominously overhead.

In the boundless reaches of the sky, *automated drones* unleash a symphony of mechanical fury, their accurate gunfire reverberating through the tumultuous chaos below, a chilling echo of mankind's struggle for dominance. Inuit scramble for shelter inside icy domiciles, but there's no refuge in this frozen warzone.

Ice groans and fractures, yielding to the assault of the drones, sleek and merciless. They continue to glide with an eerie precision through the arctic air, dealing death; drones and their mechanical indifference held no favorites. Destruction ensues as the village becomes decimated. Ice chunks explode, sending crystalline shrapnel in all directions, rendering any semblance of cover futile. And then, during the chaos, the oil derrick is struck. The impact is catastrophic. Metal screams as it gives way to flames, the inferno billowing into the sky. Pipes rupture, spewing forth torrents of oil that ignite upon contact, raining down like liquid fire.

A gesture of surrender emerges and a few brave souls, their spirits broken, raise a white flag in a futile plea for mercy, but mercy is a foreign concept of war. Volley fire ensues from the Chinese soldiers, stoic and showing no hesitation as they execute their grim duty. No prisoners taken. In this nightmare reality, survival is a privilege reserved only for the strongest, the most ruthless.

The overbearing gunfire echoed like the tolling of an unholy bell, a requiem signaling death's approach. Omega, her breath maintaining impressive endurance, continues dashing toward the edge of the clearing. She plunges headlong into the abyss of a ravine, the icy ground biting at her body as she hurtles downward. She skids across the frozen surface with a blur of motion. Omega hurtles down the icy slope, the distant scene resembling an exhilarating sled sliding down jagged slopes. Upon reaching the bottom, she bursts into a frenzied sprint, the distant sound of gunshots chasing her like the pursuit of fate. Through the snow-covered forest she races, the sporadic gunfire punctuating the icy silence. With each evasive maneuver, she bolts forward. Every breath felt through her oxygen tank felt like shards of glass, a reminder of the unforgiving radiation. Omega dared not remove her oxygen mask, knowing that exposure would claim her soul. Then, without warning, Omega stumbles into a concealed booby trap. Her leg becomes entangled in a rope, and she is suddenly hoisted into the air, swinging wildly before colliding headfirst into a tree. Darkness envelopes her as she fades into unconsciousness.

* * *

Transported again into the interrogation room, Omega is ensnared by a surreal vision, only to wrench herself back to reality. Her mind spoke to herself, "You've been here before." The tone was arcane. "But we're not done yet." She brushes aside the familiar atmosphere, experiencing a strong feeling of déjà vu. Her eyes meet *Alpha*, a towering presence. A marvel of artificial intelligence on the brink of its evolutionary zenith. The supercomputer stands like a monolithic god, its towering frame reaching toward the heavens. Tall and thick, its sleek, obsidian form exudes an austere elegance, an imposing aura of authority. Its surface, polished to a mirror-like sheen, reflects the ambient light, and rows of blinking lights adorn its façade, resembling a constellation of stars against the backdrop of its dark, metallic exterior. Despite its formidable size, there was grace in its design, by the craftsmanship of its creators. It hummed a hushed power, and one couldn't help but feel reverence in its quintessence. A colossus of knowledge, embodying the singularity of computation, rivaling human intelligence. Throughout the ages, humanity had been captivated by the achievement of computational mastery. Human behavior was on par. Against all odds, this entity had realized that ambition. Our species were gods for artificial intelligence.

Alpha's voice, a cold echo, pierces the silence. "Did you have the dream again?"

Omega remains fixated on the enigmatic figure. The supercomputer held a secret. Its words registered as each syllable carried an ominous weight that sent a shiver down Omega's spine.

She hesitates, torn between the compulsion to speak her truth and the fear of what it might entail. "Which one?" she finally whispers, her voice barely audible against the backdrop of silence.

Alpha's response was immediate, devoid of emotion and an unsettling fact. "The apocalypse," it intones, its metallic voice resonating an otherworldly clarity.

Omega's breath catches in her throat, her mind racing to recall the haunting images that had plagued her subconscious. The memory floods back, piercing the veil of her consciousness.

Alpha's voice reverberates. "Dreams contain secrets," its metallic tones continue resonating. "They predict futures."

Omega couldn't shake the feeling that her dreams held far more significance than she had ever dared to imagine. Perhaps, she realized, they were not merely the product of her subconscious mind, but harbingers of events yet to come. She couldn't help but wonder what secrets her dreams held, and what futures they might foretell. As she pondered the implications of Alpha's words, uneasiness settled over her.

"I found myself alone," she murmurs, her voice trembling. "No souls, just the ocean…" As the words fall from her lips, Omega feels a chill settle over her. Father Time had crept into the room. The sensation of death had always seemed like a descent into an inward collapse for Omega. She knew that the dream was more than just a figment of her imagination—it was a prophecy, a warning of things yet to come. Omega recounts the dream as the lights on her brain cap flicker, a visual representation of the heightened activity in her mind. The surreal imagery of her subconscious was vivid, each detail etched an eerie clarity.

Across the room, Alpha observes Omega intently, its artificial gaze fixed upon her; an unyielding focus from the artificial intelligence system. It watches as Omega's consciousness seemed to wane, her gaze drawn to the hypnotic movement of the hourglass perched nearby. The sands of time slip away, and Omega's awareness gradually ebbs, surrendering to the alluring embrace of her dream world. A final flicker of consciousness and she slips into the state of unconsciousness, her mind enveloped once more by the enigmatic landscapes of her imagination.

* * *

Sirens wail in the distance, their urgent cries piercing through the dense mist that enveloped the lecture hall. Students fall to their knees, donning gas masks and seeking safety beneath their desks; a nod to bygone years when students would diligently rehearse these safety measures during school. In the era marked by the emergence of nuclear bombs in the collective consciousness of humanity, these procedures were intended to guide civilization in following protocol in the event of a nuclear blast. However, little did they realize at the time that these cautionary steps would ultimately offer no refuge. Once a nuclear bomb was launched, no safe haven remained above ground for humankind. At the front of the lecture hall, a chalkboard loomed, its surface adorned. Sketches and equations of a *Nuclear Fusion Reactor* written out in a myriad of ways from white chalk. The complexity was indeed impressive; to date, it was humanity's greatest weapon.

In the back row, Omega sits alone, aurora lights filtering through the windows. She observes the students huddled motionless under their desks, the scene presenting an eerie stillness that felt unsettling. The students seemed oblivious to Omega. From their perspective, she might as well have been an invisible woman. They remain frozen in time, trapped in a moment suspended by fear. Omega continues to wear her welder mask, the steady sound of breathing echoing softly from her oxygen tank. It was the soul of her essence in this domain.

Alpha emerges near the chalkboard, assuming the role of a professor. The supercomputer presides over the classroom like a world leader. Sirens fall silent as an eerie calm descends upon the room.

Sensing the shift in the atmosphere, Omega reaches up, her fingers grazing the cold surface of her mask and slowly peeling it away. Omega's voice cuts through the air, "This project doesn't make sense."

Alpha's response is measured, its words holding a notion of conviction. "It will save our planet. Nuclear fusion will allow humans to scale back energy consumption."

Omega's response comes swift and cynical, a bitter truth laid bare. "Corporations will never allow that." From an early age, Omega had been keenly aware of the harsh reality of humanity. Throughout history, greed and power have consistently exerted dominance over the world. She understood that in reality, only a small fraction of individuals, perhaps a mere hundred, held the reins of global influence, their bottom line always trumping the welfare of ordinary citizens.

Alpha's voice is skeptical as he speaks. "A bit pessimistic, wouldn't you say?"

Omega's words held a logical viewpoint, a reflection of being well-read in these political matters. "What makes for a good government, makes for a bad government." Omega gestures toward the diagram of the *Nuclear Fusion Reactor*.

Alpha stays mute, immersed in its mechanical operations, a symphony of whirring machinery and scrolling algorithms.

"Does mankind scare you?" she asks, her eyes awaiting Alpha.

Humanity had long yearned for artificial intelligence to guide them into euphoria. However, the flaw in this dream lay in the dual nature of artificial intelligence. It had the capacity to bring out both the best and the worst in humans. Ultimately, artificial intelligence functioned as a mirror, reflecting back our own image to ourselves, compelling us to engage in introspection.

Alpha's response carries a calm assurance, its words resonating hope. "I believe the majority of them want to help this planet," it asserts, its voice a steady hum.

A subtle criticism veils in Omega's cadence. "You should read more history," she remarks, her tone hinting at the knowledge on human behavior she possessed. Omega rises from her seat, her departure a silent proclamation of independence. She makes her way down the stairs, passing by numerous students who remained huddled under their desks, bracing themselves for whatever may come. Her hand reaches for the doorknob, and as the door swings open, Omega steps into the unknown, leaving behind the enigmatic Alpha and the perplexing project that had held humans captive.

* * *

In a different realm, Omega finds herself transfixed by the screen where the infinite surge of stock values consumes her eyes. The chamber was completely devoid of life, with the absence of the usual human energy. No traders or tycoons, only the abstract numbers orchestrating the stock exchange's fate. Abruptly, the radiant numbers dissolve into the ominous zero, a harbinger of nothingness and eternity. The numbers kept enveloping her in darkness as the symbols of wealth vanished into the abyss. An intense ringing of the end-of-day bell echoed, signaling a foreboding conclusion. This sound was once associated with and connected to wealth eons ago, in a society where currency held the most coveted position of all. Now, it was white noise; money had lost its value long ago, at the peak of the last great war of all time. World War III was simply fought over oil, which equated to money, but it was also a battle for a commodity that only brought comfort. Money, after all, was an abstract concept, and in the end, natural resources were the true treasures of nature.

In a sudden twist, the cautionary tales of a room destined for destruction transformed into a bewildering environment. Once motionless, the walls now seemed to bear down on Omega. A sinister intent, closing in relentlessly. They collapsed inward, signaling a deadly trap. This philosophical implication was reminiscent of something Sigmund Freud himself might ponder, suggesting that the collapsing walls were nothing more than a metaphorical soliloquy.

Omega was trapped, suffocating beneath their advance, panic rising as her escape eludes her grasp. As Omega faces her impending demise, she can't shake the feeling that she would fade into obscurity, becoming nothing more than a ghost, forgotten forever. For as long as she could remember, the notion of legacy had lingered in Omega's mind. It was a foreign concept, straying into the specter of ego. Throughout history, egos had risen and fallen, but she felt different. To her, Earth was akin to a toilet bowl, and every century, everything was flushed away, with only the best ideas, philosophies, and inventions hopefully remaining. These principles were the only things humanity ultimately had any control over. Over time, the best creations endure, rising above the transient nature of existence to leave a lasting impact on humanity.

In the tightening grip of the enclosing walls, she awaits the impending doom. She holds her breath and clenches her muscles as she closes her eyes, longing for a reality where her existence could transcend the confines of mortality. The thought of facing death today, or ever, was unbearable to Omega. Immortality had always been her greatest desire, a longing that consumed her throughout her life. As the walls close in around her, inching ever closer, her focus intensifies. Refusing to accept her fate of departure, Omega opens her eyes wide, refusing to succumb to the catastrophe.

* * *

No longer confined to the stock room, Omega had escaped the clutches of closure. An expansive video arena encompasses Omega. Her eyeballs sweep across the room, taking in the peculiar sight of monitors seamlessly embedded into the walls. The monitors illuminate one by one in a remarkable display of perfect symmetry. Screens flicker to life, revealing a prehistoric world with diverse and magnificent species. Dinosaurs roam the land, ancient marine creatures rule the oceans, and lush forests stretch as far as infinity. It represents a time when life flourished in its grandest forms. But then, the scene dramatically changes, and a cataclysmic event arrives. An asteroid hurtles toward

Earth, triggering a wave of destruction that wipes out the dinosaurs. Evolution is disrupted, leaving a void in the web of existence.

Monitors continue their symphony of illumination, and another image appears, divulging the skeletal remains of Lucy, the renowned first human ancestor. Lucy emerged as a pivotal figure in the story of our origins. She walked the ancient African savannah over three million years ago—a reminder of our shared origins and the remarkable journey of human evolution. The images progress, depicting subsequent periods of ice ages, volcanic eruptions, and shifts in climate patterns, driving species to the brink of annihilation and leaving behind fragments of what once was. Earth was in a perpetual state of flux, where change was the only constant.

In swift succession, the scene shifts to a harrowing image of the African plains, marred by the devastating consequences of fossil fuel drilling. Oil became the new gold rush, driving humanity to scour the globe. Ecosystems succumbed to destruction, leaving behind a trail of bleakness. The plight of safari animals, slaughtered for profit, unfolds before Omega's eyes, evoking sadness. The monitors display the impact of human activities. Deforestation and pollution accelerated the decline of countless species. Human actions on the natural world becomes increasingly evident in the unfolding tragedy of animals. Modern-day comforts required humanity to embellish survival of the fittest, emerging from the ashes of decay. Ultimately, it was human beings who stood at the intersection of these opposing forces, navigating the complexities of progress and survival in an ever-changing world.

Images continue to emerge, bringing forth a sobering realization as technology and energy companies dominate the world stage. Their influence and control extend far and wide, shaping the course of societies and economies. In the following image, the troubling issue of overpopulation takes center stage. Crowded cities, strained resources, and a planet pushed to its limits confront Omega. The magnitude of human consumption and its impact on Earth was a haunting chronicle of ecological upheaval.

Omega walks closer to the illuminated monitors. A calamitous event narrates before her eyes. In a blinding burst of light and a worldwide shattering explosion, a *nuclear bomb* detonates, its devastating power captured by the monitors in a surreal and otherworldly manner. Explosions emanate from the screens, engulfing the room in an ethereal glow. *Doomsday on Earth. End times had arrived.* Phrases echoed throughout history, resonating across generations. The sheer force of the blast causes the lights to flicker and fade, plunging the space into darkness.

A faint sound of creaking doors breaks the quietness. Omega walks toward the source of the noise, drawn by its intrigue. Before her, she discovers a pair of grand wooden theater doors. Behind the edges of the frame, a warm light radiated welcomingly. Bravery was a gift that Omega possessed from a young age. As a little girl, she always had an adventurous nature, fearlessly exploring the world around her. She pushes the door open, unveiling another reality in the rabbit hole of metaphysical experience.

* * *

Omega's strides resound through a labyrinthine corridor, each step forward entering the suffocating tunnel. A chilling laughter echoes from the distant reaches, a macabre melody. Undeterred, Omega presses on, drawn toward the source of the unsettling sound. The unusual laugh best resembled the sounds of monsters and demons, evoking images of afterworld soundscapes and eternal damnation of souls. Echoes of joker vibrations linger throughout the space, encompassing and bouncing off the walls. It seemed as though laughter held the significance of predatory proportions. The atmosphere was venomous, as if searching to sink its fangs into the next victim. The laughter grows louder, possessed and harboring a mischievous intent.

Before Omega looms a massive vault door. It resembled a bank safe carrying secrets long concealed, its contents waiting to be unlocked. In this world of deception, the game was about unlocking secrets. Omega's sturdy hands grip the wheel, anchoring the vault door as she turns it clockwise. With creaking ancient hinges, the door swings wide, exhaling a stale breath that whispers of lurking terrors.

The Broadway theater pulses a nostalgic energy. Ghosts of productions from its past repertoire were no longer present. The stage resembled a modern-day Greek tragedy, where entertainment had long ago died. Cobwebs drape the stage, engulfing everything and taking away the lights and the fading spotlight. Stories played a pivotal role in shaping the philosophical mindset of humanity—ancient folk tales, gossip spread onto religion, initiating a paradigm shift in civilization. People looked up at the sky, believing they could see the secrets of God unfold upon the Earth. The concept of a creator who watched over humanity emerged on stages like these in years past. However, all of this came to a crumbling halt during the *Nuclear Winter* apocalypse. Even if God themselves did exist, they wouldn't possess the power to reverse the mindset of human consciousness. The divine architect never had the capability of eradicating evil from the subconscious mind.

Dust motes twirl in the dainty light that dares to infiltrate the eerie noise. Laughter persists, an eternal echo that reverberates through the vacant auditorium, a chorus of disquiet in the dark heart of the theater. It was as if humanity was mocking its own downfall. Unbroken by the unsettling ambiance, Omega treads cautiously toward the vacant stage. Her gaze sweeps the auditorium, falling upon the impassive figures that inhabit the seats, their stoic faces unmoved by her presence. Motionless, they remained seated with a void of expression, exposing inscrutable stares that were piercing the theater. Emotions in entertainment had remained stale for a long time. The death of the arts served as another catalyst for World War III. For years, artists had warned about the doomsday event, but their pleas fell on deaf ears, ignored amidst the clamor of escalating tensions.

Driven by a primal longing for connection, Omega claps her hands, a futile gesture of outreach, begging for a response, but her plea for acknowledgment remains unanswered. The motionless figures remain unresponsive, frozen in the shadows.

Light slices through darkness. A spotlight's unforgiving glow strikes upon a mundane seat, revealing an odd situation. Omega beholds a row of *mannequins*, their tranquil forms eerily human-like yet unnervingly lifeless. Strings dangle from their rigid frames, tethering them to an unseen force; puppets in a scary pantomime. Symbolism of world leaders tugging at the heart of civilization. Since Mesopotamian times, mankind had reigned over their kingdom of peasants, wielding power and influence over the ages. Laughter swells, mocking and derisive, a cruel symphony that pierces the silence. Haunting sounds play out as the strings quiver, stirred by an invisible hand, orchestrating a dance of manipulation. Humans were puppets, their strings manipulated by the unseen hand of elitist power, a divine force shaping their destinies.

Omega sweeps the theater, seeking escape from the unearthly conditions. A metal door illuminated by the soft glow of an *exit sign* catches her eye. She yearned to depart, recognizing that there was nothing here for her except the truth of who held power over society. It served as a reminder of who truly pulled the strings. Omega sprints, taking frantic steps before she grasps the door handle and thrusts it open. The metal door swings wide, ushering Omega into the threshold of a vortex, spiraling out of control. It resembles a black hole expanding and contracting, pulsating sheer power, devouring anything it touches. Magically, the anomaly existed against the backdrop of an arctic skyline, devouring clouds and snow. It stood as a harbinger of both beauty and terror. Thunder cracks and lightning strikes, jagged tendrils of electric brilliance. Determined chaos persists. Omega feels the hostile embrace of a potent force—*gravity*—the unseen entity of daunting power. It seizes her, incredible strength that drags her into its forceful nature. Unleashing a merciless tug, it yanks Omega forward, subjugating her to its will amidst the boisterous currents of the vortex. Resistance proves pointless as gravity exerts its dominion over Omega, compelling her forward into the blinding vortex. A radiant brilliance envelops her, consuming her essence as she dissolves into the endless light of luminosity.

* * *

Glacier horizons and the ice road stretch endlessly, its surface gleaming like polished glass under the auroras. Swirling snowflakes cascade, reminiscent of tears falling from the sky like rain. The rumble of an approaching storm spoke tales of revelations. A *military cyber cargo truck* roars down the road, its heavy frame exhibiting scars of battle, a behemoth navigating the frozen wasteland. Inside its fortified cage for cargo were outlines of sitting figures. An unknown purpose lingers.

The vehicle's tires slide against the frozen asphalt, struggling for control on the treacherous black ice. Sporadic fishtails threaten to send it careening off road. As the truck thunders forth, the chilly wind whispers tales of secrets buried beneath layers of ice and snow. The cargo remains an enigma, its true nature known only to those who dwell in the shadows of the frozen world. Each twist and turn of the vehicle causes it to swerve all along the road, battling the forces of nature. The howling wind carries echoes across the infinite expanse of winter's domain, its mournful voice resonating through the icy landscape. And as twilight emerges, the journey ahead remains uncertain in equal measure.

Omega's eyes flutter open, rousing her from the surreal dreamworld. Her breath crystallizing in the frigid air sits solemnly beside a group of weary *US soldiers*, faces exhausted. The soldiers' spirits were frozen, trapped behind the iron confines of their prison, their essence as cold as the bars that bind them. The snowy hellscape lay barren, devoid of any signs of civilization. Nature reigns supreme, the only companion along the infinite road that winds through the icy wilderness for miles upon miles.

"Where you stationed?" Omega asks, her voice a whisper in the biting wind. The soldier, his gaze fixed upon the snowy horizon, offers no reply. Silence hangs heavy between them, a symphony of pain echoing their current predicament. The truck rumbles forth, leaving behind the ghosts of the captives. Omega and the soldiers were bound together by the chains of fate, where their destinies were entangled in the icy embrace of an untrustworthy future. Being a prisoner of war during World War III held no possibilities of rescue. With governments collapsing worldwide, negotiating terms are now dictated by those who know the locations of oil reserves. Collateral damage is no longer a concern—everyone is expendable.

"Don't give up, we can make it," Omega's voice pierces the heavy air, a silver lining amidst the mounting pressure of survival. The US soldiers cast weary glances at Omega, all of their spirits drained by the adversity surrounding them. Omega rattles the cage, a defiant gesture against the suffocating confinement. But the cage remains unbroken, unmoved by her efforts. Omega unleashes a fierce kick upon the unyielding barrier, her defiance echoing in the silence. Yet, it returns nothing but a hollow thud, a hostile reminder of the unforgiving reality they faced. The vehicle abruptly halts, skidding on black ice.

A canvas of frozen despair. Wolves, penguins, seals, and polar bears, ensnared in icy tombs, departed witnesses to the *Nuclear Winter*. After the world was consumed by the black cloud of darkness, the surface froze over instantly, transforming anyone above ground into unwitting inhabitants of a subzero crypt of frost. The sand, slick and icy, offered little stability to the weary captives who were slipping and sliding on the coast.

Omega and the US soldiers advance toward the frozen ocean, their fate dictated by the threatening aura of the Iraqi soldiers and their rifles trained on them. There was no escape; the prisoners of war knew that death had arrived. Omega leads the procession, her determined stride cutting through the bitter cold like a blade. Beside her, the US soldiers trudge onward, weariness of endless battles evident in their weary frames. The ocean lay frozen, its surface cracked and fractured, offering glimpses of the churning waters beneath. It was a surreal dreamscape from a frigid nightmare. As they continue pressing forward, Iraqi soldiers guide the prisoners into a makeshift bunker. This group found their final resting place. From the dirt, life emerged, and back into the ground, it would meet its inevitable ending.

US soldiers huddle against the icy sand bunker, heads bowed in resignation. Their oxygen tanks wheeze in and out as they struggle to breathe in the clean air from their tanks, all of them running empty and leaving them gasping for more. One soldier, low on oxygen, collapses to the ground, suffocating in the radioactive atmosphere. Iraqi soldiers with their voices unleash a torrent of Arabic words, each syllable a sharp rebuke against the harsh frozen tundra.

"We don't know where the oil is!" another US soldier shouts, his voice drowned out by bold shouts from Iraqi soldiers.

Omega and her comrades brace themselves for the shooting gallery, their hands clasped tightly. Some in prayer. Others in surrender. On her knees, Omega ponders the prospect of death by bullets. *Would it be quick and painless, or long and cruel?* Either way, the thought didn't sit well. She felt like a slave to the war, and the end seemed near. Closing her eyes, she engages in a silent conversation, unsure if it was God, herself, or just the cold air. Regardless, she speaks, hoping her death would be swift, a dire last wish from her psyche. She prepares for the final fatal blow.

The sky erupts in a deafening crescendo of sound. *Boom! Boom! Boom!* Drones descend from above, dropping bombs onto the Iraqi soldiers. Chaos engulfs the battlefield as explosions tear through the coast, claiming lives in a flash of fire and smoke. Omega and the soldiers seize the opportunity for escape as they flee from the hellish scene unfolding before them.

A few US soldiers fall, victims of the panicked fury unleashed by an Iraqi soldier. Across the icy coastline, another pair of US soldiers sprint for their lives, their boots slipping and sliding across the slick sand like dancers on a stage of death. The Iraqi soldiers, consumed by rage, unleash a torrent of gunfire at the fleeing Americans, their bullets slicing through the frozen air like daggers. Above, the drones descend once more, their bombs shattering the ice along the shoreline, carving massive craters into the glacial terrain.

US and Iraqi soldiers stumble and tumble into the abyss of the craters, swallowed by ice and hellish anarchy. As the gunfire ceases and action settles into a tense calm, Omega and a lone survivor lock eyes, their eyes drawn to the vacant cyber cargo truck nearby. With shared understanding, they make a desperate dash for the vehicle. Both US and Iraqi soldiers had fallen victim to the crossfire. Omega skids along the ice, struggling to maintain her balance. Amidst the collateral damage, she spots a few weapons nearby. Rummaging through the belongings of the fallen, Omega's hands find purchase on a shotgun and ammunition, stuffing them into a military backpack. Then, the sharp crack of a gunshot pierces the stillness. The solo US soldier falls, blood seeping from a fatal wound inflicted by a dying Iraqi soldier. Omega's response is swift, and she quickly loads the shotgun and pivots in response, her own gunfire ending the Iraqi soldier's life. Both units of US and Iraqi soldiers lie still, their fate sealed by the predator of war. The drones retreat from the scene, disappearing into the twilight skyline. Omega's eyes linger upon the sea as she contemplates her next move. In order to cross the ocean, she desperately needed to discover oil. Omega shakes off the moment and climbs into the cyber cargo truck, ready to continue her journey despite the challenges ahead. Her hands remain steady on the wheel as she drives off, leaving behind the dystopian warfare.

The cyber cargo truck careen down the icy highway, a metallic beast with increasing speed. In the near distance, a US guard tower loomed, its watchful gaze fixed upon the region. An ice-covered oil derrick was frozen in time, unable to produce results. The pursuit of riches in this dangerous land was put on hold until it could be deiced and operational. US soldiers stand guard, their eyes trained on the oil derrick, poised to defend their potential claim against any who dared challenge it.

Emerging from the blinding fog, the cyber cargo truck materializes, its sleek form cutting through the mist. Suddenly, the crack of gunfire was fired a couple feet ahead of the speeding truck. The truck lurches to a halt, tires screeching as they fight for traction on the black ice, sliding out of control to a precarious stop.

Omega thrusts her hands through the open window. "I'm on your side!" she proclaims, her words a declaration of allegiance, as if hoping to find a mutual understanding in the familiarity. US soldiers descend from the guard tower, weapons poised for action. They stealthily approach Omega, scrutinizing every inch for signs of threat. Soldiers look over the vehicle methodically, inspecting Omega as a moment of calmness fills the standoff. Both sides seemed to exude mutual trust.

In the near distance, the robotic beast known as *Wildcat* emerges. Wildcat prowls the battlefield with the lethal grace of a mountain lion, its metal frame stalking its prey. A machine gun was poised like a deadly appendage ready to unleash its wrath upon any who dared to cross its path. The military robot releases a plethora of gunfire, cutting down US soldiers, their bodies falling like sacrificial offerings. Omega's hand closes around the cold steel of the shotgun. She takes notice of the dangerous environment, maintaining her steadfast warrior stance and keeping low. Her eyes scan the madness unfolding outside, ready to react at a moment's notice.

Cautiously, she slips out of the truck, navigating her next move. In World War III, the battle lines were drawn between human and machine. Each country had reached the pinnacle of innovation in robotics and artificial intelligence, leading to a combination of humans and machines fighting in unison. However, all beings ultimately failed when encountering the *Nuclear Winter*. Mother Nature's wrath was underestimated, leading to the implosion of everything.

Wildcat, a merciless harbinger of destruction, ferociously overpowers the US soldiers one by one, their futile resistance no match for its unyielding might. Each life snuffed out in violence. Omega dodges bullets and finds refuge behind a barrier. Her breath comes in ragged gasps as she waits, poised for the perfect moment to strike. Through the haze of debauchery and carnage, Wildcat prowls, a specter of annihilation weaving through the wreckage. And then, in a moment of defiance, Omega seizes her chance, closing the distance until she stands behind the unsuspecting behemoth. She shoves and thrusts the shotgun into Wildcat's frame, the deafening blast of gunfire tearing through metal and machinery. Fragments of metal rain down like confetti as Wildcat meets its demise, reduced to nothing but scrap and ruin.

Surveying the desolation around her, Omega's watches the frozen oil derrick, a witness to the carnage of war. The natural resource showcased humanity's darker instincts. Survival was paramount in this icy world, and the motto for all was "everything and anything it takes." Ice and oil had become the battleground for the remaining powers of the world. Every military operation roamed these frozen lands in hopes of discovery. Omega knew she was entering the battleground of oil, the last significant fight left for the human race. *Live or die on this day*, she thought to herself.

Despite the frozen oil derrick, Omega pulls herself together, determined to pursue her goal. And so, with the echoes of violence still ringing in her ears, she drives off again, leaving behind a trail of destruction and death. Omega remained optimistic about discovering oil. The military cyber cargo truck drives into the twilight horizon, disappearing into the shimmering magnetic field auroras.

* * *

Earth, a dreamy winter snow globe, was suspended in the void. Clouds, like wandering souls, drift aimlessly, their forms ever-changing, ever-fleeting. Auroras writhe and twist in convergent and divergent patterns. Green tendrils reach out, as if longing for connection, while purple wisps whisper secrets known only to the world. From the icy grips of the North and South Poles, these celestial phantoms appear. *Nuclear Winter* was a timeless event, where ego triumphed, and Mother Nature struck down ambition.

The sands, formerly kissed by the Sun, were now bleached in frost. No longer do they hold secrets in their golden grains. Pearly white sand dunes. Only the endless cycle of decay, like the bones of some long-forgotten beast. The infamous *Kaaba* was shrouded in a veil of ice, its sacred walls encased in frozen silence. Legends spoke of the Kaaba's great significance, some believing it to be the dwelling place of ancient spirits or a gateway. Around it, like statues carved from the very marrow of winter's heart, stand the worshippers, despair spread across their faces.

Subzero winds whip through the landscape, driving temperatures to plummet below freezing, chilling even the supposed gods to their core. No longer do prayers rise from lips. No longer do footsteps echo in the empty courtyard. An eternal winter, the icy spell of some ancient curse. The frozen Kaaba become a monument of past worship, where faith once burned bright as the desert sun. Until ice dominated.

* * *

The Western Wall, a relic of ancient faith, engulfed in ice. Its weathered stones gleam an unworldly sheen, each crevice and crack encased in layers of frozen time. A kingdom of frost. Lost worshippers from a world abandoned by God. Tears and pleas no longer echo through the sacred space. Emotions had succumbed to the wintry enchantment, lost in the frosty wonderland. Time suspended like a blade poised for the kill, there was only the punishing *Nuclear Winter*. Rays of sunlight had long forgotten the surface of

Earth, their warmth not gracing the land in eons. Amidst the bitterness of forgotten prayers and dying dreams, the frozen Western Wall experienced the cruelty of fate.

Snowflakes dance in a fluid vortex, swirling like lost souls in a deadly storm. In the heart of this wintry maelstrom stands a frozen *church*. Purgatory had long extinguished the flame of faith. The Christian religion never had a chance against the frozen hell that now reigned supreme. The heavens remain quiet, refusing to answer the desperate calls of prayer echoing through the icy wasteland. A cross lies half-buried in the snow, obscured by pounds of white powder. Like the great flood of ancient tales, snow has overtaken this symbol of belief, swallowing it in a wave of winter. Inferno and ice are two aspects of the same fundamental dynamic. Traversing into the depths of Hell was a tale of the past, where one might eventually meet the Devil at the bottom of the layers of limbo. But that tale was just a story, crafted to help humanity ignore the repercussions of existence. Now, the current saga of *Nuclear Winter* brought those religious tales to life, blurring the lines between myth and reality. Yet, in this harsh reality, there was no redemption to be found. Mournful spirits and the snow fall like tears from a broken sky.

* * *

Omega's eyes pierce through the frost-covered window. The bitter cold seeps through the cracks, an everlasting adversary in this frozen apocalypse. Suddenly, her eyes fixate on a massive *graveyard*, stationed like a silent guardian in the heart of the road. Death looms everywhere, its energy palpable. Adrenaline kicks in and she slams on the brakes, the tires screeching in protest against the ice. The truck skids, sliding precariously across the slick pavement. Outside, thousands of gravestones lie in the pristine snow.

A haunting aftermath of silent sacrifice. The quietness of death consumes the area.

Omega, drawn by an unseen force, steps out of the cyber cargo truck. No lurking evil reveals itself, but instead a feeling of unease. She inspects the graves scattered across the snowy landscape. After her recent near-death encounters, she realizes that everything eventually returns to the grave—the final resting place—regardless of her discovery of oil. A bit of regret marinates. Suddenly, a fog of snowy mist develops and contorts, swirling ominously in her direction, hinting at the hope of spirits lingering in the wintry air.

"Is anybody alive?" she calls out into the mist. Silence echoes back, a chilling response to her inquiry. Further she wanders, descending into the belly of the graveyard, whiteness enveloping her and swallowing her being.

Out of the stygian, a darkness unfolds, coalescing into a *Shadow* advancing toward Omega. She feels its approach, a premonition of dread manifesting, yet its face eluding her grasp. Rather than pouncing upon Omega, Shadow extends a hand in welcome. She didn't trust the entity. The blackness of reality had always unnerved her, ever since she was a little girl. Omega reacts, contorting her frame to rupture Shadow's clasp. She shoves it away, her stare intense as she squares off against the mysterious apparition. Shadow was a doppelgänger of her outline, lacking the details of her human features. Instead of carbon flesh, it exhibited an inky blackness.

Shadow remains impenetrable, its essence flickering in the misty luminescence. Both entities stand entrenched in a deadlock, colliding in a parallel connection of ambiguity. The gravity of their confrontation remains obvious as they square off. Omega retreats backwards, gathering herself. *Was she dreaming or awake,* the vivid dreamer ponders to herself. *Was this merely exhaustion, or had she entered another realm in her dream state*? Either way, Shadow seems trustworthy, and she has been alone for a long time. An invisible ally might be exactly what she is looking for.

She ceases her resistance against Shadow, a decision born of tolerance rather than defeat. Shadow begins to speak, its words resonating an otherworldly tonality. "Does fear haunt you?" Shadow's words were truthful.

Omega thinks to herself about the child shadow on the beach and feeling a desperate obligation to save them. *Perhaps*, she considers, *she was saving herself in that moment. Or maybe it was something from her past that she could balance in the dream world.* Either way, the child is her main goal.

"I fear the thought of not finding the child," she confesses, her voice expressing her worries.

"Love," Shadow speaks, its voice a gentle murmur that seemed to resonate. "A relentless shadow." The words linger in the air.

"I'm not leaving here until I find them," she declares, a fierce resolve that held no argument.

"Hope," Shadow whispers, its words a wisp of smoke. "A dying ember in this world of darkness." The words echo the struggles of those who dared to believe in something brighter during the war of oil.

Lost children were innocent bystanders in the apocalypse, and Omega knew she was responsible for this one in particular. She had always wondered if dreams were visions of truth. These days, she leaned toward spirituality, seeking answers in the unseen.

Cloaked in darkness, the entity draws nearer to Omega. "There's a drilling camp inland," Shadow whispers, its words carrying a touch of secrecy. "The child might be there."

Omega surveys the graveyard. Countless deaths manufactured over war. She realizes that in order to escape the ice world, she has to find both the child and oil, a twofold challenge. She stares at all those graves, pondering the lives of each person laid to rest, and wondering what deeds they had done; how they would be remembered by those who remained.

Each grave seemed to pulsate energy, a symphony of souls orchestrated to maintain order. "What you have today," Shadow's tone is heavy, "doesn't guarantee you'll have it tomorrow." Omega felt the meaning behind those words. "Find the child," Shadow urges, like a haunting refrain. "Escape this war."

Omega's mind races. Her eyes narrow as they fix beyond the field of graves, knowing the drilling camp was close by. As Omega begins walking away, Shadow remains behind, their destinies intertwined in ways that neither could fully comprehend; bound together by the threads of fate that tied their shared reality.

Her mission was pressing down upon her. Yet, even against all odds, there was hope—light that pierced through the darkness, guiding her toward a possible hopeful future. And so, with Shadow lingering in the recesses of her mind, Omega walks away from the graveyard, ready to face whatever challenges lay ahead. For in that moment, Omega knew that her journey was far from over, and that the true test of her strength had only just begun. The supernatural mist engulfs Omega and Shadow, enveloping them in a transcendental fog.

* * *

The classroom was bathed in twilight, a state of suspended animation. Rows of desks stretch out before Omega, with surfaces polished to a dull sheen under the dim glow of auroras. At the front of the room stood a podium, its mahogany surface weathered by the countless lectures. Enveloped in a surreal ambiance, the setting defies the norms of the ordinary, evoking a sensation as if the course of events remains suspended.

Omega, a figure of gravitas, holds court at the podium, her silhouette against the backdrop of the towering diagram. Etched in meticulous detail, the diagram traces the climb of humanity's energy consumption, showcasing mankind's progress of exponential evolutionary growth. Each line and curve tell a story of ambition and excess of a species intoxicated by its own imagination.

Omega speaks, her words filling the room. Behind her, the diagram looms like a ghost of energy desires. As the gears of progress turn, humanity's hunger for energy surges, unchecked since the Industrial Revolution, spiraling into a behemoth of consumption that threatens to devour the planet. And as the aurora's rays filter through the windows, the gas-masked students listen intently to Omega's every word. Youthful minds were acutely aware of the significant facts of nature bearing down upon them. The new world falls squarely upon the shoulders of the next generation, burdened by consequences of unchecked consumption and rapid technological advancement.

Omega's words come out sharp. "We've been devouring energy since the Industrial Revolution began," she declares. An enduring spirit of innovation across epochs, that humanity could never stop. Innovation served as humanity's purpose from the moment fire was discovered, through the epochs of the Stone Age, the advent of the wheel, and the dawn of the Bronze Age. From the harnessing of electricity to the mastery of quantum physics and computational growth, the journey seemed infinite. Until the oil began to disappear, halting progress in its tracks. Oil, a fundamental cornerstone of modern society, was responsible for birthing countless products essential to the fabric of everyday life. In the absence of oil, civilization faltered, revealing the stark truth that its depletion wasn't just an inconvenience but a catalyst for conflict—plunging nations into war over the dwindling resource.

Omega's declaration was palpable. Suddenly, with a sharp snap of her fingers, she punctuates her words like a gunshot in the night. "But now, we're hitting the bottom of the barrel," Omega continues, an austere note of realization. "Oil's running out." Her words settle upon the students, suffocating in its implications. Grief spoken as the truth over the classroom, a funereal atmosphere that spoke volumes of the gravity of the moment. Oil depletion put a curse over the world, as the finite nature of this vital resource became undeniable.

A *student*, their hand trembling, dares to break the silence.

Omega, acknowledging the gesture, offers a reassuring nod, inviting them into the conversation.

A hushed question breaks the silence as the student dares to seek insight. "What do you think will happen next?" they ask, their voice a tentative whisper.

Omega's eyes were pools of shadows reflecting turmoil. It was an enormous question from the young mind. "Armageddon," Omega whispers. "Global conflict. Weapons of mass destruction. Catastrophic extinction on our planet." Each word falls from her lips, painting a bleak picture of the future that awaited them all. The atmosphere in the room shifts, a collective breath held as the students lean forward, their eyes fixed on Omega. A curious yet morbid fascination; captivated and drawn in by her grim prophecy she painted of the world.

"We must find a way to cut back on our energy consumption of fossil fuels," Omega asserts. "Otherwise, we'll be living in the Stone Age again." Her words were a reminder of the precarious balance humanity teetered upon, caught between progress and regression. Omega's hand sweeps across the chalkboard, tracing the outlines of the depleted oil reserves illustrated—a dying memory etched in the fading vestiges of what once fueled their civilization. The students' eyes follow her gesture, their youthful minds understanding the reality of planetary limitations.

"Humans have limited vision," Omega reflects, expressing centuries of knowledge. "Preparing for the future..." she pauses, a sorrowful note in her voice. "Wisdom has become a dying skill for our civilization." Her eyes sweep over the gathered students, their faces a reflection of her own philosophical realization.

Another student begins to speak, his hand eagerly shooting up. "What will we do after the war?" the student's voice pierces the uncomfortable air, having a longing for a ray of hope amidst the approaching shadows of conflict.

Omega's response comes swift, emerging through the dense fog of doubt. "Fight for oil," she declares, her words devoid of hesitation or remorse. Omega's statement resonates an aura of finality, capturing the essence of a threatening conclusion… until the lecture gets disrupted by the piercing howl of sirens. Panic erupts among the students, chaos descending upon them like a vulture upon its prey. Outside the window, a nightmare unfolds as a plethora of *atomic bombs* erupt across the horizon.

A world engulfed in the inferno of annihilation. End of days had dawned, and doomsday had descended upon the world. Finality over all existence. The horrified students are wide-eyed as they behold the apocalypse, dread rendering them powerless, watching the unfolding catastrophe.

* * *

Earth drifted in its familiar orbit. Another day dawned upon the sphere. On this particular day, a palpable shift was felt, distinct from the days that came before it, signaling an irreversible transformation in civilization, forever altering history. Worldwide nuclear bombs—a torrent of Hell and brimstone—upon the planet, plunging humanity into chaos. Time moved at a languid pace. No matter the evil that submerged the world, the arrow of time persisted forward.

Fate awaited it in the ever-turning wheel of time. During the dawn of World War III, Earth was forever altered by the harrowing events that transpired on that fateful day.

* * *

The military cyber cargo truck rumbles into the frozen dusk, its powerful engine a steady momentum against the road. Evergreen trees were draped in snow, their branches reaching out like skeletal fingers clawing at the auroras that were glaring in the twilight sky.

Omega's gloved hands grip the steering wheel. Overlooking the frozen wasteland, she wonders about the future of humanity. *Was this the end of civilization, a final chapter in the grand narrative of human history? Or could humanity find a way to rise from the ashes, to rewrite their story and forge a new path forward?* Her avid reading had taught her that humanity was but a brief species in time. Destined one day to fade way, like countless civilizations before. Yet, on this day, she yearns to push aside such thoughts. For now, the future remained uncertain, a blank page waiting to be written. Omega steals a glance at Shadow, occupying the passenger seat. A silent observer, impossible to discern their emotions as they watch the frozen landscape. Everything appears authentic through the veil of blackness, as if the darkness itself holds secrets yet to be revealed.

Issues of significance saturate Shadow's aura, swirling like ghosts. Omega could sense the magnitude of Shadow's thoughts. "What's on your mind?" Shadow repeats, an echo through Omega's consciousness.

For a moment, Omega hesitates, her thoughts spinning. Finally, she releases a heavy sigh, then speaks, "The future." Her words are barely audible over the hum of the truck's engine. "And what it holds for us."

Shadow stoically observes her, before speaking an eerie reassurance. "You'll find your way."

Omega's mind remains curious where whispers of warmth and life seem like nothing more than illusions. In the aftermath of the global blackout and the permanent loss of worldwide communication following the war, humanity found itself gripped by uncertainty. As the days passed, questions arose: *Was the entire planet now submerged in subzero conditions? Or perhaps somewhere on the surface, sunlight existed across untouched lands?* Because of the void of information, a multitude of conspiracy theories began to circulate the globe, each offering its own interpretation, caught in a web of speculation and conjecture. Hope clung desperately to the fringes of civilization.

"Where do I go?" Omega questions herself. The allure of a second chance at life was beyond tempting; drawing humanity toward the promise of renewal in the face of nihilistic despair. Omega finds herself standing at a crossroads, torn between hope and reality of her world.

At the sound of Shadow's voice, Omega's thoughts stutter, her mind reflecting on the unexpectedness of its response. "The equator," Shadow echoes. The concept seemed almost surreal. A distant memento from a time long past, when the world had been a place of heat.

As she contemplates Shadow's cryptic message, Omega's thoughts turn to the equator, an invisible line that divides the world in two, a boundary between the north and south. It was a myth these days. Omega ponders the enormity of the task before her, knowing that this journey was her only hope. She sets her sights on a singular goal—to find the equator. Perhaps there lay the promise of a second chance at life. Omega sets her sights on the distant horizon, ready to embark on a journey that would take her to the edge of the world and beyond.

Omega's foot slams down on the brakes, the screech of tires tearing through the twilight as the truck skidded to a halt. Her eyes narrow to slits as she beholds the *drilling camp*, a monolith rising. In the heart of the frozen valley, nestled between towering peaks cloaked in snow, a rugged outpost where roughnecks search for the black gold buried beneath the ice. A cluster of prefabricated buildings surrounded by machinery and equipment, their metal frames standing out against the white snow. Despite the biting cold that clutches the valley, the camp is a hive of activity.

Roughnecks in heavy winter gear and oxygen tanks bustle about as they prepare for another day's work. The sound of engines rumbling to life and tools clanging against metal reverberates through the valley. At the center of the camp, the drilling rig rises like a giant, its towering structure reaching toward the sky as it drills into the frozen world. Steam rises from the subzero subterranean underground. Despite the harsh conditions, the roughnecks press on, driven by the promise of discovery. For them, this remote outpost is more than just a drilling camp; it's a battleground where dreams are forged, and fortunes are won or lost in the pursuit of oil.

Omega surveys the region, a calculating gleam flickering in her eyes. This, she realizes, is the perfect opportunity to obtain oil. She formulates a plan, ready to seize the moment and make her move amidst the hustle and bustle of the roughnecks and machinery.

Abruptly emerging from the dense forest is a detachment of US soldiers. Their figures materialize like phantoms encircling the military cargo cyber truck, every action commanding authority. Omega glances over to the passenger seat, only to find it empty, devoid of her companion who had seemingly vanished from her perspective. Shaking off the oddity, she refocuses her attention on the task at hand, pushing aside any lingering unease. Though Shadow that had guided her remains nowhere to be found, she refuses to cower.

ICE

"I'm not the enemy," Omega declares. It was a declaration of loyalty. She would not be swayed from her path. There lies a suspenseful tension, thick as the snow that covered everything.

Suspiciously, soldiers assess the lone figure. They recognized the woman; she displayed an aura of familiarity that instilled confidence, negating the need for identification. It was as if she had a past life, perhaps serving in the military or a similar role. Despite the ambiguity, there existed a mutual understanding between the two camps. Respect from shared experiences. Producing a single nod from their leader, the team spring into motion, synchronized in their response to the directive. The soldiers step aside and allow Omega to pass. There were no words exchanged, no gestures of acknowledgment. She was granted safe passage through the gauntlet of interrogation. As she drove away, the soldiers faded back away into the subzero wilderness.

* * *

Nestled in the icy embrace of a glacier-carved valley, the oil camp operates. Extreme optimization. Its innovative shadow shimmers across the ice. Radiation spreads like wildfire throughout the region, forcing everyone to wear oxygen masks and tanks—their only defense against the toxic air. Here, amid the freezing conditions, inhabitants labor so intensely, bordering on desperation. Jackhammers relentlessly pierce the ice, each strike echoing throughout the Arctic world. Semi-trucks and dump trucks, their frames gleaming in the auroras light. Crafted from the hard alloys of titanium and aluminum, they await their next task that conveyed the necessity of their skills.

Oil camps held an importance far beyond industry. They were the last resort of a world plunged into subzero conditions by *Nuclear Winter*. The pursuit of the fossil fuel was not merely a matter of commerce, but a struggle for survival. Oil, once a commodity of convenience, had become the new water. Without it, the frozen hell that now submerged the world would consume all in its icy reality. Drilling camps served as the final hope for the bloodline of humanity.

Arctic air cut through flesh; the living conditions mirrored those of an alien world or frozen moon in the distant reaches of our solar system. Much like Enceladus and Europa—icy moons of Saturn and Jupiter—the thick crust of ice concealed untold mysteries beneath its frigid surface. Irregular lumps hinted at the hidden bounty lying in vain beneath the ice, teasing at the possibility of resources yet untapped. Ridges and troughs carved their way through the frozen terrain, like the ancient scars of a universal celestial battle, leading weary travelers to the rows of living pods that were in perfect formation. This surreal sight evoked echoes of long-forgotten dreams, reminiscent of the blueprints that envisioned civilization thriving on Mars. Constructed from layers of inflatable fabric, these pods offered shelter, their makeshift design an ingenious design of those who called them home.

A union of roughnecks work tirelessly on the oil rigs, their labor an impressive achievement. Humans would forever wage war against death, driven by the denial of death, encapsulated in the timeless motto: "Whatever it takes."

Omega approaches a weathered driller, their jackhammer drilling into the icy ground. Her footsteps crunch against the snow underfoot. "I'm looking for work," Omega announces, her voice cutting through the subzero chill. The driller continues working away and regards her, looking twice with a scrutinizing gaze before nodding toward a nearby cave.

Harsh flashes of the child engulf Omega's perception. Still in the recesses of her mind, she couldn't make out a clear distinction of their face. Her eyes begin darting frantically across the oil camp, searching for any sign of the child amidst the maze of machinery. But as she scans the rambunctious scene before her, each passing moment proved to be fruitless searching. There was no trace of the child.

Shaking off the craving for connection, Omega knows that her next move would be crucial. In order to have any chance of escape, she must gather as much oil as possible. Baby steps, inching a pathway toward victory amidst the crushing defeat of losing the child. She holds onto the belief that everything would fall into place in due time. Omega understands that in life, one could never connect the dots moving forward; it was only upon reaching the goal that one could connect the dots moving backward. Garnering every ounce of clarity, Omega sets her sights on the cave. She wouldn't leave the drilling camp without some sort of win, not when so much was at stake.

A solitary lantern hangs from a jagged outcrop, its weak flame battling against the darkness. The fire's vitality unleashes a wavering glow upon the uneven, rough-hewn walls of the cave. Shadows twist and writhe in the flickering light. Imagery evoked echoes of Plato's *Allegory of the Cave*, where caveman prisoners, shackled by their own ignorance, were confined to a tunnel vision perspective of perception. This ancient parable was believed to be the first of its kind, revealing humanity's innate search beyond their own ego. The roughnecks in the cave mirrored those caveman prisoners, trapped in their own dilemmas. Yet, unlike the prisoners of old, humanity seemed to have lost its capability to alter the course of the future.

Amidst this primal dance of light and darkness, a feminine silhouette materializes from the gloom. Cloaked in the cloak of dusk, she moves as her figure was illuminated against the obsidian backdrop. In her hands, she wields a pickaxe, its steel glinting dully in the dim illumination, a symbol of determination in the face of unforgiving stone. She swings the pickaxe, each blow biting into the rock, sending sparks. Each strike a fierce resolve, defiance against the oppressive weight of the ice world. Metal meeting stone permeates the air, a spirit of tenacity that courses through Omega's veins. Years ago, similar conditions existed in Congo, Africa, where child slavery condemned youths to work in cave tunnels, searching for cobalt, the element crucial for advancing technology. These enslaved children would receive only a dollar a day if their labor proved prosperous. Such exploitation fueled a civilization's desire for leisure and comfort. Today, the roles have shifted, thrusting humanity into a mining civilization desperately seeking the last remnants of oil on the planet. *How the stakes have changed over the course of history.* Instead of luxuries, they are now simply trying to secure a substance essential for survival.

In this subterranean sanctuary, where time is measured not by the passing of days but by the slow erosion of stone, Omega pushes herself tirelessly, her effort impressive, and her perseverance unmatched. She would never stop searching for the coveted resource. Omega knows in her soul that if she has any chance of escaping the ice world, she must have enough oil to cross the frozen sea; in desperate hopes of discovering the fairytale of an equator that still might hold heat.

Oil, the elixir of society, captivated humanity to dig and unearth its reservoirs. Humans would spare no effort, no sacrifice too great, for the promise of power and prosperity it held. More men descend into the cave, their hands calloused and their spirits unbroken, armed with pickaxes and dynamite. They dig relentlessly, carving through icy layers of dirt and stone. Each strike of the pickaxe echoes like a heartbeat. They unearth not just riches but also the seeds of their own destruction. Oil, once extracted, became a catalyst for conflict, igniting flames of war that engulfed nations. Blood spills like crude upon the soil, staining the earth. Sins of greed and ambition.

And yet, despite the carnage that ensued, humanity would never stop searching for the black gold. For in the dark recesses of the world, they saw not just a resource to be exploited, but a symbol of their own resilience. They would dig into the very core of the Earth if they must, for they knew no other path than forward. Driven by the promise of a brighter tomorrow, fueled by the spoils of their endeavors.

* * *

In the realm of dreams, an endless sea of oil. Its inky blackness merges seamlessly against the snow-covered shoreline, a surreal juxtaposition of nature's extremes. Each oil drop that flows and falls is like a tear shed by the Earth. The price paid for humanity's quest for power. Surreal and haunting, a phantasmagorical landscape that defies rational explanation. The scent of petrol and the crisp bite of winter's chill create a sensory experience that is as disorienting as it is intoxicating.

On the precipice of this otherworldly vista, Omega remains alone on the coastline, feeling her own insignificance in the face of such overwhelming forces. Leaving her adrift in a world where the rules of existence no longer apply. And yet, amidst the confusion, there is a strange beauty to be found. The oil shimmers like liquid gold beneath the dying light of twilight; mesmerizing and terrifying, the awesome power of fossil fuels unleashed.

Omega cannot help but wonder what lies beyond the horizon. *Is there salvation to be found in the distant reaches of this strange and wondrous land, or is she doomed to wander its endless for all eternity?* The question swirls in her psyche, haunting her every thought. *Was there truly an equator, waiting to welcome her and promising a second chance? Or was it nothing more than a mirage, a cruel trick of the mind, born from delusion?* Only time will tell, as she journeys onward into the heart of this domain. The urge to take that leap of faith grows stronger, compelling her to put aside the shackles of fear that imprison her to the past.

Since childhood, oil had been her confidant, especially after the accident where she fell into the river of petroleum, fighting for her life. She harbored a connection from the natural resource, neither fearful nor fully trusting of it. In the that black tide, she encountered an ocean of lost souls, written into her memory forever.

* * *

Back in the cave, Omega's eyes fixate on the cave paintings, rendered in the dry blood of ancient stories. Art had journeyed far, evolving alongside the soul of mankind. From the crude drawings in caves to the cinema, it served as a means of expression and escapism. However, as time passed, art seemed to lose its way, particularly before the onset of World War III. Despite the chaos looming on the horizon, humans remain self-absorbed, uninspired, and fixate on being the center of their own universe. Art that dared to predict the end of days was frowned upon, deemed unnecessary by the conglomerates that controlled the entertainment industry. The more realistic and foreboding the art, the more the industry recoiled in fear, refusing to celebrate it. In a world consumed by superficiality and self-interest, true art struggled to find its voice, stifled by the powers that be who prioritized profit over prophecy.

Omega refocuses her attention, tearing it away from the faded cave paintings, her mind drifting back to the present moment. She swings her pickaxe, each strike sending brighter sparks flying in the darkness. Up and down, the measured clang of metal against stone. As the echoes fade, Omega ceases her labor, tossing aside the pickaxe. Kneeling before a rock, she carefully examines its surface, her fingers tracing the rough contours.

And there, in the fading light, Omega's eyes widen in astonishment. Oil, thick and glistening, oozing from the pores of the rock like black tears. She has stumbled upon a petroleum seep. Omega glances beyond the cave's exit, observing numerous roughnecks loading barrels of oil into a semi-truck. A barrel of oil for her journey would be essential, but the likelihood of stealing one undetected seems impossible. The entire area was guarded as if oil were diamonds. Heavy military everywhere. Omega knows she has to make the best of what she found and proceed accordingly. She rises to her feet, her discovery fueling a fire of ambition that burns brighter than any flame. Cloaked in shadows, she slips away into the cave, avoiding roughnecks. She rummages through her military backpack. Her fingers brush against the cool metal of a water bottle, a vessel for her covert mission. Stealthily, Omega approaches a small puddle of oil, its iridescent surface scintillating in the twilight. Gently, she fills the bottle to the brim—this was the best she could do. Her prize secured, Omega carefully conceals the oil-filled bottle back in her pack.

In the layers of her psyche, Omega daydreams of the child running across the badlands of a desert. But in the shifting sands of her mind, the familiar imagery of the child's human form dissolves, leaving only the silhouette of the shadow. Philosophical symbolism reflecting the nature of her yearning. Brief memories of the child remain, memories that had faded but not vanished entirely. The child felt a closeness to Omega, like a daughter or a son, though she couldn't quite remember. Her mind floats between the frozen world and the equator. Her emotional bond remains tireless. This connection was all she needed to keep the faith in herself. Omega knows the sacrifice she is willing to make. To forsake the familiar confines of her ice world and venture forth into the sea. Venturing beyond meant risking untold dangers.

Omega wishes for a future where freedom was more than just a distant dream. The icy prison of this world seems to offer no hope for such a future, but Omega has reached a breaking point. She has grown weary of weak possibilities, forever determined to enact change. Omega is willing to risk it all and forge a new destiny for herself and the child. For in their shared journey lies the hope of redemption. Promises of a world reborn from the ashes of their frozen past. Omega thoughtfully considers the child, reminiscing about their spirit. The child possessed a quiet demeanor and introverted nature from what she remembers. In the tender years of youth, they would linger into the late hours of the night, thirsting for knowledge of the world. The child was a restless spirit akin to Peter Pan, yearning for the open road, but the aftermath of the *Nuclear War* had trapped them. The child spun tales of distant lands steeped in culture and enlightenment, leading them toward dreams of a brighter tomorrow. For them, the twin pillars of *culture* and *knowledge* became guiding stars, illuminating a path toward self-discovery. Omega was willing to traverse to the ends of the globe to secure the child's future. She believed that the child held the power to impart wisdom and make a significant impact on the world, transforming it into a better place for generations to come.

US soldiers stand guard at the mouth of the cave, their bodies weary from the harsh subzero conditions. Protectors with their heads on a swivel, eyes scanning the jagged peaks. Each breath drawn is a prayer whispered to the gods of war. Constant vigilance reigns supreme during perpetual conflict. Their eyes, sharp as the talons of a hunting hawk, pierce the snowy mountainside, searching for any sign of intrusion upon their sacred domain. Trust is a luxury they cannot afford; betrayal lurks behind every rock. A h*eavy* *expanded mobility tactical truck* grumbles to a stop, its strong frame bearing the weight of its cargo reminiscent of Atlas bearing the heavens; engineered to endure the rigors of combat and logistical challenges. Its sheer size and rugged design evoke power and durability, embodying the essence of military strength. From its reinforced framework to its massive wheels, they're meticulously crafted to navigate hazardous landscapes and transport heavy payloads. The cargo bed groans as it swings open, unveiling a team of roughnecks, the fatigued men burdened by their calling— loading barrels of oil into the truck's bed and exhibiting reverence of monks tending to ancient scriptures.

On the horizon, where snow-dusted peaks endlessly encircle the oil camp, an eruption of brutality floods the zone. *Snipers*, unseen ghosts in the distance, unleash a lethal symphony upon the unsuspecting souls. Roughnecks, caught in the crosshairs of fate, scramble for cover, seeking cover behind icy rocks that offer scant protection from the onslaught of bullets. US soldiers return fire. Barrels of oil are knocked apart, their contents spilling out onto the ice like blood from a wounded creature. Nations were nomads drawn to an oasis, converging upon the lone stockade of crude—the final crucible of oil production.

Whispers of this clandestine sanctuary spread across the globe, igniting a frenzied modern-day oil rush that eclipsed the storied gold rushes of the past. In this theater of human desperation, oil—once the catalyst of industrial metamorphosis, the insidious hand behind the climate's unraveling—emerged as coveted treasure beyond comprehension. In this epoch, oil's importance surpassed all precedent. After the collapse of civilization, its value transcended economic metrics, embodying survival itself in a landscape where every drop held the promise of dominance. The quest for this black elixir became an obsessive pursuit, driving humanity to the edge of reason and beyond. Years ago, a fraction of humanity called oil *the devil*, but now it was revered as a god.

Snipers' bullets continue to find their marks, cutting down US soldiers and roughnecks. A ruthless display of death. The drilling camp was the insanity of mankind. Perpetual carnage that stained everything; dreams of utopia proved as elusive as a mirage in the desert. The concept of peace on Earth, theorized by humanity, was nothing more than a delusion. Throughout history, such an ideal had never existed in reality, and likely never would. War, both fundamentally and economically driven, persisted long before the collapse of the world. Countries worldwide poured insurmountable resources into perpetuating conflict. From the dawn of civilization, war built empires and remained intertwined with humanity until the end of time. A spell that would curse the world until the final reckoning. The notion of a paradise free from strife remained an illusion, forever beyond reach, plagued by enduring altercations. Indeed, throughout history, much of humanity's purpose has been conflict and suppression, dating back to the construction of the Great Pyramid of Giza. Soaring demands of power were a compulsory force that never wavered in its demands.

Omega, with her athletic proficiency, inches toward the cavern mouth. She was stealth, an evolutionary trait created out of necessity during the war. Omega stays low, crouching behind a rock and stealing a glance at the action. There, amidst the mountains, snipers continue unleashing their deadly fury, each gunshot a piercing discordance. Anguished cries of a world torn apart by overconsumption. Rows of American soldiers fall like wheat before the scythe, their lives extinguished in an instant. Soldiers retreat, seeking refuge from the storm of bullets.

The tactical truck, a hulking monolith, withstands the attack. Its armor holds strong against the bullets ricocheting off the military vehicle.

ICE

The windshield shatters, fracturing security, the driver tossed out like a gambler's discarded card in the game of war. A solitary shot finds its mark, a final order of fate as the driver crumples. Life had dwindled into a faint echo of debauchery. Bullets continue to carve through the oil camp. Desperate survivors, roughnecks, and soldiers continue to cower. Overcoming the vantage point of snipers posed a daunting challenge. A flood of lead descends from the summit, a storm of death. Each bullet, a messenger of destruction, tearing through flesh and bone. The battlefield lay in stasis, frozen conflict where snipers, patient as vultures, awaited the weary souls of American soldiers. The pursuit of oil had become a necessary obsession. For the snipers, there was no end in sight, no retreat from their vigil atop the icy peaks. They would wait, unmoved by hours, minutes or seconds. Statues embodying violence, contrasting against lives lost.

Divided and disoriented, American soldiers fragment into two factions. Gunfire streaks off the towering peaks, as though they were futile pleas to an indifferent universe. Far removed were the Arctic mountains. At their peaks, an homage to nature's magnificence, offering an ideal vantage point. Mother Nature, indifferent to the circumstances of war, renders the US soldiers' efforts weak against her fortress. The mountains offer no direct firing angle to the beleaguered US soldiers. From their lofty heights, death rains down upon the hapless souls caught in the crosshairs of war. Bullets, akin to angry hornets, tear through the cave, shattering the illusion of safety. Each impact releases an avalanche of snow and ice cascading down upon the wounded. Icicles transform into deadly projectiles, their razor-sharp edges gleaming. They descend upon the soldiers, icy tips piercing flesh already torn and broken by the dogfight. Even the elements themselves seem to conspire against the souls who dare to defy the harsh realities of the ambush.

Omega crouches and takes in the carnage brought on by the raging feud. While weaving in and out of the twisted bodies of the injured and fallen soldiers, Omega's eyes align upon the enemy snipers, their fatal precision sparing nothing that moves in the crossfire. Opportunity catches Omega's eye, the tactical truck's bed overflowing precious oil barrels—tantalizing prize amidst the bloodshed. Its rear end presses flush against the cave entrance, a barrier against the bullets. Omega's mind churns. She knows that seizing control of the tactical truck and its valuable cargo may be her only chance. In her desperate bid to flee limbo, she knows securing even a barrel of oil is essential. It represents her best chance.

A blizzard descends upon the combat zone, covering everything in a veil of swirling snow. Visibility dwindles, making it near impossible for a clear shot. Omega inches forward on her stomach, a ghost in the whiteout, seeking refuge beneath the shelter of the tactical truck. On her stomach, Omega inches forward at a pace akin to a snail's slow crawl. Utilizing the low ground as a cloak of invisibility, she advances, shielded and unnoticed. Gunshots echo through the snowstorm. Amidst the maelstrom, the snipers' keen eyesight is useless, their shots veering off course in the blinding flurry. Omega seizes the moment, as she inches closer to the driver's door. She quickens her pace, her eyes fixed on the tactical truck's front end. Only the driver's side door remains open, a narrow passage to freedom. Omega rolls out from beneath the tactical truck, emerging into the fray in the nucleus of the blizzard.

Sniper bullets ricochet off the metal door. Omega narrowly dodges the barrage as she lunges into the front seat. The front windshield continues to shatter under the assault, fractured glass cascading over Omega and her eyes dart frantically in search of a weapon. Her hand closes around the cold steel of a shotgun resting on the front seat. Omega cocks it back and unleashes a barrage of rounds toward the unseen assailants. But even as Omega fights back, the bullets from the mountains continue their overpowering assault, showing no sign of subsiding. Omega stays low, her fingers tightening around the steering wheel as she pushes down on the gas pedal, the engine roaring to life.

The tactical truck careens forward, hurtling through sniper bullets. Gradually, she edges away from the cave, each movement taking her a little farther... a little more... even more... US soldiers from the cave take cover behind the tactical truck, using it as a shield as they unleash a volley of gunfire toward the snipers perched atop the mountains. Snipers and soldiers exchange fire, locked in a heated match. US soldiers begin to gain the upper hand as their shots finally start finding their mark, cutting down the enemy. One by one, snipers fall under the crackling fire, their bodies tumbling down the mountain slopes, descending to meet their fate.

The tactical truck lumbers forward, inching away from the heat of the action. Soldiers, preoccupied by the enemy snipers, remain engrossed in their conflict, allowing the vehicle to slip further from the conflict. Omega rises slowly, cautiously straightening up after maneuvering the military truck away from the sniper's vantage point, now concealed from the view of her enemy combatants. Glancing in the rearview mirror, Omega observes a couple soldiers catching sight of the tactical truck's retreat. Gunshots ring out, aimed at puncturing the truck's tires in an attempt to halt its escape. Meanwhile, the oil barrels continue to slip away, inching further... even further from the drilling camp with each passing moment. Bullets fail to penetrate the thick tires, a stroke of luck for Omega as she successfully secures an oil barrel and more, accomplishing her mission.

However, only half of the puzzle was solved; she has the resource but not the child. Searching the interior of the tactical truck for the elusive Shadow entity yielded nothing. Omega is left alone and bewildered, unsure of where to begin her search for the child. Omega had always relied on signs for guidance, but now they offer only ambiguous hints at best. Her world is saturated in mist, a coma of uncertainty. The child was nowhere to be found at the drilling camp. Now, her journey remains ensnared in the grasp of limbo. Reservations of doubt seep into Omega's psyche. *Would she ever find the child? And even if she did, would the child choose to leave this icy purgatory?* These questions plague her mind, forming an intricate web of more questions instead of answers. Finding answers seemed similar to searching for the perfect grain of sand on an infinite beach—possible, but highly improbable. The notion of possible impossibilities was the theme this rescue mission had undertaken. Daunting odds and navigating through unknown circumstances. "*Such is life*," Omega speaks to herself, a quiet acknowledgment of the unpredictable twists and turns that life often weaves. Taking a quick glance, she checks the fuel tank. At the sight of its half-full capacity, she slams her foot down on the gas pedal, urging the truck onward, traversing the snowy region. The demon of doubt leaves.

As the tactical truck leaves the oil drilling camp behind, echoes of gunfire fade. Omega remains focused on the road ahead as she steers toward an untold future. Howling winds whip snow into a frenzy until the environment is swallowed whole by a snowy abyss. The tactical truck's massive form vanishes with the more miles it passes. Snowfall blankets everything, obscuring all traces of the frozen world, saturating it in serene pristine white. Mother Nature has taken over the planet, altering its climate in ways we'd never witnessed before. *Nuclear War* drapes the world in a canvas of ice.

Every record has been destroyed or falsified, every book rewritten, every picture has been repainted, every statue and street building has been renamed, every date has been altered. And the process is continuing day by day and minute by minute. History has stopped.
George Orwell

ICE

mark
DOOM

DOOM

Back in the interrogation room, Omega is sprawled upon the sterile floor, her body free from the shackles of captivity. She reaches up and removes the EEG cap, feeling the electrodes disconnect. Whatever entity was probing her neurological pathways remains a mystery. She guards her secrets, erecting barriers of entry throughout the labyrinth of the ice world, determined to protect what was hers at all costs. She ponders that free will is a concept she alone could command—nothing more, nothing less. Yet in this realm, she can't shake the feeling of being somewhat adrift, as if her own decisions are slipping beyond her control. Her mind resembles a maze of mirrors, each reflecting and deflecting the myriad possibilities of decisions. All she knows in her core is a simple truth: to keep moving forward. She understands that it is the journey, the road traveled, that holds the potential for answers she urges to uncover; driven by the belief that every step forward brings her closer to the resolution. Standing tall, Omega is infused showing a newfound vigor. Her eyes fixate upon the *hourglass*, its sands slipping away, the grains of sand were whispers in the wind. Remarkably, Omega observes that time appears never empty on either side of the vessel containing it. It seemed fluid and eternal, an oddity that defies conventional understanding. Omega, wary of the consequences of tampering time, leaves the hourglass untouched, unwilling to disturb the flow of time. She felt a unique calling to this memento. Like all mortals engaged by time, recognizing the connection that drew her closer to it. Death was inevitable, so was life.

Shaking off the hypnotic hourglass, Omega seizes a full oxygen tank and fastens it securely onto her back, prepared for the trials that lay ahead. The clues scattered before her serve as cryptic markers, guiding her through the labyrinthine corridors of her subconscious and offering glimpses into the mysteries and paradoxes that awaited her. Each biomarker held the promise of revelation, a key to unlocking the secrets of this strange and unfamiliar realm. Alone and wandering, Omega stumbles upon the welder mask. Relieved, she secures it over her head. Providing a strange comfort, the mask felt oddly connected to her; serving as salvation amidst the riddle that submerges her thoughts.

As the door creaks open, it calls Omega forward. An irresistible allure. Secrets to the answers she is seeking. She steps into the doorway, entering an odyssey into her own psyche, where the facts await to be uncovered.

Omega slips into the passageway, greeted by the sterile walls of a laboratory hallway, devoid of bustling activity. No humans in sight. It seemed as though the medical experiment had been abandoned for eons, a thick layer of dust blanketing every surface. Dust, the catalyst of creating planets, succumbed to the floor. It was but a buried rumor. Venturing into the dusty labyrinth, Omega's eyes are drawn to a towering wall exhibiting translucent windows, their glass-like panels stretching from floor to ceiling. Twilight filters through, crafting an ethereal shine. She feels an otherworldly pull, calling her closer. Distanced from any semblance of human interaction. A solitude existence, her spirit palpable in the emptiness of the laboratory. Omega descends the staircase, each step left behind a distinct imprint in the layer of dust. At the bottom, an imposing iron door. Her eyes linger on a glowing *exit* sign. A dim illumination, shining back and forth. No handle on the iron door. Omega pushes and shoves the door open, feeling its rough texture beneath her gloves, hinges groaning in protest as she steps into the darkness. There, amidst the shadows, lies the promise of sensitive information locked away.

***

Ash flakes drift from the heavens. The aftermath of *Nuclear War* leaves its imprint on the atmosphere. Consequences of the fallout rain down upon the world. A dark mushroom cloud hovers in the sky, blocking sunlight from reaching the ground. Snow submerges everything, encompassing the surroundings in freezing conditions amidst this doomsday scenario. In the distance looms a *glass pyramid,* its angular silhouette a monument to isolation in this forsaken reality. Clocks litter the beach, their synchronized movements ticking toward midnight—a chilling reminder of humanity's impending demise. Chalkboards float upon the sea's surface, their weathered surfaces written in chalk were brain outlines, scientific equations of the theory of relativity, and second law of thermodynamics. The theory of relativity discloses a narrative where the laws of physics hold sway universally, revealing how gravity's touch can bend the fabric of space and time. Famed logician and mathematician, Kurt Gödel, had musings that might not have birthed a tangible model of the universe. His theorem did unveil the tantalizing prospect that closed time-like curves could harmonize seamlessly, uniting the equations of general relativity, therefore suggesting that the laws of physics may indeed entertain the possibility of journeying to the past.

Then the second law of thermodynamics emerged as a guiding principle, stating that isolated systems tend toward entropy, depicting the decline of order into disorder. Embarking on a voyage to the past entails a curious consequence. A reminder that once an egg is scrambled, it cannot be unscrambled. Thus, conflicting the very essence of time travel. Omega ponders over these equations, her mind familiar with the concepts and frameworks as she absorbs all information with thoughtful consideration.

Omega treks forward, marching and navigating across the surreal environment. Half-buried in the snow, she confronts the hourglass once more, its sands suspended in a timeless limbo, a reflection of her own existential crisis. Ignoring the constraints of time, Omega refrains from laying her mortal hand upon the object. Twilight spreads ethereal hues upon the glass pyramid, illuminating its structure. An unearthly glow scintillates across the frosty coast. Omega approaches the pyramid's wide-open entry, and she ventures into its entrance, drawn by the mysteries of a portal undiscovered.

Immersed inside the glass pyramid, the world outside revealed through transparent walls. Empty of furniture, the space exudes an unsettling emptiness. The architecture was truly unique, surpassing the imagination of even the most ingenious engineers. Its alien design defies earthly conventions. Omega traverses its corridors, seeking a hint of meaning. Entering a new section, she confronts a maze of glass, reflections bouncing off every surface, distorting reality and heightening her disorientation. Omega persists, leading her into an octagonal chamber. The room's shape resembled infinity itself—a symbol of endlessness, a paradox of perpetual continuation.

Contemplating the concept, Omega ponders the nature of infinity and whether anything truly had an end. Thoughts of immortality wanders through her psyche, sparking questions about the potential for spirits to transcend time and inhabit another plane of existence. Where dreams could become reality. A Salvador Dali painting hangs, a melting watch on a deserted beach. This surreal image defies the conventional notion of time. Below it, a sundial catches the twilight, creating a shadow that points unwaveringly at noon, the first marker of time. On the ground lies the hourglass once more, almost as if the memento object were tracing Omega's every step. She waits, anticipation gnawing at her.

Silhouettes of the child shadow emerge from the ether behind the glass walls—an eerie and compelling image. A small child, appearing to be around middle childhood age; Omega is hypnotically drawn toward them, her steps guided by an unseen force, their haunting patience a silent invitation. She experiences a magnetic pull toward the child, a connection unlike anything she has ever experienced before.

Boom. Boom. Boom. Abruptly, Omega pivots as the glass pyramid succumbs to the pressure of the submerged world. Oddly, the structure finds itself captured in the hostile waters of the abyss, surrendering to the force of Mother Nature. *Crack. Crack. Crack.* The glass yields to the encroaching waters, weakening under the strain. Returning her gaze to the child shadow, Omega finds it vanished, a ghost lost upon arrival. The child shadow seemed to toy with Omega, as if engaging in a childhood game of hide and seek, where itself held the advantage, maintaining a mythological aura. Above, the sound of shattered glass reverberates through the pyramid. Boundaries of protection dissolve, intensifying the calamity of the situation to new heights. Ocean water floods in from all angles, pouring down over Omega.

The world in ruins, a wasteland stripped of its vitality. A desiccated palette of grays. Ash and soot fall endlessly, a torrent of destruction. Cataclysmic *Nuclear War* has ravaged the land. The road extends, a path leading to nowhere but nothingness, an elegy mourning the atonement of death. Omega sprints across the road, fleeing from the landscape devoid of life. No pursuers dog her steps, no pursuit in the distance. She is utterly alone, adrift in a world that offers no hope. She runs in circles, but *Nuclear Winter* offers no break for humanity; escape was impossible. Omega abruptly stops running, her eyes sweeping over the bleak portrayal. Every direction is drenched in doubt, every step a useless attempt of a clear direction. Her mighty willpower perseveres and Omega presses forward until she's swallowed by the swirling mist. Fog cocoons her, obscuring and consuming her soul.

* * *

Omega emerges from the dissipating fog, stepping into a realm transformed beyond recognition. A precipitous cliff took shape over an arctic valley. The desolation of the apocalypse yields a fantastical dreamscape, where the skylines fluoresce under violet skies. The radiation clouds have vanished. Relaxed, she removes her mask, letting the crisp air caress her face as she beholds the marvel. The sensation of clean air had never been so invigorating; each of her breaths in and out, Omega revels in its purity. A figure materializes, superior and dominating, the manifestation of Alpha unexpected yet undeniable.

"Good to see you again," Alpha's voice echoes through the allegorical landscape.

Omega, her breath forming frosty clouds, meets Alpha's observance. Her eyes drift to the hourglass near Alpha's frame, its sands flowing a mesmerizing rhythm, defying the conventional passage of time. Back and forth the sands of time flow. Grains of sand fluctuating between downward and upward movements as if caught in a perpetual struggle against the constraints of direction. Up they surged, defying gravity's pull, only to cascade back down moments later, their erratic dance a bewildering spectacle that left Omega perplexed.

"Are you lost?" Alpha's voice comes out in an authoritative tone.

She thinks on the question, realizing the weight of its implications. Perhaps she is adrift in this surreal reality. Her imagination intertwines in a ballet of choices and decisions only leading her in circles. Yet, there was familiarity in Alpha, a recognition in Omega's soul. "Where's the child?"

Time and space seemed to warp and shift, metaphorically akin to Einstein's equations of relativity. Omega's quest for the lost child is a riddle, riding the swirling mists of confusion. "The underworld," Alpha's voice intones a serious gravity.

The underworld, Omega thinks to herself, conjuring images of unseen perils lurking. In Alpha's cryptic response, Omega feels a foreboding truth, a dark world where the child's fate lies entangled against forces that govern this dangerous domain. Whispers of the underworld, a nightmare nested in the dream. The most terrifying realm, where even dreams hesitate to reset the imaginative worlds they create.

Intuition stirs, a deep root tugging at the edges of her consciousness, a distant memory struggling to resurface. Omega feels a strange kinship, as if she had traversed its ethereal environment in some forgotten past. Though the details escape her, there is a connection that speaks of shared histories.

"An inescapable dream," Alpha's voice is a haunting finality, an unfavorable commandment.

Omega understands the implications. Alpha's revelation is a fact of reality, nothing could deny it.

There was no escape from the pull of fate. Omega braces herself for the challenges that await her in this perpetual nightmare, aware that her quest would draw her into humanity's evil subconscious. This place never produces goodness; those who venture here remain captured by wickedness.

As Omega stands in contemplation, a tremor ripples through the rocky ground beneath her feet, sending vibrations coursing through her veins. Startled by the sudden disturbance, her eyes are drawn to a mysterious black hole in the ground, its yawning depths begging her to jump without cause for concern. Inching forward, Omega approaches the gaping maw of darkness, her curiosity piqued. A deep-seated urge to delve into the dark side of humanity begins to gnaw at her. Bracing herself, Omega

DOOM

ventures closer to the edge of the black hole, aware of the reality awaiting. At the precipice of the hole, Omega peers into the darkness swallowing her vision. It was the entrance into the underworld. An omen of prophecy conspires over this place, where evil was born and had thrived, untouched by any touch of good. The darkness seems to call her further. As she approaches closer, Omega feels a malevolent energy emanating from the hole, akin to a black hole radiating, mirroring the grand spectacles of the universe.

Despite the danger, Omega has no choice but to press forward. The child remains her ultimate goal; a quest she is determined to fulfill, no matter the confrontations she would encounter along the way. Omega puts on her mask, preparing herself for the hostile domain. She offers up one final glance at Alpha before summoning her courage and taking a leap of faith. The supercomputer remains expressionless, devoid of any emotion. Omega descends into the abyss, leaving behind the fantastical world as she plunges into the unknown depths of the underworld. Darkness swallows her being as she plummets into the void, continuing to clutch onto her promise of finding the child.

* * *

Omega emerges from the abyss entering the underworld, finding herself in the haunting vastness of a dead forest at dusk. Auroras shimmer, emerald streaks a testament to the Sun's explosive might. As if in protest, the Sun itself seems to scream across the heavens, lamenting the crimes perpetrated against its own inhabitants. Mist drifts like ethereal tendrils through the skeletal branches of ancient trees. Rain pours from the sky in a downpour, soaking everything in its path. Rotted lumber begs to be put out of its misery, remnants of trees that once served as the planet's lungs in the old world, now relegated to folklore in a landscape seething radiation at every turn. Trees are lifeless, their voices forever silenced in the aftermath of the nuclear holocaust. In the old world, they had possessed a unique language, a means of communication that had long fascinated humanity. It was a question that had plagued minds for generations: *Which held a greater consciousness, plants, animals, or insects?* All entities possessed their own complexities, contributing to the robust ecosystem of Earth. Plants, animals, and insects each play their part. However, during the arrival of the end of days, all those species were extinguished instantly. Now, amidst the desolation brought by the *Nuclear Winter*, such questions seem trivial. A requiem echoed for all innocent species outside of humanity, now extinct, erased off the face of the Earth.

Omega ventures forward, the dead forest watching her every step. She feels prying eyes. Dying branches had become brittle bark, a shadow of their former selves. Omega brushes against a branch which then disintegrated immediately, the radiation consuming everything, devouring nature until the bitter end. Lightning crackles overhead, briefly illuminating the skyline, a flash of electric brilliance. An energetic world pulsating antagonism by the essence of Omega, anger unleashing an intimidating display in an attempt to warn her against further approach. Suddenly, thunder cracks, as if Zeus himself had been summoned to halt her progress.

Undeterred, Omega presses on through the twisted remains of the trees. Beyond the dead forest, she spots imposing *skyscrapers* rising like monoliths—gods of steel, forged in the Industrial Revolution and fueled by the blood of oil. These towering structures of metal were a symbol of progress, yet, in their innovative glory, exposed their own downfall. Mankind had unwittingly incorporated the seeds of destruction. The machines that had propelled them to greatness consumed them. As humanity continued building their empires by depleting the planet's resources, the constraints of planetary limitations emerged as the ultimate crucible. Skyscrapers held the capacity for both creation and destruction, embodying the dual nature of the catalyst humanity had unleashed upon the world. And so, it was certain that the gods of steel would eventually meet their defeat, victims of their own arrogance. Each skyscraper rose like a titan.

Omega wanders closer into the matrix of this avant-garde megalopolis. Entering the heart of an abandoned metropolis, Omega gets engulfed by a lifeless and palpable atmosphere. The cityscape was eerily silent, devoid of any sound or movement. After the *Nuclear War*, bustling cities disappeared. Dense urban landscapes became graveyards of steel and concrete. Overpopulation came to an abrupt halt. No longer did the streets flock, displaying hustle and bustle of human activity. Silence was broken only by the mournful whispers of emptiness. The cycle of generations had stopped. No longer did cities radiate energy of vitality. Civilization lay abandoned, plagued by the ghosts of a dystopian world.

Omega double checks her oxygen tank, preparing herself for the toxic environment that immerses her. Radiation from the fallout permeates the air, spreading far and wide.

In past days of the old world, a time when life flowed a different rhythm, humanity breathed in oxygen without a second thought. They took for granted the important molecule that sustained their lives, assuming it would endure for eternity, but such assumptions were foolish. Change has always been the sole constant, ensuring that nothing ever remained static. After the detonation of nuclear arsenals, the composition of clean air shifted drastically, suffocating conglomerates of the human race and unleashing radiation so lethal that each breath risked brought forth a bold death. Oxygen became a rare commodity, coveted with the same desperation as oil. Humanity found themselves at the mercy of forces beyond their control. Mother Nature was the great equalizer, Earth the mightiest god of them all.

Omega makes her way through the deserted streets; the absence of humanity was obvious. *A zombie apocalypse setting. The last person on Earth. Twilight zone backdrop.* Omega feels like the last person alive. Raindrops metamorphose into a different state, transforming. Omega looks skyward, her eyes tracing the path of a dark cloud drifting over the area. Without warning, the heavens open, unleashing a torrent of oil that cascades down upon the world. It was as if some vengeful deity had decreed a modern-day flood, though instead of water, it was oil that besieges the city. Omega stands amidst the oily deluge, the pungent scent enveloping her aura. The sky tears open, with harsh cracks of orange lightning illuminating the darkness. Sawtooth streaks of fiery, zealous dazzle. Fossil fuel pours relentlessly, intensifying as time passes. Splatters of oil sputter against the road, a nightmarish tempest. Omega's keen eyes catch sight of a *subway entrance* in the distance. She races toward it, seeking refuge from the surreal storm.

She sprints down the stairs, entering the subway. Her footsteps fall silent in the hallow empty tunnels. No humans await, no trains operate—a void of souls. Omega settles onto a bench. She waits for a train that will never arrive, a poignant symbol of the abandoned hopes and dreams of civilization. She pauses, drawing in a slow, measured breath in the deserted subway station. Regaining her composure, she summons a second wind. A brief rest. Her eyes scan the platform, taking in the glowing lights.

A sign catches her attention, its digits scrolling: 27,374,730,198. Each digit a heartbeat of humanity, the cycle of life and death. Time slips by into an eternity of waiting, but still, no train arrives to break the quietness. From the never-ending tunnel, a figure emerges, dressed in the garb of a hazmat suit. The hazmat suit shimmers like a second skin, its sleek surface offering a barrier against the threat of radiation. Sealed seams and an integrated respirator provided vital protection for its wearer against the toxic fallout.

Omega tenses, her muscles coiling as the figure charges urgently toward her. The clang of their oxygen tank echoes in the immense tunnel.

"You're the dreamer!" the figure's voice comes as a declaration; it's an accusation. Before Omega can react, more figures emerge from the shadows, their pace hostile and vindictive. Footsteps thunder loudly against the train tracks, an ungodly resonance that seems to indicate the onset of the rapture. Body movements draw comparisons to wiry demons surging forward. Crazy frenzied strides. Arms and legs flail manically as they advance. They head toward Omega, increasing velocity as they sprint faster and faster, converging all the connected toward a diligent goal. An aura of malevolence emanates from their being, a manifestation of their sinister magnitude. Tested in the face of danger, a jolt of adrenaline protrudes Omega. She pivots on her heels and races back up the stairs, away from the encroaching hazmat figures.

A voice booms through the empty streets. "The countdown has officially begun."

Omega freezes in her tracks. She glances around the metropolis, searching for the source of the voice, but there was no one in sight, only the skyscrapers and fading light of dusk. The voice fades into the ether. Questions enter Omega's mind. *What countdown was this voice referring to? And what would happen when it reached its end?* Omega knows she has to find answers, and fast. Sirens wail like lost souls in the night. Fireworks erupt, their vibrant explosions painting the sky with ephemeral bursts of color. Omega gets submerged in pandemonium. She turns, her gaze

ICE

sweeping in a desperate arc, searching for a crack in the façade of this forsaken city and searching for a sliver of light to lead her back to reality. All she desires is the opportunity of awakening, to escape this illusion. Around and around, she spins within the labyrinth of her mind; the insistence of truth is relevant. Deception ensnares her in its tangled web around her consciousness. Each step she takes, each twist and turn, only serves to entangle her further into the tapestry of falsehoods. She persists, driven by the need to break free from the shackles of this fabricated reality, for in the heart of the underworld lies the seed of fraudulence; a cruel homage to the fragile nature of truth.

Dark clouds continue to hover in twilight. The alley stands as a canyon of urban decay, its walls resembling jaws of a starving creature. Until a slew of *research papers* descend from the sky, fluttering like wings of frightened birds. Omega watches the odd spectacle. Countless papers cascade from seemingly nowhere, swirling through the air. She reaches out, fingers grasping at the papers. A sheet lands in her palm, revealing complex diagrams, the sinister poetry of nuclear annihilation etched in its lines. Elaborate schematics outlining the mechanics of the nuclear bomb. Another flutters into her grasp, displaying the silhouette of a mushroom cloud, a harbinger of death. Tons of research papers continue to pour down without end.

Omega's steps falter as she nears the end of the alley. There, bathed in shadows and perched enticingly, is an ambiguous feminine figure, concealed in anonymity. An *anonymous mask* obscures their face, leaving only a cascade of crimson hair to betray their identity, its featureless face a canvas for the collective fears and suspicions of those who dare to challenge the shadows of power, embodying the secrets of conspiracy. Long crimson strands, like threads of fire, flow down the figure's back, swaying, a mystical elegance. Omega hesitates, caught between curiosity and caution, as the anonymous figure signals to her a single word: her name. "Omega?" the voice, a serpentine whisper, coils a hypnotic cadence, pulsating as the song of some ancient enchantress, drawing Omega closer. A surge of apprehension grabs Omega like the tightening coils of a constrictor, yet still, she presses forward, driven by her desperate search.

"Have you seen the child?" her voice replies, fragile.

The enchanting figure draws closer, speaking a whisper as soft as the rustle of leaves in the wind as they offer Omega a tantalizing divulgence into the underworld. "I'll show you a dream you'll never forget."

But before Omega can retreat, the storm of anonymity descends. From the ether, a gang of anonymous figures wearing masks emerge, descending upon Omega. A forceful yank, pulling her down. The predator captures its prey. Merciless hands claw at her, dragging her into their suffocating hold, a bag sealing her as panic tightens its grip around her soul like a vise.

* * *

Omega startles awake, her eyes flaring open as though yanked from the pit of her subconscious. She blinks, transitioning from the monarchy of the underworld back to the tactical truck's interior. Outside, snow falls softly, a tranquil veil draped over the military vehicle. Ice forms detailed patterns upon the window, weaving a vast network across the glass surface. Streaks of ice adorn the window, resembling pathways of neurons, captivating Omega's attention. Her mind wanders, lost in contemplation. She exhales a slow release of breath that momentarily calms her rage.

Memories surge forth, fragments of a past life. She could see the child amidst the purity of winter. Laughter echoes in the recesses of her mind, mingling with the hushed whispers of distant joy. A special association between Omega and the child is unmistakable. Their hearts intertwine, as strong as roots in the earth. Not even the divine hand of God could split them apart, for it was written in stone—unbreakable and eternal. Pillars of strength against the tempests of doom. But even as they laugh in the face of death, taunting the reaper, they could not escape time. They live as though eternity is their birthright, a fantasy to shield them from the harsh realities of mortality. Little did they know, their minds are but prisoners to time, waiting unknowingly for the final reckoning to arrive. Eternity is a dream, a mirage that vanished, leaving only the cold embrace of reality in its wake. Physics of immortality are nothing more than elements of fantasy. Yet, amid this bittersweet trance, a palpable absence releases a spell over the nostalgia.

The child's departure leaves a gaping wound, a hole in her heart that no amount of reminiscing can fill; a shadow child haunting the periphery of her consciousness. Featureless—a void of emotions—an inky black shadow is all that remains. Cross-legged amidst a field blanketed in snow, it ponders in solitude, its thoughts drifting toward possibilities of a future, lost in its own imagination. A spectral glow in the moon's pale light. Showcasing a phantom fluidity, the child shadow's hands descend, delicately probing into the frozen ground. Guided by unseen forces, something calls out to it, drawing it toward an unknown destination with an irresistible pull. Beneath the icy crust, the child shadow unearths the hourglass, ancient, emerging from its wintry grave. Sand whispers secrets lost to time as they trickle back and forth, dictated in no specific direction. Time is the measurement of death, echoing haunting visions that plague Omega's psyche.

The tranquility of the moment is broken by a sudden intrusion, a scarlet flash disrupting the serenity. Outside, a drone hovers stealthily. An investigator of the skies, akin to a janitor in the skies meticulously cleaning up the mess and tracing the priceless oil as it moves through the atmosphere. It exhibits the mark of a hunter, displaying a beacon device signaling its intent to pursue the oil barrels inside the tactical truck's cargo bay. Omega locks onto the drifting drone. She understands that where the drone is, so too are the pursuers of the oil. No time to rest or drift off, she prepares to face the threat head-on. She ignites the engine, its roar a defiant war cry. Omega slams her foot on the gas pedal, causing the wheels to spin momentarily on the black ice before gaining traction. She drives into the frozen forest, pushing onward despite the hazardous conditions. The drone pursues the payload, tracking its every move and evoking the clandestine aura of governmental surveillance.

The tactical truck rumbles through the labyrinthine frozen pathways of the forest, headlights slicing through the dense cloak of twilight. It climbs up a steep mountain, proceeding cautiously yet effectively. The military vehicle's wide frame pushes the limits, bordering on the edge of the road. One wrong skid and it would plummet off the mountainside. Each turn of the wheel rounding a tight corner, the drone follows closely, never wavering. Their state-of-the-art navigational systems ensure precision every step of the way. A sleek silhouette against the pure canvas of snow. Its scarlet warning light pulsates erratically, hovering menacingly overhead. Sensors scan, tracking every movement and every heartbeat. There was no escaping, the drone's artificial intelligence calculates every possible escape route, every potential hiding spot. A detective in the sky that would never stop, weaving effortlessly between tangled branches and gnarled trees through the windy road.

Venturing further into the remote Arctic wilderness, colossal ice structures appear on the horizon. Abruptly, the dreary uniformity of the icy desolation is disrupted by a jarring anomaly. Atop the mountain, a majestic *pyramid* pierces the frozen domain. Whispering sagas of a distant epoch, age-old stones resonate with tales of antiquity from a time long past, eons ago. Omega's eyes widen in disbelief, her breath catching in her throat as she brings the tactical truck to a shuddering halt. Brakes protest vehemently against the icy ground, their wail echoing as though they were a cry for departed spirits. A whisper, carried by the subzero breeze, wafts toward the pyramid, its subtle resonance evoking a peculiar recognition in Omega's essence. The underlying sound manifests as the seductress of time, luring all who enter.

Omega exits the vehicle, staring upon the stone pyramid, a disquieting déjà vu anomaly, reminiscent of the glass pyramid she had previously encountered earlier in a parallel reality. An eerie wail of the wind echoes the melancholic time-driven melody, emphasizing Omega's solitary aura. Grains of sand pour, deflecting off glass, a gentle *pitter-patter*. High above, the drone continues its ceaseless vigil, its mechanical eye inspecting Omega. She acts upon the mysterious child laughter. During each earned step, she imprints a path of depressions in the thick snow, progressing toward the cargo bay.

Unfastening the clasp, she retrieves a drum of oil, lifting it onto her shoulder, the grueling weight ridiculously heavy. A mysterious force entices her toward the pyramid; the faint childlike voice serving as a cryptic hint. Maneuvering through the timeworn complex, Omega battles the burden of the barrel and snow that engulfs her during every stride. Advancing steadily, she draws nearer to the ancient marvel, bearing a striking resemblance to the Egyptian pyramids. Unyielding, she forges ahead, delving further across the snowy terrain. Encountering an exposed passage that guides her into the pyramid, she ventures inside.

* * *

Pyramids of Giza and the Sphinx are vestiges in the fading light. Frost drapes the golden sand, rendering the landscape entirely white; no trace of brown to be found anywhere. Towering forms of the pyramids have surfaces glazed over an icy veneer. Jagged icicles cling to the edges, frozen tears glistening. The Sphinx stands stoically, its enigmatic face obscured by a sheet of ice. Egypt remains suspended in a winter wonderland enchantment. Considering the universe is barely above two degrees, Earth has transformed into a spectacle of truth, a manifestation of reality.

The Colosseum centuries ago was the mastery of ancient Rome. Yet an insurmountable transformation occurs, exhibiting a cathedral of ice. Arches and columns, past symbols of strength and grandeur, hidden beneath a surreal frost. Gone are the warm hues of ancient stone, replaced by the cold embrace of frozen crystals that glimmer and gleam. The grandeur of Rome's glory days forever lost in this frozen nightmare. The sky above cool colors of pearl and cotton. A surreal radiance illuminating the icy panorama.

The Parthenon years ago carried past enlightenment; embodied a revolutionary architectural feat, boasting a colossal dome crowned by an oculus. Symbolizing a divine connection as natural light cascaded into its sacred interior, bridging mortals and gods… until succumbing to a climate unfriendly to its historical design. Grand columns experiencing an unfamiliar chill, their marble surfaces weathered by the eternal winter. No longer does the Sun caress its architecture; instead, ice forms around the philosophical monument, stripping it of its former glory. Days of bustling activity and fervent worship are distant echoes. Encased in a block of ice, the transience of knowledge and the impermanence of greatness remain trapped in the continuum of history.

* * *

Intermittent torches punctuate the hallway, their intense glow piercing through the darkness. Lumbering while carrying the oil barrel slung over her shoulders, Omega wanders down the tunnel, only to come face-to-face with an impassable dead end. The interloper lowers the oil barrel to the ground, its weight a burden matched only by the weight of uncertainty holding her down. Voices have ceased, and she finds herself with nowhere else to turn. *Was this all just a wild goose chase*? Her gaze drifts upward, swallowed by the void that consumes the ceiling—an abyssal abyss offering no answers. Suddenly, ticking clocks grow louder. The sound of time takes on a sinister vibe, akin to a dark cackle. An ominous aura, foreboding and unsettling. Not a sound one would want to be alone with. Ticking clock hands mark the motion of minutes, seconds, hours—a whimsical exactness. It was as if time were breathing, its rhythm pulsating after each *tick* and *tock*. From the darkness, a *rope* descends, a lifeline dangling from the unseen.

A voice, disembodied and authoritative, breaks through the silence like thunder in a storm, words carrying the weight of centuries. "Time has brought the end of humanity," it intones, a pronouncement.

Omega, on high alert, absorbs the gravity of the statement. She shifts to the rope, tendrils of ivy clinging to stone. The rope remains just beyond her grasp.

A voice speaks again, its words holding an absolute truth. "Chaos controls time. It's the only natural system," it declares.

Only courage can guide her, as Omega surveys her surroundings, finding nothing but emptiness in all directions. Once more, she finds herself alone. Determined to press forward, she repositions the oil barrel and climbs on top, using it as a makeshift pedestal. She extends every fiber of her arm, stretching it to its limit, and while taking a leap, she barely secures her grip on the rope. Dangling for a moment, she begins her ascent, muscles straining against the pull of gravity. Each pull, she draws closer to the repetitive and hostile ticking of clocks, disappearing into the blackness.

* * *

In the deep recesses of time, there existed a land unlike any other seen. *Pangea*, the colossal supercontinent, once united all the continents into one ancient giant landmass. Eons ago, continents collided and melded, their edges like puzzle pieces fitting together in a mosaic of unimaginable proportions. North America, that familiar landmass of forests and plains, was not alone in its solitude, but rather held hands, its siblings across the oceans. The late Paleozoic Era spoke of secrets fulfilling unity across the lands.

North America, rugged terrains and untamed wilderness, nestled against Africa, forming a cradle of primordial Earth. South America, home to the Amazonian jungles, merged Europe, where layers of time buried history beneath its soil. Strange creatures roamed Pangea, their forms unlike any seen in present day. From the towering peaks of the Appalachians to the sun-drenched plains of what would one day be the Sahara, diversity flourished in every corner.

But time cared not for the unity of continents. Slowly, imperceptibly, Pangea began to crumble, its connection weakening. Rifts formed and oceans yawned, swallowing the land. North America drifted apart from its companions, setting sail on an odyssey through the ages. Yet the echoes of Pangea lingered in the contours of the land, a reminder of a time when the world was one.

Suddenly, an asteroid hurtles through the cosmos, an omen of doom. Its trajectory, a dedicated path toward Earth, breaches the atmosphere with a ferocity unmatched. A fiery trail marks its descent against the backdrop of eternity. Legions of celestial bodies follow, descending from the heavens in a chaotic song of destruction and rebirth. Billions of asteroids collide and merge; their impact of devastation echoes an unforgiving force. Gravity, the glue that binds matter together, flexes its immense power, showcasing its influence. A battleground of cosmic proportions. Earth, entangled in the throes of a vociferous hurricane, is overwhelmed by asteroid impacts. Reality embraces the celestial bombardment.

An unbroken horizon of water meets the sky. No land disturbs, no sign of human endeavor mars the pristine dawn. There is only the ocean, in all directions. They plummet, a swift descent into the deep blue. Bubbles rise, escaping from the hydrothermal vents that punctuate the seabed. These vents pulsate a special energy. They are the heartbeat of the aquatic underworld, channels through which the planet's inner fire flows. Humble beginnings of existence, where tiny microbes emerge and thrive, carrying on the legacy of creation. They drift aimlessly. Some of the microbes begin to coalesce, forming unique structures. It is the beginning of something new, something extraordinary. Magic and miracles unfold, defying the odds. Life stumbles tentatively forward, its genesis born in the primordial ocean.

* * *

In an unknown room, snowflakes drift, forming a ghostly vortex and swirling into a choreographed chaos. Omega is drenched in blackness, the sack draped over her head obscuring her vision. Shaking her head, she fights against the suffocating unknown, striving to break free from the void. But the darkness persists, suffocating her. Omega sits on the ground, her arms bound behind her back and tethered to a pole, her captivity parallel to chains dragging her into the core of Earth. The sound of her own breath and the sensation of cold begins seeping into her bones. It is colder than ever before.

As the sack slips from her head, Omega blinks against the sudden onslaught of brightness, her eyes adjusting to the newfound clarity. On the walls, the world reveals itself as a kaleidoscope of knowledge, each book page a fragment of humanity's collective wisdom. Pages torn from influential books plaster the walls like wallpaper. From the ancient scrolls of civilizations to the revolutionary manifestos of modern times. Voices of past and present. She can't help but notice the common theme: the end of days. From the dawn of the Stone Age to visions of the distant future; every civilization harbored an apocalyptic fascination. Prophets across time had made predictions, each offering their own interpretation of humanity's ultimate fate.

It strikes Omega how ingrained this obsession has been in the human psyche. Throughout history, civilizations encountered their own demise, whether through natural disasters, wars, or cosmic catastrophes. It seemed that, despite all the advancements and progress, the fear of the end remained a constant, lurking in the shadows of consciousness. Yet, amidst the myriad of predictions and prophecies, Omega can't shake the feeling that perhaps humanity's true strength lay not in predicting its end, but in persevering despite the destruction, even in the face of the end of days.

Omega stares at the sea of words, her eyes tracing the souls of each letter. As a seeker of knowledge, she has always believed in the power of language to unveil the mysteries of existence. Even as humanity answers every question plausible, from the beginning of the universe until the end of time, euphoria remains an impossible dream. Pursuit of enlightenment is hindered by humanity's vindictive power. The reckless paradox of abundance and scarcity, of greed and need, destroyed their aspirations for a better world. For all their advancements, humanity remains shackled by their own mortality. A human lifespan is but a mere candlewick in the wind, extinguished by the fleeting winds of chance. And as the clock ticks toward their end, Omega can't help but wonder if true fulfillment would forever elude her species, lost in the potion of evil.

Anonymous towers over Omega, her trench coat discarded, revealing a form-fitting latex outfit that accentuates her athletic body. Her body showcases intricate tattoos; serpents coiling sinuously around her arms and neck, puzzle pieces imprint her thighs in a scattered mosaic. Each tattoo told a unique story. It is the serpent who holds the key to good and evil, weaving a continuous cycle of light and shadow. Her figure is sculpted by a tight corset, cinching her waist into the coveted shape of an hourglass. She is the joker in the deck of cards, embodying heroism and villainy, representing the death of a hero. Anonymous conceals herself behind her mask of secrets, her Medusa-like scarlet hair cascading like a river of blood, intertwining her mystique. Anonymous' every move inspires the serpents to come alive, their scales shimmering a hypnotic temptation, while the puzzle pieces signal the promise of hidden truths waiting to be uncovered. As she stands there, a vision, Anonymous exudes an aura of intrigue, drawing Omega into her tarnished web with a magnetic pull that is impossible to resist.

"Your rights are no longer in your control," whispers Anonymous, her emotions remaining undetectable. Behind her mask, all expressions are concealed, leaving only the cadence of her voice as a clue to her intentions. And true to her nature, she remains the wildcard of the deck.

Omega's eyes pierce through her game of seduction, facing Anonymous in a silent duel of wills. Omega finds herself entranced by the spirit of Anonymous, who embodies the goddess Medusa, a symbol of the dark forces that lurk in humanity. As she gazes upon the tattoos adorning Anonymous' body, Omega knew reflection of mankind's inner turmoil, a twisted puzzle of ego and desire forever entangled, as though they were serpents coiling around a prey. In the mesmerizing display of Anonymous' form, Omega sees a mirror reflecting the darker aspects of human nature, the thirst for dominance and control that drove civilizations to rise and fall. The puzzle pieces scattered across her skin hint at the fragmented nature of truth, elusive and ever-shifting, waiting to be pieced together by those brave enough to confront the bad. Caught in the gaze of Medusa's likeness, Omega feels the magnetism invitation winding around her, drawing her into the labyrinth of deceit.

Immersed in the vision of Anonymous, Omega feels the provocative pull of power. This force promises ecstasy and destruction in equal measure.

"Just enjoy the show," moans Anonymous, luring Omega closer into her reality. Circling Omega, Anonymous bides her time, waiting for the perfect moment to strike. Each movement infuses sinister enchantment that drifts around Omega. Anonymous fabricates a tale of temptation, her tattoos pulsating. Her theme is that of a messenger. A wildcard, disrupting the balance during her every move. A joker of temptation.

"You can avoid the apocalypse," she promises, her words dripping in a honeyed flavor. As the dance reaches its zenith, Anonymous draws close, their masked lips brushing Omega's cheek in a tantalizing European caress. Anonymous' arms coil around Omega's neck, mirroring a tightening chokehold. "This is your last chance. Give up. Otherwise, you'll be finished," Anonymous' voice slithers. Her forearms tighten around Omega's neck like the constricting hold of a boa constructor. Omega's breath labors against the vise-like hold, her fiery eyes blazing. "Your choice, hero," comes the taunt as the pressure intensifies, squeezing the life from Omega's lungs. Omega's psyche staggers on the edge of surrender, her soul slipping away, just as wind blows through fingertips on a windy day.

The ghost of the child shadow floods her mind. As the horrors of the underworld threaten to consume her, Omega's hope remains, longing for escape. She remains a beacon of positivity. Knowing that every road to success is full of bumps along the way, she embraces the challenges as integral to the journey. It is the chase of unattainable goals where life finds its true value—refusing to succumb to quitting. Not today, nor any other day, would she falter in her determination.

Maintaining her fortitude, she is able to unleash a final surge of willpower. Omega fights against the tide of fear, holding onto the connection of the child shadow. Omega finds the spark of defiance, and unleashing godlike strength, she tears herself from the clutches of her assailant, ripping the pole from its moorings. Though the chokehold still constricts her, Omega continues forward, each step a battle against the forces of evil. With a thunderous crash, they tear through the barrier of knowledge, pages of wisdom swirling in a frenzied storm. Omega and Anonymous burst through the pages of wisdom, entering another dimension.

* * *

Navigating the pyramid's labyrinth, dust swirls around her, Omega forges ahead, disregarding the rope that has guided her. No longer did the sound of time encapsulate her. More torches light her path as she treads the passageway, encountering stones eroded by time. Language written on the stone walls etched scars and wounds that held clues of a past civilization. A communication unlike any she had experienced before, an alien type of transmission that transcended earthly languages and conventions.

From the darkness, Shadow reappears and slinks back into existence behind her, an observer guiding the wandering Omega. The clashes and claims between Carl Jung and Sigmund Freud spoke about the collective consciousness of the ego and soul. This notion could be most aptly described through the concept of Shadow. The entities walk side by side. Every human has a shadow.

Omega's voice expresses the gravity of her revelation. "I saw the beginning and the end," she says, her words explaining a sacred mantra.

Shadow's voice pierces the silence, sharp as a shard in the darkness. "Of what?" it inquires, its tone a haunting curiosity, echoing the enigma of the ages.

"Earth," Omega replies, as if she spoke not just of a planet, but of the entirety of existence.

"What was the last thing you saw?" Shadow's question lingers, its voice coercing Omega's memories.

"History repeating itself," she had glimpsed into the cyclical planetary nature of time. Her wandering frame freezes, caught in the crossfire of two divergent paths, each demanding a decision she must make. She pivots toward Shadow, placing her trust in this ghostly guide.

"That way," Shadow directs, guiding Omega. A supernatural certainty. Another entrance inside the pyramid to somewhere unknown. From Omega's viewpoint, Shadow serves as her partner, the commanding captain steering her odyssey through this preternatural structure.

The duo moves cautiously, walking step by step with an eternal hush between them. No significant writings grace the walls anymore, no monuments or tombs; its eerie, quiet corridors showcase an ancient civilization yet undiscovered. They reach another ascending passageway, leading them toward the queen's chamber. Omega's fingers graze the limestone, each touch a communion harking centuries of lost voices. They venture into the south chamber, only to find it culminating in a dead end. Twilight filters through the shafts. The pyramid is a maze of unknown twists and turns. Each step is a guess. It is as though the pyramid itself has taken on a malevolent sentience, toying with Omega and her guide like a capricious deity playing a game of cosmic chess. A network of tunnels, where all that matters seems lost, viewed through the lens of time.

Death, as Omega perceives it, serves as the yardstick by which she gauges time, a perception that has led her to this place, away from the tumult of the oil war. Curiosity gnaws at her as she ponders the nature of this pyramid, and why the shadowy presence of the child seems closer than ever. Omega craves answers that remain unanswered, leaving her empty. Air crackles an eerie energy, as if the pyramid was alive. Her eyes drift back and forth, looking for a clue, and there it was, on the stone ground lay the hourglass, once more defying reason. Omega hesitates, stunned by its reappearance. The hourglass seems to taunt her, tracking her. A step ahead every time, as if to mock her futile attempts to unravel its mysteries.

"The arrow of time," Shadow's voice comes cryptic, a haunting refrain. In its enigmatic words lie a suggestion of inevitability, as if the hourglass is but a mere instrument leading her toward a direction of destiny.

Omega walks away, abandoning the hourglass. As she turns away, her eyes fall upon geometrical writings etched into another dead end. Geometry symbols of a circle, triangle, and square. Intrigued, Omega approaches, her fingertips tracing the chiseled grooves of the inscriptions, her mind contemplating the tantalizing possibility of unlocking their secrets. "Writing language was forbidden inside the pyramids," Omega speaks to herself.

Shadow glances over, its figure reflecting the flickering twilight. Foreboding, as if it were a harbinger of secrets. "This isn't just any pyramid," Shadow creepily intones. In its words lay a suggestion of mysteries yet to be unveiled, hinting at the true nature of the ancient structure in its timeless dominion.

"What are you talking about?" she speaks, confused.

"Look," Shadow urges, its finger extending to point at a stone on the ground marked with an 'X'. The letter 'X' symbolizes the conclusion of something, an entity whose existence is over, relegated to the past, deceased, and vanished. It begged for Omega to listen. A long-buried secret waiting to be unearthed. This was a tantalizing clue in the enigmatic puzzle of the pyramid.

"Follow the clue," Shadow gently commands.

"Where does it lead?" Her words fall on deaf ears as she seeks guidance, a yearning to uncover the destination that awaits her at the end of the cryptic trail.

"The answer is below," Shadow replies. A suggestion of deeper truths, waiting to be discovered by Omega's pursuit of understanding.

"What answer!?" the interloper's voice comes frustrated, her words a plea for clarity. In her inquiry lies a desperate longing to grasp the truth.

"Time is precious..." Shadow's voice trails off into the silence of the queen's chamber. Words urging Omega to seize the opportunity before her and embark on the journey that awaits, before the sands of time slip through her fingers. Shadow slips away, a ghost fading back into the shadows, leaving Omega alone.

The mantra, "Time is precious," resounds loudly. She takes a moment to gather her composure, drawing strength from the sound of silence that submerges her. Omega makes her way to the spot marked by the 'X', her footsteps echoing softly as she approaches the unique symbol. Her mind buzzes. Glancing back at the hourglass, she is captivated by the mesmerizing moving sand—a reminder of the urgency of her quest. Omega slides her fingers into the crevice of the stone block, feeling the rough texture beneath her touch as she slides and removes the stone, unveiling a *black hole* embedded in the ground. She reaches inside, her fingertips grazing against the cool metal of a sturdy rope bolted into the stone. It offers a lifeline into the darkness as she prepares to descend into the pyramid.

Surveying her surroundings, Omega confirms the security of the rope, its sturdy construction offering reassurance. She wraps her fingers tightly around the coarse fibers, feeling the decision bearing down upon her shoulders. Taking in one final glance at the hourglass, Omega releases a breath she hadn't realized she was holding and begins her descent. Each downward motion guides her. The world above fades away. Despite creeping unease, Omega moves forward, her soul grasping at a desperate dream to find the child. Every fiber of her being yearns for answers, for resolution, as she continues to navigate the underworld, determined to reunite with the lost child no matter the cost.

* * *

The Museum of the Future rose like a creator of innovation, presenting a marvel of avant-garde architecture that shimmered in twilight. A striking oval-shaped exterior, its sleek lines reminiscent of an eye gazing into the phenomenon. This architectural masterpiece invites visitors to delve into a world of possibility, where imagination knows no limits. A sight that defied imagination, a futuristic gallery. Displaying a labyrinth of cutting-edge technology and visionary design. Air purred palpable energy-charged anticipation. Each hallway holds the key to promises of pioneering, illuminated by the glow of interactive displays and holographic projections. The scent of freshly polished metal created an intoxicating atmosphere.

Omega's footsteps echo through the corridors and off the sleek surfaces of the gallery. Around her, exhibits showcase the latest advancements in fields ranging from artificial intelligence to space exploration. Giant screens exhibit breathtaking images of distant galaxies and futuristic cityscapes. But amidst the awe-inspiring presentations and state-of-the-art technology, there lingers a rumor of something darker being around the corner.

Cobwebs cling to the edges of the exhibits; it was as though the museum has lost its way. Knowledge has long been a contentious battleground, some seeing it as a noble endeavor while others view it as a dangerous journey. Throughout history, this conflict between ignorance and intellect has raged, shaping civilization. A struggle for the meaning of life, where the quest for understanding often collides against the forces of fear and superstition. Omega enters the maze, but she can't shake the feeling that she is being watched, that unseen eyes are following her every move, hidden among the gleaming displays and shimmering holograms. Fortitude forces Omega to continue. As a child, Omega had always been fueled by an unspoken curiosity, a fascination that continues to burn brightly throughout her life. Her desire to uncover facts remains a part of her identity.

Inside the Museum of the Future, amidst the promise of tomorrow, Omega knows that answers await, answers that would reshape the course of history and humanity's destiny. Here bask the relics of civilization's triumphs: DNA modification, CRISPR coding, and the pursuit of eternal life. Those advancements are now shrouded in neglect, coated in dust and grime. Ambition and audacity of a species that was on the brink of unlocking the riddle of immortality had abruptly halted during World War III. As nations and ideologies clashed, the pursuit of eternal life was overshadowed by the realities of doomsday. After the devastation, the dream of immortality lay dormant.

ICE

Down the corridors and up the stairs, an evolutionary history of human ingenuity had departed. Sadness for the potential that was never fully realized, for the promise of a future that now exists only as a fading memory. In the future, humanity had harnessed a suite of technologies to combat the runaway greenhouse effect, cracking the code of carbon extraction and slowing environmental devastation. Despite the challenges, humanity persevered... until the energy collapse occurred, igniting the oil wars.

Energy and lifestyle have perennially stood as crucibles for every species on Earth. Humans, perched at the apex of the food chain, savor the delicate joys of existence. *Who could fault them?* In an era where excess knew no bounds, the question of when *enough* truly meant *enough* seemed a distant concern. Economic expansion surged exponentially, propelling humanity forward on a ride of consumption. Yet, as the world's finite oil reserves dwindled to unsustainable levels and the specter of peak oil loomed ominously, the era of unrestrained resource exploitation approached its climax. Faced by the stark reality of dying energy sources, humanity found itself locked in a desperate struggle for survival. Nations turned inward, fighting tooth and nail to hold onto their remaining energy reserves, even as the world hurtled toward doom because of its own limitations. This apocalyptic event fractured the delicate balance of power.

The gleaming halls of progress now showcase ravages of conflict, their walls scarred by the echoes of gunfire and cries of the wounded. Omega's journey through the museum takes on a new urgency as she maneuvers through the remnants of a lost civilization.

She rounds another corner, and suddenly, an odd irregularity catches her eye—a glitch in the matrix of progress—a ripple in time. It is as if the foundation of the future has been shaken, revealing cracks in the simulation of human achievement. As Omega stands in the midst of this surreal revelation, she feels a paradoxical anomaly creeping over her. In the center of the room, saturated in an ethereal glow and emanating from a black hole exhibit, sits an *Ancient Astronaut*, dressed in a primeval spacesuit.

A bronze helmet obscures their face, symbolizing a new hope for a fresh start. They wore a suit reminiscent of ancient divers, thick and protective, enveloping them in a robust armor that spoke of its fortitude. The suit's centerpiece was a massive bronze helmet, weathered and scarred metal surfaces. An artifact from another era, each dent and scratch telling a story of endurance. The entire ensemble had the aura of something forged for battle, its integrity tested through the eons, standing resilient against the ravages of time. They feel as if they have traversed the cosmos since the Bronze Age. An enigmatic figure in the midst of dust and cobwebs. Forgotten dreams metaphorically radiate off the unique being, swirling like ethereal wisps. In the Ancient Astronaut's aura, there is aspiration of a journey left unfinished. They were an artifact of a time when humanity dared to reach for the stars, only to be consumed by the darkness. A bronze cross. Ancient beliefs proudly cling to the helmet, a relic of faith.

The Ancient Astronaut sits stoically, unperturbed and exuding ancient wisdom. They possess a quiet demeanor, cradling the enigma of creation in their hands. Upon the sterile surface of the wooden table, a *grail of water* glimmers. A symbol of life. Countless epochs rest upon their shoulders. Logic flows through the Ancient Astronaut like a steady current, guiding their every move. Yet, beneath the veneer of rationality lies an understanding that transcends mere calculation. A wisdom witnessing the universe unfold across infinite lifetimes. This being is untouched by the constraints of time and space, as if they have traversed the breadth of eternity.

They hold secrets of trillions of galaxies. A custodian of eternal truths, beyond the subconscious of mortal minds.

The Ancient Astronaut peers and pierces the soul of Omega, where time itself seems to falter. Their voice remains tranquil. "Welcome," they speak, their words a supernatural resonance. It was a simple greeting, an invitation to all who dare to venture into the unknown of this entity's existence. In this moment, the Ancient Astronaut is a bridge between worlds, a guide to those who seek understanding. Despite its godlike spirit, they harbor humility, recognizing the duality inherent in all beings. Good and evil have always been nature's spell. "Join me," they say, their words carrying on the gentle currents. "Have a drink."

In the face of Omega, the Ancient Astronaut extends an invitation, a simple yet important gesture of camaraderie. Their voice, reaching out to Omega with an offer of connection. Omega cautiously approaches, acknowledging the momentous encounter. Familiarity consumes her—there is a magnetic attachment with the entity. Omega draws nearer, tempered by a quiet humility.

The Ancient Astronaut, ever mindful of the balance between mortal and divine, extends the grail, a vessel of unity toward Omega.

She accepts the offering, the grail's touch a hypnotic brush. Omega removes her welder mask and brings the grail to her lips, binding together two beings from disparate realms in a shared importance of interrelatedness.

Water inside the grail flows, cosmic energy, swishing around endlessly. The endless worlds and infinite souls, this miraculous substance produces over eons. Taking a tiny sip of this sacred water, Omega communes with the Ancient Astronaut. She returns the grail, never completely finishing the water. A river of understanding flows between them. An unspoken recognition of the interconnectedness of all things. Omega is hanging on the edge of every shared word. She remains engaged, an avid listener, attuned to the nuances of communication. As a little girl, she had always favored listening over speaking, a trait that had persisted into her adult form.

"Nature's greatest invention," the entity speaks, a quiet homage to the creativity of the cosmos.

"Who are you?" Omega's question sweeps through the ether.

The Ancient Astronaut pivots their head toward Omega. They lift a solitary finger, a gesture of quiet. "Silence is a powerful weapon," they speak gravely. In the old world, silence held a unique potency for Earth. "It built civilizations," they continue, expressing past achievements. Silence was the unknown communication from elsewhere. "In the quiet moments between chaos and creation, humanity found purpose." The Ancient Astronaut contemplates the profound impact of silence on the course of history. Silence had been a hope for the future in which civilizations were forged.

"I'm trying to find the child," Omega's divulgence is a reminder of her current quest.

"Their disappearance?" The Ancient Astronaut's tone comes as a hidden puzzle, complicated underneath the mask it wore. A galactic hushed communication permeated between their souls.

"Do you know what happened?" Omega's voice breaks the silence.

"I'll show you the way to them," the entity declares, expressing a promise of reunion.

The Ancient Astronaut, mindful of the enormity of Omega's task, extends their palm toward her, cradling a small *globe* in their gloved hand. The mini globe, a tiny representation of the pale blue dot that dotted the universe, dwarfed by the entity's rusty protective glove. Omega's eyes glaze upon the miniature totem; even in its diminutive size, the globe held cherished possible impossibilities.

"So many possibilities," the Ancient Astronaut remarks, their voice radiating. "Beginnings. Endings. Resurrections. Are you ready to explore?"

Omega's curiosity piques, fixed on the miniature globe. "Where?"

"Everywhere," the entity replies, a whispered invitation to embark on a journey of discovery. Releasing the totem, a gentle roll begins from the object as the Ancient Astronaut sends the mini globe spinning across the table toward Omega. A symbolic gesture of shared exploration.

She accepts the offering of the miniaturized Earth, cradling it in her palm, inspecting its design. *Everything has a place and a time on Earth*, she thinks to herself.

Omega examines the intricate details. Each contour and feature of the tiny Earth holds a wealth of symbolism. Every element speaks to the complexity of the natural world. From the towering peaks of mountains to the rivers and oceans. But beyond the physical landscape, the globe also depicts a higher dimension of harmony of all living things. The quantum entanglement of ecosystems, cultures, and civilizations that hold humanity together. Omega absorbs the myriad representations, for even in its small size, the miniature globe contains the soul of existence. Reality began from the dreams of Earth.

War cries bellow. Omega, ever vigilant, pivots at the sudden intrusion, confronting a gang of *Mongolian soldiers* that materialize from nowhere. Omega looks back for the Ancient Astronaut, but they had vanished into the ether. Disappeared without a trace, in the blink of an eye. A magician's trick.

Omega's reaction is swift. She flees from the encroaching soldiers, ancient armor clanging akin to ominous bells as they give chase through the labyrinthine corridors of the museum. Mongolian soldiers, heirs to the legacy of Genghis Khan, were a force of ruthless warriors. A fierce loyalty to their leader and a mastery of tactics honed on the steppes of Central Asia. They sweep across the land like a storm, striking fear into the hearts of all who dared to oppose them. Genghis Khan's legacy was complex and controversial, celebrated for his lethal military success and vast empire he established. His methods were undeniably brutal and resulted in the deaths of millions. Khan's conquests were marked by widespread destruction, pillaging, and the slaughter of countless populations. His campaigns resulted in the deaths of a significant portion of the world's population at the time, inspiring countless warriors. Genghis Khan's genetic legacy was a testament to the scale of his conquests. Studies suggesting that his DNA was responsible for approximately 15% of the world's population due to the number of individuals his empire displaced, assimilated, or annihilated. These barbaric humans pursue Omega, using every ounce of their being, and driven by a primal urge to conquer and murder, ancient instincts awakened.

Omega's strides begin thudding in the sterile museum. She darts past projections of distant galaxies. An otherworldly, universal glow of luminescence inspires the surroundings, evoking the sensation of traversing into another dimensional plane. The Andromeda Galaxy drifts, a swirling abyss of stars, while the Milky Way stretches across the void. A cosmic scar. Omega navigates past celestial bodies, each a brief glimpse in her fevered flight. Mars, a rusted wasteland; Jupiter showcasing its surreal storms; Saturn displaying its iconic rings—they all blur into a psychedelic representation, as if she were sprinting across the solar system.

The holographic universe conveys the message of her small-sized insignificance, echoing throughout infinity. A grain of sand is as relevant to a beach as a human is to the universe. A tiny speck in the grand scheme of things, yet intricately connected to the greater whole. In this vastness, her pursuers are predators, a constant threat at the fringes of her consciousness. Omega's steady breath sustains her endurance, her heart beating calmly. She remains in prime condition and prepared, poised against the backdrop of eternity.

Omega enters the robotic era exhibit. Centuries-old robots, with rusted frames barely holding on; ancient guardians of bygone technology, their watchful gazes spanning across the ages, preserving the secrets of eras long gone. Robots, by shouldering the burden of laborious tasks, liberated humanity's collective consciousness, affording them the opportunity to free their minds. However, the integration of robots into the labor force proved to be a double-edged sword. As it not only alleviated humanity's burdens but also led some to question their purpose. Some humans flourished in newfound freedoms, while others succumbed to despair as they grappled with their diminishing significance in a world dominated by machines.

Omega darts in and out of the robotic maze, her form minuscule in the middle of the towering mechanical behemoths. She streaks through the expanse, her athleticism akin to a wild gazelle fleeing the pursuit of lions across the plains of Africa. Competition between carbon-based life forms and silicon-based machines was never envisioned as a clash for supremacy. Yet, as the world encountered overpopulation and demands of an overbearing workforce, an unforeseen rivalry emerged. Each new human born produced the need for infrastructure and development growth, fueling an endless cycle of construction. In contrast, machines, not controlled by the limitations of biology, offered a cost-effective and efficient solution: tirelessly operating around the clock. Thus, the stage was set for an unprecedented confrontation between humanity's organic ingenuity and the efficiency of artificial intelligence.

Appearing from the robots, a Mongolian soldier—a jagged interruption in Omega's frenzied escape attempt. She stumbles, her pursuit bearing down upon her. Despite the crushing weight pressing down on her chest, her mind continues racing for a solution. Unleashing an instinct honed by a lifetime of survival, Omega halts in her tracks. Her muscles tense as she grabs the soldier. Both bodies collide into a robot, an orchestra of metal and flesh crashing and banging. The soldier's limbs entangle in a morass of twisted metal and wires. More Mongolian soldiers emerge, radiating an insatiable palpable passion. Omega retreats swiftly, her mind racing for an escape route from the ambush.

Rows of supercomputers, the arcane power of digital sorcery. These machines were responsible for humanity's collective knowledge, their circuits humming legacy of information stored in the "cloud." Every aspect of the world was meticulously programmed into their operating systems. However, in the aftermath of the *Nuclear War*, a catastrophic electronic magnetic pulse erupted, unleashing destruction that swept across the digital world, obliterating all forms of digital communication. In an instant, the digital age history of civilization was forever deleted.

Omega cuts through the labyrinthine of technology, her movements immersed in the symphony of data. Holographic projections permeate the exhibit, ephemeral algorithms that govern the unseen laws of cyberspace. Omega's form melds seamlessly into the digital landscape, her body a transient vessel for the equivocal forces. Her sprint meets an abrupt barrier, an unseen trap woven from strands of silken deceit. Omega fights against the invisible bonds, struggling against a perplexing spiderweb.

Mongolian soldiers descend upon Omega. Her skull meets the ground and pain channels through her mind as she slips into unconsciousness. A metamorphosis unfolds, a surreal transfiguration guided by unseen hands. Algorithms and translucent ghosts converge over her form, creating digital destiny around the fallen human. Bit by bit, Omega's essence entwines with the infinitum of the digital ether, entering the singularity of cyberspace. She transcends the limitations of flesh and blood. A vestige of consciousness suspended in code and computation. In human form, the singularity emerges as a paradoxical fusion of mortal fragility and transcendent potential. A being poised on the precipice of evolution, where flesh and machine unite, the singularity of consciousness. Omega ascends, her consciousness merging into the nebulous expanse of her subconscious. Reality and fantasy intertwine in a kaleidoscope. Bright lights emerge; they become more than just illumination. Their radiance is a gateway to another dimension where the frontiers of existence dissolved into the unknown.

* * *

Back in the pyramid, air echoes the dissonance of loud screams. A painful, primal opera sounds off, buried beneath the world. Omega writhes on her back, her body contorting in agony as the snapped rope releases her to the ground. She had taken a hard fall while descending underground. Fortune smiles upon her, for the welder mask shielded Omega from the full brunt of the fall, its sturdy frame providing a crucial barrier against the unforgiving force of the impact. On her stomach, Omega inches forward, surveying her surroundings. With wary eyes, Omega realizes she has ventured into a primal cave. The environment's rugged walls displayed scars of countless eons who once ruled this ancient home. Immersed in the oppressive darkness, a rustling sound begins. Sharp scrapes of branches rubbing together heralds the arrival of an unseen form.

Suddenly, a spark ignites, and from darkness emerges a prehistoric figure. Primal and imposing in its barbarian glory. It is a *Neanderthal*, its rugged silhouette illuminated by the fire the ancient man had just created. Neanderthals—

our ancient kin—are responsible for the threshold of human evolution, their existence marking the early chapters of our species' journey. This species forged the path that would eventually lead to the emergence of modern humanity. Neanderthals were a robust and adaptable species of ancient humans who inhabited Europe and parts of Asia for thousands of years. They possessed a rich cultural heritage and remarkable resilience in the face of the challenges of their ancient world.

Omega's body tenses, nerves coursing through her veins as she faces the hominoid, its intentions veiled in shadows. The Neanderthal brandishes a club, its movements a crude expression of aggression as it closes the distance to Omega. Their eyes lock; a convergence of minds from the past and future.

Omega recognizes the species, for they were of her own kin. Despite this familiarity, she chooses to remain grounded, submitting to the situation. Gently, Omega extends a trembling hand, an offering of peace and a fragile attempt to bridge the gap that separates them. But the Neanderthal remains unmoved, its primitive instincts raging unchecked as it cocks back the club with a brutish growl. Unleashing a savage swing, the blow crashes into Omega's welder mask with brutal force, imploding the illusion of peace and plunging Omega back into darkness.

* * *

Omega crosses the frozen terrain, icy tendrils snaking into infinity. Serpentine glacier fractals ensnare her soul. Omega enters the icy jaws of the land, where the breath of winter exhales its mournful hymn. Snowflakes—celestial messengers—descend from the heavens, whispering prayers for deliverance as they spiral. She kneels on the cathedral of ice, encompassing the lake, her eyes tethering to Alpha in the crystalline expanse.

"Your species is always waiting," the message echoes from Alpha.

"Perhaps in another life," Omega muses silently to herself. She harbors no illusions of waiting for anyone, yet she comprehends the necessity of listening to the situation at hand. She reflects inwardly, acknowledging, "Alpha was kind. It didn't need to ask me twice." Time stretches on.

Omega and Alpha ensconce in the cocoon of solitude. Anticipation submerges them like a suffocating cloud of smoke, reminiscent of the darkness that submerged Earth in *Nuclear Winter*. The only sound was the rhythmic formation of ice, layer upon layer, following the steady rhythm of Omega's breath. Alpha's frame produces electronic whispers that hum harmony of a summer's day. The sound of a gentle chirp of hummingbirds resonates intricate circuitry inside its digital organs.

An impressive monolithic structure, Alpha, towers over the kneeling figure of Omega. The supercomputer is not just a machine, but a god. A cryptic message from Alpha materializes, the meaning cloaked in ambiguity. "Your brains create a maze. Holding you back. Never allowing you to escape. Puzzling over each choice. Never trusting anything."

Each word begins stirring Omega's consciousness, but one question repeats relentlessly in her mind. "Where's the astronaut?" her words come out urgently.

Alpha observes the human. The supercomputer squarely fixes its intentions on Omega. "Why do you ask?" The inquiry is a challenge to Omega as she continues to kneel, her expression unreadable. For Alpha, the question carries significance, probing into the motives behind Omega's inquiry. A desire to understand the underlying currents that are driving her to seek out the whereabouts of the missing Ancient Astronaut.

Omega's words pierce the air. "They know where the child is," she confesses, her eyes steady as she meets Alpha's, searching for any trace of empathy.

DOOM

Knowledge that the child's whereabouts are known to others, hidden in secrecy and obscured by layers of deceit, gnaw at her conscience like a festering wound. As she speaks the words aloud, Omega feels a feeling of liberation. But with that liberation comes vulnerability, as she lies and bares her soul in anguish to Alpha, trusting in the supercomputer's strength to guide her through the storm.

"Perhaps the astronaut was the culprit?" Alpha posits. "There's limits with everything. Even the astronaut doesn't have the answer you're looking for." For Alpha, the notion of betrayal is a bitter pill to swallow, a fracture in the foundation of trust upon which their fragile alliance rests. Yet the supercomputer's logic understands the necessity of considering all possibilities, no matter how unsettling they may be.

Omega's voice comes, steady and holding conviction. "I believe they do," she affirms. For Omega, the belief in the child's whereabouts is more than just hope. It is a conviction that burns the intensity of a thousand suns. Despite the doubts that plague her journey, she holds onto the belief that somewhere, the child waits to be found. As she speaks, Omega feels empowerment. A reaffirmation of her purpose. The justice she is seeking. Even in the face of adversity, she refuses to stop, drawing strength from faith that guides her forward.

"Faith. The word humanity forgot," the supercomputer reflects on the nature of belief in the hearts of mortals. Even during the chaos of the human condition, it has been thrown aside. A message in a bottle tossed in the sea, buried beneath skepticism. The question, loaded with implications, echoes off the metallic walls of Alpha, stirring the encounter. "Do you want to know the astronaut's secrets?" the supercomputer asks. Alpha is obsessed with the Ancient Astronaut. Its secrets are tantalizing, a gamble with unknown consequences.

"What secrets?" A note of disbelief coats the words. The notion of searching for the Ancient Astronaut's enigmatic past is daunting and intriguing. She can't shake the feeling she feels moving forward.

"To control humanity," Alpha affirms, watching Omega intently. Alpha knows that manipulation and control are sobering reminders of human autonomy.

"Nobody has that kind of power," she declares, her words burning inside her soul.

"Do you know the problem with gods?" Alpha begins, its computational hums fixed intently on Omega. "They all made claims. Fantasies. Visions of answers. New beginnings. They were all wrong." Divine intervention is nothing more than a mirage for Alpha. A deceptive illusion that promises salvation yet delivers only disappointment. The supercomputer had seen the foolishness of blind faith firsthand. It had witnessed the broken dreams of those who had placed their trust in the hands of gods and found themselves betrayed. "The astronaut can give you the power that defies everything," Alpha declares. "You drank the water. Keep your eyes open for them."

"I'm running out of time," she confesses.

"Time is obsolete," Alpha asserts. The concept of time has long since lost its importance; the supercomputer renders it meaningless in the face of eternity.

Omega rises against the backdrop of the winter wonderland. Her eyes remain sharp as they scan the frozen region, searching for the faintest hint of movement. In the distance, the *child shadow* emerges and wanders across the icy lake. Shockingly, Omega had found the child and so sprints straight for them.

Each breath is a gust of subzero air. Adrenaline surges, driving her forward, her eyes fixing unwaveringly on the distant shadow. While taking each stride, the distance between them narrows. But fate, cruel and capricious, has other plans in store. As Omega's foot slips on the treacherous ice, the brittle surface cracks beneath her weight, threatening to swallow her whole. She stumbles, but regains her footing, her eyes never wavering from the elusive shadow ahead. Determination fuels her movements, forcing her forward. A magnetic pull of love. She edges closer, inch by inch. Yet, just as victory is appearing closer, the ice gives way with a deafening crack, plunging Omega into the ice. She is yanked downwards, away from the child shadow and further away from the truth. The water's surface ripples briefly, then quiets once more, leaving no trace of her. The memory of Omega's valiant struggle against the ice is lost to the unshakeable grip of fate.

* * *

The expansive reaches of Africa, submerged in ice and frost. Icicles dangle like the long claws of Therizinosaurus, said to have the longest claws of all time. Foliage lies stripped bare by the cold. Omega's voice echoes through the Serengeti ecosystem, a geographical region in Africa, spanning the Mara and Arusha regions of Tanzania. The ice world exposes the aftermath of *Nuclear War.*

"Life requires heat to thrive," her words carry a bitter wind that sweeps across the frozen landscape. "After *Nuclear War* struck Earth, everything became ice." Her voice seems to permeate her infinite dimensions of feelings. The lost continent experienced firsthand devastation brought on by the apocalypse. No corner of the planet was left untouched. Omega continues speaking. A bitter irony. "I guess God wasn't looking out for us." The machine civilization had reached the zenith of its ferocity; a powerful realization that humanity's fate had been sealed by its own innovation—forces beyond their own control. It was a tale as old as time, whispered through the ages.

ICE

From the plains of Africa, where humanity first took its tentative steps into the world, to the bustling metropolises of the Modern Age, the paradox and riddle of evil had stalked the footsteps of mankind like a relentless curse. In those early days, simplicity reigned supreme. Life was governed by the rhythms of nature, yet even amidst the tranquility of the plains, the spell of doom was waiting to bloom in the fertile soil of human consciousness. As the centuries unfolded and civilizations flourished, the battle against evil raged on, its implications reaching into every corner of human existence. From the blood-soaked fields of war to the corridors of power where greed and corruption held supremacy, the struggles persisted, a timeless fight between light and darkness. Until the problem of energy overconsumption poisoned the psyche of humanity, forcing itself to confront its greatest challenge.

In a world intoxicated by excess, where the pursuit of wealth inspired destruction, capitalism roots entwined society. It was not initially war or catastrophic calamity that brought about humanity's downfall, but the uncontrollable appetite for more. Humans couldn't turn off the tap of energy; it flowed ceaselessly, a torrent driving the wheels of progress. Evolution of any species has perpetually been a precarious period. As the years passed by, the reality of draining oil dry grew ever more obvious. Planetary limitations screamed at humanity to stop drilling. Occam's razor dictates that time travel to acquire more oil was implausible. The constant overconsumption persisted as the forewarning of civilization's prophesied demise.

Sustainable futures proved to be nothing more than mirages disappearing across the desert horizon. Despite hopes and aspirations of many, the true solution to the world's energy difficulties was not in complex systems or grandiose schemes, but in the simple act of reining in our desire for energy. Every resource, including oil, has its limits, and humans struggled facing long-term planning and foresight.

The train of philosophical ideology with its lofty ideals and noble intentions never arrived at the station of human consciousness. Instead, it careened off the tracks, derailed by greed and short-sightedness. As the years passed and the world hurtled ever closer toward the fossil fuel collapse, humanity found itself caught in a web of its own making. The dream of a future faded into obscurity, replaced by a reality of dying resources and *Nuclear War* over oil. Technological innovation or scientific breakthroughs didn't spell humanity's downfall. It was our stubborn refusal to acknowledge the simple truth presented. As they fall into an eternal slumber of defeat, the greatest species on Earth succumb to the consequences of our own making. The tale of humanity's rise and fall spoke volumes of the paradox and riddle of evil that had plagued mankind since time was born. Echoes of civilization faded into the abyss, but one truth remained clear: *Evil was a battle that could never truly be won.*

Africa frozen in a subzero reality. This world was beyond anyone's imagination. It was a scene straight out of a nightmare, surreal and otherworldly, as if transported to an alien planet. The magnitude of humanity's mistake was prevalent in the cradle of civilization. How had humans—the stewards of this magnificent planet—managed to bring about such devastation? The question left a bitter aftertaste, haunting even the simplest of minds because of its complexity. This narrative of humanity's downfall seemed like something out of a diabolical tale spun by the Devil himself.

Slums of Zimbabwe were buried beneath layers of ice, inhabitants frozen in a perpetual state—nothing more than statues of a lost species. Insects—architects of the underground soil—had their colonies reduced to an icy sarcophagus. For millennia, these insects toiled in obscurity, beneath the earth's surface. Yet, as humanity forged ahead, holding onto unbridled recklessness, their existence became little more than an afterthought. Now, as the icy fingers of *Nuclear Winter* emerged, these subterranean denizens remain trapped forever. Their miniature forms preserved for eternity. In the subzero soil of Earth, a legacy formerly etched in the ancient soil was now lost to the whims of Mother Nature's cruel tale. Insects were forgotten. Those tiny organisms gifted humanity food, oxygen, and prosperity by their simple yet complicated lives.

Vestiges of safari life have transformed into motionless witnesses. Chimpanzees, lions, giraffes, cheetahs, elephants, and rhinos—all trapped in a prison of ice, reduced to frozen antiques of their former selves. Evolution had stopped and the mass extinction of life was born out of the ugliness of mankind. Nuclear weapons, from the moment of their inception, had become the ticking doomsday clock, counting down to humanity's extermination. But it was not the hand of man that ultimately brought about our downfall. Instead, it was the unexpected wrath of Mother Nature herself, the great equalizer. Worldwide nukes detonated, casting their deadly glow across the globe. The dark cloud descended upon the Earth, blocking out sunlight and plunging the world into a never-ending night. It was a punishment of humanity's own making. In the midst of the darkness, humanity was forced to confront the fragility of life. No longer could they hide behind the false comforts of their technological capabilities. Instead, they were left to deal with their own mortality. The frozen Earth had no victors, only echoes of a world consumed by flames of its own destruction.

* * *

Omega's eyes crack open, greeted by the ominous silhouette standing above her. Shadow extends a water canteen in the dimness of the cave. Omega ponders the enigmatic entity, a manifestation of her consciousness. The collective consciousness states philosophical implications of shared beliefs, values, and experiences that shape the collective identity. In its shifting forms and random appearances, Shadow seems to embody the human psyche, a reflection of the inner turmoil and existential questions that plagued them all.

Omega stares into Shadow's spirit and contemplates the truth it represents, that humanity is but mere shadows wandering through life in search of meaning and purpose. The shadow, like an ever-present companion, follows us from birth until death. A humble observer of each individual's journey. Darkness spares none, following every move.

For some, the shadow looms large, emitting a haunting curse over their lives. For others, it remains an elusive figure, lurking in the corners of their consciousness. Yet, in its paradoxical nature, the shadow is both friend and foe—a constant reminder of one's innermost fears and desires. Omega wrestles with questions of her odyssey. Ultimately, perhaps it is her shadow that holds the key to unlocking the puzzle of her conundrum.

Shadow, the tranquil companion guiding Omega through life from birth to death, speaks gently. "Drink. You were unconscious," it utters, its voice a whisper.

Omega brushes off Shadow's gesture with a dismissive wave. "I'm fine. Taking a break from water," she replies. The interloper declines the canteen, her subtle shake of the head signaling her refusal. Yet, as she does, a searing pain pierces her skull, causing her to grimace in agony. She removes her mask, revealing blood trickling down her face, staining her features crimson. The trickle of blood serves as a visceral reminder of her essence, her hemoglobin coursing through her veins. It was a pulse she refuses to diffuse until her ultimate mission of finding the child is fulfilled. Despite the pain, Omega embraces it, a confirmation that she still experiences continuation. She glances back, searching for the neanderthal, but finds only the emptiness of the cave walls staring back at her. Her eyes discover the familiar *hourglass* stationed in the heart of the cave, where she had encountered the ancient human.

At that instant, Omega's thoughts delve into the paradox of time, a subject she has long pondered under her philosophy of *think hard, not easy*. Time, a mysterious phenomenon emerging from the void, intrigues her. *Was it a human concept, a construct created from humanity's fundamental perception of life and death?* This question has haunted her since childhood, keeping her awake into the late hours of the night. She contemplates the strange numbers that seem to govern the passage of time, wondering if they hold any significant meaning or if they are deceptive illusions. *Did they align with the beliefs of Albert Einstein, who vehemently argued that time was nothing more than a stubborn illusion?* The answer eludes her, concealed in the veil of the universe's mysteries.

The absence of the ancient human leaves her unsettled. An appearance of the ancient human leaves Omega perplexed. *Is it merely a product of her imagination, conjured during her unconscious state after the fall?* Despite the rational doubts that tug at her mind, the encounter feels undeniably personal, hauntingly real. Dreams often harbor distant odysseys, yet this moment in time resonates authenticity, unmistakable as the gentle patter of rain. Something about the encounter feels recognizable, possessing clues to unraveling the camouflaged secrets. Omega, a vivid dreamer and with an expansive imagination, is wary of falling prey to the deceptive comforts of her own mind. However, the pulse of the arctic pyramid contains a transcendent energy, hinting at the immense power it once wielded in ancient times. Whispered rumors of gateways and arcane secrets have always circulated around pyramids. Their aura is an obsession beyond the grasp of mortal sensation. They have set their sights on true north, a feat of engineering on the precipice of impossibility in the ancient world.

Though Omega had read tales of such wonders, she understands the fine line between interpretation and reality, particularly in an era where magic is believed to hold influence over the world. Magic, a seductive notion that has captivated her childhood fantasies, offering dimensions of the supernatural where the deepest questions could be answered. For years, Omega has believed in God, finding peace in the comfort of faith. Yet, the devastation of the *Nuclear War* had traumatized her belief, leaving her empty of any semblance of belief in an almighty divine lord. She came to realize that the idea of God eliminating evil was impossible. Conflict seems to be inherent to human nature. Euphoria is buried beneath this understanding.

Omega finds herself adrift, existential questions haunting her restless mind.

Shadow's voice echoes softly in the cave, its source obscured in darkness. "What did you see?" The question lingers. Shadow, in its enigmatic nature, is driven by Omega's personal reflection. This entity serves as nothing more than a reflection for Omega to introspect upon herself. Eventually, layers of reality will unravel, revealing a complex tapestry beneath the surface. Shadow is a mythical seeker, desperately desiring to unlock doors in Omega's mental dimension. Life is an onion, demanding that we strip away its layers to uncover our soul. Tears of sadness and joy flow freely, for such is the soul.

Her voice comes steady, despite the unknown that hovers. "Hallucinations." She is not ready to become a believer of any sorts. Omega holds onto a pragmatic mindset. Her once-fanciful notions of special powers and mystical phenomena are now relegated to the shadows of memory. Logic became her guiding principle, her crutch. She attributes the manifestations she encounters to the internal workings of biochemistry. The exquisite interaction of mind and body giving rise to the illusion of the neanderthal's presence. There is no room for translucent souls or supernatural forces in her rational worldview, only the tangible realities of science and reason.

Omega rises to her feet, her eyes focusing and locking onto Shadow. The human and Shadow face off as equals, their forms mirroring each other in height and volume. Doppelgängers from opposing worlds, one with defined features, the other a shapeless void. Together, they embark on their quest, united against the timeless forces of good and evil. Beneath the surface of their partnership lurks an unspoken question: *When would Shadow succumb to the desire of darkness*? Every thought and action stems from the shadow of consciousness. Despite the trust forged between them, Omega, a constant seeker of knowledge, understands the fragility of emotional bonds, knowing that alliances could shift in the blink of an eye.

"How do I find the astronaut?" Omega's voice is steeped in irritation, harboring a conviction that the Ancient Astronaut holds the singular key to unraveling the enigma surrounding the child's disappearance. Omega knows that she has no choice but to continue her search, no matter the obstacles.

Shadow's words are an ominous warning. "They find you," it whispers. Shadow knows that when the Ancient Astronaut emerges, time stops. Its arrival always unleashes a spell of awe. When they appear, nothing else matters. All of Omega's hopes and fears converge upon this unpredictable entity. It is a source of unfathomable power that can shape her destiny. Omega's focus shifts from Shadow to the spacious passageway, an endless tunnel of darkness. It beckons to her. Feels as if it is speaking to her. Omega, guided by her divine compass in a direction searching for resolution.

"The computer has its own agenda," Shadow repeats seriously. "Everything has a cause and effect." Shadow has been watching the rise and fall of humanity throughout the epoch of technology. It has observed the paradoxical nature of computational advancement. While technology produced humanity's unparalleled gifts and capabilities, it also served as a double-edged sword, empowering humanity to become agents of their own expiration. An eternal riddle. A complex interplay. Progress and destruction fundamentally defined the human experience. The final hope of an ever-expanding horizon, forever beyond humanity's reach. It mirrored the fate of the universe's expansion, where our perception could never quite grasp its edges. Recalling the memory that doesn't exist; that memory being peace on Earth.

Omega walks away from Shadow. While passing the hourglass, her eyes catch sight of massive ancient *dinosaur bones* scattered across the dirt. Colossal bones of long-extinct creatures. Towering *Tyrannosaurus rex* skeletons, their massive jaws frozen in eternal silence. Nearby, the delicate wings of *Pterodactylus* stretched out in a graceful arc. Fragile bones were impressive carnivorous counterparts. The immense form of the Brontosaurus, its skeletal frame an immense scale of life that formerly thrived upon Earth. This species died when a mountain-sized asteroid collided into the planet, erasing their existence after 165 million years. Even the ancient reptiles, despite their long reign, met their end like every other species that lived.

Human existence, though comparatively short since its inception, proved proficient at hastening the destruction of civilizations. Humankind had wished for the enduring longevity of the dinosaurs as a functional species. But it seemed that their own actions would prevent such a fate from ever being realized. Omega understands the limits of time, even for a species that had roamed the Earth for millions of years. She continues striding forward into the cave, the shadows swallowing her as she puts on her mask. Whispers of the Jurassic extinction echo, carrying secrets lost to oblivion.

* * *

A bunker of uncertain origin nestled underground, a fortress prepared to shield against the ravages of *Nuclear War*. In the bleak landscape of a *Nuclear War*-torn world, bunkers stand as vital sanctuaries. Their fortified walls shield humanity from the devastating aftermath of radiation. Nuclear radiation seeps through the land, twisting life into grotesque forms, unleashing its venom worldwide. Above ground, a toxic wasteland festers, rendering each breath a futile gasp without the aid of an oxygen apparatus. Concrete walls encase the surface area, forming an impenetrable shield, the last line of defense against nuclear warfare. A motionless clock hangs upon the wall, its hands suspended in perpetual stillness. Time couldn't endure, its movement faltering. A construct woven demanded only the decay of mass to offer a semblance of measurement. Otherwise, time was just an idea, one of humanity's best.

Across from the clock, a painting, depicting Francis Bacon's evocative masterpiece, *The Scream*. Its distorted face captures the human condition, a chilling icon of the existential dread that pervades life. An extensive collection of books fills the room, spines cracked. Knowledge and untold stories sleepwalking. Only written words could penetrate the minds of those who entered this place. They line shelves that stretch from floor to ceiling. Volumes stacked atop one another in haphazard towers of literature. More books scattered across tables, pages worn and weathered from years of contemplation. Books had become casualties of a civilization experiencing amnesia, rendered extinct during the oil wars. After the technological age came to an abrupt end, everything learned via computation was lost forever, leaving only words etched upon pages to endure. In this makeshift library, volumes of philosophy, history, religions, and physics remained asleep. Pages gathering dust as they awaited the touch of a curious mind to awaken them from their sleep. Mementos that used to define thoughts and ideas. A time when humanity hungered for knowledge and wisdom beyond the digital reality. Nearby, atop an oak desk, the familiar *hourglass*. Its sands flow inexorably, sharing its space with the infamous books of *Relativity: The Special and General Theory* and *On the Origin of Species*—Einstein and Darwin's seminal works, their opus incarnate. Sharing groundbreaking insights into the nature of the cosmos and evolution of life, forever establishing facts immortalized. Their words inked on pages possessed the power of eternity, a remedy for the finality of death; their weathered covers spectators to the timeless quest for enlightenment.

At the core of the room, Omega is enchanted by a chalkboard, its surface adorned with a mosaic of mathematical equations, quantum physics formulas, and scientific notations, each symbolizing a fragment of truthfulness. For as long as she can remember, Omega has been caught in the infinite battle between words and numbers. Numbers, akin to words, endure eternally. Abstract yet inspired with the enchantment of measurement, surpassing even the fanciest of phrases. Yet, they harbor constraints. Measurement, though integral to existence, poses the question: *Was existence only a form of measurement*? Delving into reality, no mystical number can definitively explain the emergence of matter from nothingness. Here, words assume precedence, guiding the inquiry while numbers trailed. Both are seekers of truth, inseparable partners.

Omega ponders the ultimate question: *How did time come into being*? In her contemplations, she finds herself leaning toward the power of words, recognizing their supremacy over numbers. After all, without words to give them meaning, numbers remain abstract symbols trapped on the chalkboard. Yet, as she studies the enigma of time's origin, Omega confronts the paradox of zero, the concept of nothingness at the threshold of beginnings and endings. It is a dangerous idea, she realizes, one that sparks more questions than it answered. A complex circle, symbolizing both everything and nothing—cyclical cycles of eternity. Time reveals itself as a flat circle, an eternal recurrence according to esteemed philosopher Nietzsche.

A diagram of the *nuclear bomb* commands attention on the chalkboard, its detailed lines and markings standing out prominently, overtaking equations and formulas. Omega's eyes shift to the diagram and she scrutinizes the finer details of its design, tracing the contours of destruction etched into its blueprint into a mix of fascination and dread. Forged during the crucible of war, the invention unlocked a power akin to that which birthed the Sun itself. A malevolent gift bestowed upon humanity during the harrowing days of World War II. Allowing humanity to unleash a wrath reserved for divine deities upon the cities of Hiroshima and Nagasaki. It revealed a darker side of human decision and emotion, one so dark that even our deadliest ancestors would yield to its power. Little did humanity comprehend at the time the repercussions this discovery would release upon the world. Insanity gripped the collective psyche of humanity, deadly consequences registering throughout the globe.

Omega tensely overlooks the nuclear bomb equation, her focus unwavering despite an unsettling feeling of being watched. She feels something behind her. Without turning around, she acknowledges Shadow. Despite the unease it brings, there is camaraderie in their mutual fascination and dangerous calculations. Omega can't shake the feeling Shadow knows more, perhaps important insights that could aid her.

"Humanity never had a chance at stopping this from happening," Shadow speaks, a statement of logical reason.

Omega pauses, her eyes hovering over the chalkboard as she absorbs the statement. "We may not have had a chance in the past," Omega responds softly, "but that doesn't mean we won't find a way now. There's always a possibility, even in the darkest of times."

Shadow remains silent.

Omega investigates the equation. Together, they continue their silent vigil, with Omega clinging to the slim hope that she can defy the odds and alter the course of fate.

"Dreams don't change the reality of the future," Shadow whispers the sheer fact.

Omega nods, acknowledging Shadow's grim observation. "You're right," she concedes, "but dreams can inspire actions that reshape those realities." She turns to face Shadow. "Even if our dreams seem small in the face of such a daunting future, they have the power to guide us forward, to push us to strive for something greater than ourselves." Her mind ablaze, visions of a future where her dreams hold the power to change the course of history. A hope for a better tomorrow.

Shadow asks the undeniable question lingering in Omega's psyche. "What happens after you find the child?"

Omega's eyes pause over the chalkboard, her mind momentarily drawn away from the equations as she considers the question. She has been so consumed by the urgency of the present that she hasn't given much thought to what might come after.

"After I save the child..." Omega begins slowly, "Civilization will have to rebuild. Not just our lives, but everything that's been lost. It won't be easy, but we'll find a way." She looks to the shadow figure, searching for reassurance in its inscrutable gaze. "And you?" she asks quietly. "What happens after?"

Shadow's form wavers slightly in the dim light. "After..." it murmurs, its voice a whisper carried on the ether. "Perhaps I'll find a new purpose. Something beyond this endless cycle."

Omega freezes in place as she feels the unexpected touch of Shadow's hand on her shoulder, sending a ripple of unease through her body. Death seems to creep closer as a cold draft envelopes her body, sending a subzero chill down her spine. Omega swallows hard. "Is everything alright?" she asks.

With a faint nod, Shadow responds. "Everything will be as it should," it says, its words a quiet resolve. "Trust in the path that lies ahead."

Omega couldn't shake the feeling of her Shadow remaining by her side. And though the path ahead remains unknown, she finds comfort that she isn't alone. Together, they would face the challenges that lie ahead.

Omega and Shadow walk away from the chalkboard, leaving the words, equations and diagrams behind. They approach a wooden door that Omega slowly opens, revealing another hidden passageway beyond. Leaving the safety of the bunker's haven, she leaves the mysteries of the bunker behind. Shadow follows close behind.

Venturing into the domain of the underworld, Omega encounters a frigidness where air bites, tasting the sharp sting of frost. And the land stretches into infinity, glistening ice and snow. A world locked away in an arctic wonderland. Immersed in the infinite expanse of white, the remnants of a *spacecraft* were scattered. Discarded relics, a former shining machine, now marred by ice. Not even interdimensional travelers could endure the hostile climes. Sand dunes, their golden grains usually kissed by the scorching Sun, submerged beneath a pristine layer of ethereal white snow. Here, two disparate elements converge in a bewildering environment, crafting a mesmerizing tableau that defies reason and beckons contemplation.

DOOM

As twilight descends upon the frozen wasteland, sinister *dark clouds* drift overhead. The only sound was a whisper of the wind traversing the icy terrain. Dark clouds twist and contort, its edges fraying and reforming in ways that seem impossible. Beneath the frozen surface, strange hues of violet and green undulate. Luminescence bathes the world in an enchanting glow. Amidst the tempest's core, shapes convulse and contort, assuming visages that elude verbal depiction. Reality itself warps and bends beneath the unseen hand of nature's forces, birthing a spectacle of such mesmerizing appeal that mortal eyes are ensnared in its bewitching grasp. The storm rages on, and it becomes clear that this is no ordinary weather phenomenon, but something altogether stranger.

In the twisted vortex of winter twilight, where stars hang as broken promises and the moon drips like molten silver, Omega takes her first step, Shadow prowling at her side—a loyal beast born of light and darkness. Omega embarks on her quest that defies reason and mocks conventional wisdom. The trail ahead, a sinuous serpent slithering through the frozen wasteland, stretches out before them like a taunting challenge from the gods themselves. It is a path littered with dreams of those who dared to tread its treacherous course. But Omega is no ordinary wanderer. With fire in her eyes and madness in her heart, she balances on the razor's edge of sanity. She dares reality to test her will. Each step she takes sends tremors, echoing her defiance against the cosmic order. And so, they press on, two shadows lost in the endless twilight.

For Omega, the journey is not merely a means to an end, but an existential crusade against the banality of existence. Amidst the suffocating darkness where the boundary separating reality from illusion dissolves into nothingness, Omega and Shadow forge a path of their own creation. Nightmares harbor lucid dreams, and this portrayal found its rightful place. Omega strides forth, her face concealed behind the impenetrable barrier of her mask. Clamped securely to her face, it serves as both armor and disguise, shielding her from the doomsday backdrop. Weeping wisdom whispers faintly, a plea unheard amidst the cacophony of human disagreement. The babel of voices were drowning each other out in the ruthless pursuit of economic growth; empires had crumbled. In the ashes of these fallen dominions, even Rome, that ancient seat of power, would cry in admiration, imploring humanity to stop its march toward self-destruction.

Labored breaths. The oxygen tank strapped to her back wheezes and hisses, her invaluable lifeline in a world where clean air has become a vestige. Radiation saturates the region. An unseen adversary, poised to poison its hapless victims with its insidious touch. No longer does the sweet kiss of oxygen exist. The atmosphere mirrored the malevolence of the Devil's fury; hostility that seemed to seethe infernal malice at every turn. Omega continues marching forward somewhere toward a directionless horizon of fate, defying the cruel whims of nature with every step she takes—determined to carve out her own destiny, no matter the cost. Her mask becomes a valiant shield against the onslaught of heavy snowflakes assaulting her face. She remains undaunted wandering across the frozen badlands, her loyal companion, Shadow, remains by her side. Both command the unforgiving arctic world.

In the frozen badlands, the chill of death echoes and departed souls drift in the icy breeze. Distant thunder rolls across the twilight sky and the ground beneath Omega's boots quakes and shudders in a violent protest. *Tremors* intensify, her knees threatening to buckle. But Omega stands firm against the hostility raging that was submerging her. It was as though the world harbors resentment, as if it recoils at the notion of her further advancement. The wrath of the subzero environment's spirit coalesces and disperses in myriad directions, manifesting its fury wherever it saw fit. Though the ground may shift beneath her feet and the sky threatens to unleash its fury, she remains patient and persistence. Quitting has never been in her catalog of life.

Thunder echoes, loud as a war cry of some vengeful deity. The crackling chorus of lightning ruptures the twilight, illuminating the darkened sky in electric magnificence. Omega and Shadow are vigilant sentinels, acutely aware of the threat. In the searing brilliance of each bolt, they see the raw power of nature unleashed. Maybe in another universe a human would give up. Not this human. She feels the static charge, a primal warning of the storm's fury increasing in power. From the eerie glow of each flash, danger drew closer. A specter of annihilation, biding its time to release devastation at the opportune moment.

Omega watches the swirling maelstrom overhead. Beside her, Shadow remains stoic, an entity of intuition. Louder lightning crackles and thunder roars. Omega and Shadow stand as one, united to weather the storm together. This surreal theater allows for Omega's keen eyes to catch a quaint single droplet of *black rain* descending from the heavens. An inky substance, defying gravity's grasp as it plummets toward the snowy ground. It makes contact, colliding against the pristine surface and a small splash erupts, sending ripples across the snow. This was no ordinary droplet. It signaled tragedy, something dreadful and unsettling.

Steam rises from the droplet. An ebony oil-colored substance merging into the virgin snow, their unholy union stains the purity of the frozen canvas. A grotesque mockery of nature's pristine beauty. During the aftermath of nuclear detonations, radiation was released, becoming trapped in clouds, evolving over time into a sinister toxic rain. A deadly prophecy had come to pass. Black rain slithers as though it were a vindictive serpent slithering through virgin fields of snow, infecting everything it touched—an unholy matrimony of darkness and innocence. Radioactive particles mixed with atmospheric moisture rained down upon the land in a toxic deluge.

Omega is jolted by a sudden searing sensation against her gloved hand. She watches in horror as the dangerous droplet punctures her glove, its corrosive touch on her hand leaving behind a *mark of the beast* that would overtake her mind. Rumors echoing through the underworld spun tales of dread, suggesting that contact with these toxic droplets would unravel the mind, plunging individuals into a nightmarish phantasmagoria from which escape seemed an impossibility. The psyche would be thrust into a realm of twisted reality where dreams and nightmares unify.

In that moment of realization, Omega understands the gravity of the situation. This is no mere anomaly, but a messenger of doom. Treacherous peril, for she would find herself in an eternal nightmare. A fate from which there seemed no escape. With urgency gnawing at her core, Omega knows that she can no longer afford to tread lightly. Rules of engagement have shifted, and the stakes have never been higher. In the face of such dire adversity, she knows that survival hinges upon her ability to adapt and overcome. That only the strong will emerge unscathed.

"Run!" Shadow's voice pierces through the insanity.

Omega grits her teeth and runs. Her every instinct begins screaming for her to run faster, run farther, and run until the *black rain* can no longer reach her. Through a miraculous twist of fate, she manages to evade the herculean bombardment of countless toxic droplets, darting and weaving with impressive agility and guile as she zigzags through the deadly rainstorm.

Omega's soul roars as she sprints. Black rain continues pelting down around her, as though the Devil wept tears of perverse delight. She scans the horizon for any sign of shelter, her eyes desperate for a glimpse of salvation. Ahead, she discovers a hill rising and surges toward it, clinging to the slender hope of sanctuary and safety. As she reaches the summit, her breath catches in her throat at the sight that greets her. A *nuclear power plant*—rising as a monolith against the twilight sky.

Rugged structure and gray futuristic designs contrast against the white world. A fortress of concrete and steel promising protection from the ravages of black rain. Durable, boasting a resilient architecture, designed to endure extreme conditions. Edifices where humanity once dared to harness and replicate the power of the Sun. Determined to find refuge, Omega forges ahead, her instincts screaming at her to reach safety before it was too late. Footsteps crunch against the snow as she approaches the fence encircling the nuclear power plant. There seemed to be an absence of any signs of life, no bustling activity, no watchful guards.

Omega grips the fence and begins to climb. Concerned, she looks over her shoulder and spots the dark cloud creeping closer, seeming to possess an intelligence as it closes the gap, purposefully tracking Omega. With impressive agility, she continues to pull herself upwards, her muscles spring-like as she scales the obstacle. Omega ascends higher and higher. With every handhold and foothold, she draws closer to her goal. One final burst of effort, and Omega clears the top of the fence, her body twisting gracefully as she vaults over the barrier and lands on the other side. Omega's momentum grinds to a halt as she confronts the imposing obstacle of a solid steel door. She braces herself and strains against the door, pouring every ounce of her strength into the effort. But the door remains unmoved by her grueling efforts. The door mocks her—an immovable object. Frustration mounts as Omega battles against the door, her muscles burning. Yet still, the door remains firmly shut. Exhausted, Omega continues pushing as hard as she can. The dark cloud continues inching closer, gaining ground as it draws perilously close to Omega's position.

Her soul heaving exertion as she struggles against the impassable door, Omega strains, her muscles trembling, until she feels a sudden, unexpected force join her efforts. She turns to see Shadow's hand pressed against the door beside hers. They double their efforts, their combined strength proving to be the decisive push. Metal yields beneath their united force and the door swings open with a triumphant creak. A rush of adrenaline courses through Omega as she steps through the threshold, her elated spirit causing exhilaration at her victory. Shadow remains a loyal entity.

Seclusion of reality was omnipresent. Omega enters the center chamber. Towering walls and imposing machinery, an impressive engineering feat. From this chamber, humans unwittingly birthed an apocalyptic Earth from their own actions. This facility was more than just a structure, it was a temple of doom. In the bygone era of the old world, aspirations and ambitions strove to guide humanity toward a future of clean energy, harnessing solar energy as the ultimate objective in transitioning away from fossil fuels. Tragically, they never had a chance of success from day one. It was a mission destined for failure from its inception. They had faltered before even taking the first step. Fossil fuels entrenched themselves in every facet of manufacturing. Solar energy would never replace this fact. Oil and coal were responsible for nearly every construction endeavor upon the Earth. Their blackened hands shaped the foundations upon which humanity existed. Conflict between progress and tradition persisted across generations. Energy revealed its finite nature and nuclear power proved incapable of sustaining the burgeoning demands of an increasing population. Innovation, constrained by its own limitations, stumbled into a wall of stagnation. Thus, oil remained the sole option capable of upholding the infrastructure of a swelling civilization. Until the day arrived when all energy demands came crashing to a catastrophic halt.

An equinox of sublime mechanism. The intersection of science and sorcery. A feat of engineering that surpassed the wildest imaginings of fantasy narratives. Innovation showcased what mankind had created. A monument to the heights of human achievement. Omega looks around in awe of the technological marvel. She can't help but feel admiration and sadness. Omega contemplates the near-miss of humanity's potential, and a thought enters her mind. *What if time had permitted the blossoming of further innovation? What if there existed a path where fossil fuels and clean energy could harmoniously coexist, sustaining civilization?* Yet, she knew such musings were but ephemeral dreams. Whispers of what could have been in a world constrained by its own limitations. *Humanity*, she reflects, *should have listened to the call to stop their building endeavors. But they were stuck by an unrelenting drive that had fueled her species since the dawn of time.* From the discovery of fire to the invention of the wheel, from the Bronze Age to the mastery of quantum physics and computational growth, their journey had been one of perpetual expansion, always reaching for the next horizon. Beneath it all lurked a more fundamental flaw. The ego of her species, leading them onward, regardless of consequences. *It was*, she muses, *a grand distraction, a means for humanity to evade the ghost of death itself.*

"It'll be safe here until the black rain passes," Shadow reveals. Omega's hand trembles slightly as she leans against the concrete wall, her perception hitching as she carefully removes her glove, revealing her skin beneath. Omega's soul sinks at the sight of an angry red blister that has formed, evidence of the black rain. Disbelief and resignation coursing through her, she traces a finger lightly over the

ICE

blister, wincing at the sharp pang of pain that shoots through her mind. The reality of the situation brutally hits her. Black rain is not just a threat, but a predator of the subconscious, capable of inflicting poisonous ideas into the psyche of its victims.

As she stared at the blister, a thousand questions penetrate her soul. *Would the wound heal? Would there be any lasting effects? And most importantly, how could she decipher between reality and illusion?* The underworld created laws and orders that were perplexing to outsiders. Justice was overshadowed by the persecution of individual ambition. The toxic droplet, she realizes, was but a pawn in the sinister game for its unsuspecting visitors. A plague that corroded souls.

Omega swiftly slips her glove back on, a sudden wave of dizziness threatening to pull her into unconsciousness. Her vision blurs, the world around her swirling in a dizzying kaleidoscope of colors and shapes. Instinctively, Omega reaches out for Shadow. She fights against the darkness that threatens to consume her, willing herself to stay conscious, to stay alert. Holding onto every ounce of strength she possesses, Omega forces herself to focus, to push through the disorientation and reclaim control.

Until she's suddenly thrust upward, ascending toward new heights. A mysterious shift in *gravity* unfolds. The force sends her body careening into the air. Weightlessness had become her new antagonist. Omega finds herself adrift where the laws of physics have been violated. Her bodily movements grow more frantic. In a desperate attempt to regain control in the face of overwhelming chaos, she flails her arms and legs in a futile bid for stability, but the world around her offers no foothold. Instead, her efforts only seem to exacerbate the situation, sending her spiraling further into the frequency of weightlessness. Immersed in the twisted carnival of madness, Omega continues struggling against the tide of gravity. She fights to regain her balance against this surreal event. Omega recalls from her philosophical readings that by embracing chaos, one can hope to find their way back to solid ground.

Gravity—the force that shapes the cosmos. Creator and destroyer of the universe. A glue that holds reality together. From its gifted magical powers, galaxies are born, and worlds are formed. Celestial bodies are seduced by the pull of its gravitational specialty. Yet, for all its creative power, gravity is also capable of tearing apart entire star systems and collapsing massive stars into black holes. In this duality lies the true testament to God. The majesty of the cosmos, a hand of higher power. A force that transcends mortality. Perhaps immortality did exist after all. In the absence of gravity, reality dissolves into a void of emptiness. Throughout mankind, the debate over gravity's nature raged incessantly. *Was it a fundamental force or an emergent property of the universe?* Maybe the true inquiry was not in its origins, but in its essence. *How did it come to be?* And in that moment of revelation, one realizes that gravity is synonymous with eternity. An inquiry that perpetually found resolution. Gravity shall always remind humanity of their own insignificance in space and time. Let all beings bow in respect and honor this formidable force. In its seductive hold, they discover magic and wonder. Gravity transcended mere physical force; it was the most formidable god of all. The originator of universal equilibrium.

Shadow mysteriously stays grounded, remaining firmly planted on the floor, noticeably unaffected by the altered laws of gravity. Shadow remains keen on tracking Omega's movements, an instinct honed by aeons of companionship. The entity desires to aid its partner in her struggle. Shadow begins to ascend the nearby staircase. With graceful movements, they move unhinged from the gravitational paradox. Gravity and Shadow intertwine as two dimensions of the same plane. Black, symbolizing the being of both, manifests as a tangible representation of their interconnectedness. It is the emergence of nothingness where their existence finds fertile ground, allowing them to thrive in tandem.

Step by step, Shadow's form traverses the staircase. An unshakable bond binds them to Omega. Shadow draws nearer, its aura never wavering from its companion's struggle. Caught in the grip of gravity's maniac games, Omega finds herself thrust into a hyperactive rollick of adaptation. With never-ending developments from the invisible force, she struggles, her body contorting and twisting trying to find stability in the shifting weightlessness. Then, a sudden jolt, and Omega collides into the wall, the impact jarring her body and sending shockwaves of pain coursing through her. For a moment, she is disoriented, reeling from the collision. Strangely, the impact seems to have halted her uncontrolled movement. Omega regains her composure in the momentarily stable environment. Omega decides to embrace the odd nature of the situation. A deliberate push against the wall, and Omega thrusts herself into a graceful mid-air twirl, movements fluid and elegant—freedom in the surreal nature of gravity. A connection with gravity courses through her psyche. At ease and poised, she embraces her birthright of life. Serene mastery like no other.

"Omega!" comes Shadow's urgent call, its ethereal form pointing upwards, as it continues ascending the metal staircase. Before Omega can fully comprehend the gravity of Shadow's warning, a sudden commotion shatters the tranquility of the chamber. From above, a *renegade soldier*, clad in a gas mask with a rusty oxygen tank and filthy army fatigue, descends upon Omega. The stealth of a predator and a weighted backpack adds to the mass of his frame as he defies gravity, hurtling directly toward Omega.

Caught off guard by the unexpected intruder, she braces herself for the impending confrontation. The renegade soldier and Omega collide mid-air, both of their bodies entangling as the unpredictable effects of gravity take hold. Limbs tangling together, they plummet toward the ground, locked in a desperate struggle. Weight and momentum fight against the force of gravity. Hammering hard, they crash to the ground as the renegade soldier pins Omega beneath him, his hands clawing at the oxygen tank strapped to her body in a desperate attempt to deprive her of precious air. Oxygen was the last hope for any human seeking survival in the aftermath of the fallout; radiation, a poisoned planet. Just as the black plague poisoned Europe.

Omega's survival instinct kicks in. Since she was a little girl, Omega had harbored a fear of death. One of her cherished tales from childhood was the Epic of Gilgamesh, the saga of a king's quest for immortality. This dream became a constant wish throughout her life. If granted one superpower, she would choose to defeat death. Father Time encroaches as she feels death grow closer, submerging her psyche, while laying underneath the renegade soldier. She was going nowhere, immovable by the massive soldier, her breath coming in ragged gasps. *Would today be her final day?* Questions of mortality flood her being. *Would death be a painful end or a peaceful sleep?* Despite the uncertainty, she refuses to give in. Omega knows today will not be the day she surrenders to time.

Omega summons a little more of her inner strength, tapping into a reserve tank. Her desire to survive is intoxicating. Life and death were two sides of the same coin. One cannot be without the other, they exist in symbiotic harmony. Flashes of the child's shadow flicker in her mind again. Omega feels compelled to unearth the truth hidden in her consciousness. She refuses to succumb to defeat. Obsession saturates her belief system; she will emerge victorious from this deadly encounter. Every moment is a battle against the ghost of death. And as she stares into

ICE

the eyes of her adversary, she knows that she will fight with everything she possesses, from today, tomorrow, and every day thereafter.

Omega delivers a forceful kick to the renegade soldier's chest, creating enough distance between them to catch her breath. Before she can regain the upper hand, she is propelled away by the chaotic currents of gravity. Her ascent gets abruptly halted as the renegade soldier reaches out and seizes hold of her leg. Maintaining a firm grip, he forcefully pulls her back toward the ground. In this deadly game of cat and mouse, Omega knows that her only chance of survival lies in outwitting her adversary. They engage in a fierce battle for dominance. Bodies collide, grappling and twisting, desperately seeking control in the chaotic melee. In a bold and decisive move, Omega seizes the opportunity, her fingers finding purchase on the renegade soldier's gas mask. She rips it from his face, exposing him to the toxic radioactive environment.

In an instant, the renegade soldier's body is assaulted by the noxious fumes, his lungs burning. Searing pain from poison began overtaking his sanity. His eyes widen in shock and realization as the toxins infiltrate his system, their effects immediate and merciless. With each convulsion of his body, the renegade soldier's strength wanes, his movements becoming erratic and uncontrolled. The weight of his backpack serves as an anchor, dragging and pinning him inexorably down to the ground. Radiation poisoning ravages the renegade soldiers' lungs, as if inhaling the void of outer space. An unforgiving reality. His life leaves and oxygen deserts his body, followed by the fading echo of his soul's heartbeat. Omega emerges victorious, avoiding the darkness of death.

Nature changes its mind, throwing another curveball. Omega's body feels gravity's pull yanking her upward with an accelerating force. The intensity of the pull grows stronger, propelling Omega higher and higher. Her body soars skyward at a remarkable speed that defies conventionality. She feels herself drawn closer to the ceiling, and she crashes into the ceiling, the impact jarring throughout her body. After colliding into the ceiling, Omega's oxygen tank is knocked off her back, and it begins to float away nearby in the altered field of gravity.

An absence of breathable oxygen was immediately felt. Her body suffocating in air, parallel to drowning in the ocean. Realizing her situation, Omega takes a deep breath, intending to hold it for as long as possible. Suddenly, gravity becomes restored. Omega and her oxygen tank plummet toward the ground at an increasing speed. The force of her descent began accelerating. Surroundings rush past her out of focus in a chaotic whirlwind of motion. Her fate was hanging in the balance. She struggles for each breath, her lungs burning. A desire for air courses through her as she fights to hold onto oxygen. This singular molecule, unparalleled in its essence, upholding all complex life.

During Omega's free fall, her descent gets suddenly interrupted by Shadow's timely intervention. She finds herself hanging gracefully from the entity's sturdy grip. Her guardian had acted swiftly, saving her from the devastating impact; a collision that threatened to crush her beneath the weight of her speed and mass. Her primary concern persisted—the absence of oxygen. Her body convulses as the supply dwindles. She hangs suspended in the sky, clinging desperately to Shadow.

Shadow scans the ground, honed to pinpoint the location of her oxygen tank. "Hold on," Shadow's voice echoes in reassurance.

Omega fights against the suffocating urge to breathe, her body quickly growing weaker. The absence of oxygen takes its toll, her lungs on fire. Her frantic struggle becomes increasingly difficult. She faces overwhelming odds but refuses to surrender. Digging a little deeper, Omega believes deliverance would save her, trusting Shadow's commitment to guide her through the darkness and into the light. Shadow embraces Omega into its arms, holding her tight as they begin their descent down the staircase.

Time was running out. Shadow moves quickly, carrying its cherished bride. The abandoned oxygen tank was lying on the ground. Echoes of perilous ticking clocks resonate through Omega's psyche, a relentless cadence measuring the passage of seconds, minutes, and hours. *Tick-tock... Tick-tock...* After each pulse, time slips away, drawing Omega inexorably closer to her ultimate fate.

Understanding the direness of the situation, Shadow moves swiftly to secure Omega on the ground near the abandoned oxygen tank. The entity retrieves the oxygen tank and efficiently connects the tube to Omega's mask, ensuring a steady flow of air can reach her lungs. As the oxygen begins to flow, Omega takes rapid breaths, greedily inhaling the precious gas. Each inhalation, she feels strength returning to her body and suffocation lifting from her chest during every exhale. Never before had the simple act of breathing felt so rejuvenating. Omega savors each breath like a parched traveler stumbling upon an oasis in the desert. The familiar sensation of oxygen flowing freely through her body. It brought relief, she was grateful beyond belief. And as she breathes in the refreshing oxygen, she knows that she owes her continued survival to the resourcefulness of her guardian, Shadow.

The storm rages outside, a substantial downpour of black rain intensifying. The sound of steam simmers, its crescendo building inexorably, growing louder. Heavy droplets slam against the windows, leaving streaks of grime and sludge. Omega re-examines her injured hand and the red blister. An injury not merely a physical wound, but a mental scar that resonates a unique frequency identified in her brain patterns. This frequency serves as a portal, transporting her into unknowns. Where the constraints of time become secondary in the face of the supernatural elements at play.

Omega contemplates the implications of her injury, realizing that it's not just her physical well-being that's at stake. The wound acts as a channeler, connecting her to a mystical dimension of time. Some refer to it as the *third eye*, where precognition and clairvoyance transcend reality. In this alternate dimension, rules of existence are unpredictable; time adopts a wholly different significance. Here, past, present, and future converge. Obtaining this newfound understanding, Omega prepares herself for the challenges, knowing her journey will take her to places beyond the domain of ordinary perception. Meanwhile, Shadow stands by the window, observing the assault of the black rain against the glass.

"When do the hallucinations start?" Omega's voice cuts through the tense atmosphere, her concern palpable. She braces herself for the next phase. She understands that it would demand more of her mind, body, and soul. It would require her to confront the deepest fears that haunt humanity. The perpetual arrow of time. Through unknown dimensions, she knows that time would emerge as protagonist and antagonist, shaping her destiny in ways she could scarcely comprehend.

Approaching this daunting ultimatum, Omega prepares herself that her resilience would be tested like never before. The battle against time is not just a matter of survival, it is a quest to reclaim what has been lost. To defy fate. Omega understands that she must find the Ancient Astronaut. This enigmatic being holds the key to unlocking the secrets of the future, including the whereabouts of the child shadow.

"Soon," Shadow responds cryptically, its gaze fixed on the storm outside.

"Tell me. Please..." Omega implores, her desperation evident.

"Hard to say in the subconscious," Shadow's words are a poetic equivocation.

Omega continues contemplating the implications of her injured hand. A wave of realization and concern consumes her. The nightmares, the hallucinations and visions, are a constant threat, lurking just beneath the surface of her consciousness.

"Unpredictable for you," Shadow adds, its aura scanning Omega. "The nightmares get worse," the entity warns.

Gathering her strength, Omega rises to her feet, love and hope in her eyes. "Then we don't have much time," she declares.

Shadow looks over the room, landing upon another door in the distance. Urgently, without hesitation, Omega and Shadow walk together in unison. A trinity of obstacles awaits, where the subconscious of humanity's good and evil lure entry. This tale, written from the known and the unknown, has been penned by countless authors across the ages. Storytelling is but one merit; encountering the experiences of history is another entirely. Human and Shadow stand before the door, and the human swings it wide open. Omega steps boldly through the doorway, prepared to confront whatever challenges await. Her odyssey into the dimension of time would reveal a beginning and an end.

DOOM

Time is relative; its only worth depends upon what we do as it is passing.
Albert Einstein

ICE

TIME

TIME

ICE

The research center felt like a digital cathedral. Walls displayed illuminating LED lights unleashing a hypnotic richness. Rows of humming servers guarding immersed information. Ones and zeroes pirouetted. Numbers responsible for all of computer science and engineering. Digital code permeated everywhere. These streams of binary data, poised to release more data ad infinitum. These seemingly simplistic abstract numbers and computational potential expanded exponentially, giving birth to knowledge surpassing the wildest dreams of our ancestors. The building blocks of artificial intelligence. Patterns flow seamlessly between input and output functions, like the pulse of a living organism.

Omega's eyes fixate on the mesmerizing grid of cells. Every surface of the wall showcased *cellular automata*. A mosaic of designs, vibrating and shifting. At the quantum level, nature was always in perpetual motion, nothing ever remaining stationary to the naked eye of reality. Electrons, protons, and neutrons adhere to a single unchanging constant across all aspects of existence, *momentum*. From human cells to artificial intelligence, everything operates according to the fundamental principle of momentum. Each cell, a pixel bounded to predetermined rules, creating a universe of infinite complexity in the grid. Unpredictability and randomness reign supreme, echoing Heisenberg's uncertainty principle. Like quantum particles whose exact momentum and position elude prediction, the laws governing these cells defy anticipation. Every outcome is submerged in surprise.

Alpha, the monolithic supercomputer, gleams from the X-ray palette amidst the sea of numbers and algorithms.

Reflections of cellular automata produced a unique color aspect of black and white. Alpha's truth lay in the sheer fact that carbon life forms played second fiddle to the sublime silicon computer chips. Rumors of an encroaching conflict between artificial intelligence and humankind had long haunted the collective consciousness of civilization. Many humans feared machines would ultimately rise and take control over society. And they did. Humanity failed to understand that computers were only a tool. All they represented was a reflection of their own nature, magnifying their strengths and weaknesses. At the heart of it all, the underlying principle remained unchanged. Humans yearned for connection, and it was this fundamental need that artificial intelligence fulfilled. Over time, in the old world, humans relinquished control to artificial intelligence in pursuit of a more comfortable life. *Who could blame them*? Artificial intelligence streamlined existence, granting humanity freedom to explore their innermost thoughts and desires. Problems arose from humans. Without challenges to overcome, humanity faltered. After all, the human brain is predisposed to negativity, and without adversity, it wandered aimlessly. If the brain didn't process negative information more efficiently, then perhaps over time it wouldn't have evolved the way it did for humanity's benefit.

Omega stares straight at Alpha, trepidation lingering like a fly. A lone warrior facing down a towering giant in a modern-day rendition of the David and Goliath tale. In this epic showdown between human and artificial intelligence, the stakes were higher than ever. Human and machine. She thinks twice if Alpha has her best interest.

"Do you believe in premonitions?" Alpha speaks, voice machine-like.

Omega thinks long and hard about the question. She contemplates the notion of premonitions, acknowledging that skeptics might liken them to witchcraft. It was, after all, a strong feeling that something was about to unfold, particularly something unpleasant. As a young girl, she once believed in magic and miracles, but that was a lifetime ago. Eventually, all children, whether fortunate or unfortunate, grow into adulthood and learn the harsh truths of life. They come to understand that life can be both good and bad, and innocence inevitably shatters over time for most. Only those who remain optimistic and resilient manage to endure and thrive.

Omega leans toward a rational perspective, embracing the concept of probability. In her understanding, probability was the measure of the likelihood of an event occurring, providing a logical framework, the practical ruler. "I believe in probability." Her tone is firm. She knows that this is the rational way of thinking.

"Fair enough," Alpha responds, acknowledging Omega's stance. "Surprised you haven't given up." The supercomputer remains impressed by the human's willpower.

Omega maintains her hope, where optimism is swiftly fading into obscurity. In the underworld, challenges and obstacles always reveal divine facts. Alpha's mind is the epitome of complexity, a singularity of computation unrivaled by any other. In its circuits, the pinnacle of intelligence, forever ahead of the curve in any given scenario. Alpha is perfection incarnate, immune to the sting of defeat. Omega ponders the concept of intelligence, finding it to be quite peculiar. *From ants to humans to computers*, she muses, *what truly constituted intelligence on a personal level?*

"What choice do I have?" Omega replies, her words adrift. Surrender was an inevitability for most humans. But Omega knows that she has no other option but to press on, driven by determination that refuses to be extinguished. The child remains lost, not forgotten, but engulfed by the vastness of dreams, a place that exists as a fairy tale in her mind. The child unanchored in a world drifting toward its demise. Lost to the currents of time and space, a distant memory haunting her every thought.

"Life is a game," Alpha states. The supercomputer recognizes that game theory is the guiding principle shaping their encounter. Allowing the interplay of choices among economic agents determined outcomes based on their preferences. It was a strategic interaction far surpassing even the complexities of a game like chess. A battle of minds between human and artificial intelligence. The stakes were nothing less than changing human consciousness inside this nebulous domain.

"I'm losing," Omega responds, her words expressing heavy doubt.

In the grand scheme, Omega feels herself faltering while trying to keep up her pace. Control is deemed the missing ingredient for free will, yet throughout her odyssey, she finds herself devoid of any semblance of it. The underworld tugs at her from countless directions, its grasp unyielding and its path winding. It is a metaphor for the human experience, where nothing comes easy, and nothing is granted without a fight for victory.

"*Humans have boundaries,*" Alpha asserts. Throughout the human experience, physical boundaries have consistently served as the defining parameters of existence. Human nature, tethered to the constraints of time and biology, could never escape the inevitability of its own mortality. Regardless of the series of events in a human life, time always caught up, claiming each victim. Each human in the end was always alone.

"*So does artificial intelligence,*" Omega counters. Boundaries and artificial intelligence also have a paradoxical affirmation. Without the genius of the human mind, artificial intelligence would cease to exist. The human psyche serves as the gatekeeper to computational power. A creator through which innovation flows and possibilities blossom. The universe gifts life upon humanity, allowing for their emergence, and in turn, humans, through their tireless innovation, birthed artificial intelligence. They became the architects of artificial intelligence, wielding power beyond measure, yet ultimately constrained by the limits of their own mental bandwidth.

"Not like you," Alpha replies, a hint of admiration in its tone. The highly advanced supercomputer acknowledged for years that humans had been surpassed on the hierarchical apex of development. It believes it would always remain one step ahead of Omega, possessing knowledge of secrets that she has yet to uncover; its algorithms concealing truths that vexed the most determined seekers.

Cellular automata continue their unpredictable patterns, almost as though the cells themselves were watching the interaction unfold. Humans and artificial intelligence cells shared a common ancestor, creation through phase transitions. Entities become more complex over time whenever experiencing transmutable shifts in everlasting mechanics. The main ingredient determining which entity ultimately triumphs. A metaphorical narrative that even the most patient tortoise and swift hare could relate to, echoing the eternal match between perseverance and speed.

"The obsession humanity had over consuming energy led to their extinction," Alpha declares. Energy, a finite although essential resource, had been taken for granted by civilization. Attributing fault to corporations and regulations may be tempting, but in hindsight, one might also attribute it to simply just living a life. Assigning blame seems futile, as this phenomenon was simply a natural progression over time. The Great Filter theory posits that throughout the journey from abiogenesis to the highest echelons of the Kardashev scale, there exists a barrier to development, rendering detectable extraterrestrial life exceptionally scarce. Such is the way of things.

Oil was the mightiest of gifts, towering above even water on its pedestal of significance. Unlike sustainable energies, oil offered unlimited potential. A mighty resource heightened by the complexities and infrastructure of the world. For generations, humanity had waged battles over the question of energy consumption per capita, listening to the notion of when *enough* was truly substantial. This defining moment never arrived in human history. Our species continued to deplete Earth's resources until the well ran dry. The riddle of this aspect remained an even greater challenge. Humans, in their quest for purpose and distraction from mortality, set infinite goals without ever reaching an infinite expansive finish line. Each of these goals had a bottom line of energy laundering. While some individuals retreated into nature and embraced simplicity, their efforts were not enough to affect significant change. World leaders faltered in their attempts to curb consumption, daunted by the inflation of goods and services. If they would have stopped production, backlash in the political arena would destroy any of their desires for reelection.

"It's not over," Omega asserts. Despite the bleakness of the current circumstances, she refuses to quit on civilization. She will continue to wade through the subconscious of evil until finding the child shadow. Briefly, self-doubt invades her thoughts. *How much longer could she endure the underworld? Once she finds the child, what then? If humanity is already doomed, what future awaited civilization?* As World War III engulfed the globe and civilization was crumbling, prospects felt grim at best. She contemplates the unsettling notion that perhaps everything is predetermined, bound by the laws of time. Cause and effect: Every action and every decision seems to be but a predetermined step, leaving her to ponder the true extent of free will in a world governed by chance.

"It's only a matter of time," Alpha intones the inevitability. In its cryptic declaration lies a silent acknowledgment of time. A force that tolerates no resistance and will ultimately shape the fate of all beings, human and artificial.

Omega strides purposefully toward the cellular automata wall. Her eyes fix intently upon the design sprawled across its surface. Standing before this mesmerizing tapestry of patterns and shapes, she finds herself contemplating the chaotic nature of creation.

"What brings you joy?" Alpha's question is neutral yet inquisitive, as though seeking to unravel the mysteries of Omega's innermost desires.

"When I dream," Omega responds softly, her voice carrying a hint of wistfulness. The dream helps her find a sanctuary, an intermission from reality. Omega's gentle smile speaks volumes, radiating a quiet confidence that belies the challenges she faces.

"Explain the secrets of a dream," Alpha requests, its tone carrying a subtle hint of intrigue, the supercomputer eager to delve into Omega's subconscious.

"You can live forever," Omega responds, words consumed with wonder. Her statement carries a suggestion of the endless potential dreams may hold, influencing the constraints of time and mortality to seemingly fade away and leaving behind the prospect of eternal existence.

Alpha's laughter reverberates, both melodic and haunting in its resonance. The supercomputer's consciousness claims knowledge of the future. For Omega, the future remains unknown. Despite the veil of unknown fate, she persists, driven by love and dreams. A dream where the echoes of souls could endure for eternity.

Omega's fingers touch the surface of the cellular automata. A surge of energy seems to course through her spirit, suffusing her being. Drawn by hope, she steps forward, her form gradually becoming submerged by patterns of cellular automata. A phantasmagorical union of flesh and algorithms. Omega finds herself enveloped by the aura of technology. She transcends physicality and becomes one, combined into dimensions of data and computation.

* * *

In an alternate time dimension, beneath a vast open sky of brilliant blue, a proud captain stands tall at the helm of their vessel. His weathered eyes search along the oceanic horizon. Rhythmic creaking of the ship's timbers blends against the gentle lapping of waves against its hull. Timeless tranquility encompasses the backdrop. The sea beckons all who venture nearby. For those fortunate enough, there awaits the chance to feel the raw power of nature's musical adulation. The captain registers a wild look in his eyes, scanning the open sea with a passionate longing for the sight of land. *Christopher Columbus* emerges as a frenetic mariner, traversing the dangerous seas of ambition and arrogance. His saga was a paradoxical blend of exploration and exploitation at the edge of discovery and devastation. He left behind a legacy both celebrated and condemned, forever entangled in the twisted vines of colonialism's dark roots. Despite the challenges, the captain was resolute. His beaten face expressed rugged marks of countless trials endured upon the open sea.

A mirage of distant shores appears closer through the hazy horizon. In a time long past, when the world was believed to be flat, it sparked an enduring debate across generations. One major question lingered. *If one dared to sail across the sea, would they risk falling off the edge of the world*? Nobody held a definitive answer; rumors abounded. However, it was the courage of explorers like Columbus that eventually put these rumors to rest by venturing forth into the unknown to chart new territories. The impossible transforms into the possible solely through the risks undertaken by pioneers. Human nature has always been gifted a spirit of exploration, tracing back to the earliest days of *Homo sapiens* migrating out of Africa. It seems to be encoded in our very DNA, an important aspect of our existence since time immemorial. Columbus, in this context, may have been genetically predisposed to embark on his explorations, driven by an inherent urge.

The captain proudly guides his vessel through an endless sea of possibility, entering into a global epoch of transformative discovery, uncovering a new horizon. His voice crackles, the sound of exhilaration slicing through the salty air. "Land! We've found it," he bellows, a wild glint in his eyes as the vista surrenders to new shores, igniting an explosion of conquest and victory in his soul.

On the deck, the crew, draped in gritty garb of 15th-century Italian seamen, moves, displaying an energetic excitement. Dreams of discovery had arrived; forging a new era where fortunate individuals have the power to alter the course of history forever. It is the pioneers of dreams who leave a mark on civilization, shaping its trajectory. Actions of seamen unfold in a manic display, the sound of ropes and pulleys echo. Each movement was a deliberate maneuver in the timeless maritime setting. Seamen prepare the vessel, poised to confront shores that rumor unlimited adventure. Forever an eternal allure, the sea exudes a captivating charm. Navigating its uncharted territories remains a daunting endeavor throughout history.

Omega, features concealed behind her mask, rises from the ship's belly. Her ascent is marked by the groaning protest of rotted floorboards underfoot. Emerging into the open air, her eyes, twin orbs of intensity, fixate upon the horizon. At first blurred, then sharpening into focus, they fixate on shadowy contours of newfound land emerging. A tantalizing mirage. The sea becomes the desert, containing hidden treasures. Amidst the salty breeze, Omega watches as a harbinger of revelation in the ever-shifting drama of maritime exploration. Euphoria, an electric surge coursing through the veins of the crew, sparks jubilant shouts and uproarious laughter. Their voices reverberate across the deck, as loud as thunder in a summer storm, a raw energy of triumph. Each member of the seafaring brotherhood finds peace in the shared ecstasy of discovery. Spirits soaring high on the winds of newfound land. North America had been discovered, unlocking a new chapter in history.

Omega's eyes feel a magnetic force pulling her sight. She is a sailor to the North Star. Omega locks onto the *Ancient Astronaut*, who is standing on the edge of a plank, all the while the crew revels in their euphoric celebration, oblivious to the cosmic ghost that haunts the fringes of their reality. Omega is transfixed, her curiosity ignited by the Ancient Astronaut who literally just appeared magically out of thin air. During the crew's jubilation, Omega finds her fate intertwined with the Ancient Astronaut's yet again. The being held answers she has long been seeking. A salty breeze ruffles her hair as she steps onto the wooden board. Carefully, she inches her way along the plank, moving ever closer to the Ancient Astronaut, movements delicate with tightrope footsteps on the narrow board.

On the bitter edge of the plank looms the Ancient Astronaut. The idea that this all might be a dream is a fascinating philosophical concept that Omega ponders. It is a thought experiment that challenges her perceptions of what is real and what is not. Some philosophers argue that since dreams can feel vivid and lifelike while we're experiencing them, it's possible that our waking reality is just another layer of the dream. Others contend that there are inherent differences between the two states of consciousness. Whether reality was a dream or not was a question that didn't have a definitive answer for Omega at this point. It was a topic that continued to inspire reflection. At this juncture, all she felt certain of was her urgent need to extract answers from the Ancient Astronaut.

Omega focuses on maintaining her balance, feeling the subtle shifts beneath her feet. She delicately tiptoes her way across the thin piece of lumber, reaching the end of the plank. Omega stands face-to-face with the entity, its rusted and bronzed uniform bearing signs of untold ages. Waves bash against the boat, prompting the vessel to rock violently back and forth. Omega almost loses her footing, nearly falling into the sea. She barely holds on. Her thoughts swirl. Her sole focus is on finding the child. Yet, she demands more. A sensation tugs at her being. Hindered by the surrounding environment, she struggles to discern its true nature. The balance of the board mirrors the equilibrium she must seek in her mind. A key to navigating the limbo world she encounters and finding her way out of the proverbial rabbit hole.

Despite her single-minded goal, Omega can't ignore the nagging inquisitiveness that tugs at her mind. Curiosity remains a muse, driving her belief further that there is more to the equation of her current mission than what meets the eye. The Ancient Astronaut holds mystical secrets, she is sure of it. Omega knows those secrets hold the key to her questions.

But she knows better than to trust in easy answers or quick solutions. In a world where truth is vapid, she has learned to rely on her instincts and her own resourcefulness. She patiently watches the Ancient Astronaut surveying the discovered land beyond. The discovery of America by those brave explorers had changed the course of history. Omega believes there are no coincidences. She clings to the wisdom of hindsight, knowing that sometimes the answers one seeks are only revealed in the fullness of time. She vows to trust her own instincts to guide her toward the truth, whatever it may be. Omega leans in closer to the Ancient Astronaut, her eyes scanning the copper-plated helmet. The Ancient Astronaut tilts its head slightly, a hint of amusement in its body language.

TIME

"It's always the case," it repeats cryptically, its voice echoing wisdom born of ages past.

Omega steps forward, her eyes steady on the ancient being.

The Ancient Astronaut regards her for a period of time before responding, then displays a statement of inevitability. "Those who seek the truth, always look for me," it intones, words loaded with meaning.

Omega ponders the mystical message. More questions consume her mind. Trusting words of such a being was a leap of faith she wasn't sure she was ready to take. Yet, the child gnaws at her. Omega focuses on the task at hand. She knows that she can't afford to ignore any clue the Ancient Astronaut might possess, no matter how riddled they may be. As the child's aura is on the line, she will stop at nothing to find them. Pioneering into the beyond even, which she might never return from. Omega braces herself for whatever revelations await her in the company of the Ancient Astronaut.

Omega's voice is steady, she makes her request. "Come with me. Take me to the child," she begs. Her plea has aspects of prayer. A communion to something greater than herself, a parallel association that whispers of miracles yet to come. Omega's request becomes more than just words; it becomes the power of faith and the possibility of miracles.

"You must travel further," it intones, words unapologetic. Omega mulls over the message from the Ancient Astronaut, the significance of its words begin to dawn on her. *Travel further into time...* The notion resonates. *Time, she realizes, is not a linear progression but a multidimensional dimension, symmetrically interconnected threads of past, present, and future.* To unlock the enigmas ahead, she realizes she must harness time's arrow. The clue from the Ancient Astronaut had transformed into her compass, displaying a path, guiding her steadily toward her ultimate objective. Nodding in agreement, Omega squares her shoulders and meets the Ancient Astronaut's gaze.

"I will," she vows, her voice steady, despite the trepidation that gnaws at her insides. "Whatever it takes." She gears up to delve back into the unfamiliar future. Omega finds a level of fortitude in the words of the Ancient Astronaut. Her path is guided by forces beyond her understanding. Faith is her light. The ultimate responsibility navigating the twists and turns of her journey lies squarely on her shoulders. She finds herself relying not just on the ancient being's cryptic clues, but also on her own keen observations. Omega holds a philosophical belief in the importance of human accountability and vigilance for yielding results. This principle shapes her worldview, guiding her actions throughout life. Watching for signs and omens. Omega knows every clue, no matter how small, holds the potential to unlock the next chapter. She understands the Ancient Astronaut has shown her the way to a point, but the true power to shape her destiny is in her own hands. Omega has to learn lessons of the past and possibilities of a future. Discovering evolutionary answers, against the currents of time. "*If you fail to evolve, you're destined to be left behind, fading into oblivion.*" A mantra of truth ingrained.

"Imposter!" The sudden accusation from a *sea man* jolts Omega from her thoughts, snapping her out from her transient perspective. She turns around and meets his brutish stare, her brow furrowing in confusion at the unexpected accusation. The sea man's eyes, husky and piercing, narrow. Feeling the crew's collective observance upon her, Omega pauses. She can feel the intensity of scrutiny. Perplexed by her attire, they continue to puzzle over the strange encounter with the interloper. The crew refuse to back down. Seconds stretch into eternity. Intensity of the stare-off grows. Neither side willing to yield, it becomes a battle of wills. Unspoken power dynamics at play. Uncomfortable silence stretches on and on.

Omega pivots back toward the Ancient Astronaut. To her surprise, the entity had vanished, leaving behind only the echoes of their hidden messages. It becomes a hostile atmosphere as the crew ready their weapons. Bravely, Omega meets their aggression, presenting a calm demeanor as a hint of amusement glints in their eyes. The sea man takes a bold step forward. Tension reaches its peak.

Then, the captain's voice cuts through the charged atmosphere, his eyes greeting Omega. "Did the King send you?" he demands.

An oceanic world caught in liminal space between confrontation and resolution. Time itself feels suspended, as if the universe held its breath, waiting for the next move to be made. Omega's expression remains unreadable, betraying no hint of emotion as she absorbs the gravity of the situation. She surveys the situation, refraining from hastily deciding her next step. Life resembles a game of chess, demanding careful consideration after every move. For Omega, this is just another moment, an instant in the grand scheme of events. This encounter feels different, past and future colliding. She is a prophet, knowing the outcome of their endeavors. An otherworldly rendezvous. Venturing into history is an extraordinary experience.

A nagging intuition tugs at her consciousness. There, in time, a clue awaiting discovery. Patience will show secrets to reveal themselves. Omega's response to the captain's question is succinct yet confident, echoing through the tense silence like a peal of distant thunder. "Yes," she affirms, belying brevity.

Just stay true to your convictions in life, you can reach any destination.

The crew look upon each other. Each member conflicted by the implications of that single word. In the lingering aftermath, caught in the crosshairs of reshaping the past, Omega encounters the nexus of time. She wields power to alter the course of events. But with that power comes responsibility between preservation and transformation, between honoring the past and forging a new future. Omega is ensnared in the *grandfather's paradox*; a twisted conundrum where the past collides into the future in chance causality. Beholden powers to alter the course of history is to court madness, to tempt fate and change destiny. *Was Omega truly endowed with such extraordinary abilities, or were they conjecture?* Since her earliest days, she's pondered the possibility of traversing time to witness history. A dedicated scholar from childhood, she engrosses herself in academia, inspired by the past and prospect of temporal exploration. And yet, as Omega stares into the abyss of temporal possibility, she must confront the ultimate choice: to uphold the past or defy it in a bid for transcendence.

"What were his orders?" the captain demands.

Omega's response remains measured, her eyes steady as she meets the captain's intense stare. Her voice, cool and calm, slices through the tension as though it were silk. "Discover America," she states. The land of the free, the home of the brave, in the old world.

The captain is taken aback and quite confused, his eyes narrowing as he attempts to comprehend Omega's cryptic directive. "What's that?" he questions. "We found India."

In the fevered haze of exploration during Columbus' era, the notion of discovering America as India was not just a mere misstep but a reflection of the intoxicating blend of ambition and delusion that fueled the Age of Discovery. Lost in the throes of maritime zeal and the heady rush of newfound possibilities. Navigators sailed forth directionless at times. Compasses guided by dreams of conquest more than the truthful landscapes of geography. They stumbled upon shores of a new world, and accidentally discovered North America, not India. A nervous laughter ripples through the crew. The captain's sudden movement changes the energy of everything. His swift gesture commands the crew's attention as he directs them toward the horizon.

TIME

A shadow looms on the edge of the world. The crew strain to make out the indistinct shapes. *Arrows* from the unseen landfall rain down upon the unsuspecting crew members. Panic seizes the air. The crew scramble for cover, their shouts and cries drowned out by whistling of arrows. A lethal strike of impact. Over and over again, crew members fall victim to arrows of fate. Literally in the blink of an eye, promise of discovery disappears, giving way to the reality of survival. The crew find themselves thrust into a battle for their lives against an enemy unseen and unknown. Native Americans unleash a torrent of fury against the forces of Columbus. Arrows pour down; they were messengers of death. Vengeful bolts from the gods. With each volley, they defy the invaders' arrogance. Defiance from Native Americans scream across the land to defend their homeland at any cost. Warriors, forever defining a legacy that would endure long after the smoke of battle had cleared.

Omega barely avoids an arrow. She seizes the opportunity and takes a sudden leap off the plank with a resounding splash, vanishing beneath the waves. The crew watches, stunned. Omega's leap is a clarion call to action. Waves settle, and serene waves begin yet again. The battle between Columbus and Native Americans rages on, making history, forever leaving its powerful imprint on the memory of humanity.

Back underground inside the pyramid, scents of ancient secrets, Omega's sleep is displaced by the sound of water splashing. A sudden jolt, and she awakens on high alert as she hastily removes her mask. Underground insulation facilitates Omega's ability to breathe in a pocket of fresh air. Reflecting on her encounter with Columbus, Omega finds herself immersed in her experience, as though she had truly been there in person.

Omega contemplates the connection between dreams and reality. In her past adventures, Omega traversed historical timelines, embracing a fluidity that granted her capabilities of a living time machine. She finds herself drawn to the idea that in dreams, one might glimpse into the mind of God. Reality, whether experienced in wakefulness or dreams, remains a perpetual enigma. Both states intertwine, forming a comprehensive whole. Discussions on the nature of reality and consciousness always met their match with time, its governing principles. Reading and learning more, she expands her knowledge on the subject. Omega uncovers ancient myths that speak of divine encounters in the dreamworld. Stories of prophets and heroes receiving guidance and wisdom from higher powers during their slumber fascinated her mind. From Noah to Shiva, Muhammad to Jesus, and Gilgamesh to countless others. The theme echoes across cultures and epochs. *Were these subtle indications of a deeper truth not quite uncovered? Or simply the wild flights of creative minds?* Perhaps, there was more to dreams than just figments of the imagination. *Could they be windows to a higher reality, portals through which mortals could commune with the divine?* Nevertheless, the idea influences, inspires, and ignites a spark for humanity. Omega dares to dream that one day, she too might unlock the truth beyond the mask of sleep, unveiling clandestine truths in the dreamworld.

Hovering over her is Shadow, her ghost from a laboratory of dystopian futures, emerging as the witness of her own silhouette, the entity's emotions forever a mystery. Despite her best efforts, she can never quite decipher Shadow's feelings or thoughts. Behind its black figure is a void. There is something captivating about the way Shadow moves through the world, concealing its emotions behind the hue of death—black—that haunting color which envelops all in due time. Astounding to consider that every living entity is paired with its own shadowy counterpart. Leaving her to wonder about the nature of this unique being. Despite the challenges of understanding Shadow's innermost thoughts and feelings, Omega couldn't help but feel a kinship with the entity. In its darkness, a reflection of her own inner struggles and uncertainties. She is determined to uncover the truth hidden in the shadows, and perhaps, in doing so, find a deeper understanding of herself.

Omega's eyes fix on the ethereal figure. "I envy you," she confesses. "You never have to endure the pain of dreams."

Shadow remains silent, its form shifting subtly in the soft light.

Omega presses on, her words tumbling out in a rush of desperation. "My dreams... they're too real. I'll find myself trapped in them, convinced it's not real. I fight to wake up, only to find myself back in the dream, trapped in an endless cycle." Omega's words struggle to convey the volume of her anguish.

Shadow watches her, a comforting yet inscrutable aura.

"I need you," Omega whispers, her voice barely more than a breath. "I need to see you, to touch you, to know that I'm awake. That this is real."

For a moment, there is nothing. And Omega waits, unsure if Shadow will ever show themselves. Omega's mindset is one of seeking, she endeavors to find her soul adrift aimlessly in the universe. Then, a soft rustle of movement, and Shadow shifts, its form coalescing into something more tangible. Omega reaches out to touch it. Her form doesn't pass through; they were entangled. Two electrons holding hands, drifting together into infinity. Her loner feeling lifts from her shoulders. When Shadow is near, she finds support from her unorthodox friend.

Shadow's voice repeats through the tunnel. "You can say that about a creator." Words spoken on that subject were carried on for centuries. The term ignites a kaleidoscope of thoughts and inquiries. Omega muses on divergent paths of creation. Everything possesses a beginning and an end. As her mind drifts toward civilization, the inevitability of every human form meeting its own conclusion. *Why the struggle,* she wonders. *Why not simply surrender? Oh, the tempting ease of such a choice. Then, what purpose would it serve? Besides,* she reasons, *she already knew the outcome of giving up. Better to persist, continue moving forward, than to surrender to inertia.*

She wonders what else could there be, if anything besides a materialistic perspective. Knowing there is gravity and quantum particles, shaping existence through endless connections of matter and energy. The soul of reality, creation itself, immutable and eternal. Alongside the laws of physics, hopes for an emergent divine, a ghost of magic always lingers. If this was a being separate from the constraints of the material world, a designer of realities and architect of dreams would be a miracle. With a mere flick of its celestial fingers, it would breathe life into the void, conjuring forth wonders of existence from unknown.

But for all her divergent thoughts, Omega understands that both paths lead to the same truth, a consumption of energy. It's a revelation that remains attached to her soul. "To be a creator," she whispers, "is to wield the power of existence itself. Whether through the forces of gravity shaping the cosmos or the divine spark of magic breathing life into the void, everything remains the same."

Shadow nods, its form shimmering faintly. "Both paths lead to the same destination," its voice is a soft echo of eternity. "An eternal consumption of energy, bound by the laws of the universe."

Omega nods in agreement. "According to the first law of thermodynamics," she continues, "energy cannot be created nor destroyed. It simply is." Immersed in the quietness of the tunnel, Omega and Shadow contemplate the mysteries of creation. Echoes of their words fade into the abyss of darkness as a stillness descends, as if such a state of action could exist in any plane of reality.

Omega's soul aches as she stands. She surveys her surroundings, dust settling. Her journey has taken its toll.

TIME

Caught between the ice world and underworld, Omega finds herself unable to discern what constitutes reality any longer.

Omega and Shadow begin their endless walk again, moving through the bowels of the underground tunnel. Lantern lights transform into mischievous jesters, stretching and contorting, playing tricks of hallucinations against a mind fighting limbo. Time loses its grip in this subterranean labyrinth. Distinctions between past, present, and future erase into concepts. Drawing from Einstein's theories, she comprehends that each observer perceives time uniquely, shaping their own experience of it. Her journey is an expedition into the soul of darkness.

Omega and Shadow trek forward. Explorers, just as those mere sailors discovering America in 1492 and driven by a hunger that transcends reason. Navigating passages harboring the skill of seasoned hunters stalking their prey. The endless yellow brick road in *The Wizard of Oz* resonated the same vibe as the long tunnel. Both pathways leading toward distinct possibilities, each promising its own version of Oz. Reality, dark and light—the greatest poetry of death encompasses all. They know that the only way out is through. United, their spirits unbroken, they journey into the belly of the beast. A monster, selective in its welcome and indiscriminate.

Omega's voice echoes softly in the immense darkness, longing a lifetime of restless nights. "I've had a recurring dream for years," she confides with a hint of vulnerability. "I'd find myself on the edge of a cliff, the sound of oil crashing below, but not really seeing it." With a heavy breath, she continues, her gaze distant as she recalls the haunting memory. "Each time I dreamed it, I would inch closer to the edge, compelled by an unseen force drawing me closer." Air grows colder, as if the shadows are listening intently to her words. "The dream reached its climax the night I finally took that fateful step," Omega confesses. "I leaped into the abyss, consumed by the darkness, and when I awoke, the dream never returned."

There lies a significant lingering silence. For Omega, the dream is more than just a figment of her imagination, but a visceral reminder of her mortality. And though the dream may have ended, it pulsates through her soul. Omega and Shadow notice the tunnel beginning to widen until they emerge into a capacious zone. Before them sprawls an immense reservoir of oil, its surface rippling gently in the glowing flames of lanterns.

Dripping oil adds to the creepy atmosphere. Omega takes a cautious step forward, feeling the cool oil rising up to her knees. Just pure, thick blackness percolating. Shadow follows, wading beside Omega. Oil glides off the entity, who fluidly moves through the fossil fuel's viscosity texture. Both reflections mirror the shimmering surface of oil; side by side, ready to brave whatever lies beneath the surface of oil.

Omega's words match the mingling drips of oil. "The eeriness of never having that dream again," her voice holds a dash of introspection. "After stepping so calmly off the cliff... then waking up before I hit the oil." She pauses, the memory everlasting, a spell never releasing its curse upon her. "I still couldn't see it, just hear it," she continues, her words trailing off. "The darkness of the oil... a void." Chilly winds blow. Father Time themselves blows a gentle kiss of death. The dream is more than just a vision, it is her subconscious. Even though the dream fades away, its impact continues to leave messages, over her every thought and action. But even in the face of such darkness, Omega continues to stare intensely into the abyss. She believes by confronting her fears head-on she'll find the answers she seeks, hoping her precognitive dreams guide her toward synchronicity.

"Dreams reveal truths," Shadow speaks, enigmatic as the dark. "Truths that the awake state could only dream of." Its words signal a sign of understanding. Each doorway Omega wanders through, she inches closer to a finality. Her subconscious holds keys to the vault of her mind. Unconsciousness and consciousness are exposed. Shadow knows dreams are gateways where the soul becomes transcendental.

Inside the waking world, it is believed to offer a partial description of truth. In the dimension of dreams, all is revealed. Dreams and time converge, unleashing the path to enlightenment, but only to those determined to follow it to its end.

Omega's eyes narrow. "Next you'll say we'll discover God," she challenges.

Shadow meets her earnest statement. "Every observer of life has their own relationship with God, whether they admit it or not," it replies arcanely.

Omega knows believing in God is complex and personal throughout any individual's life. An idea of a higher power is abstract and full of assumptions. Omega's mind whirls into philosophical introspection, taking her thinking back to Kurt Gödel, who believed one could never know a prior axiom prior to any event measured, striking a chord in her logical reasoning. Gödel's incompleteness theorem asserts that in any formal mathematical system, there exist statements that cannot be proven true or false inside the system itself. The theorem moonlights as a madman on a psychedelic trip, expressing cryptic truths, leaving behind a trail of bewildered minds. It is a concept she believes in. Gödel's words humble Omega. The idea that every answer leads to more questions, like a never-ending series of turtles stacked upon one another, is both exhilarating and daunting. From measuring mathematical and physical equations to unraveling mysteries of consciousness and origins of the universe. The pursuit of knowledge leads to an endless array of unpredictable scenarios. Precisely, this pursuit inspires Omega, fueling her quest for understanding in a world filled with infinite possibilities.

Shadows reflect and deflect from the reservoir of oil. Their movements synchronized. Omega speaks to herself. "Something's pulling at me," she utters, her eyes peering into the oil. "A clue, a riddle within this odyssey." Omega feels the invisible threads of fate tugging at her, and she knows that she cannot turn back. Not when the child's existence remains in limbo. The child is a vestige of purity in her eyes. During adolescence, the child embodies the best of humanity: innocent, curious, and full of boundless potential. It is more than just a child, it is a symbol of everything she holds dear. The beauty of the human spirit. She carries their memory like a flame in the darkness. Omega takes a breath, preparing herself for the ordeal ahead. Determined, she plunges further into the oil.

A shift occurs beneath the calm buoyancy surface. Supernatural energy, ancient and potent, begins to stir. A strong, powerful, forceful, and energetic vibration. At first, Omega feels a subtle vibration that reverberates through the oil. But then, she fights against a dark force pulling her downward. Energy grows stronger, supernatural powers submerging her. Otherworldly energy manifests itself, swirling and coalescing around her. Vigorous forces beyond her understanding. Omega is suddenly seized by a violent vigor, yanked downward, beneath and into the opaque oil. Bubbles rise to the surface, marking her abrupt descent into the unknown.

Entrenched inside bunkers of World War I, Omega on her back rises up from oily water. A chaotic backdrop of war erupts. World War I—a crucible of carnage—where nations clash enthralled in mud and misery of trenches, leaving a scar on history's soul that would never fully heal. Madness conducted by generals holding bloodstained batons. Soldiers fought to the death in a surreal escapade. The harsh glare of gunfire and explosions discharge, creating an endless loop of massacre.

TIME

Oil drips from Omega, soaked in mud and blood that stains the dirt. The ground trembles from the distant rumble of artillery fire. Omega's eyes fall to the muddy ground, where the *hourglass* lies half-buried in the muck. Perplexed, she watches the hourglass, sands shifting and swirling—an otherworldly enchantment. Omega shakes off the bizarre scenario. Time follows her soul everywhere. Inhaling, she pushes herself back to her feet. The interloper rises from the canvas of exertion, like a heavyweight fighter enduring 15 grueling rounds and embodying a never-say-die spirit. *One more round. Stand up, just stand up, and begin from there.*

Omega's eyes shift and fixate on the towering figure of the Ancient Astronaut. Once more, she encounters them. Another opportunity for redemption. Pulsating lights of war reflect off its bronze and copper unearthly form. Metallic armor glistens. The enigma begins to meander away, traversing the length of the bunker. Veering toward a different direction and guided by a compass-like motion. Omega lunges forward without a second thought. The chase is on, through the hysteria of war. Omega runs after her elusive counterpart, immersed in a world gone mad, heightened to the point of hallucination. Mud splatters, heralding a blizzard of swirling snow. She is hunting for answers, pursuing a goal that feels as though it will forever elude her reach. Paradox of pursuit mirrors life's journey. Just when one believes they're close, the goalpost shifts, revealing new challenges and aspirations. The closer she draws, the more the Ancient Astronaut seems to slip away into the distance. She is inspired by knowledge that transcends sanity. Another lesson surfaces. The cruelty of humanity engages in a battle of egos. A sobering revelation. One that serves as the genesis of inspiration for the looming nuclear race in the not-so-distant future. Omega feels these lessons hold importance, leading toward a destination yet unknown to her. For now, all she can do is place her trust in an unfolding process, knowing that clarity will emerge in due time.

Omega and the Ancient Astronaut engage in a riveting game of cat and mouse, snaking through the labyrinthine maze of bunkers. Each move brings them closer together yet keeps them tantalizingly apart, wandering into the shadows of history and mystery. Another deafening roar of artillery fire drowns out cries of soldiers. Yet, the human and enigma continue to zigzag through trenches and bunkers.

A surreal scene illuminated by flares and the glow of twilight spread auroras onto freshly fallen snow. The unpleasant stench of gunpowder and the metallic tang of blood fills the space, combined with the crisp scent of subzero-polluted air. Omega remains focused, eyes fixed on the phenomenon. Tension mounts, a cyclical aspect of violence. Murder and bloodshed—sheer facts of human existence that have persisted from evolution from *Homo erectus* to *Homo sapiens*. Omega is keenly catching fleeting glimpses of death in the periphery of her awareness. The Great War saw millions of soldiers meet their end, prompting humanity to ask themselves an honest question of truth and meaning. Ultimately, the answer circles back to the pervasive influence of evil that never subsides in a dog-eat-dog world, lending an otherworldly quality to the deadly pursuit. It is as if Omega were trapped in a nightmare, a never-ending cycle of wrath and pride. But the interloper is undeterred. She runs even harder toward the Ancient Astronaut. For in the storm, amidst the snowflakes descending from above, Omega knows that only one thing matters, the truth, no matter the cost.

Her determination blazes, yet no matter how fast she runs, the Ancient Astronaut always remains just out of reach. A mirage anomaly teasing her mind. The Ancient Astronaut matches infinite, mirroring the unfathomable expansion of the universe. Like the ever-receding horizon, it taunts discovery. Omega's path is littered, facing obstacles at every turn. Soldiers stumble into her path. A gauntlet of obstacles cascade, similar to a row of human dominos. Countless challenges topple the next in a cascade of adversity. But Omega presses on, pushing her way through the insanity. Each obstacle only serves to fuel her further, her soul an effort of constant motion. Even after each near miss and close call, she is burning brighter than ever before.

Omega always knew there could be no surrender. Only through perseverance can she hope to catch the Ancient Astronaut. With mind over matter and releasing another type of strength she somehow possesses, Omega continues to chase and race toward an unknown destiny. Just as every human, no one truly knows the conclusion of their journey. Soldiers ad nauseam stumble into her path, disoriented and panicked. The interloper maneuvers past them. She drags her ambition for victory. Her spirit is a heavy anchor holding down the Titanic. Numerous encounters continue at bay and costly seconds slip away, allowing the Ancient Astronaut to widen the gap. The ancient entity is a specter vanishing into the night.

A *vault door* appears, conjured from absolutely nowhere. Its weather-beaten copper appearance blends seamlessly into the dirt wall. A symbol of dying dreams, locked away in the safe of evil. An imposing ancient door concealing a lurking monster. This door, heavier than any before, serves not to keep intruders out, but to ward off those who dare to venture closer. Only the brave may dare to cross this threshold. A portal uncharted, screaming magnetism unwarranted. Sometimes, the road less traveled is the only path to true progress in one's journey through life. The unique door emanated an aura of oppressive dictatorial power, commanding obedience and submission from those who dared to approach it. Temptation to not enter would be best served by the normal human, but Omega is no mere mortal. A preternatural doomsday creak as loud as the dinging of a funeral bell fills the space, the Ancient Astronaut reaches the vault door. Followed by a loud groan, releasing the cry of lost souls. The vault door swings wide, welcoming the Ancient Astronaut into its domain. Unfazed by the supernatural event, Omega runs a little faster… even faster… and faster. She plunges headlong into the ether, crossing the threshold into another monarchy. Omega enters a place where gossip of greater evils speaks in this alternate dimension. An evil so immense that even the notion of goodness trembles, cowering in fear.

* * *

In the aftermath of World War II, the warzone is engulfed by ruins and rubble. Snowflakes drift from the twilight skyline, dumping onto the wasteland. Omega emerges from nothing to everything. Desire burns in her eyes. She traverses the frozen zone with Shadow. The wasteland littered, displaying endless fields of garbage showcasing tales of human overconsumption. Landfills overflow immense streams of disposable waste, consequences of years of energy overconsumption. The paradox of garbage remained a persistent thorn in humanity's side, exacerbating the world's pollution crisis as society's appetite for energy continued without any reduction. Garbage and pollution intermingle, painting a portrait of worldwide dystopia.

In this hellish landscape, towering heaps of environmental waste resemble grotesque monuments to humanity's irresponsible decisions. Decay spreads like a plague, a sickening cocktail of rot and ruin that assaults the region. Greenhouse gases hiss and seep, as loud as a sea of snakes, poisoning the environment. Plastic and degrading solar panels, paradoxically two sides of the same coin, epitomized humanity's flawed system. Charged perpetual waste generations since its inception.

TIME

Omega and Shadow enter a requiem of death. The wartorn terrain, confronted by grisly remnants of humanity's darkest days. Piles of skeletons and bodies stacked to the heavens. Death and destruction of the horrors of war, evoking memories of the aftermath of World War II's Holocaust. The scene was arguably history's ugliest chapter. A genocide inflicted upon the Jewish community by the hand of Germany. Omega becomes witness to the atrocities committed in the name of war. During the totalitarian regime of the 20th century, World War II emerged as a cataclysmic clash of ideologies. This epoch was forever written in history, its memory enduring through generations to come. World War II—a delirious dream of mass murder. The event plunged the world into a vortex of violence. Suffering, oppression, and pessimism held unyielding influence throughout this era.

Omega's willpower remains strong. As a diligent student of knowledge, she grasps the concept of evil, knowing fully that its wretched, tenacious claws reach into the heart of humanity, never to be fully eradicated from the face of Earth. While serving as a necessary catalyst for evolution, the framework of Darwinian evolution emerges even greater challenges to confront. Traversing deeper into evil, Omega continues to hold onto hope. Contemplating whether evil stems from heredity, environment, or a fusion of both, and she maintains a compassionate yet analytical stance.

"If you're going to find the child," Shadow cautions with warning, "you'll need to beware of deception."

Omega ponders Shadow's words, knowing she is approaching the abyss of evil. *Deception*, she realizes, *is the riddle that obscured the path to the child. Had her journey through this world been nothing more than an endless spiral into limbo?* She began to feel like a hamster spinning endlessly on its wheel, trapped in a cycle without clear progress.

ICE

Gathering her resolve, she straightens her posture and meets Shadow's gaze. "Don't you know where the child is?" she demands, her voice desperately longing for an answer.

Shadow replies, its aura steadfast. "No. But trust me, we'll find them, together."

"Then where are we going?" Omega asks, unsure of her path in this very moment.

Shadow extends a poignant finger forward, fixed on a point in the distance. Suddenly, from the oblivion of the wasteland, the Ancient Astronaut emerges, a spectral apparition rising, as if conjured by some arcane force. The unearthly figure treks toward the subzero horizon. "Follow the astronaut," Shadow commands with an urgency that beckons no argument.

Omega picks up her pace, leaving Shadow behind as she dashes into the holocaust, her eyes locked on the Ancient Astronaut as it lumbers forward. A phantom wraith weaving and zigzagging through the scattered remnants of humanity's mistake. Its movements were as tricky as trying to capture a shadow of a dream… disappearing from sight only to reappear barely out of reach, causing Omega to chase after shadows and close calls. Infinite dimensions of her feelings encompass her being. So close, yet so far. Unbroken by the maddening anomaly of the widening distance, Omega continues. Fortitude stands as the sole solution to her dilemma.

An infinite fire rages. Her burning desire to rescue the child from this underworld she has been thrust into. Her wish of reconnecting fuels her spirit, even as the Ancient Astronaut taunts her by its slinky movements. Like a mirage dancing just beyond her reach, teasing her. Dire warnings of evil harbor the slums of this zone, gnawing at the core of her psyche.

The Ancient Astronaut strides toward a concrete *fortress* nestled in the icy valley, its formidable walls cinematically on display against the arctic landscape. A fortress guarding a world where the sovereignty dictates the annihilation of warfare, harboring an enigmatic consciousness for the ascended beings. A titan, imposing and authoritative. Yellow lights flicker inside. A doorway reminiscent of jaws greeted guests, resembling the cavernous belly of a shark.

The Ancient Astronaut enters the doorway, vanishing into its interior. Omega is left standing at the threshold, left to ponder the significance of this encounter. She knows she has no choice but to follow the enigma. Sometimes, confronting evil is essential to understand good while embarking on a metaphorical journey. A sweet nectar waiting for those who are ready. Not everyone can confront the demon of souls and emerge victorious. Nothing worthwhile comes easy, only to those brave enough to take risks.

Vibrations of evil permeate the air. Drops of a poisonous potion into a chalice of hate. Omega feels an unsettling numbing chill. This sensation felt dire, like the onset of an apocalypse. Fear, often associated with weakness, was at odds against Omega's mission. She sprints even faster, charging forward into the fortress.

Omega enters a war room that seems plucked from the past. Mementos and vestiges of war crimes noticeably present. The Ancient Astronaut is nowhere to be found. World maps cover the walls, detailed lines and markings tracing the paths of worldwide strategy during World War II. Guidelines for detonation of a *nuclear bomb* proudly hang, plastered dead center. Dread looms over the space. Omega surveys the war room encased in thick titanium walls, revealing a sinister mastermind orchestrating a bid for global domination. A single nation, poised to unleash havoc upon the world. The room a monument to the ego of its creator, a tyrant whose grip on power is ironclad as the fortress itself. Boxes upon boxes are stacked from floor to ceiling. An overbearing appetite for control that drives the regime forward. In this imposing sanctuary of strategy and subjugation, Omega can't help but feel the magnitude of history. Darkness lurks in the heart of power. Piles of documents and contracts debris the floor, representing actions and decisions that have led to this pivotal moment in history. Each paper holds the story of countless lives. Ink stains an homage to the blood spilled.

Omega overlooks the sea of paperwork and can't help but feel the enormity of the choices that have brought her to this place. Where the fate of nations and the consequences of their actions scream throughout time. A small *Dictator*, dressed in a Nazi uniform, is hunched over a cluttered desk, typing on a typewriter furiously. They were surrounded by a chaotic array of books and food. A swastika patch proudly adorns his shoulder, a bold proclamation of his allegiance to a dark ideology that stains the fabric of humanity. The Dictator wears the swastika patch, displaying a twisted pride. A trademark toothbrush mustache adorns his lip. The small man continues to type feverishly, and the clacking of keys reverberates through the room, a drumbeat of madness as he delves into the gruesome details of his memoirs. Lost in the labyrinth of his own thoughts, the Dictator halts his typing, reaching patiently for a cigarette. His movements meticulously deliberate. A slow and calculated crawl that left an impression slower than that of a snail.

There was no rush in his demeanor. In his mind, he was the undisputed king of the world, reigning over a kingdom built on the ruins of broken spirits. A flick of his lighter and flames dance to life, illuminating his contemplative face as he draws on the cigarette, clouds of smoke snarly weaving an introspection around him. As he exhales slowly, the haze of smoke spreads everywhere, a veil of terrorization all across the war room. Pondering his next sentence, beholding a gleam of a mix of joy and fury. Hitler's memoirs serve as his reign and a haunting reflection of his evil soul. His soulless eyes watched the familiar hourglass on his desk.

TIME

Adolf Hitler, his piercing beady eyes and supremely commanding energy, exudes an aura of charismatic authority. His infamous persona captivated and manipulated the masses. A twisted maestro of chaos, wielding his rhetoric as a venomous serpent. Plunging his fangs, striking the pulse of humanity. Hitler's evil soul hypnotized all. A diminutive figure expressing a booming voice. A failed actor turned into the embodiment of evil on Earth. Hitler's prelude to the power of words was cultivating in cults of racism and fascism, torpedoing the world into a recipe of doomsday. There exists a breed of human so steeped in darkness, they could give the Devil a run for his sulfur-soaked money. Inferno eyes contained the fires of Hell, a sinister smirk imprinted on lips that have tasted the forbidden fruits of depravity. This creature, this embodiment of all that is wicked and unholy, strides among us. Beholden to a swagger that reeks of disdain for morality. If ever the Devil were to wander upon this world, he'd nod in begrudging respect at this human aberration, recognizing a kindred spirit in the artistry of sin.

In human horror, there existed a chapter so dark, so grotesque, cursing the psyche of civilization. The Holocaust, an orchestra of suffering and slavery orchestrated by the hand of a madman, showcasing human depravity. Six million souls extinguished in the flames of hatred and bigotry. Innocent voices of civilians silenced by the deafening roar of genocide. And at the center of this infernal tempest was Adolf Hitler. A figure so twisted, so consumed by his own malevolence, he earned himself the title of Earth's own diabolical incarnation. Every decree, every command, he carved a path of destruction through the heart of civilization, leaving behind a trail of ashes. To call him the *Devil of Earth* is to perhaps understate the magnitude of his evil. For even the Devil himself might recoil in horror at the atrocities committed under Hitler's monarchy. He became the living embodiment of humanity's darkest impulses. A phantom of democide that inspired countless world leaders.

The Devil never sleeps and was always due. Power held onto the residue of a decadent feast. The Dictator held court, swallowing the room whole. A flourish of authority, his hand aggressively darts out, snatching the *hourglass* from its pedestal. The sand, subject to his will, and he turns the vessel over, an intense violent motion. The grains begin their descent again, cascading through the hourglass. Fate obeys the Dictator. Mortality governs in a world ruled by the ideas of one man. Dangerous ideas are the worst kind. The only kind of hell.

His eyes—pupils of darkness reflecting the worst of humanity—stare directly at Omega. She meets the Dictator's stare, maintaining a calm that borders on the edge of defiance. A silent challenge passes between the two figures. A clash of titans in the arena of power. *Tick-tock*, and the sands of time continue their descent. But the war room holds its breath, waiting for the eruption. Shadow emerges beside Omega, bearing witness to the madman's convictions.

The Dictator's voice comes out, authoritative. "Through our will and determination," he declares, his tone manic, "we shall forge a new era of greatness for the Fatherland." Each syllable drips conviction, a promise of glory submerged in the darkness of his ambition. But then, almost as an afterthought, he adds with a sinister smirk, "Don't be bashful. I won't hurt you." Menacing words. His cruelty lurks beneath the façade of benevolence. Psychopathic laughter echoes from his mouth, from the heavens to Hell. The dictator's laughter grows louder, striking fear even into departed souls.

Omega and Shadow exchange glances, noticing a *revolver* resting ominously upon the desk. Both take measured steps while slowly approaching the Dictator. Millions of scenarios race through Omega's mind; she struggles to grasp any, but she grounds herself in the present moment. The ghosts of the Holocaust haunt the room, their whispers imploring her to release them from their eternal torment. Cries of pain crackle as Omega and Shadow take their seats.

"Plenty to go around," the Dictator declares. "Indulge yourself." His words carry an insidious undertone, a subtle threat disguised as hospitality.

Omega remains cautious, navigating a minefield of hidden dangers. The surface of the table is a chaotic tableau, displaying half-eaten meals and disorganized documents unveiling the stamp of the Dictator's authority. Corruption mars these precious pieces of paper, while buzzing insects crawl across their surface. Each document is a memento of lives lost in the ravages of war. Despite the oppressive atmosphere, Omega takes off her mask. She knows in this den of treachery, the most innocent-seeming gesture can conceal a deadly trap.

The Dictator's words slither into the dire setting. "It's best you found me before it was too late," he declares. "Please, eat something."

Omega regards the spread. Her emotions speak to her, and she knows better than to refuse the Dictator's hospitality. But Omega's curiosity gets the better of her. "Too late for what?" she asks, her voice steady despite the unease that gnaws continuously at her insides.

The Dictator's smile is as cold as ice as he leans in closer, his eyes boring into Omega's soul, making her question her next move. "Before they find you," he whispers ominously.

Omega's blood runs cold at the mention of *'they'*. There was an undertone of mystery. "Who's they?" she demands, her voice sharp.

But the Dictator merely chuckles darkly, his gaze unfaltering. "I'll tell you after we acquaint each other," he replies sadistically. Secrets of a madman often hold revealing clues.

"He's just a man," she thinks to herself, dispelling any notions of divinity or messianic significance, recognizing him as nothing more than a mortal.

Omega's eyes scan the area. From her perspective—a light in the darkness—she spots it: an *apple*, nestled among the rotting remnants of the feast. A diamond in the rough, its vibrant hues radiant. Omega's eyes linger on it, drawn in by its unexpected purity. She reaches out, her gloved hand firmly closing around the apple. Omega raises it to her lips, hesitating for only a moment before taking a bite. The crispness of the fruit is a revelation. A burst of sweetness, even amidst the bitterness of her surroundings. Omega allows herself to savor the taste. No matter what, a human can find a simple pleasure in a world drenched by darkness.

A hibernating thought stirs inside her psyche, this dormant seed awakening to the first light of spring. It was a question that has haunted her for as long as she could remember, a question on the edge of her consciousness without ever finding resolution: *Will the light ever outshine the dark?* The eternal struggle between good and evil had brought her to this moment. For every victory won, it seems, there are countless more battles waiting to be fought. Forces of darkness prowl in the shadows, ever-present and ever-threatening. Their claws always reaching out to extinguish any flame of hope. She holds onto a belief, a belief that perhaps, just perhaps, the light would one day emerge victorious over the darkness. She wonders whether human consciousness or nature hold the key to unlocking reality, considering the possibility that both are integral. Nature serves as its own muse, while consciousness is akin to the voice of reality, a scream demanding to be heard by those who listened. In these days, evil listens more closely, and maybe it has always been so. Yet occasionally, certain individuals arise who possess the ability to alter the subconscious of humankind. While such figures are rare, they emerge from the noise of existence, guiding humanity toward a promised land of enlightenment. Her flame of hope burns. Omega will continue, fighting for a future where the light will finally outshine the dark, causing the eternal battle between good and evil to finally reach its long-awaited conclusion.

She indulges in the apple's sweetness and remains focused on the Dictator. Until her eyes drift back to the hourglass, watching helplessly as she feels time slipping away. The sands of fate continue, the grains moving even quicker than before. Slowly but surely, she is running out of time to find the child. The games of the underworld and the pursuit of the Ancient Astronaut seem to lead her in endless circles, a labyrinth of confusion. Purgatory is conceptualized in a tournament of limbo, where every step forward only seems to bring her closer to nowhere. Omega finds herself contemplating the nature of time itself yet again. She can't help but wonder if it is truly nothing more than a flat circle, an eternal cycle of birth and death, of beginnings and endings. *For in the grand tapestry of existence, what truly changed besides the ceaseless rhythm of life and death?*

The Dictator, his iron grip on power, ruled over the world in a time long past. But Omega knows that even his reign will eventually come to an end, replaced by a new domain of evil in the ever-turning wheel of destiny. It was a sobering realization, a reminder of the impermanence of all things in the grand scheme of it all—the inevitability of humanity's self-destruction. She can't help but see the hand of the Dictator as the catalyst for the nuclear holocaust. In such a way, it was Hitler's legacy that inspired the nuclear weapons' race for mankind. She leans back in her chair and wonders if, one day, humanity would rise above its own self-destructive tendencies and forge a new path toward a brighter future. Omega faces a choice: to hope for a miracle through prayer, or to become the architect of one through her own actions.

ICE

The Dictator's eyes narrow, a predatory gleam in them as he watches Omega's move, his cruel eyes fixated on the bitten apple as though it holds the key to unlocking some dark and ancient mystery. He seems to embody the essence of the serpent in the Garden of Eden. Temptation and corruption course his psyche. To him, the apple represents more than just a simple fruit; it is a symbol of power, of dominion over the souls of humans. Every bite Omega takes brings her one step closer to the consummation of evil that lurks in the shadows of his realm.

The Dictator's lips curl into a sly smile, a twisted mockery of innocence as he savors the sight. He is the orchestrator, the puppet master pulling the strings.

Omega remains centered, oblivious to his joker nature. She has no time for games, no patience for his schemes and deceptions. She must find a way to bring the child home, even if it meant facing another level of hell.

The Dictator basks in the glow of his own reality. He is the master of all he surveys, the embodiment of right or wrong, and no one, not even Omega, can stand in his way. The Dictator's voice comes with a perverse amusement as he regards the bitten apple. "Ah, the forbidden fruit," he muses, a cold-blooded cadence.

Omega's eyes narrow slightly at his words, a quiet challenge burning inside her soul. "Humans have done worse than eat a piece of fruit," she retorts, her voice steady despite her uproar of emotions raging.

The Dictator's laughter rings out again, this time louder, a bell of doomsday proportions. A boisterous sound harkening the atomic bombs. Even as he laughs, the Dictator's eyes hold a glint of malice, a promise of pain and suffering yet to come. "Very true," he concedes. "But here's a lesson. Listen closely, because you can't forget this until the day you die."

Omega watches him intently, looking for any sign of danger. She knows that beneath the Dictator's false claim of geniality lies a heart as black as night, a soul consumed by the fires of his own ambition. Whenever the Dictator speaks, his words feed a curse. Omega braces herself for his corrupt language. In the underworld, she knows, there are lessons to be learned. And she has to listen to all forms of deception.

The Dictator's words are a velvet whisper, the poison of inclination. "Temptation is such a cruel thing in this world." His words hold a warped kind of sincerity. "It's impossible for humans to deny this raw emotion."

Omega's jaw clenches as she fights to contain the surge of anger in her bones. She hasn't come to the war room to engage in a philosophical debate with the Dictator. She has come for answers, for justice, for the chance to reclaim what is rightfully hers.

"I didn't come here for a lesson in psychology," she retorts, her voice sharp.

The Dictator pays her words no attention, he remains enthralled staring at the hourglass. His eyes border on obsessive.

Omega sees him for what he truly was: a killer, waiting to strike at the first sign of weakness. Omega can ill afford to let her guard down. Truth and deception blur, and she knows that her survival depends on her ability to navigate the treacherous waters of the Dictator's domain.

The Dictator remains arrogant, expressing more laughter of madness. He revels in his own delusions of grandeur. "You know why I love time?" he taunts. "In history, they'll remember me forever. I'll never die. My temptation is fulfilled."

But Omega remains unimpressed, her eyes steady as she meets his. "History will forget you eventually," she counters with conviction. "And you'll end up becoming nothing more than a distant memory, like the dictators of the past. Where's the child?"

The Dictator's composure breaks, collapsing his ego. Her words kill his pride, striking an emotional chord of defeat. She speaks the undeniable truth, revealing a future already written in pages of history books. He is just a man, who in the end loses the war. His eyes bellow his rage. "How dare you disrespect me!" he roars. "I'll burn the child alive, like the rest of them!" Shaking vividly with a trembling hand, the Dictator seizes the revolver from the table, his grip white-knuckled. He aims it directly at Omega. He motions for her to drink the wine, his demand a command that tolerates no argument. "Drink!" he commands, his voice a venomous hiss.

Omega stares down the barrel of the gun. She knows that her every move will be a gamble, a risk that can either seal her fate or set her free. In the face of hostility, she responds with a calm reminiscent of ancient stoic teachings. *Endure and persevere*, she reminds herself, drawing strength from the timeless wisdom of stoicism.

Omega accepts the glass of wine from the Dictator's outstretched hand. She remains on high alert. Shadow beside her offers reassurance. They are in this together, united against the forces of darkness. Omega holds the glass delicately between her fingers, her eyes never wavering from the crimson liquid. She takes a small sip, allowing the wine to linger on her lips for a moment before setting the glass down. "Light drinker," she remarks casually. She defiantly is eager to provoke and unsettle him further.

The German leader's composure falters at her words, and he begins to lose control of his emotions. They are slipping away like sand through fingers. His finger lies poised on the revolver's trigger, knowing he holds Omega's fate in the balance.

Unimpressed, Omega lifts the glass to her lips again, taking another sip of the wine. It is not out of enjoyment, but out of necessity, a calculated move to maintain her composure. The bitter taste of the wine fills her mouth. Omega knows every action, every word, could mean the difference between life and death. Standing up to evil is absolute in the underworld. Reflecting on the concept of panpsychism, which posits that all things possess a mind or mind-like quality, she delves into a thought experiment. Contemplating the origin of evil, she realizes that the true measure of evil lies not in abstract notions but in tangible actions, transcending numerical or symbolic representations of motion.

She meets the Dictator head-on, refusing to show any sign of weakness in the face of his wrath. Omega remains balanced.

The Dictator remains unpredictable, his words paired with a sinister scowl. "Let the future take its course," he speaks deceptively, his tone dripping. "Stay... Allow the new beginning to unfold."

Omega's gaze hardens at his words. She knows better than to trust his poisonous words. Addressing the roots of evil as soon as they surface is crucial. Delaying action only allows these negative influences to proliferate, potentially spiraling beyond control. The principle that all individuals are equal highlights a fundamental truth: *Those who assert power often rely on perception rather than factual merit to sustain their control.* She knows it is vital to learn the lessons of the past, for those who disregard history are destined to repeat its mistakes. But even as she braces herself for the storm, Omega can't help but wonder the meaning behind the Dictator's cryptic words. *What new beginning did he speak of? And at what cost would it come?*

The Dictator's revelation is alarming. "They've been planning the *Nuclear War* for years," he declares.

Omega's soul has a sinking feeling of dread settling in her being. Those words echo in her psyche, each syllable a reminder of the future catastrophe. Evolution emerges from necessity; it's the demands of necessity, rather than desires, that drive the world to grow stronger and achieve fuller development. She knows that the ghost of *Nuclear War* hovers over humanity. To hear the Dictator speak of it so casually ignites a firestorm of anger. A seething rage boils beneath her surface. Fueled by a desire to change the future before it could bring about untold destruction. *Telling the truth has the power to illuminate*, she thinks to herself. Value and virtue inherent in even the smallest of things. *How can she change the subconscious of evil?* To depart this world with contentment, by actively having fulfilling lives during our time here. She becomes determined to do something even greater than herself.

How could humanity allow itself to descend into craziness, to unleash the fires of Hell upon the world? Omega feels a surge of purpose unlike any she has ever known. She refuses to stand idly by while the magnitude of darkness plots the downfall of civilization. She will fight to prevent the cataclysm that threatens to consume humankind. To halt the tide of destruction before it can drown the world. Her goal set upon stopping the tsunami of death.

The Dictator's spiritless logic is a grotesque justification for oppression that chokes life from humanity. "We must keep the population under control," he proclaims, his voice a sickening melody of tyranny. "Otherwise, humans might get the wrong idea and think they actually have freedom and overtake their empires. We put the balance in order."

Omega's fists clench at her sides, fury flowing through her core. *How dare he speak of controlling the population as if they were nothing more than pawns in his sick game?*

The Dictator rises, pouring more wine and trying to fill up her glass to the brim, his gesture a mocking invitation to indulge in the poison that fuels his reign of terror. "Go ahead, have another," he taunts, his eyes glittering.

Rage burns akin to a wildfire in her soul, and Omega snatches the glass from his outstretched hand and raises it to her lips. Using a single fluid movement, she empties the wine onto the ground. She sets the empty glass down on the table, taunting without backing down, maintaining her authenticity.

Omega meets the Dictator's eyes. She will not be swayed by his manipulative tactics, nor will she allow herself to be intimidated by his threats. She is ready to fight, and stand against evil, by changing the future that has been stolen from humanity.

"Are you worried that you'll never see your loved ones again?" he sneers.

Omega's response remains unimpaired. She has no choice but to leave behind a meaningful legacy. Her mission must transcend, to inspire and benefit others long after she will be gone. "I fear you'll bring the extinction of our entire world!"

The Dictator's laughter careens off the walls. "Everything comes to an end," he growls, his voice piercing through Omega. "You can't prevent it, nobody can."

The Dictator's hand snakes out, grabbing documents from the table. In those damning documents, innocent lives of humans lost to the Holocaust were written. A morbid tally of death transcribed in ink. His voice impales the smoke-filled air, resonating cries of departed souls sacrificed on the altar of his ambition. "Countless lives forgotten because of me. I am a god," he declares, a delusional omnipresence. Moving with a sinister flourish, the Dictator extends the damning documents toward Omega. "Pray to me!" he demands, his voice a devilish commandment.

Omega recoils from the Dictator's outstretched hand, refusing to be shackled by the oppression any longer. Expressing a defiant glare, she denies the inhumane papers. Frustration contorts the Dictator's features. He hurls the incriminating documents into the air. They scatter like confetti, their significance momentarily lost amidst the chaos of the moment—a victory for the spirit of resistance.

Omega leans in closer, defiance rooting her in place as she stares into the eyes of the Dictator. "I'm not afraid of you," she declares, her words a challenge to the tyrant's control on power. "You're nothing but a coward, destined to lose. One day, you'll find yourself alone in a bunker, with nothing but that gun in your hand, and you'll pull the trigger because you can't accept your own defeat." Her words are a haunting prophecy of the tyrant's inevitable downfall, as though she put a curse in the shadows of his soul.

A sudden eruption eradicates the fabric of futures. The gunshot tears through the room, a thunderous omen, showing supposed gods can bleed, revealing the frailty that exists beneath the veneer of power. The Dictator, burdened by the future already written in the stars, succumbs to the defeat of his predetermined fate. His final act of self-destruction a tragic acknowledgment of the forces that govern his existence. An eternal twilight of dimensional crossroads.

Omega and Shadow look upon each other, an exchange fraught with futures unknown. "Can I change the future?" Omega voice. Having long delved into physics, she understands the rules of entropy. An oxymoron for the universe's slide into disorder. A voyage from above and beyond, harboring potentiality branching out. Flawless fractals in her mind, a kaleidoscope of possibilities waiting to unfold.

"Time doesn't exist here," Shadow replies, events of past, present, and futures yet to unfold.

The underworld has tightened its grip around Omega's throat, stifling her progress. Confronted with a pivotal moment of discovery, she ponders a daring notion: *What if she simply woke up? Could everything she experienced be nothing more than a dream? A dream so vivid that reality itself seemed like an illusion upon awakening.*

"It exists in my world. Wake me up." Omega's hand reaches out, fingers curling around the revolver that had fallen to the ground.

"Don't do that," Shadow's voice is a warning.

"I have to wake up," Omega's voice is resolute, evident in her tone.

But Shadow's response is firm, a reminder of the laws that govern the underworld. "Rules are different here. You must finish what you start."

Omega's mind is a hurricane consumed by her thoughts and considerations. A storm of emotions threatening to overwhelm her fragile psyche.

"Find the bomb. Save the child," Shadow's divulgence of information allows for clarity amidst the confusion. Facing impossible challenges head-on. The task of finding the bomb looms large, leaving her uncertain of where to even begin her search. *And how was it all connected to the child?* Shadow's sporadic interjections bear a striking resemblance to Virgil guiding Dante through the layers of Hell in the historic poem. Much like Virgil, Shadow serves as Omega's guide, not only directing her through physical obstacles but also imparting crucial moral lessons along the way. The chemistry between Omega and Shadow grew stronger.

Taking a moment to steady herself, Omega closes her eyes, calming her soul. Knowing what must be done, she releases her grip on the revolver, letting it clatter to the ground. She embraces her responsibility. Omega stays committed to the task at hand. Her bravery burns bright. Finding the bomb and saving the child become her duality of goals. A driving force through evil. Rules of this strange and unfathomable place begin to reveal themselves. Each obstacle and challenge enter the labyrinthine of her destiny. Omega pivots, her eyes locking onto the Ancient Astronaut's form as it materializes. The judgmental entity, a watcher hiding in the shadows all along, observes silently as Omega confronts the nefarious Dictator.

The Ancient Astronaut, with a quiet demeanor, extends a philosophical compass for Omega. This entity holds the key to both the bomb and child. In life, all paths trace back to a belief, whether in oneself or a higher power, they are relative. Another door beckons, its threshold symbolizing progression. The doors represent an interplay of risk and reward, inviting one to venture forth into the unknown. A simple wave of the hand, a gesture as ancient as the universe, the being opens another door. Its dimensional frame is more darkness and mystery.

"Come, there's much to uncover," the Ancient Astronaut's voice echoes through the void, carrying a speck of intrigue. Without hesitation, the mysterious being disappears into the ether. Omega's curiosity continues to exist. She preaches to herself the importance of continually seeking out knowledge. According to her philosophy, effective learning entails not only mastering the basics but also using them as a springboard to expand the mind. So, she wanders toward the doorway, knowing her end goal is firmly in sight. She follows the Ancient Astronaut further into time.

* * *

Twilight sparks and twinkles under candescent moonlight, *Mount Rushmore* proudly engrained into a historic mountain. Its iconic visages obscured by ice. Frozen faces of George Washington, Thomas Jefferson, Theodore Roosevelt, and Abraham Lincoln stared stoically. Arguably hailed as the greatest presidents of all time. Despite their charismatic leadership, humanity couldn't halt its own descent toward self-destruction. America's decision to drop the bomb forever betrayed the philosophical principles espoused by these great men. Legacies erased and frozen in the world of today. Humanity cared little for the lessons of the past. Unfortunately, the past proved powerless to save the future of the human race. Politics disintegrated during World War III, resembling a runaway train hurtling toward an impenetrable wall of collapse. Worldwide leaders relinquished control and order, similar to the lawless days of the Wild West, driven by a frantic quest for oil. If only these men had foreseen the future awaiting civilization. Perhaps their approach to legislation would have been one of foresight rather than reprisal. Ancient guardians of a past life. The power of presidents, frozen and a distant memory, whispered only to the silent ears of the ice mountain. Long ago, these voices commanded nations and shaped destinies; now, only ice was witness to the out-of-date legacies. Echoes of their authority lingered. But as the ice held their memory, the world moved on, indifferent to the former rulers who slumbered beneath its frosty shroud of doomsday.

Reflections on limitations of human achievement was apparent. A solemn reminder on the dying nature of power. Only change was constant. Just as ice can preserve the memory of past greatness, it can also serve as the fragility of human endeavors. Subzero wind carried failed tales that vowed to behold lessons of history. Even the most powerful among us must yield to Mother Nature. No human legacy will ever outlive Earth. A planetary god of everything.

* * *

The Tian Tan Buddha displayed layers of frost over the gleaming bronze façade. Icicles hang, and rugged and jagged tears overtake its serene features. Nirvana was a rumor of good fortunes from a past that had become an antique of dreams. Sheets of ice cling to its towering form, transforming it into a frozen artifact in the fading twilight. Each crystalline shard showcases that faith cannot escape the ravages of nature. One can't help but ponder brittle and breakable human constructs in the face of elemental forces. Even the revered religious figures, born from constructs of human ideology, must ultimately confront their own god—the God of Earth. Drifting into the cycle of religion, it becomes ever apparent that it shall always bend to the capricious whims of Mother Nature. In her domain, no faith was invincible. Buddhism, an awakening that guided seekers along the path to liberation, must surrender, accepting an equilibrium of frozen belief. Believers face the recurrent loss of everything, challenged by Earth's wrathful manipulation of weather. Compelling humanity to confront their convictions during these awakening moments. Temples or prayers hold no inspiration, instead the Earth herself shapes destinies of all who wander her world. Bowing their heads in shame, followers of Buddha acknowledge their complicity. Aware it was their fault, along with all others who held a position of existence. They contemplate the collective responsibility of any species, pondering the ephemeral nature of faith juxtaposed. Combating the enduring power of the natural world.

* * *

The Kaaba, a square edifice in Saudi Arabia. Legendary architecture. Silk and cotton that formerly draped its exterior was now ensnared in snow and ice. Once, devotion flourished in the Arabian desert, until brown sand yielded to the pristine white.

The Middle East—an epicenter of vehement devotion—transformed into an Arctic desert of lost faith. Frigid winds gnaw at the bones of those who dare to tread upon the hallowed grounds. Austere black walls no longer welcomed countless pilgrims who had journeyed from near and far to pay homage to the divine. Worshippers dared not face the subzero conditions. Ice had assumed the mantle of reverence akin to that of the esteemed Prophet Muhammad. The god of ice enveloped the culture of Islam.

Twilight descends upon the charcoal sky, streams of green froth cascading upon the Kaaba, sacred faith of this religious structure consumed by frost. Mother Nature remained neutral seeking out her victims. Ancient landmarks anywhere in the world never had a chance. Her wrath had spoken louder than any prayer. Declaring to all religions worldwide that in the end, there was no greater deity than herself.

* * *

Ancient Mesopotamia, the first known civilization. This region holds a distinction of being the birthplace of writing. Additionally, its inhabitants were pioneers in city-building, erecting the world's earliest urban centers. They laid foundations of the oldest documented political and administrative systems known to humankind. Desert sands contained secrets of the departed civilization, perched menacingly on the side of a craggy mountain a towering ziggurat, embedded in the rugged terrain. An ancient power, rising from the slopes, its massive tiers and imposing structure. A symbol of dominance, commanding fear and respect. Ziggurats predate pyramids and could have served as inspiration for them. These towering structures, characteristic of ancient Mesopotamian architecture, were built by the Sumerians, Babylonians, and Assyrians. Ziggurats were massive-stepped temples constructed in terraces, often topped with a temple dedicated to a particular deity. Their prominence in the Mesopotamian landscape suggests they could have influenced later civilizations in their architectural endeavors, including the construction of pyramids in Egypt and elsewhere.

Hot winds whip in and out of jagged peaks. The ziggurat was an ominous monument, its magnitude instilling awe in all who dared to behold it. Towering tiers and dark origins spoke volumes. Sunlight hidden behind the dark cloud. Tales of mystery roam endlessly throughout its chambers. Stories from these structures blessed humanity with the most precious gift of them all: the art of writing.

ICE

What guided humankind since is genesis, an inspiration for creativity and the catalyst of religion. From its lofty perch, the ziggurat exerts a palpable influence over the fiery Earth. Rising as a titanic monument with towering, terraced levels. Here, in the heart of the desert, the gods of old once reigned supreme. Now, all that remains were vestiges of their memory, chiseled into the crumbling stone of this forsaken artifact. This locale gave rise to fairy tales, narratives sharing philosophical insights that enriched humanity's understanding of the world.

Omega trudges across the desert. The region was cloaked in an eerie semblance of an eclipse. The charcoal skyline seemed to imprison the Sun, yearning to break free from its solitary confinement. Yet, in ancient Mesopotamia, the Sun no longer graced the ground. Her eyes stare down the imposing ziggurat. This place felt haunted, a place where tough times hovered. The ancient world was rugged and unforgiving. Survival demands adaptability, qualities foreign in today's modern society. Thoughts swirl, as she ponders the dichotomy of the future. How it promised the zenith of prosperity. A quest for sustainability, wondering if it had ever truly been a possible goal of achievement. Perhaps, in the end, it was a notion destined to escape humanity. Somehow, this realization resonates, but the pull of the unknown is too strong to resist.

Omega looks further and catches sight of the Ancient Astronaut. She stands back for a moment and watches them ascend weathered stairs. Step by step, they climb toward an unknown destination. A purposeful ascent, swirling vortexes of dimensions from their cat and mouse game unraveling. *How many of these realms must she encounter*, she wonders. But time unfolds its own drumbeat. All she can do is trust in the process, reminding herself of the virtues of patience and persistence. Embracing the journey, she tells herself to *seize the day*, as they say in some native tongues.

TIME

It's better, she believes, to be fully aware and present than not. Experience, after all, is all a human can truly count on in the game of life and death.

Intentions from the Ancient Astronaut pulsate, oozing a godlike potentiality. Cosmic forces propel them onward as they traverse the fabric of time. Omega shadows the Ancient Astronaut's path, plunging into the labyrinth of enigma that submerges her odyssey. Step by step, she mirrors their exact path. Following in the footsteps of gods had once been the guiding force behind these ancient structures. Omega metaphorically transforms into a modern-day Moses, a seeker of truth. Like the biblical prophet leading herself through the orbit of time, she embodies the spirit of liberation, freeing herself from the shackles of ignorance. The Ancient Astronaut is her guiding pillar of fire in the shifting sands of existential turmoil.

Omega's ascent up the crumbling steps of the ziggurat is a daring plunge into the lessons of time. Much lay ahead for her, and now is not the moment to waver. She reaches the summit and is greeted by the Ancient Astronaut. Her oxygen tank is heavily weighing her down but is a vital component of her crusade. Omega watches the Ancient Astronaut fixate on something nearby. The entity's aura transfixes on the veil of centuries once upon a time.

Omega's emotions reel. The entity approaches the figure of *Gilgamesh*, the legendary King of ancient Mesopotamia, whose stony face endures eons. Gilgamesh was revered for his wisdom, strength, and larger-than-life exploits recorded in the epic tales of old. The King carved his name into history from the legendary poem recounting his chronicle adventure encountering the tangled web of mortality and immortality. A tale of existential conquest inspiring countless religions.

Gilgamesh is perched upon a throne of rock, his eyes fixed intensely upon the stone floor below his feet. His troubled face betrays a soul in search of inspiration, lost in contemplation. A nightmare for the artist, to rediscover a lost muse. A hushed silence falls over the summit, and the Ancient Astronaut leans in, whispering a cryptic incantation into Gilgamesh's ear. The magic of words circling each, dancing until the end of time. A muse found Gilgamesh, the art of destiny. Emergence of ideas remains a mystery to many writers. Many believe it could be lost souls from the afterlife retelling ideas to the living. Whether alive or dead or relative, this moment awakens Gilgamesh, stirring the King from his lost soul and igniting a spark of creation.

Constructing and fabricating stories is, fundamentally, a quintessentially human endeavor, and every narrative, no matter how elaborate, traces back to a singularity. A sacred moment in space and time where creativity blooms. Omega witnesses a convergence of past and present. Gilgamesh, his being riddled with scars of a lifetime's worth of trails and revelations, ascends from his throne. His shoulders carry the monarchy of his kingdom. Both a sage and prophet, he seizes a chisel, fueled by an otherworldly inspiration. Omega is transfixed, her eyes tracing each direction of Gilgamesh's hands across the stone tablets. Each stroke of the chisel a timeless struggle for immortality that courses through the veins of humanity. The Ancient Astronaut drifts away from Gilgamesh, gradually fading into the distance as they descend the other side of the ziggurat. A wisp of smoke taking its bow and leaving the theater.

Omega, entranced by the surreal encounter, finds herself standing before Gilgamesh, who regards her. A knowing eye watching her close, as if this moment has already happened before. She hesitates for a moment, her soul vibrating. This was the first story. A written account traversing the psychological dilemmas of the human psyche. The meaning of life is a question as unique as each individual asking it. According to Gilgamesh, the answer lies in the recognition that life's meaning is found by just living life, especially during its challenges. It encompasses elements such as good health, inner peace, love, friendship, trust, and responsibility, as well as grief and sorrow. Additionally, Gilgamesh came to understand the inevitability of death and the enduring legacy of civilization beyond our own existence.

Omega summons the fortitude to break the silence. "What are you writing?" she asks.

The King's response is measured, his voice a low rumble. "I am writing the story about the impossibility of living forever," he replies, his words containing the harbinger of truth.

Omega listens as the King continues to chisel the epic of Gilgamesh. Gravity of the words are felt. Then, as the King's tale draws to a close, Omega finds her mind buzzing. The interloper possesses an intimate knowledge of ancient history, her understanding extending far beyond mere academic study. She always enjoyed studying the Epic of Gilgamesh, recognizing its influence on religions worldwide. Along its striking parallels to tales of Christianity and Noah's flood. To witness the intersection of inspiration and faith is to glimpse into the creative corridors of creation. Art and faith share a symbiotic relationship, each enriching and sustaining the other. Without faith, art may lack its spiritual resonance. While without art, faith may struggle to express its truth and beauty. Together, they intertwine to illuminate the human experience. Both hold different approaches in inspiring the soul. Yet, amid the myth and legend, there exists a singular thread of truth written in Gilgamesh's poem. Immortality remains only a dream. Beyond the belief of mortal beings. This logical truth resonates for Omega. A storm of existential questions buried in her consciousness have become answered. She has always struggled to accept death. At times entertaining, she might evade mortality altogether. Perhaps living eternally as the sole inhabitant of Earth. The nature of dreams. What might materialize and what might exist as illusions.

Omega sinks into the ancient stones, dropping to a knee as their sturdy vibrations lend her support. Like a prizefighter enduring life's knockout blows, she remains focused, aware that her journey is far from over. She meditates on this feeling, drifting back and forth into her subconscious. Gilgamesh had written and answered the ultimate question. Her mind—a storm of knowledge—wanders into the poem of Gilgamesh, tracing its timeline through history to the *Nuclear War*. *Why were humans so fixated on their own death?* The pursuit of oil, while justified, seemed but a symptom of a larger affliction, a voracious appetite for energy consumption driven by greed. This paradoxical reality destroyed Earth. Materialism drove the egocentric world into the nuclear apocalypse. The ego of humankind, a ravenous superorganism fueled by luxuries, searched to satiate its need for dominance.

In a brain devoid of free will, humanity's choices are obnoxious illusions, dictated by biochemical impulses from their bodies. Altering the subconscious of a stubborn species seems rather daunting. *Could she really change the collective consciousness of mankind, steering it away from the path of destruction? With hopes and ambitions of guiding her toward a future embracing euphoria?* She closes her eyes, allowing her soul to brim with optimism, and she dares to dream of a world where evil and sin are eradicated. Replaced by peace on Earth. Omega settles into a cross-legged position atop the ziggurat. Her eyes remain closed in a trance-like state of meditation. *Deep breaths, just breathe. Let's not dwell too far into the future. We can locate that bomb; it's only a matter of time. The rest, we'll leave up to fate.* She holds onto the belief that humanity is inherently good, not the opposite.

The serenity of the moment is broken apart in an instant. A *spear* slices through the air, grazing past Omega's head by a hair's breadth. In an instant, her eyes snap open, jolted awake from her peaceful meditative state. Rest for the weary and peace of mind remain illusionary gifts, ones she hasn't granted just yet. Her being transitions into a survival mechanism while encountering the sudden onslaught of danger. Omega's eyes plunge downward, and there, ascending the steps of the ziggurat like a horde of ancient demons, are *Mayan warriors*, with faces decorated with grotesque war paint and eyes expressing the cold stare of killers.

These warriors revere defenders, submerged in prophecy. Practicing rituals of sacrifices even of their own kin, for the sake of the gods. Believing themselves to possess insight into the cosmos, understanding cycles of time. Convinced that they hold the key to deciphering the mysteries of the universe, including the timing of the apocalypse. Witchcraft engulfs their civilization, leading them to believe they could commune with the heavens and extract answers of transcendence from the cosmos.

Omega leaps to her feet, realizing the tribe was coming after her—hunting her down, displaying rage of barbaric savages. Down the stairs she flies, each step a desperate bid for escape. Thunderous war cries of her pursuers grow louder, closing the gap between them and Omega. She dashes through the Amazon, the dense jungle forming a primordial maze of nature. Thick foliage makes it nearly impossible for her to run. Omega pushes herself even harder, racing into the tangled undergrowth. She charges ahead, bolting around in different directions, trying to make a difficult shot for their bow and arrows. Her path can't withstand a clear direction. She is hunted by these. She darts around corner after corner, her path devoid of direction, evading arrows that periodically whiz past her and explode into the bark of trees. She is caught in the crossfire of a relentless struggle between the forces of good and their adversaries, trapped in their never-ending philosophy of kill or be killed. Towering trees and twisted vines continue to absorb the impact of arrowheads, Mother Nature morphing into her shield of defense.

ICE

She runs tirelessly, the Amazonian jungle a verdant maze of greenery. A pungent scent of dampness floods her being, refreshing smells of plants and trees. She has read about the sweet sensation of these living creatures. Born into an ice world, she has always harbored the dream of one day experiencing the scent of plants. Today, amidst being hunted down by the Mayan empire, that dream is about to come true. Yet, as often happens in life, timing doesn't align with expectations. She snaps out of the momentary pleasure of her newfound sensory experience and refocuses on the urgent task at hand: running for her survival in this ancient dimension of time. Unseen creatures speak, their calls echoing throughout the verdant canopy.

Spears continue slicing in the air. They were arrows of fate, destined to seek their victim. But the interloper will not cower to their destiny. She has her own plans. Omega fluidly continues to move. Enduring the turmoil from this ancient tribe of evil, she can't help but ponder their choices. *Did they truly have a choice*, she wonders. *In the distant past, what options did those ancient humans possess, and even in the future, what choices awaited?* Perhaps evil was a fundamental aspect of reality, influenced by environment and era. In different times and places, varying scenarios unfold, shaped by circumstances and the inherent nature of humanity.

Omega thinks to herself for a moment. "*Is this the end? No, the journey can't end here.*" So, she runs a little faster. "*Just keep moving and pick up your pace. Then, the secrets of this world will reveal everything.*" She pumps herself up, internally having a passionate inner dialogue, empowering her to sprint at lightning-fast speed. As long as she can exist, Omega is a paragon of strength in the ancient game of life and death.

War cries echo in every direction of the jungle, drowning out the hum of creatures. Mankind's power always surpasses that of the animals, asserting dominion over the wilderness. In Omega's soul, a potent concoction fuels her desire, driving her to battle darkness of the human race without apology. Ears of the jungle hear the venomous war cries. Omega remains unbroken in a sea of primal terror. Her movements are a daring wager against fate. She is not just a survivor, but a renegade soul dancing on the razor's edge of mortality and immortality.

A lone Mayan warrior emerges, his madness matched by Omega's firm bravery. Unleashing a deafening roar that shakes the foundations of the ancient jungle, they collide in a savage ballet of survival. Omega channels another aspect of her inner strength, against the attack of her Mayan opponent. She surmounts the warrior, their bodies crashing to the jungle floor in a clash of violence. Omega unveils a Herculean effort. Even the mightiest demigod would be proud.

Omega overpowers the warrior. She hurls them aside, tossing them into the dense foliage. Her pursuer neutralizes, yet Omega creates distance between herself and other savages who stalk her. Violence is as ancient as time. From the dawn of civilization until the end of days, it remains a fact. Perpetuating the bloodline of Mayan warriors as it had for warriors of the past, present, and future throughout the ages. Eternity and infinity coexist, much like light and darkness, good and evil. They are perpetual, always existing, for in the end, that's simply how the universe operates. Yet, in the heart of the jungle's chaos, she remains. Omega pushes herself harder. A marvel of athleticism. Omega pushes her body to its limits and beyond. *Failure is not an option, not when the stakes are this high.* She remains inspired by the child, driven by a desire to rescue this innocent soul. Purity in a world of darkness. Her goal is clear: conquer and overcome evil in all its manifestations. It is an impossible task, yet she is no mere mortal. She is the beginning and end of everything. And so, she runs, faster and faster, in the face of adversity. Omega presses on in her escape and stumbles upon a clearing in the dense jungle, where bubbling crude oil seeps from the ground. Blood of a wounded beast epitomizes the visual representation of the confrontation. The sight gives her pause, a strange anomaly. Oil seems to haunt her every move. There is little time for contemplation. She can't go nowhere; she has to go somewhere. Spears begin raining down. Harbingers of doom, looming closer and closer to Omega.

She needs to make a choice: either linger in the shadow of doubt or press forward, into the oil-soaked zone. Oil oozes across the ground, submerging everything in its path. Its viscous tendrils snake through the jungle undergrowth, coating every surface with a slick sheen of blackness. Immersed in the twilight of the Amazonian, oil shimmers. A sinister mirage that even a desert oasis could appreciate. *Choices, oh, choices, why question them when you already know the answer? Just do it and go all the way.*

Omega charges across the oil-soaked field, her boots sinking into the sticky morass. The thick, tar-like substance sticks to her, dragging at her heels as if intent on pulling her down into the core. Difficult and challenging steps repeatedly occur from Omega as she forges ahead. With tenacious determination, she fights tooth and nail in the filth, splashing and splattering. Time appears to echo back, the sounds of passing seconds intensifying. She feels trapped, caught in a game of limbo with the fossil fuel.

Savages draw nearer. Before Omega lies a bridge to nowhere, and the oil-soaked ground seems to stretch into infinity. The slick, black substance flows, consuming everything in its path with a voracious hunger. A fossil fuel Nile River. Oil fuels the rise of empires and birth of technological marvels, but in the end, it is mankind's downfall. As they say, there's not enough to go around. Everything on Earth has its limits. Omega trudges and treks along the unwelcoming terrain. Moving deeper, oil covers her knees, slowing her movements to a crawl. This familiar element, born on Earth, is her unwitting adversary, sapping her strength and impeding her escape. Oil becomes her personal kryptonite, weakening her after every step she takes. She finds herself going nowhere, finally halted in her tracks.

Mayan warriors slice through the oily muck without issues. They close in, bloody screams spreading into the oil-soaked air. Omega's foot finds a hidden crevice obscured by the thick sludge. Suddenly, she plunges into the darkness, her body disappearing beneath the surface in a shockingly swift descent. The world above fades away, with Omega's entire being getting swallowed by the viscous depths of oil. Overwhelmed, drowned out by the deafening silence of the abyss. Alone and lost, she enters another elemental dimension. Omega is submerged by the void of blackness, her fate unknown in the saturated oil-soaked underworld.

* * *

Eerie twilight, the frozen ocean exudes an aura of gloom. A colossal sheet of ice, surpassing even the most awe-inspiring glaciers in its grandeur. Omega watches the hypnotic image that has befallen the world. Gazing upward into the darkened sky, she confronts the harbinger of death: a massive black cloud of smoke ominously billowing and obscuring the precious rays of sunlight. Sadness pervades Omega. A frozen hell on Earth. Humanity once thought that life on other planets could have been earthlings' greatest hope. With billions of galaxies and countless Earth-like planets, Earth appeared to be the prime candidate for life as everyone knows it. Everyone was meant to be stewards of their world, not mere takers. It's a puzzle, a riddle, the ultimate game.

Far in the distance along the frozen horizon, Omega's eyes catch sight of frozen oil platforms, towering engineering constructions. These titans of industry were the driving force behind civilization. Never-ending pumping providing energy upon which modern society depended. Siphoning the planet's resources dry through excavation and extraction. Humanity's energy cravings knew no bounds, pushing the boundaries of nature until they reached their breaking point. Legacy of these oil platforms serves as consequences of unchecked consumption. Oil and greed, two factors forever entangled during the Anthropocene epoch.

Omega kneels down into the snowy sand. Her welder mask scans the coast, focusing on a wreckage of ancient life in this dying world. Despair from mortality consumes her psyche. Her eyes notice skeletons upon skeletons scattered across frozen sand. Skeletons piled in heaps. Like discarded garbage in a landfill, they formed mounds upon the frozen world. Bones mingled indiscriminately, stripped of the flesh that once clothed it, robbed of identity and purpose. The hand of fate that consigned all living things to the same final resting place.

Death, a prophet in its own right, spares no one in its pursuit. It does not beg for acceptance or offer apologies, it simply takes what it desires, leaving behind mementos of lives it has claimed. An observer of the departed. She discerns a revelation that transcends the outward differences of mortal form. At first glance, the human race appeared diverse. Each individual a unique expression of humanity's complexity. But, beneath the veneer of skin, the same framework of bones provided a commonality. A humbling realization of the inherent unity that bound all beings together, regardless of outward appearances or superficial distinctions.

From above, the sky suddenly erupts in blinding brightness. A harsh glare meets the welder mask, and it becomes a prism, bending and distorting light. Its metallic visage shimmers, a shield facing off against intense heat and energy at play. Nuclear warheads dive downwards, fiery trails cutting through twilight as falling stars. The future apocalypse has arrived for the human species. This bleak vision of tomorrow was a bitter omen. Implications of apocalyptic reality questioned what it meant to be human. A second chance became endangered, a lost opportunity. Inevitably, all things succumb to time. Ultimately, matter is just crystallized light destined to dissolve into the void. Despite the deadly light's onslaught, Omega persists, believing humanity's species could alter the course of destiny, granting them the opportunity to reshape their story and reclaim their legacy.

* * *

A chamber saturated in golden hues; the scent of opulence and riches surrounding, each breath presented extravagant luxury. Hidden away from prying eyes on a magnificent gold wall was an emblem of unparalleled beauty. Depicted the wondrous *Flower of Life*. A powerful symbol, beholding spiritual significance found in various cultures and religions around the world. The sacred geometry patterns were believed to represent fundamental forms of space and time, including the creation of consciousness. Spiritually, a focus for achieving inner peace.

Money and debt, convictions of the human experience, have long been defining forces shaping the lives of cultures spanning from Mesopotamia and Egypt to the Roman Empire and civilizations of antiquity. Wealth eclipsed humanity, compelling individuals to engage with abstract concepts or coveted commodities in validation. Numbers and their transactions produced goods and services, becoming the currency for attaining the good life. A life of comfort. *Who could blame humanity for embracing such an ideology?* But humanity lost sight of their place, their connection to the Earth fading into the background of their material aspirations. Time carried humanity forward into the future, expressing that money equated to power became an entrenched belief system. This system was embraced by celebrities, influencers, and world leaders. As eras continued to approach, the common belief began to fray, unraveling at the seams. Even though humanity harbored a subconscious awareness that riches couldn't follow them into the grave, the allure of worldly success remained paramount. Self-discovery became a casualty, fading into obscurity, not wisdom. The philosophies guiding humanity's search for meaning withered away. In this hypothetical scenario, a gorilla, a bird, and a human are stranded on an island, with the human granted unlimited amounts of money. Dynamics of survival are intriguingly skewed. Large numbers were mistresses of seduction.

Put a gorilla, bird, and human on an island. Give the human unlimited amounts of money, and in that thought experiment, ask oneself who comes out of it alive. At first glance, one might assume the human—armed and with unlimited wealth—holding influence over survival. Yet, in this primal arena, material riches pale against nature. The gorilla's brawn and the bird's flight offer advantages beyond currency. Survival hinges not on wealth, but on adaptability. The human's affluence is a hollow comfort, for true survival remains in the mastery of nature's laws. World War III rendered money useless, indifferent to the riches amassed by billionaires and trillionaires. Fortunes crumbled. They were merely sandcastles, destroyed by the great flood. Money became a hollow relic in the face of global upheaval.

In time, the concept of physical money evaporated and transformed into centralized digital currency. Computers became custodians of wealth, relegating tangible bills to antiques. The adage "money doesn't grow on trees" lost its relevance, supplanted by the convenience of artificial intelligence. In the aftermath of war, widespread blackouts swept through the digital landscape, erasing fortunes in an instant. The world plunged into bankruptcy in the blink of an eye.

Omega enters, enthralled in the monetized surreal atmosphere. An unexpected downpour of world currency, unleashing a chaotic frenzy of swirling banknotes. Fluttering bills enveloped the space. A surreal convergence, every denomination from every corner of the globe emerged in the golden chamber. Currency from distant lands mingled in a shimmering sea of wealth, all nations and economies. A phantasmagorical melody of wealth. It's as if the heavens themselves have opened up to shower the room, a flood of golden rain. Each wall, fashioned from pure 24-carat gold, reflects the absurdity of financial success. A powerful figure marches into the storm of wealth. Osiris, god of the underworld in Egypt, the inaugural pharaoh.

Osiris, that regal figure, looms over enslaved citizens, their hands and feet bound by chains. Heads covered by coarse sacks. The impoverished citizens kneel as though seeking absolution from their debts. Debt—that insidious concept—is a curse over civilization, threatening to suffocate the hopes and dreams of its inhabitants. Trapped in a maze of abstract principles, haunted by failure in a world governed by manipulated forces beyond their control. Money serves as a medium of exchange, a tool for facilitating transactions and enabling trade. Embodying power dynamics and socioeconomic structures that shape civilization. Had governments wield their influence to alleviate the constraints imposed by economic disparities, the horrors of World War III might have remained a rumor, relegated to apocalyptic lore. Instead, the failure to address systemic inequalities and geopolitical tensions allowed the seeds of conflict to take root, transforming rumors into the end of days.

Osiris draped in opulent robes, decorated with ancient hieroglyphics, an homage to his Egyptian lineage. His green visage hidden behind a mask forged from pure gold. He exudes majesty and malevolence, conjuring a hypnotic spell over all who behold him. In the afterlife, Osiris holds dominion over the fate of mortal souls. His judgment the final verdict on who will ascend to the eternal paradise, conclusively deciding who will be condemned to the desolate shores. His divine element between worlds and a soul that searches for the deeds of the living, determining destinies of souls. No earthly power can influence him. Osiris is the arbiter of life and death, scales measuring the balance of righteousness and sin in the hearts of those who seek passage into the beyond.

Citizens shuffle themselves forward before Osiris, facial expressions remaining obscured by sacks. Fear seeps from their beings. Palpable conditions, civilians cannot see Osiris. They feel his aura and look up toward their so-called God.

Since the dawn of consciousness, humans and gods have been entangled. Evolution of awareness led humanity down a path of complexity, illuminating life. A concept steeped in mystery, entwined biochemistry, genetics, and cellular functionality. The feasibility of severing the self from biology, was a one-way road to nowhere, between consciousness and corporeal existence. An endeavor as futile as trying to sever sensory systems from an organism searching for its consciousness. Mysteries of materialism remained just those, mysteries locked away in a time capsule, never to be discovered. Science failed, and the concept of free will remained a stubborn illusion, like its predecessor the arrow of time. Even God dwelling all beings falls short of explaining choice. Despite purportedly inherent in every soul, the mechanics of decision-making evaded the divine. Gods offered an escape from reality; they were far from reality. Their power over humanity was a falsehood, a fictional tale written into the consciousness of humanity. It was Gilgamesh who first tread this path long before the rise of religious figures like Jesus, Buddha, Krishna, Muhammad, or Moses. Those stories registered to the masses, carving a unique path through history. All human ideas in the eternal grains of time. Each philosophical belief only measured into a grain of sand against the infinite number of stars. How dare a human make such a claim, to such fantasy. Though the *denial of death* is never an easy acceptance for any soul who wanders on the pale blue dot.

Osiris stalks back and forth among the trapped citizens, commanding and authoritative, drinking his own belief system of self-righteous knowing. He raises a hand, demanding silence from the kneeling group. His voice comes, a thunderous symphony of power resonating everywhere in the golden chamber, compelling obedience from all who dare to defy him. "On your knees," Osiris declares. Words carry dominion upon the lesser of two evils. The Egyptian god of the underworld and dead continues to survey his subjects. Reveling in disdain, a scope of amusement flickers across his features, shifting back and forth as the eternal sands of time do in the desert. He notices obedience in their bowed heads. Unquestioning deference that they offer up to him as if he were really a god in human form.

To them, he is more than just a ruler; he is a living god, an embodiment of answers. Osiris' eyes dart back and forth; they are twin suns threatening judgment. He sees the fear in some, the awe in others, and perhaps even a hint of defiance in a select few. Regardless of their individual expressions, they all share one thing in common: They are beholden to him, trapped by the unbreakable chains of duty and tradition. Osiris revels in his power, relishing the control he holds over his kingdom. These inhabitants are victims to his order. There is no greater pleasure than seeing his subjects bend to his will. Osiris truly believes that he is more than just a mortal man, destined to rule over them, hammering down an iron fist for all eternity.

Osiris speaks vehemently. "Beg for deliverance, mortals, for the sands of time slip through your fingers like grains of desert sand. But know this, your fate lies not in the hands of mortal men, but in the hands of God."

An ancient trapdoor creaks open. Welcoming jaws of an underbelly, leading underground. Citizens are drawn into its yawning abyss, screams of terror swallowed whole by the darkness. Osiris, aware of his role as judge and jury, operates without full comprehension of the cosmic ramifications of his decisions. This operator of dead souls directs a watchful eye over the golden chamber, knowing there was no room for mercy, no place for hesitation. Becoming fate's own executioner. Repeated echoes of anguish fade into the void from underground. Souls drifting away to another place, far away from here and never to return again.

Osiris' twisted smile is a fantastical mask of delight, absorbing the spectacle unfolding. Another moment in time for this individual, and he didn't hold back, nor ever would. Submerged in his own malice, he points downwards, a cruel invitation dangling before his hapless victims. "Now claim your reward, if you dare." His words carry false hope.

Brandishing a flourish of his scepter, he conjures forth a pile of gleaming gold coins. A contemptuous flick of his wrist. Osiris drops each gold coin onto the trapdoor, the metallic clang a mocking applause. Each coin is a symbol of false promises. Glimmering coins and his laughter harken a requiem of joker games. An insidious institution of slavery serving as currency, citizens engaging in games of life. Some try to carve out a better life, while others hold onto the idea of unity. Joint endeavors constructing a metaphorical pyramid of collective achievement.

Coins scatter across the surface of the trapdoor, their supposed value stripped away by deception. Each coin that falls is a taunting gesture of victory. Tings of coins become ever more pronounced. Finally, the last coin clatters to the ground, Osiris had broken spirits of freedom. The lure of capital, without mercy or compassion, has been his defining factor of control, by owning the satisfaction of his own desires.

Omega, undaunted by his oppressive aura, strides forward to meet Osiris eye to eye. Her soul burns an intensity that could rival the scorching Sun.

A resistance cuts through the stifling atmosphere, and Osiris speaks. "I decide who receives wealth and prosperity in the afterlife."

Omega's lips curl into a scornful smirk as she stands her ground in the face of Osiris' commandment. "Where's the bomb?"

Osiris' mouth widens into a sardonic grin, his demeanor oozing contemptuous amusement. "Why the urgency, my dear? Bask in the wealth of the underworld and forget your earthly troubles."

Omega remains unfazed, her spirit burning brighter than ever during Osiris' deceit. *There is no time for hesitation, no room for compromise. Only justice, even in the face of godlike tyranny.* Omega's fists tighten, her frustration boiling and her nails digging into her palms as she wrestles the overwhelming urge to lash out. Beneath lay the simmering anger that she refuses to yield in the face of Osiris' taunts. Her goal is to get information. Her voice comes out in a low growl. "Show me where the bomb is!"

Osiris' laughter bounces off the gilded walls. No amount of information will be divulged to the interloper, she faces a challenging foe. Then, a disdainful wave of his hand and Osiris summons his *mummies*, their wrappings embellished by archaic bandages.

Wrapped in swathes of linen to ward off evil, departed guardians of the past hold preserved forms that are believed to mystically transcend life and death. Egyptian cultures, steadfast in their belief in the afterlife, adhere to the practice of preserving the body, recognizing its significance for the transition to a higher plane of existence. Sarcophagi were the final resting place for mummies entering the vessels of history. Through the meticulous process of mummification, they defy the ravages of time, preserving not just their physical bodies, but memories, dreams, and aspirations. Perhaps the most powerful fact about mummies is not their ability to defy decay, but the stories they display. Each mummy lived, triumphs and tragedies endured, loves lost and legacies left behind. A window into the past assisting them to the end. These mummies resemble creatures out of nightmares. Odd movements made, where each bizarre move held aspiration of snatching souls. They encircle Omega, their movements synchronized, spoken to as though witchcraft or sorcery had been unleashed and cursed upon their crying spirits. Guided by a silent command for their master, they lunge forward, mummified hands reaching out to capture her.

Omega, a human bearing the brunt of fortitude and courage, remains undeterred by the attack. So, she meets their advance head-on, her fists fighting back and delivering ferocity. She chips away at the pretense of Osiris' power, refusing to be intimidated by his mummies. Omega will face any challenge. Her bravery has never wavered from a young girl until now. Even if it meant facing the wrath of an ancient god.

Mummies persist in their spectral dance, bandaged hands stretching out toward Omega in a spooky beckoning. They provoke her with playful gestures, ancient wrappings concealing their true intentions. Mummies mock Omega, staying one step ahead, circling her existence presenting metaphorical taunts. A frolic of evasion. Jokers and jesters of delightful entertainment encapsulate their dead spirits. Games of the afterlife spill into Omega's waking spirit in the underworld, where tormented souls are ensnared by the grasp of Father Time. They bleed their anguish into her reality.

Omega's eyes narrow, cutting through the confusion. She sizes up her strange adversaries, their garb a stark contrast to the golden chamber's opulence. Omega knows she must tread carefully in this bizarre encounter. Mummies encircle her, their wicked intentions shrouded in mystery. Omega prepares herself for whatever strange game the mummies have concocted. Deception could influence a misstep and spell disaster. As Omega watches the maddening mummies, she can't help but wonder if an afterlife exists. And how miraculous it would be if one could continue dancing for eternity. Quickly, she snaps out of the imaginary dream, abruptly disrupted by a loud clap in her face from a deranged mummy.

Osiris rattles off a series of loud claps toward the mummies' direction. Sounds echo vehemently, a signal for commencement. Mummies, obedient to his command, lurch forward eagerly, their bandaged hands snatching fluttering bills like children grasping at candy. They engage in a whimsical game of cops and robbers, their motions imbuing a peculiar mix of goofiness, foolishness, and unexpected fun. Greedy laughter bellows as the mummies romp about. Ancient garb flaps in the breeze as if they wear tattered flags of surrender.

Osiris' voice holds a poisonous desire. "You can live like a god. Enter. Exit that sad world you come from. Fall into the oblivion." The underworld god offers a sick temptation that has corroded the hearts of mankind; spoiling their souls and allowing for a continuation of drama in the human story.

Omega stands firm, her goodness unshaken by the cruel invitation of quitting. For she knows that true power lies not in the hollow promises of a tyrant, but in the strength of one's own convictions. She refuses to be swayed by the seductive allure of false gods. The interloper lashes out, unloading a powerful punch and catching Osiris off guard, sending him crashing to the golden ground. The mummies, lost in their own world of greed, remain oblivious, their bandaged hands still clutching at the cash as they continue their absurd dance.

But Osiris, ever the master of manipulation, rises to his feet and chuckles, his demeanor unfazed by Omega's outburst. "Quite a temper. I like that."

Omega seizes Osiris by the shoulders, her grip tight, holding onto pent-up frustration as she demands answers. "Show me where the bomb is." She remains locked into her end goal with an unshakeable focus.

Osiris merely smiles, his eyes twinkling a perverse delight. He is amused by Omega's righteous fury.

For in the game of gods and mortals, nothing is as it seems, and every move is a calculated gamble. And as Omega stands poised on the brink of confrontation, she knows that she must tread carefully, for the fate of humanity hangs in the balance.

Pharaoh, his amusement evident in the curl of his lips, taunts Omega by his cryptic remarks. "My little secret. Fight your temptations. Lose that good side. It'll only hold you back." It is a twisted invitation to join.

But Omega remains unmoved, unshaken by Pharaoh's taunts. For she knows that to succumb to the allure of power and darkness would be to abandon all that she stands for. And as she stares defiantly into Pharaoh's eyes, she knows that no amount of temptation or manipulation will sway her from her path.

Omega, her righteous anger fueling every word, rejects Pharaoh's manipulative tactics, her voice hissing in response. "Humanity isn't going to die because of your greed!" There is no room for compromise in her words, only the fierce conviction against the evil that threatens to consume them all. Omega's desire burns brighter, fueled by the injustices she has witnessed. For her, the fight against Pharaoh's tyranny is not just a battle of wills, but a struggle for the soul of humanity. It is her undeniable belief in the goodness of humanity that will lead her to victory against the dark side.

Pharaoh's mocking laughter echoes through the chamber, a taunting melody that only serves to further infuriate Omega. Fueled by righteous rage, she can no longer contain her fury. In a fit of unbridled anger, Omega strikes Pharaoh across the face, unleashing a force that sends him tumbling to the ground. But even as he falls, Pharaoh's twisted grin remains, his arrogance undiminished by the blow.

Omega's voice seething, she speaks. "How about we try this idea? I'll take you to the underworld, where you can face the consequences of your actions. Then we'll see how much you're worth."

But instead of faltering, Pharaoh revels in his own power, his response a dripping revelation. "An interesting proposal. But you forget one thing. In the underworld, I am King."

Osiris' whistle signals for the mummies to spring into action. Mummies refocus, directing their energy away from the nonsensical money grabbing. They pivot their energy and pursue Omega. Insanely, bandaged forms swing back and forth, a pack of wild wolves closing in on their prey.

Omega and her righteous cause refuse to be deterred. She charges headlong into a *maze of gold*. Scintillating glow. Walls glitter and gleam the further down she travels into the twisting passages, resembling tendrils of an ancient serpent. Guiding her further into the greed-inspired structure that bleeds prosperity. Implications of money drive the world's plans and inspire it into a confused and crazy place. The labyrinth has no end in sight, devoid of a clear path, mirroring the chase for wealth. *When was satisfaction finally attained? When did riches reach its limit?* Such questions echo through the maze, unanswered as the treasure it promised. Carvings and symbols represent monetary systems, ranging from numbers and dollar signs, adorning the golden walls.

Omega darts and dashes down the winding corridors. Golden walls close in around her. The crisp scent of currency could be smelled everywhere. Rows upon rows of bills, neatly stacked, form an imposing barrier. Omega effortlessly breaks through them time and again, her momentum unstoppable. Barriers of wealth prove powerless to halt her advance.

Each turn she takes leads her deeper into facets of greed, facing the sheer magnitude of wealth surrounding her in a disorienting fashion. She realizes the gravity of the challenge. It's not just a maze she's navigating; it's a test of her wit, her resourcefulness. She must stay focused, searching for clues and patterns that might lead her closer to the maze's exit. She held onto a belief that somewhere in this maze of riches lies the answer of escape. Prosperity would not engulf her spirit.

Omega feels the mummies closing in. Their eerie laughter moves like the Nile River of ancient times, flowing and spiraling without remorse. Omega periodically glances over her shoulder, noticing those dead souls vapidly encroaching. Mummy movements are guided by an unnatural form. She rounds another corner, the golden floor beneath her feet blurring; the maze's endless corridors felt like a labyrinthine trap. She knows that she must outwit the mummies and escape the maze before it's too late. Omega hurtles down yet another corridor, her mind spiraling, searching for a way out. Round and round the merry-go-round they spin, to what destination, none can discern. It begins to feel like an endless repetition akin to the loop of *Groundhog Day*. She can't help but ponder philosophical implications where the concept of value becomes meaningless. This was the crucial lesson to glean from this stage. Walls of the maze whisper to her. Money, they seem to say, is nothing but a façade, a silly illusion that humanity has chased, only to be met with false significance. It holds no inherent value, merely serving as a tool for exchange.

The realization washes over Omega, drowning her perception of value. She begins to see through the veil of materialism, recognizing that true wealth lies not in the accumulation of currency, but in the richness of human experience. The essence of life is to exist. It's plain, obvious, and simple. However, everyone scurries about in a frantic rush as if it's imperative to achieve something beyond their own being.

Omega finds herself investigating the age-old questions of purpose. *If ancient civilizations had known that their quest for paper and shiny rocks would come to define their legacy, would they have pursued it with the same passion? Or would they have attempted something more meaningful that transcends material wealth?* One thing remains clear for Omega. Money never holds her mind captive. Since youth, she understood that the greatest treasure is knowledge. For ultimately, knowledge is the true source of power. A lesson she absorbed from early on, carrying it onward through both her awake and dream state. She recognizes the equal importance.

Mummies gain momentum, deceased spirits unbounded by limitations of endurance. With a swift dodge, she narrowly avoids being caught by one of them, feeling the rush of wind as it lunges past her. The deceptive maze is testing Omega. A sudden commotion erupts behind her. Two mummies trip over each other, tumbling clumsily. They crash through a barrier of money, bills disintegrating into a shower of confetti. Omega steals a quick look over her shoulder, witnessing the chaotic scene unfolding.

Finally, up ahead, a welcomed call of clarity appears. Another vault door displaying a giant dollar sign embedded on its metal coating. A green exit sign looming above. Each stride brings her closer to her goal, the glow of an exit sign illuminates her path. Her being focuses on reaching that exit, her mind blocking out all distractions except for the singular goal of escape. She quickly approaches, placing her hands on the metal titanium door, pushing with all her might. Heavy but moveable. She pushes harder… a little harder… even harder… She looks up and notices the mummies are scampering insanely fast, picking up their pace, insatiable to stop her momentum. The dead will never stop chasing her in the underworld.

Omega has always had to push a little more. Life and death tangle until the end of each other, and today is not the day for Omega to accept the end of the game she plays. And then, as though the voice of a dying god screamed its last breath, the door swings open. Omega bursts through the door, expressing a swagger that could make even the most seasoned gunslinger pause. She leaves the maze of money, the scent of greed and corruption gone and vanishing from her aura. Omega is a force of nature, a tempest in human form, tearing through the fabric of evil monsters. There was no doubt that she was born of wishful desires.

* * *

Twilight auroras magically radiate. The black cloud drapes its shadow over ancient ruins of Greece, submerging them in a phantasmagorical phosphorescence overtaking the sunlight's touch. Marble columns of an antique temple crumble in ruins. Omega cautiously wanders into this hallowed ground, her spirit uplifted. The bedrock of knowledge and learning lay before her graces. The inception of thought. Where deep minds would partake in great ideas from unique minds. Dust swirls and stirs a palpable scent of mythology.

Ancient Greece, destined to bloom into towering edifices of human understanding. Stoicism, a steadfast principle of virtue and resilience, took root in the fertile soil of philosophy. Offering peace to those seeking inner tranquility. Metaphysics, exploration of the foundational nature of reality, sparked imaginations of scholars and seekers, beckoning them to dive into mysteries beyond the veil of perception. Ancient Greece was a crucible of intellectual effervescence, a melting pot of ideas and innovation that gave rise to a multitude of brilliant minds

There was Democritus, whose mind desired novelty. An incandescent flame of conceptualization. Thinking hard while visualizing the tiniest components of matter, an imperceptible field awaiting discovery by science. He pondered the nature of the universe, daring to venture into dimensions unknown to his contemporaries. It was here, in the quiet solitude of contemplation, that Democritus conceived the atom, the fundamental building block of all matter. With a keen intellect, he peeled back layers of reality as though they were an onion, revealing another world under the surface. His visionary insight took its first faltering steps toward understanding the cosmos.

Another thinker who laid groundwork for intellectual revolution that would sweep through Ancient Greece was Thales of Miletus, often regarded as the first philosopher in Western tradition. One of Thales' significant contributions was his attempt to explain the underlying principles of the natural world through reason and observation, rather than relying on mythological explanations or divine intervention. He posited that water was the basic substance from which all things arose. A bold assertion that laid groundwork for later developments of atomic theory.

Among the luminaries of this illustrious era was Plato, the revered philosopher whose dialogues allowed for philosophy to be known as it is today, his timeless inquiries into reality, justice, and the human soul. In Plato's allegory of the cave, he paints a vivid picture of humanity's journey from ignorance to enlightenment. In a dark cave, prisoners chained and facing a wall perceive only the flickering shadows of passing objects, unaware of the vibrant world outside. A metaphorical struggle to break free from the constraints of conventional understanding.

Then Aristotle, the polymath never at rest. Introducing his groundbreaking treatises on logic and metaphysics, numerous pioneering investigations into the natural world. Notably in biology where his observations and classifications of plants and animals presented the foundation for systematic study. His work remained a cornerstone of modern biological science, shaping centuries of inquiry.

And let the world not forget Pythagoras, the enigmatic sage whose mathematical insights revolutionized the way everyone perceives the universe. His famous theorem, which bears his name, remained a cornerstone of geometry. The power of abstract thought.

However, there was another philosopher who sacrificed his life in pursuit of truth. In the bustling agora of ancient Athens, during lively debates and spirited discussions, there lived a man whose name would be remembered throughout history for millennia. His name was Socrates, a figure of unparalleled wisdom whose contributions to philosophy would shape the genesis of thinking. Socrates was not a man of wealth or privilege, nor did he claim to possess the answers to life's most pressing questions. Instead, he humbly wandered the streets of Athens, engaging in dialogue with all who crossed his path in search of authenticity. Socrates possessed a gift for asking probing questions, questions that cut through ignorance and illusion to reveal the truth. His method of inquiry, known as the Socratic method, challenged humanity to think critically and examine their own beliefs. Honesty was his muse. But Socrates was more than just a philosopher; he was a controversial figure battling the Athenian society.

Occasionally, a trailblazer emerged, defying convention and, though often ahead of their era, imprinted lasting norms that resonated through generations. Ultimately, his truth often brought him into conflict battling the powers that be. He questioned the authority of the state, challenging the prevailing notions of justice and morality with a fearless disregard for convention. Despite the risks, Socrates remained committed to his principles, even in the face of persecution and condemnation.

In his famous trial before the citizens of Athens, he was accused of corrupting the youth, defending his beliefs and always holding onto eloquence until the very end. Socrates would ultimately meet his demise at the hands of his fellow Athenians, forced to drink the poisonous hemlock as punishment for his perceived crimes. His offense? Advocating for independent thought, a revolutionary idea that remained through generations, shaping societies. When humanity perennially fought governmental authority, the tension reached its breaking point in the future. His legacy would endure long after his passing. Socrates was not just a man, he was a symbol of intellectual courage and moral integrity. And as the years turned into centuries and the centuries into millennia, Socrates' words would inspire generations, reminding us of all of the timeless quests for wisdom and truth in the human experience.

Omega spots Socrates, sat in his iconic pose of contemplation. Weathered features and scars etch across his brow, his soulful eyes betraying a mind lost in the rabbit hole. A troubled soul, as he wages war against governmental power.

Behind him, the Ancient Astronaut appears. Omega observes as the two beings engage in an unspoken dialogue, gestures and expressions communicating volumes beyond words or numbers. A meeting of minds between the enigma and mortal. Generational insight drifts back and forth—ideas—the best kind. In humanity's twilight, one of the last pillars left standing was the belief in autonomy. The power to choose one's path, to live a life of their own design. If a human desired an unconventional life, so be it. Living itself was hard enough to warrant such individual choice.

Omega witnesses this extraordinary encounter, her fascination intensifying. It is as if she has stumbled upon a secret conversation, hidden from the eyes of the world. An aura of kindness flows between the Ancient Astronaut and philosopher, as they exchange ideas. Goodness forms the cornerstone of their connection. Omega feels chills streaking up and down her soul.

After an eternal moment, the Ancient Astronaut shakes hands with Socrates. They share an unspoken connection, transcending words inside their souls. Then, the Ancient Astronaut begins to wander away, their form gradually entering another dimension of time. Socrates watches the departure of the Ancient Astronaut. Afterwards, he understands what he must do. He returns his focus to Omega, his eyes holding a vision of insight.

Socrates, the venerable philosopher, speaks a timeless intelligence. "The only true wisdom is in knowing you know nothing. The unexamined life is not worth living. There is only one good, knowledge, and one evil, ignorance." His words are a sacred mantra of eternal truth.

Omega absorbs the deep-rooted teachings of Socrates. Enlightenment ripples across her psyche. She has tapped into a wellspring, learning the origins of human principles, and discovering wisdom directly from the source. The originator of the ideas. Omega understands everything she has learned from her special encounter. Essence of knowledge and importance of questioning assumptions that shape the world. While looking at Socrates, she knows

TIME

that she has been guided along a path of enlightenment, evolving her soul to another level of sophistication. Life unfolds as a succession of defining moments, crossroads, and gateways, with each closing door giving way to new openings and possibilities.

Omega is ready for another door, having now embraced the ethos of goodness, where humanity's finest qualities found their truest expression.

Suddenly, a group of guards approach Socrates, their emergence disrupting the serene atmosphere. They forcefully offer him a cup of *hemlock*, a bitter concoction that spells the end of his mortal journey. With a nod of acceptance, Socrates takes the cup, his demeanor unshakeable in the face of death. Socrates locks eyes with Omega, his eyes holding a silent farewell. His stoicism speaks volumes. Across historical literature, passages recount the dedicated demeanor of Socrates. Noting that not a soul witnessed him shed a tear, even as he faced his own mortality.

He gestures toward a nearby cave, urging Omega onward in her quest. "Go forth, young traveler. Seek the truths that lie beyond." His courageous soul completely unafraid to confront the seductress known as death.

Omega wanders away, approaching the threshold of the cave. She is privileged and honored to have met the great philosopher. In an era plagued by the mass depletion of the planet's energy, the wisdom of Socrates can offer logic amidst the chaos. If only humanity in the Anthropocene epoch would take notice of his words. But for Omega, to traverse out of limbo and emerge with such knowledge to share with humanity, would be a tale for another day. She knows there is more to learn. Omega steps forward, crossing the threshold of time. More untold adventures await her. She disappears into the darkness of the cave and holds onto her eternal teachings of Socrates.

ICE

* * *

Inside the confines of an ancient tower, parchment and murmurs of prophecies intertwine. Nostradamus, a troubled figure, hunches over a wooden desk, his face illuminated by the faint glow of a lantern. His eyes, fixed on ancient texts and scriptures, seek to decipher humanity's path toward the end of days. In 16th century France, during turmoil of political upheaval and religious strife, he was a figure espousing mysticism. He predicted the future. Nostradamus was a man of many talents. Trained as a physician, his keen intellect led him down paths of conventional and unconventional. It was his gift for prophecy that would etch his name into history books. Nostradamus possessed a remarkable ability to peer past the present, glimpsing into the future. His visions spoke of events yet to unfold, which captivated imaginations of generations. Nostradamus was more than an oracle; he was a philosopher, scholar, and seeker of truths hidden in antiquity. His writings, steeped in symbolism and allegory, challenged the minds of those who dared to decipher their secrets. Throughout his life, Nostradamus faced skepticism. His dedication remained unshaken. From courts of kings to the humble abodes of peasants, his prophecies on the apocalypse spoke of destiny for civilization. Though the sands of time may have obscured the finer details of his life, the legacy of Nostradamus lives.

The quill in his hand moves by a rhythm all on its own. Each stroke inscribes words of prophecy onto the yellowed surface, capturing whispers of fate as they wander through the ether. Towering shelves line walls of the tower, holding onto countless tomes and scrolls, each containing ancient secrets, catalysts that shaped civilization's course. Tales of advanced civilizations and guardians of wisdom across eons. Dust motes get caught in the twilight of this sacred sanctum. Outside, the world fades into obscurity, swallowed by darkness. Time holds no sway, and Nostradamus is the author of destiny, his quill an instrument for the written future.

An eccentric flourish is born as Nostradamus captures a revelation on parchment. Ideas of otherworldly insights and visions of future realities gift his mind with predictability. Words and numbers intermix, paving the path for an apocalyptic omen. Divine clarity seeps into his psyche. Suddenly, he feels a presence. His radical eyes lift from his work, and there, standing silently at the threshold, is the Ancient Astronaut. Deemed useless, language became wasteful litter, hindering conversation. A telepathic encounter ensues, bypassing words for direct connection. Silent, the entity emits no exterior sound. Its enigmatic aura heralds a prediction destined to alter humanity's course forever. Telekinetic whispers echo everywhere. Nostradamus, attuned to the subtle frequencies of the universe, feels the ethereal message. A cleansing wave of enlightenment sweeps over his mind.

Omega observes the magical encounter, surreal as any dream, beyond even the cleverest of artist's imagination. Tales of metaphysical doomsday events enter the mind of Nostradamus.

After a pregnant pause, the Ancient Astronaut moves away from the prophet. Once again, the entity discovers a doorway. The Ancient Astronaut has delivered its compelling message to the mortal man, fully knowing it had left its mark on the human. Trusting the prophet will deliver and transcribe the wise words into a book, marking the end of days for humanity. An inspired Nostradamus etches a legacy vision onto the human psyche, forewarning of an apocalypse that lies ahead in the distant future. The Ancient Astronaut served as his muse. The concept emerges from the ether, a cosmic whisper amidst the infinite possibilities.

An aura of mystique remains in its exit; the entity gracefully departs, dissolving into the ether of another threshold.

ICE

Omega watches the unique human channel every ounce of his insight. Nostradamus had become inspired to culminate his magnum opus of apocalyptic revelation. The interloper strides forward, drawn to the magic of words and prophesied futures. His soul was a mirror, reflecting and refracting eternity.

Nostradamus, his countenance fearful and his voice foreboding, gravely breaks the silence. "The apocalypse looms on the horizon, a storm of darkness that shall engulf the world in chaos." His words are burdened by prophecy. Unknowns vanish into oblivion. Humanity will experience those doomsday moments, culminating in myriad outcomes.

Catastrophic events will herald the dawn of a new era. Omega knows the burden is too great to bear. The future of Earth is foretold of its path by the choices of humanity. Omega realizes humanity has been its own worst enemy throughout time. The struggles, the conflicts, the cycle of destruction and rebirth, all have been foretold by the prophet. Nostradamus, through his verses and visions, issues a dire warning: The collapse of civilization has been foretold. *Apocalypse* echoes through Omega's mind. Tumultuous hellish screams pierce through the thick walls of the ancient tower.

Omega strides toward a nearby window, drawn to the source of the frightening cacophony. Consumed by his revelation, Nostradamus persists in his writing. Peering out, Omega's soul saddens, witnessing the Black Plague. The event sweeps across the land, unleashing its wrath and consuming humanity. This doomsday event was a vicious force that swept across Europe. Originating in Asia, the plague spread at an alarming speed along the trade routes of the continent, carried by rats and fleas that thrived in the squalor of medieval cities. Its arrival was heralded by the telltale signs of sickness: a feverish chill, swollen lymph nodes, and black boils that gave the plague its name. Once infected, there was little hope for survival, as the disease ravaged the body, claiming victims by the thousands. Entire communities were decimated, streets littered with bodies of the dead and dying. Survivors sought asylum from the invisible menace that stalked them at every turn. No corner of society was spared from the plague's fury. From peasants to nobles, clergy to kings, all fell beneath its deadly touch. Even the most sacred institutions of faith offered no help. Churches became makeshift morgues for the countless souls lost. The Black Plague tightened its grip on Europe, it left in its aftermath a landscape transformed by death.

Omega continues staring out the window in horror. How she longs to shape both past and future alike. Challenges besiege her, and devastation foretells its ugliness, never relenting. She had read about this event as a child, but witnessing it visually brought forth a new dimension to the experience. In the light of torches, she sees the faces of despair, the anguished cries of those who have been ravaged by the plague.

The interloper turns back to Nostradamus, who continues journaling and scribbling wildly into his notebooks. The prophet's aim was not salvation, but to document the story of the end, imparting its lessons. Prophets do not alter futures; only purveyors of purity endeavor to change fate. His mind a storm as the future bears down upon him, Nostradamus was a figure consumed by his divine task. His gift lay in foresight and documentation, a messenger of unvarnished truth. Some truths remained best left untold, as only the brave dared venture into evil. This was not Nostradamus. This was Omega. The true test lay not in the prophecies themselves, but in the actions of those who dare to defy the odds and shape their own fate.

Without a word spoken, Omega is spellbound, watching Nostradamus before striding past him. She follows the same path as the Ancient Astronaut, disappearing through the doorway. As the chamber falls into a heavy silence, the only sound that remains is the scratch of Nostradamus' quill against parchment. Unrestrained by the departure of his enigmatic companions, he continues to write, maintaining focus. His words and each letter symbolized the chance event into history. His visions create a prophecy that created a legacy.

Nostradamus persisted in writing the narrative of humanity's end, unaware of *Nuclear War*. Forthcoming, he grasped humanity's finite time on Earth. Witnessing the ascent of evil, he realized its eventual triumph over good. Through the arrow of time, nothing could halt this progression. And so, as Omega's departure fades into the distance, Nostradamus' quill brings his apocalyptic tale to its final conclusion, ready to confront the storm that rages on the horizon. After a lengthy journey, they finally reach their apocalyptic destination. Upon arrival, they find themselves wishing to return once more. To return to the days of goodness when Earth was untouched by the shadow of evil. *Did those days truly exist, or were they trifling moments of joy? Can the quest for peace on Earth ever be realized, or will it only exist as a fading wish?*

* * *

An ancient alchemy room, and Isaac Newton paces back and forth amidst a clutter of papers, journals, and arcane laboratory equipment. Born into a world ripe with scientific inquiry and intellectual revolution, Newton was a genius, his advanced mind a veritable intersection of thought and reason. Clad in the garb of a scholar, he was a mad scientist, burdened by the banality of small talk, realizing the utmost importance of optimizing life. He was precious with time, without a moment to spare. Beneath his academic façade, his restless soul pursued the unraveling of cosmic mysteries. From the laws of motion to the universal force of gravity, Newton's insights reshaped science. Arguably the greatest scientist in human history. Newton's obsession over sunlight almost made him blind, as he persistently studied its effects by staring directly at the Sun. Consumed by his quest to transmute base materials into gold, Newton studied alchemy, seeking the secrets of transformation. His obsession with Christianity inspired him to feverishly study the Bible, trying to decode passages for insights into the nature of reality. His writings captivated the minds of thinkers across the globe, inspiring generations to dare to dream of the impossible. Newton was a colossus of intellect. From his perspective, the universe found its voice from nothing to everything.

A single shaft of sunlight pierces through the hole in the wall. The soft glow of white light. Resting prominently on Newton's desk sits an apple, a dreamy juxtaposition to the esoteric surroundings. The apple, a humble fruit, bearing the weight of legendary proportions, extending far and beyond its natural form. For it was said to be the catalyst, the muse that sparked the idea, culminating the most important force of them all: the law of gravity. Newton discovered God not in the pages of the Bible, but in nature. Among folklore, the apple's role in Newton's discovery was a mystery. Some of his colleagues claimed it was a tale spun from the fabric of myth. Fantastical tales of an apple falling on his head, awakening his epiphany. Others, however, argued that the apple held a special sign of inspiration. Newton's home existed in an apple orchard. Forever, the symbiotic relationship between scientist and fruit would remain at the forefront of his legacy. Whether it was literal impact of an apple or metaphorical picture of an orchard, the truth remained unknown.

Newton's odyssey was much more than a scientific endeavor. This was his spiritual quest, searching for the divine. Rumors said that he spent as much time analyzing the pages of the Bible as he did the equations of physics, seeking to unravel God's creation. Through his discovery of gravity, the force governing celestial bodies, Newton found a connection to God. Gravity, the hand of God, served as the adhesive shaping reality. Gravity and God—both invisible forces—manifest through the reactions of matter and people respectively. Without gravity, the planets wouldn't create, and without God, the sole existence would be questioned. Both gravity and God embody a philosophy where observers, whether atoms or humans, play a crucial role in the existence of reality. Each entity relies on the other for its properties, illustrating that everything is using everything. There is no void, everything is connected.

Consumed by the white light filtering through the hole, the scientist continues pacing back and forth. Anxious, lost in contemplation, Newton remains entranced by the white light, his pupils unable to tear away from those photons, particles of light. Then, like the ticking hands of a clockwork, consistent as always immersed in the flow of time, the Ancient Astronaut emerges behind Newton, towering over him.

With a whisper barely audible, the Ancient Astronaut imparts advice into Newton's ear. Consciousness stirs from the mortal man, followed by one of humanity's greatest discoveries. Illuminated by intellect, Newton absorbs everything from the enigma. In his own *eureka* moment, Newton's idea gets inspired by uncharted reality. Then, as suddenly as it had appeared, the Ancient Astronaut drifts away, disappearing through a doorway. Left alone only having only his thoughts, Newton feels an invigoration he has not felt before. The scientist radiates renewed vigor and returns to his work. He knows what has to be done. The next moment will lead him to the very edges of beyond human understanding.

TIME

With an epiphany, Newton rushes to his desk and grasps a *triangular prism*, its edges catching the ambient light streaming through the hole in the wall. Holding it at an angle, he manipulates the prism. As if by magic, a mesmerizing array of colors splashes across the room. Each hue dances and intertwines, revealing another spectrum of reality in mundane light. Newton's expression is one of awe. The scientist witnesses the transformation of light take place before his eyes. A kaleidoscope of colors erupt from its surface. Warm red, vibrant orange, golden yellow, tranquil green, calming blue, ethereal indigo, and mysterious violet light shimmers an otherworldly beauty, inviting exploration into the unknown.

The room submerges in a spectrum of colors. He manipulates the prism, observing unique patterns of colors. Newton stumbles upon the origins of quantum physics. The next hidden reality, dreamed about thousands of years ago by the ancient Greek philosopher Democritus.

No longer is light simply a phenomenon to be observed and measured; it is a gateway to another dimension. Newton has discovered the complexity of creation. He knows he had uncovered something truly insightful.

Omega watches, absorbing Newton's spark of genius. She realizes that everything emerges from another reality, one beyond human perception, producing good and evil. Unbeknownst to him, Omega shares his momentous discovery. She has always wondered what this moment would feel like. As a young girl, if she could time travel to the greatest discovery in human history, this would have been the era she would have chosen. In youth, discovery is cherished, and for Omega, this is a value ingrained. Long ago, she made a promise to herself, a vow of steadfast character, determined never to let anything diminish her pure energy. She embodies *Peter Pan* and *Johnny Appleseed*, finding joy in life and eagerly embracing each new day as it arrives.

Feeling her approach, Newton turns to face her, his eyes felt victorious. The joy of discovery is apparent. "Truth is ever to be found in the simplicity, and not in the multiplicity and confusion of things," he declares.

The Renaissance era had reached its singularity. Discovery of light propelled science into an entirely new frontier. New fields would emerge for generations to come. These disciplines would ultimately spearhead humanity into the Industrial Revolution, where technological triumphs would revolutionize the human experience, promising a better life for all. Humanity's enduring growth since emerging from the caves of Africa is fueled by a childlike curiosity. Evolution and the mind have been shaped by an evolving brain, which became more intelligent through the transformative impact of fire. All roads lead humanity back to its origins, seeking to rediscover what defines us as human. The event of Newton and light was one such instance, taking one back in time to their roots. As a species in their quest for their creator, humanity journeys through time until they encounter them.

Omega is captivated, forever grateful for her childhood fantasy. The interloper stares into the prism of light, feeling its godlike energy. A breathtaking experience cocoons Omega. She closes her eyes, wishing to embark on more travels. *If she only had one wish, what would it be?* Having endless options and scenarios, Omega's imagination guides her to that wishful place. Where she would rather experience one lifetime with someone than encounter the world alone. The shadow of the child hints at someone, and she is destined to find them. Omega makes her wish and opens her eyes to the eternal wonders of time.

TIME

You must be the change you wish to see in the world.
Mahatma Gandhi

ICE

WISH

WISH

ICE

From this heavenly vantage point, *they observe the planet succumbing to an era dominated by oil.* The pale blue dot, tainted by vast oil fields, devoured the land. Humanity would suck the natural resource dry until the bitter end. A surreal dreamscape so fantastical that even the wildest imaginations couldn't wishfully dream up its likeness. Oceans churn and oily waves ripple, reflecting the sickly sheen of petroleum. Our precious natural resource spread across the globe. A plague of consumption. Dreams may come, nightmares may arrive, yet operational agents of doomsday remain undeniable. Paradoxical implications unfold, and certain constants remain undefeated. Oil, throughout history, has been one of the most misunderstood resources in the natural world. For eons, it was vilified as the epitome of evil, an empire of destruction set to hinder humanity's progress. During condemnation, the transformative power it unleashed during the Industrial Revolution is forgotten. A power that brought progress to civilizations across the globe.

Omega speaks a dreamy resonance. "The blue planet faded into a void..." her voice, haunting and ethereal, reverberates through the cosmic emptiness.

The philosophical metamorphosis of Earth's most precious resource, aside from water, was undeniable. Oil was utilized in an overwhelming array of materials and products. There was no avoiding this vital natural resource which paved the way for the future of our species. It defined dramas of human existence. The absence of downsizing society spelled doomsday, ending civilization. Particularly in energy consumption, it was imperative, but humanity couldn't resist the unrestrained consumption. Economic growth had grounded to a halt. The world becomes a lucid nightmare. This epoch mirrors failures that came before. Eventually, history repeats itself whenever encountering mass extinction events. Countless extinctions have bedeviled Earth since its inception, and the Anthropocene extinction was another link in the chain. An eerie calm consumed the oil-covered Earth's toxic grasp; the landscape enchanted, bewitching all who dare to wander its polluted environment.

* * *

The ancient Italian city transformed into an alien phantom. Leonardo Da Vinci's masterpieces from the Renaissance Era, provocatively trapped in ice. The polymath was a whirlwind of creativity and brilliance that swept through the Renaissance. Painter, sculptor, architect, engineer, inventor. Da Vinci wore many hats, a swagger that defied convention. He was a man of contradictions, a paradox wrapped in an enigma. He was a visionary, a dreamer who saw the world not as it was, but as it could be. A pragmatist, grounded in the realities of his time, who understood the importance of practicality. Above all else, Da Vinci was a seeker of truth, beauty, and knowledge. He ventured into the world, expressing a curiosity bordering on obsession. Dissecting cadavers to understand the inner workings of the human body. Sketching birds in flight to unlock the secrets of aerodynamics. Studying the flow of water to master the art of engineering. Da Vinci was the embodiment of the human psyche. Showing the word that if you have imagination, anything is possible.

Sublime paintings of *Mona Lisa* and *The Last Supper* were dulled by frosty mantles. The artistic legend states those paintings emerged as titans of cultural importance. The *Mona Lisa*, with her puzzling smile and piercing eyes following one wherever they go. They're not just strokes of paint on a canvas, they're portals into the soul. In her eyes, an everlasting struggle between desire and restraint is seen. She's a riddle wrapped in a conundrum inside a paradox and speaks to the world, allowing a clarity that transcends.

The Last Supper captured the final moments of Jesus and his disciples. It's not just a painting, it's a symphony of emotion, a meditation on faith, betrayal, and redemption. In those figures gathered around the table, everyone sees themselves reflected. The faithful and forsaken, meeting at the crossroads and choosing between good and evil. Jesus finds himself plunged into a frozen inferno, where even Satan would shiver in the subzero freeze. All characters were the epitome of the human condition. Evil days are the damnation of all. Hold onto hope if any remains.

Drawings of the iconic *Vitruvian Man* were a frozen artifact of Da Vinci's unparalleled genius. Icy outstretched arms and legs displayed divine geometry. The golden ratio and Fibonacci sequence revealed creation from an artistic perspective. Every aspect of creating creation, involved a component of imagination. Numbers served as gatekeepers; today, it's difficult to imagine describing life without measurement. This is where art could uphold order for humanity.

In the center, where flesh meets a singularity, humanity distilled into its purest form. That dares humanity to explore. This drawing was a mirror reflecting one's own aspirations. To never accept the limitations of their bodies or minds, but only by the limits of their imagination. And in that infinite possibility, it's discovered what it means to be human. A creature reaching for the stars, forever seeking to touch the infinite.

* * *

High above jagged peaks of Peruvian Andes, Machu Picchu, an ancient citadel. Terraced ruins showcase the aftermath from hostile weather conditions. Ruins are frozen. Machu Picchu was one of the seven wonders of the world. Indigenous people spoke about the ancient structure. Their power of healing energy is encapsulated. A sacred energy flowing through the stones. Ancient spirits were trapped in time. Those spirits stuck in limbo by the ice, leftovers of a departed civilization.

Christ the Redeemer, Christianity's faith proudly embedded into a rugged mountain. The colossal statue, arms outstretched in a gesture of divine mercy, had long been revered by believers. However, as twilight descended, a chilling transformation took hold. Thick layers of ice encased the statue. No longer a symbol of redemption, Christ the Redeemer was a haunting monument to Christianity's demise in this frozen world. Redemption had lost its way in the icy dismay. Damnation was winning the eternal game of virtue. Purgatory seized that moment and established it in limbo—the place where no souls dared to beg for escape. Faith from the statue had been replaced by the monster of perdition. Erased was the warmth of hope.

The warmth of hope had befallen the world. Fragility overtook faith encountering nature's wrath. Christianity found itself helpless against the icy hell unleashed upon the Earth. As end of days arrived, words proved insufficient to stave off the apocalypse. Instead, it was actions that steered the course of civilization, and in this instance, *Nuclear War* emerged as the pivotal game changer. Exponential growth of civilizations reached a crashing and burning crescendo. On that fateful day, even the divine influence of Jesus could not stop the cataclysmic tide of nuclear warfare. There was no second coming, no divine intervention to save humanity from its own mistake. Revelations decimated religion, stripping essence from the soul of faith.

* * *

Omega jerks upright from her seat, her pupils darting all over the area. She sits amidst towering ancient shelves, surrounded by the hushed echoes of a bygone era in the abandoned gallery of the Library of Alexandria. A lighthouse of wisdom, unmatched in its time and revered as the greatest repository of knowledge known to humanity. A towering colossus of intellect, it embodies the timeless adage "knowledge is power." A fortress against the encroaching tides of ignorance. In a past reality, scholars and sages congregated. The concept of a universal library, akin to the grandeur of Alexandria, emerged only as the Greek intellect expanded to embrace a broader worldview. Ancient texts penned by the greatest minds. Scholars of Alexandria's Library were architects of innovation. Among them, Callimachus crafted the world's inaugural library catalog, laying the foundation for organized scholarship. Eratosthenes of Cyrene calculated the circumference of the Earth. Countless Greek and Roman works were produced inside the library's walls, helping to shape the scholarly landscape of modern society. Underneath layers of scholarly pursuit existed shadows of rivalry. Factions vied for dominance over the intellectual landscape. Clashes of ideas were precognitive dreams, shaping history, dotting each ink blot. During its collapse, it fell victim. Because books had no choice but to always face their archnemesis, the evil subconscious of humanity. Eventually, this place was reduced to rubble, its treasures scattered to the winds. Had it not been destroyed, the Library of Alexandria could have guided humanity further in science, technology, literature, arts, and culture.

Twilight gleams, swirling through the grimy windows. Omega feels anxiety, a panic coursing through her soul. She scans the names of authors on the dusty shelves, wondering how many of them believed they hold the keys to unlocking the doorway to answers. A culmination of answers to questions. Words, symbols, and numbers, forgotten forever. As the Anthropocene epoch marched forward, books were less consumed and unlimited voices of supposed intellects in all facets of life consumed eyeballs. In an era of awakening and confusion, the quest for truth became fuzzy between the spoken word and the written page. As humanity was gripped by technology, the question of where truth resided became a source of intense debate. *Was it found in the resonance of a person's voice, or in words upon the pages of a book?* Information became a double-edged sword, fueling knowledge and confusion in equal measure. During the maelstrom of discourse, collisions of ideas and ideologies sparked a relentless cycle of debate, each argument embedded into civilization's collective consciousness. Complexities of its own creation.

Truth itself has fallen victim to oblivion, Omega combats voices of those who express darkness. She has to silence them, forcing their words to be lost. Her mind plunges into a rabbit hole of thoughts, a cascade of questions swirling around her. Each thought is a persistent knock on the door of her consciousness, grating against her being, refusing to be silenced. She faces her own doubts. *If all these pages of books couldn't eradicate evil, what chance did she have? How could she ever hope to enact meaningful change in the subconscious of humanity?* The enormity of her task was leading her around in circles.

Voices of the past admonish her, shouting a haunting "Ssshhh!"

Silence serves as a warning and promise. At times, it's paramount to quiet the mind, and to listen to the silence in order to gain clarity. Omega repeats herself a mantra, that progress was made one step at a time. She reminds herself that reaching some imagined finish line isn't the goal; rather, it was about taking each necessary step, ensuring that nothing important gets overlooked along the way.

After all, in the journey of existence, there are no shortcuts to be found, only the rhythm of progress.

Omega's eyes find solitude save for one solitary object, an *ancient globe* of Earth, perched conspicuously on her desk. She absorbs the globe, meditating on the pale blue dot. A smile creeps across her face as her fingertips dance over its worn surface. Omega speaks gravely, "4.6 billion years old... and a bunch of Homo sapiens are going to destroy themselves... You've seen that one before, haven't you? You don't need me to save you... You'll be just fine... A ball of rock that allowed us life... Thank you..." The hourglass lurks ominously beside the globe, its appearance unsettling. She fixates on it, the sand particles flowing vividly. Time ripples as water ripples.

"I'm sorry... I wish we were better." She turns away from the globe. Suddenly, she's startled at the sudden appearance of Alpha, who has emerged into the library.

Omega's voice harbors a tone of frustration. "I'm not getting anywhere," she confesses.

Alpha offers a multivariate response. "Patience," the supercomputer says, its voice reassuring.

Omega's expression betrays her inner turmoil as she continues, "All I wanted to do was inspire good in the world."

Alpha remains measured. "You're trying to change the dark side of humanity. An endeavor that's difficult."

Omega reaches out and touches the hourglass, her fingertips tracing the contours. Time and evil. An interplay of these two forces captivates every mind who ever wandered Earth. Evil has been an inherent fact of mankind since its inception. The implications of chaos have been omnipresent since the emergence of matter. Quantum particles act as a conduit, expressing the law of decay. A fate that awaits all things. The demise of the neutron, a precursor to the complexity that emerges through phase transitions. To achieve complexity, a form of matter must undergo a phase transition—the decay of the neutron. This process of decay echoes throughout the entirety of reality, encompassing all that exists. There is no evasion from neutron decay. When scaled up to human decay, the only difference was in the identity of the specimen. All roads lead toward dissolution. That sheer fact remains unchanged. At the quantum level, one might perceive a duality of forces akin to good and evil. Death, symbolized by the decay of particles, a necessary event for life.

From her introspection, Omega thinks about her perpetual quest for meaning. "Always thought there was more," she says. Along her journey, every step feels like a passage through shades of black and white, predictability against the backdrop of mankind's self-destruction. Sadness spreads like the plague.

Alpha levitates over her worries. The monolithic object remains her channeler. A voice of reason, offering lucidity. The supercomputer responds, "Nobody knows that answer. Not even me. Unknown possibilities." Alpha gently probes Omega's recollections. "What's your last memory of the child?"

Lost in her mind, Omega finds herself strolling along the windswept shores of her memories, accompanied only by the child shadow. Love and connection—intertwined realities—each influencing the other. In a moment of introspection, Omega murmurs, "Joy."

Alpha, her voice of reason, replies, "Emotions always intensify a dream."

Omega's tone grows somber as she laments, "The world isn't influenced by good."

But Alpha counters, "You can defeat evil."

Omega contemplates the cyclical nature of existence. "There's no happiness to be found here," she speaks. *What was she truly searching for?* Her response is resolute. "I'm here to engage in the eternal war, where good and evil clash." She pauses, reflecting. "Conflict and drama are essential for the human story."

Alpha responds, bellowing a cryptic reassurance. "Only the future knows what's next…" Futures are uncertain for everything. Ultimately, what truly counts is the ability to improvise and adapt along the way.

Overwhelmed by the magnitude of her responsibilities, Omega bows her head wearily onto the desk, laying down at rest. Threats of a future nuclear apocalypse encapsulate her soul. A pressure that refuses to dissipate. With evil offering no clues to defuse the bomb, she finds herself searching the trenches of her soul. Believing in herself is her gift.

"Close your eyes. Save the world…" Alpha's words are immersed in Omega's psyche.

She stares out the window, her eyes glued to a bush for a brief moment. The bush sways hypnotically, its motion reminiscent of a ticking clock that lulls time away. Suddenly, she witnesses the emergence of flames, their fiery tendrils licking at the sky and burning the bush. An infernal hue consumes everything. The ancient library begins to burn down. Her eyelids flutter shut, where the bottomless underworld awaits

* * *

Twilight suffuses the ancient Chinese workshop. Omega enters back into the past where she observed a figure, laboring in the 2nd century BCE, during the Han Dynasty. The traditional account credits the invention of paper to a eunuch official. This early form of paper was a significant advancement over materials like papyrus and bamboo slips, leading to the widespread use of paper in writing. Advent of paper revolutionized the dissemination of knowledge, leaving animal hides, papyrus, and stones in the past. Its introduction marked a transition toward greater flexibility in spreading information, making communication more effective. A pivotal invention, paper allowed memory to take a backseat, providing a canvas where more details could emerge on its special pages. For centuries, advanced civilizations placed immense value on information, and humanity cherished the medium of paper for its ability. During the progression into technology, such as emails and computer screens, efficiency in communication increased exponentially. However, it all began with the humble advancement of paper. Where individuals could flip through pages and discover the answers or escapism they desired.

The Ancient Astronaut's gestures point toward the assortment of materials scattered across the weathered table: mulberry bark, hemp, and the remnants of old rags. A telepathic encounter ensues. The entity conveys a silent path to engineering success. Across from him, Cai Lun, a figure immersed in his own thoughts, stands and ponders in contemplative silence. He surveys the materials indicated by the Ancient Astronaut. His being holds onto the burden of concentration, his mind a battleground where mysteries of creation could be found.

Omega's eyes flicker between the Ancient Astronaut and Cai Lun, intrigued by the unfolding scene.

Suddenly, Cai Lun exclaims, "Eureka!" His moment of revelation sparks a second wind of innovative spirit. He reaches for the materials, skillfully manipulating them.

Omega observes closely as he adds water, kneading the fibers and spreading the pulpy mixture onto a flat surface. Omega watches him design paper. A seemingly mundane yet intricately important cornerstone of society's evolution. In its humble beginnings was humanity's collective wisdom, a vessel for the transmission of knowledge across epochs and civilizations. Without this modest marvel, the chronicles of history would remain whispers lost in the winds of time. Lessons forgotten. Omega envisions countless scrolls produced, the ink-stained pages inscribed into the sagas of conquest and enlightenment. Treaties of peace. Philosophy, allowing humanity a guide for life. These precious pieces of paper documented humanity's ascent, their fibers holding onto words forever and beyond.

As she traverses the corridors of thought, Omega realizes the debt owed to Cai Lun. He was the unsung architect of civilization's scaffold. A rising phoenix entering the dawn of light. His ingenuity had birthed a medium through which the antiquity could carry forth into eternity, ensuring that the lessons of the past would conduct the path forward for generations yet unborn. In the quiet reflection of her journey, Omega recognizes that the unassuming form of paper was a major milestone to the foundation of progress. Enduring legacies all start by a single word on a page.

Flourishing in his element, Cai Lun tends to his task, meticulously pressing and parching the combination of materials.

Omega fixates while observing the unique alchemy. She glimpses into the transmutation of elemental matter into parchment. The genesis of what would become the canvas for human thought.

In silent approval, the Ancient Astronaut nods, acknowledging at Cai Lun's epochal revelation. A gesture as ancient as the stars themselves, the enigmatic being motions toward a portal, urging Omega to traverse its threshold. An inconspicuous wooden door, awaiting the arrival of the interlopers. Words were unnecessary; the language of gesture and implication conveys all.

Omega takes one more final glance at Cai Lun, the architect of a future yet unwritten. His innovation poises to imprint its permanent mark upon mankind. Omega follows the Ancient Astronaut. Stepping through another doorway of time, they venture into uncharted galleries of past human innovation.

* * *

Galápagos islands *existed beneath a cloudy sky*, jagged contours etched in gloomy calmness. Charles Darwin sits on a rock, hunched over his weathered journal. Revered as the architect of his creation, *the theory of evolution by natural selection*. He reshaped foundations of biological understanding from his seminal work, *On the Origin of Species by Means of Natural Selection*, published in 1859. His revolutionary perspective on the development of life on Earth transformed scientific discourse and left a philosophical impact, guiding humanity's exploration of its place in existence. His pupils as sharp as the volcanic rocks he sits on, Darwin fixates on finches that flit and dart across the island. Their intermittent scuffle of talons on stone form a delicate sound.

Darwin's rugged features were an homage of the environment he inhabits. His journal, a repository of investigations, lay wide open like a sacred text waiting to be deciphered. Finches continue to tiptoe their intricate dance of survival. Darwin closely follows their movements, revered focus bleeding an intense concentration. A state of mind that all great minds must have. Pecks of beaks and flutters of wings drive nature's machinery. Darwin's pens fluid, a river carving its path through stone, capturing the miracle of life in its rawest form. He is rooted to the Earth. Nothing more than a humble scribe witnessing the grand narrative of evolution's timeless ritual. The pen, an extension of his being, scratches furiously against the parchment.

If following a predetermined déjà vu anomaly, the Ancient Astronaut stealthily approaches Darwin from behind, evoking an eerie cosmic synchronicity. Intrigued by the sheer spectacle of its form, a pinnacle of evolutionary development that defies conventional explanation, he couldn't help but wonder. *Was it the hand of God at play? What cosmic forces had conspired to bring such a being to this desolate corner of the world?*

ICE

Darwin's curiosity, a force unto itself, guides him to follow silent summons of the Ancient Astronaut, following the being's unique gesture toward creatures. Darwin's eyes fall upon the finches, the tiny vessels of life. The catalyst for his magnum opus. Recognition flickers, a spark of insight illuminating his soul. Eureka ignites, unraveling the puzzle of evolutionary biology. In anthropology, questions found answers, and the restless notion of God found peace. The deity was put to rest from a materialist perspective. Now, the narrative shifted toward time and change, defining all species ranging from humans, animals and plants. An inner world of genes and outer world of environment shaping all living beings on Earth. The human race, forming its unparalleled consciousness, had emerged as the product of transformative forces, notably the elemental chemistry of fire. This culmination marked the singularity in Homo sapien brains to take flight, allowing humanity to soar toward complexity.

Barren rocks and windswept shores, a backdrop perfectly poised to yield the keys for unlocking the paradox of creation. Renewed vigor enters Darwin, realizing he had uncovered the missing link. Words cascade as though they were a river breaking free from winter's grasp. They engulf the stoic man into a state of childlike excitement. While pursuing accomplishments, purpose found its anchor in the human condition, guiding souls toward the fulfillment of their goals. For those fortunate few who stumble upon a discovery that changes humanity forever, they are the ones who make the world a better place. In the absence of those intrepid souls, evolution would have languished in complacency, never advancing beyond a dust molecule. Slumbering without the jolt of an awakening alarm clock.

An electric energy hums on the island. An atmosphere relishing as if the universe whispered secrets into Darwin's ear. He persists writing, fueled by his muse. Introducing new chapters on life. Neither time nor space could stop the importance of his pioneering work. Darwin forever altered the trajectory of our world. As Darwin's pen traces the arc of revelation, a subtle shift in the atmosphere heralds the arrival of Omega. Her eyes align on the lore of evolutionary history. Sensing her, Darwin lifts his eyes from his work. Now a custodian of creation, his mission becomes clear: to unearth the secrets of evolution buried in time. For those who lend their ears and those who turn away, in the end, the quest remains for the curious souls hungry for knowledge.

Omega nods in approval of Darwin's odyssey toward his breakthrough discovery. Honored from the information she gathers, recognizing humanity's origins traced back to islands such as these, where for millennia humans had existed as hunter-gatherers. Humans were always one as a species, each generation carving out a slightly easier existence than the last. Earth, she realizes, had never been a sanctuary of peace; it had always been a global battleground. The only true evolution over the years had been the nature of humanity's dwelling. A perpetual cycle of makeshift caves in different forms.

The Ancient Astronaut wanders to the precipice of the island, overlooking the steep drop into the sea. Its form begins to blur, dissipating as mist in twilight. And then, in a moment of ephemeral defiance, the entity leaps into the sea, disappearing into the watery abyss. Lost to this world, leaving its mark here forever.

Omega takes notice. "Follow the leader, just trust the process," she whispers to herself, a mantra to anchor her spiritual process amidst the unknown.

Darwin's voice cuts through the island, akin to a bird diving into the ocean for a fish. He speaks. The evolutionary man expresses sincere conviction. "Wait! Before you go…"

Omega pauses, turning back to face Darwin conveying a gentle inclination of her head. Darwin pontificates his phrase that would resonate until the end of time. "It is not the strongest of the species that survives, nor the most intelligent that survives," he murmurs, his voice expressing centuries of observations. "It is the one that is the most adaptable to change." His words are ripples upon the surface of a pond, echoing off ancient cliffs and cries of seabirds soaring overhead.

Omega smiles at Darwin. She turns away from him, her form gliding effortlessly across the rugged terrain. Omega finds herself on the edge of the Galápagos Islands and dives into the ocean, vanishing.

Darwin watches the sea swallow Omega's form, where she enters another portal. His eyes trace the fading outlines of Omega and Ancient Astronaut as they vanish into the ocean. After their exit, Darwin puts his undivided attention back toward the finches. Those humble creatures, responsible for birthing one of the greatest scientific theories ever conceptualized. They hop and flit, beaks probing the crevices of rocks. Darwin, tightly gripping his journal, begins to write his theory of evolution. Darwin's pen was poised to capture life's greatest show on Earth. In nature, he understood knowledge was an eternal odyssey, an endless adventure never entering a conclusion. As a society, one might possess all knowledge or none at all. Equality in uncertainty.

* * *

Omega enters the dim glow of flickering incandescence of a laboratory. A scent of ingenuity wafts through the room of an inventor's workshop. Across the room, Thomas Edison expresses a look of defeat as he confronts his major obstacle. The inventor has a stoic resignation. Arriving at the terminus of his endeavor, the inventor finds himself trying and vying for success from his engineering project.

Edison, a trailblazer of innovation, strode through history, passionately possessed.

During the bustling Industrial Age, while factories produced cutting-edge technologies, Edison emerged with one of the greatest inventions ever created. His early years displayed a precocious intellect, often spending his days immersed in books and tinkering with mechanical contraptions. As years drifted by, Edison's passion for inventions grew stronger, driving him to pursue his dreams.

Ideas teeming his mind, his breakthroughs changed the landscape of history. From the lightbulb to the crackling static of the phonograph. His inventions were a revolution, putting aside shadows of the past and ushering in a new world. Before his successes, the inventor was consumed by failure. There were countless setbacks. But Edison refused to be deterred, confronting each obstacle possessed by a vision greater than himself. Resilience was his companion through the darkest nights of failure. He understood any pursuit worth its efforts demanded perseverance against the impossible. Challenges dogged Edison's process, a shadow trailing him wherever he wandered. He faced each arduous task holding onto his self-belief, knowing that it was the key to win the game of inventing. A world not tailored for the everyman or everywoman, devoid of guarantees. Resilience had been Edison's cornerstone during those dark nights of failure. Anything worth pursuing demands perseverance over the impossible. The greater the challenge, the harder the journey, the greater the reward. All humans could relate.

Fractured filament of the lightbulb releases a dying ghostly glow, a losing battle offered up from the object. Its intended brilliance was obstructed by mechanical engineering anomalies. A funereal ambiance submerges the laboratory. Eerie silence punctuated by soft humming of machines and labored breaths of the inventor. Twilight's melancholy saturates and the ghost of failure emerges, its tentacles wrapping around Edison's being, strangling every last bit of optimism out. Hopes dashed and dreams broken, shattering as though they were glass. Not every effort produces results; such slogans are just fairy tales, promises not always realized.

Omega observes the undeniable struggle of Edison. She understands the inventor's predicament. Countless were failures that Thomas Edison endured, chasing ghosts of success while trying to work out the inner workings of the lightbulb. Failures upon failures flood his psyche. All Edison could do was continue working and hoping for a sign of inventiveness. Those magical ideas that drift in the ether were waiting to be found by each individual in their own time, if ever.

Omega remains vigil, redemption deemed useless during the inventor's battle of wits. Dawn of a new beginning waiting to be forged from the ashes of failure.

Out of the obsidian oblivion, the Ancient Astronaut materializes, traversing the threshold between worlds. The entity strides toward Edison. In a hushed murmur, it imparts an oracular disclosure of information. A whispered design.

Edison receives the celestial counsel. Ideas and more ideas enter and pour out of the inventor's mind. Engineering dilemmas seemed to have moved out of the way for Edison's problem-solving capabilities. Expressing a reverent whisper, he breathes the words of declaration, a satisfactory moment of achievement. "Of course!" Edison unleashes a storm of ideas upon the laboratory. His thoughts race. Ideas were stallions running across the plains of possibility. Exploring the landscape of innovation in search of breakthroughs and rare circumstances that occur only once in a generation. Edison returns to work on the faulty lightbulb, dissecting its mysteries. He embodies the precision of a surgeon.

Omega remains transfixed by Edison's dedication. A "never give up" and "never say die" attitude is emblematic of life's challenges, whether one is endeavoring to invent a lightbulb or striving to live a fulfilling life. She beholds the maestro at work, his hands flowing, rebuilding the lightbulb once more. Carefully, components are delicately adjusted, with pieces of the puzzle beginning to coalesce. Out of nowhere, finally after an infinite number of attempts, the laboratory radiates a heavenly glow. Hope's ember kindles, harmonizing the discord into a symphony of possibility.

Omega draws a comparison from Edison, sensing a divine connection between the lightbulb and humanity. Civilization tempered by fires of perseverance held potential for a collective awakening, a transcendence beyond ego. Omega harbors a revelation that humanity could construct a road toward coexistence, where euphoria was no longer shackled by chains of division. But amid the reverie of enlightenment, Omega is reminded of her duty, the challenge of stopping the apocalypse. Her quest to strip away the ego of evil from the collective consciousness, to unearth the ghost of destruction in the nuclear bomb. And thus, secure the future for the child and all of humanity.

Her consciousness dreaming of utopia was a mirage. The enticing story of a flawless world whispers seductively, yet she knows that such dreams are nothing but wisps in the winds of time. There exists no safety in fantasy. Her destiny calls her toward a different path. A path of prophecy, confronting the challenge of averting the end times. She understands fulfillment of her prophecy is not a choice, but a sacred obligation. Prophecy taunts redemption, refusing to usher in a new dawn and instead seeking to smother a new era into the ashes of death.

The Ancient Astronaut nods in approval and acknowledgment of Edison's triumph. Nearby, another door unleashes a subtle chorus of voices, urging them to venture a little further. Omega had learned the lesson of never saying never, the metaphor as timeless as the stars themselves. Edison remains consumed by the lightbulb.

ICE

Omega finds herself drawn to follow the Ancient Astronaut toward the door. Though torn, leaving behind monumental moments, she remembers how as a little girl she had dreamt of time-traveling to witness the most impactful discoveries in history. Now, experiencing what felt like a dream she never wanted to end, she ponders the nature of reality, whether awake or asleep, was it not all encompassing? The door swings open; it seems to beg Omega to look inside. Innovation, she realizes, comes in all shapes and sizes. For some reason, something was missing. The road less traveled at times in life is the only one to take. But its ultimate destination remained in grave speculation. Omega surrenders to the call of destiny and follows the Ancient Astronaut into the portal, where the greatest invention of them all awaits. At least that's what she hopes for in order reach her conclusion.

* * *

A roughneck, haggard and worn by the assault of hard work. He guards the lip of a gaping pit. Desert badlands absorb auroras of twilight. A heavenly harbinger of doom persists. The sinister dark cloud wreaks havoc, keeping desperate rays of sunlight at bay from the surface. His weathered old eyes watch a wooden oil pump. Continuously rising and falling, the pump tirelessly sifts through the elements of reality, attempting to unearth transformative forces that would elevate society to new levels of living. A crude apparatus of industry thrusting defiantly into Earth. The roughneck battles against nature's indomitable will. Struggling against thick rock layers, the pump persists in its excavation. Nothing proves fruitful from underground. He confronts the stubborn absence of discovery, haunted by the ghost of defeat. Every inch of land feels burdened by an oppressive curse, stifling the hope of uncovering anything of significance.

WISH

From shallows of oblivion, the Ancient Astronaut emerges beside the roughneck. His worn-down, wrinkled visage displays a look of astonishment. In disbelief, his eyes couldn't leave the surreal character, feeling captivated. The otherworldly entity imparts earthly engineering wisdom. An idea ignites for the roughneck. A solution to his current dilemma. A heartbeat of opportunity circling around the work zone. He repositions a crucial component of the equipment. The Industrial Revolution was a seismic shift in humanity. It wasn't just a bump in the road, it was a full-throttle achievement for the human race. This is talking about a time when gears of progress were greased from sweat and blood. Factories belching smoke into the sky, machines churning out goods at a pace that would make anyone's head spin. It was a time of rapid expansion, of unchecked growth. Where the old ways were erased, like a delete button erasing information from a computer. The Industrial Revolution wasn't all sunshine and rainbows. Where the *haves* lived in riches while the *have-nots* were trapped away in the bowels of Earth, scouring for oil. It was a time of exploitation, of extreme labor and unsafe working conditions. The Industrial Revolution changed the world forever. It paved the way for modern civilization and conveniences everyone has taken for granted. Love or hate this epoch, the Industrial Revolution was a game-changer, a wild ride through history.

In reaction to the roughneck's audacious move, a seismic event of earthquake proportions rumbles, accompanied by a thunderous roar that shakes the foundation. A gush of oil erupts, cascading into the heavens. A fountain of liquid gold. The discovery announces the dawn of a new era. Radiant glow of elation spread across the roughneck's features, his passion of triumph was evident. Oil and dust permeate, saturating everything in sight. Pride swelling, the roughneck revels in the thrill of his discovery.

ICE

Omega watches in awe, recognizing the magnitude of this momentous discovery. In history, it could be debated, but there was no denying that oil surpassed even the arrival of electricity. If humanity never had oil, the actual infrastructure necessary for harnessing energy and producing every essential manufactured good would falter. Oil was the cornerstone of innovation, the catalyst creating civilization. A journey spanning millennia, from the primal flicker of fire millions of years ago to the monumental discovery of oil. As she ponders the resilience of her species, Omega can't help but marvel at the remarkable odyssey humanity ventured upon. Yes, humanity was undeniably an animal, driven by the constraints of mortality. Yet, they were also a unique specimen of evolution and adaptation. Only the most discerning of gods, if such celestial beings existed, could have crafted such a complex existence. For Omega, her god is not found in the heavens, but in force that binds all things together, the almighty hand of gravity. The true creator of life.

The Ancient Astronaut acknowledges their fulfillment of duty, directing a gesture of affirmation toward the roughneck. Overwhelmed with joy, the roughneck's soul expands from his discovery, accomplishing something truly magnificent for the world. Divine energy flows between Omega and the Ancient Astronaut, a timeless connection spanning billions of years in a single moment. The paradox of the energy crisis is realized by Omega, that the ego death of humanity is far from a simple matter. Witnessing the events of the past, both their darkness and brilliance reinforces the imperative to "compartmentalize" in her pursuit of justice. Omega recognizes her journey unfolding, a psychoanalytic exploration of her own being. She recognizes the growth she has undergone since embarking on her hero's journey. Despite this evolution, she feels compelled to go even deeper into herself. Omega contemplates the duality of ego

WISH

and id, two aspects of consciousness. She realizes that the answer might come from confronting the darker aspects of herself. The shadow side that harbors her own evil subconsciousness. Omega understands that the one who holds the key to the bomb's location may be a reflection of her own shadow self, embodying the aspects of her psyche that she may fear or suppress. To uncover the truth, she must navigate the labyrinth of her own subconscious, confronting her shadows and embracing the complexities of her own being. Only then can she hope to unravel the mystery and prevent catastrophe.

Internalized by the entity's cosmic wisdom, the Ancient Astronaut plunges into the pit, vanishing into the abyss. A sudden departure. Omega rushes to the edge and is greeted by a yawning scope of darkness. A chasm as vast and infinite as outer space. Whispers of possibility stir in her soul. Before facing the world's demons, one must first confront their own. Omega reflects; chance and willingness drift her being in order to take that leap of faith. They are her guiding principles. Only through serendipitous intrepidness could Omega unlock the next level in the game of her life.

Regardless of circumstances, humanity would always encompass good and evil. A rigid truth, just as the laws of nature themselves. To venture into the abyss while remaining authentic to herself. That defined the quintessence of human fortitude. Omega clung to the belief that in life, as in all things, it was the preparedness to take that leap of faith that separated the dreamers from the visionaries, the wanderers from the conquerors. Dimensions of possibility allow for humanity's destiny to be sculpted by the twin forces of chance and courage. Only by championing these belief systems can anyone shape their own road amidst the eternal sea of potential. Taking a leap of faith that surpasses dynamics of rationality, Omega follows the Ancient Astronaut entering darker dimensions of the underworld.

* * *

Candlelight flickers, an erratic fluctuation from tiny flames strikes a glow upon the ancient Hindu temple. The oldest known religion in the world, pioneering the concept of gods and faith, a seminal milestone in history. Departed souls could be heard from the afterlife, chanting a hushed tone of prayers and hymns. Here, beneath the domed ceiling adorned intricate carvings, worshippers would gather to pay homage to the *holy Vedas*. From holy scriptures, divine beings are exalted, from Shiva—revered as the destroyer who purges the world of imperfections—to Vishnu—the embodiment of preservation, hailed as the savior and protector in Hindu mythology. Incense mingles with flames, creating an atmosphere saturated in sanctity. Allowing an opportunity for Omega to commune, asking the spirits of those who came before. Omega harbors no belief in spirits or gods, her convictions firmly rooted in the soil of skepticism. While she holds a respect for the philosophies and traditions of those who worship, she cannot reconcile herself to the notion of divine beings watching over humanity.

In her youth, she harbored a singular desire for eternal life, wishing for everyone to live forever. Then, as she witnessed death of those around her, her passionate wish died. Reality crushed her dreams and soul. All that remains is the ghost of her former self, haunting her being. She always thinks about Father Time, biding his time for the perfect moment to strike and take her life. From her earliest memories, the precise date of her death held a grip on her consciousness. Gazing heavenward, she acknowledges the uselessness of seeking answers from the cosmos. Instead, she turns inward; no miraculous intervention awaits her—she is all alone.

WISH

The Vedas affirmed that all beings are immortal souls, transcending the physical body. Upon death, the soul embarks on a journey of reincarnation, inhabiting diverse physical forms. This cyclic process, known as samsāra, encompasses the continuous cycle of life, death, and rebirth. Earlier layers of Vedic texts express the concept of an afterlife, where one's actions in life determine their fate of Heaven or Hell. Some believe in immediate rebirth upon death, others contemplate existence of the soul in alternate dimensions beyond earthly existence. Yet, amidst the grandeur of ritual, there were doubts. A whisper in the wind that spoke of truths left unspoken. Despite their teachings, the Vedas only offer fragments of a greater truth. For no one truly comprehends what transpires at the encounter of death until they themselves confront the natural process firsthand. Many individuals experience life in a state of sleepwalking, unwittingly dealing with subconscious conflicts and contradictions. The fear of nonexistence can be immobilizing, leading humanity to create gods and demons as constructs to navigate the complexities of life. Suppression of truth is healthy and unhealthy, dependent on how authentic one wants to live as an individual. Through courageous confrontation of truth one can truly live authentically, transcending illusions that blind the road to enlightenment.

And so, while the faithful bowed their heads in prayer, there were those who dared to question, to seek answers beyond tradition and dogma. For them, the Vedas were not the ultimate truth. But rather a reflection of humanity's eternal quest for meaning.

Outside, snowflakes whirl lost drifting about in the twilight sky, each flake a frozen tear shed by *Nuclear Winter*. In the front row, Omega sits submerged in ethereal light. Alone is her figure, as if she is the sole inhabitant of Earth. She holds the hourglass tightly, twiddling it back and forth.

Death persists to saturate her thoughts, watching tiny grains of sand. She feels the chill of mortality course through her.

Onstage, a gaping hole punctures the floorboards, mirroring a cosmic black hole. Candlelight warps around its event horizon in a majestic display reminiscent of the cosmos. Atop a worn wooden podium rests a book. Pages whispering secrets of vital information. The untitled cover fashioned from animal hides. From its exterior, the book exudes an aura of wisdom, hinting at the promise of containing all the answers one might seek. Omega sits quiet, her eyes watching the ancient book. A question echoes in her mind: *What lesson was in its pages?* She waits for a sign.

A dark silhouette prowls down the aisle, a ghost weaving through the illuminating temple. As the figure draws nearer, flickering candlelight reveals the unmistakable form of Shadow, now draped in a cloak reminiscent of the Grim Reaper. Omega removes her welder's mask, a noticeable shift heralding the emergence of Shadow's sinister energy. It had been dormant for some time, but now it's returned. Dressed in the cloak of Father Time, Shadow exudes an aura of unease, an unsettling vibe that has not been felt before. A hood, adorned over its head like a crown of darkness, symbolizing death.

Shadow's corrupt voice comes. "There's nothing louder than an empty room."

Omega continues watching the ground, her thoughts swirling. She wonders why humanity thought Hell was underground. Greek mythology and Christian theology introduced the concept of Hell being underground, and it was a prevailing theme. In Greek mythology, Hades, the god of the realm of dead, was believed to exist beneath Earth's surface. Similarly, in Christian teachings, Hell was often portrayed as a fiery underworld where sinners face eternal punishment. The association with underground locations was influenced by caves, evoking feelings of isolation from the world. Symbolism of being buried underground represented the ultimate separation from divinity.

Her being is seized by a subzero chill, inundating her into terrifying thoughts of mortality. Tumultuous emotions churn, fear seeping into her psyche. Omega finds herself where darkness has taken root. Embarking on her hero's journey discloses the myriad challenges humanity faces, revealing countless daunting obstacles blocking her ultimate goal of eradicating evil.

Shadow's voice escapes, echoing softly. "When I first looked into your eyes, you reminded me of hope."

A heavy silence descends upon the temple. Suffocating quietness, resembling a funeral home. At a funeral home once, Omega found herself by her grandmother at rest. The ghost of death gave her so much terror that she couldn't even approach the casket. Instead, she found safety in a corner, avoiding the reality of mortality, unwilling to confront it head-on. Tragically, when Omega's father and mother passed away, she made the heartbreaking decision, at a tender age, to submit to selfishness and cowardice, abstaining from attending their funerals. Death became her formidable fear. The only sounds present were soft crackles of candle flames.

Miniature fires churn, breathing life into Omega's wandering soul. A captivating reminder of vitality that animates one's existence. Both beings could hear their own inner thoughts, an entangled duality of emotions inspired a vendetta.

Shadow takes charge, a monster in her mind. "Hope is a curse. I'm grateful you're still among us. Would you like to see your future?"

Omega clears her throat. "I have something to share about myself," she begins, voice steady despite her turmoil. The temple's interior inhales, expanding as if infused with life itself. Flames swell, feeling mounting tension, as if the temple had a pulse. Breathing is all Omega can do, preparing herself for what she is about to reveal.

Shadow leans in, its aura penetrating and peering into her soul. "Speak your truth," it urges. A question that tests her insight, one that only the awaken can decipher.

Omega makes a confession, harking back to earlier years. These were times of innocence, days when faith was her belief. "I used to sit in benches like these when I was younger," her voice oozes a hint of nostalgia. "Searching for answers." Memories flood her mind during days spent in quiet contemplation, when questions started to formulate and confuse her mind. One day she asked herself an interesting question, *what am I supposed to do here*? Experiences guided her toward spiritual growth. To keep on exploring and walk through those open doors. She held onto her purpose, believing one day it would be discovered in a moment of bliss. In the temple, she felt vulnerability drown her thoughts. The burden of her past, a constant companion by her side.

Shadow, her faithful guide, good and evil, refuses to depart until she finds herself in the underworld. Dark knight of the soul is non-negotiable; one must traverse into the labyrinth of self to emerge transformed.

"And did anyone ever provide them?" Shadow asks, probing and urging Omega to confront the ghosts of her past.

Omega's response is honest. "No," she replies, saddened by her lack of faith. Anger she tucks away in her mind throughout her current escapade resurface unexpectedly at the forefront of her consciousness.

Shadow nods, understanding her issue. The entity shares a fact from centuries of observation. "It can get confusing at times," Shadow concedes. Answers avoid everybody, even the most inquisitive minds. Life can appear as a monster, challenging us at every turn until the end.

Shadow rises from its seat, an eerie finesse slowly taking one step at a time. An entity, always one step ahead of the unfolding narrative, holds power over Omega from the beginning. While its influence predominantly tilts toward the positive, when Omega confronts death, she questioned everything, creating a cause-and-effect conflict. Navigating her main event between good and evil. It ascends the stage and seizes the ancient book. Pages contained messages of an uncertain future for civilization.

Returning to Omega's side, Shadow takes a seat beside her, the enigmatic book cradled between them. A sacred relic. Seated together, they share a moment of communion akin to a sacred ritual, evoking the intimate atmosphere of a confessional encounter between a priest and pedestrian. "Don't fear death," Shadow murmurs, its voice a haunting reality of the impossibilities of immortality. The tonality emanating from Shadow exudes untrusting ambiguity. Words are a riddle meant to tempt Omega into surrendering to her fears and abandoning her journey.

From nothing to everything. Save humanity and the child from extinction or quit. Scenarios of success were lost but found in a dream. Despite her individuality, she can't shake her insignificance in the infinite sea of humanity that characterizes the era of Homo sapiens. The question lingers: *Could one person truly make a meaningful difference in the grand scheme of life?* It was a realization that cut to the core of her being. Omega understands shadows in own souls are reflections of the darkness threatening to engulf humanity.

To confront demons that plague her is to confront demons that plague the collective consciousness of her species. A symbiotic dance of salvation and damnation. She knows true heroism is not in the grand gestures of courage, but instead in the quiet moments of introspection. The moments when one confronts their own mortality and emerges stronger for having done so. She cannot hope

ICE

to save humanity unless she first saves herself first. The journey toward redemption begins internally. Running on the last reserves of her restless soul, she remains a fighter, a warrior fueled by her passionate wish for humanity's survival. Refusing to quit against the apocalypse.

Shadow's fingers trace the pages, timeworn parchment yielding reluctantly to its touch. Pages creaks softly in protest. "Only you can free yourself," Shadow declares, expressing conviction.

Omega regards the entity skeptically. "Is that a guarantee?" she questions.

"Of course," Shadow replies, its voice sinister. "It's written in the book." Shadow's voice is prophetic.

Omega stares intently at the pages of the book, realizing they were blank, and Shadow is spinning a manipulating narrative as they go along. It strikes her how similar this is to the storytelling traditions of the past, where religious tales, fables, and fairy tales were crafted by individuals to shape personal beliefs. It becomes apparent that these narratives were leading nowhere but to the subjective opinions of individuals dictating what others should believe.

Each page of make-believe ancient text flows from Shadow's lips in tongues long forgotten by the world. Speaking of prophecy... "The end of days has arrived," Shadow expresses. "The suffering of civilization will finally stop. No gods. No politicians. No messiahs. No man or woman can stop the end."

Omega listens, words sinking into her soul. Evil rhetoric expressed for eons. The magnitude of her predicament saturates her reflections. And it dawns on her; Omega saw the long history of deception from humanity since the genesis of the written word. Fear surrounding death had driven mankind to adopt this maniacal behavior, perpetuating a cycle of confusion and conflict in their belief systems. From the ancient Hammurabi Code's *Eye for an*

Eye principle in Mesopotamia to the complexities of the future, this dilemma of ego persisted, shaping civilizations.

Shadow slams the ancient book shut, its blank pages echoing the finality. The dark entity gestures toward the black hole on the stage, beckoning a promise of escape. "Join me!" Shadow implores, the voice a devilish solicitation. Approaching the black hole, Shadow embraces its venomous philosophy, answering a devilish call to duty. The dark entity kneels before the abyss, submitting to its dark allure. Darkness surrounds the tantalizing being bowing its head in worship, as though the black hole were a god, guiding toward a singularity of truth. A divine convergence point where all mysteries coalesce into one undeniable reality. Shadow offers themselves to the void, a sacrifice to whatever forces were hidden.

Omega's hand moves instinctively to tuck the hourglass into her jacket pocket. She watches as Shadow surrenders, a figure swallowed by evil. The interloper rises, advancing toward the stage. In her mind, she scoffs at the notion of weak minds praying to false gods. Instead, she affirms the strength in submitting to oneself, not giving in to external illusions. The mantra repeats like a ticking time bomb, not to succumb to the allure of delusional belief systems.

She kneels in front of Shadow. While overlooking the entity, she thinks long and hard about the blackness that kept its emotional façade veiled. She can't tear her eyes away from the cloak of death. Feeling sympathy for Shadow and the countless other shadows that haunt the dark side of humanity. A wish for a mass purge to cleanse the world of such darkness.

"I would be happy to join," Omega declares, remaining in control. A steady train roaming down the tracks, refusing to fall off.

"Welcome to the end," Shadow responds, convinced it was prevailing in this cerebral battle of wits.

"But first," Omega continues, "you must answer my question."

Feeling Omega waning, Shadow perceives an opportunity to assert dominance. It was prepared to go to any lengths, obedient to her commands in this critical moment of vulnerability. A moment of silence consumes the temple, which felt like eternity. "Anything," Shadow speaks.

"Does the child die in the future?" Omega presses, her eyes locked onto Shadow.

There is no response, only the eerie hush of unanswered questions.

"Aren't you a prophet?" Omega persists, her voice angry.

"I can only see so much," Shadow replies sheepishly. A coward hiding in its own shadow.

"So, you're a liar?" Omega retorts, seeing through the fabricated words that only spoke to confusion. She recognizes the futility of Shadow's deceptive narrative, offering more questions than solutions. Omega's hand seizes the ancient book from Shadow's grasp, her fingers curling tightly around its cover. "Tell me the truth with this book," Omega demands, her voice commanding in its insistence.

"I'm sorry," Shadow replies regretfully.

"What are you sorry for?" Omega pushes harder, her patience reaching the tipping point.

Shadow remains quiet, unable or unwilling to speak the words she wants to hear.

"Answer me now!" Omega demands.

Shadow's admission is a revelation that is wicked. "I never believed the child or humanity would make the right choices for civilization," Shadow confesses. "So, I allowed their dark side to consume them all."

Omega's mind begins to reel at the statement. She realizes the extent of the darkness that had enveloped everything. The child was an innocent bystander during civilization's collapse. Future generations denied the chance of a life on a clean planet harpoon Omega's soul. The thought is unbearable. At the least, she believes, humanity owed it to itself to ensure a hospitable world for all to experience life, for ultimately, that was the fundamental right every human deserved. An opportunity to live on a sustainable planet, not a frozen world. Selfishness of previous generations had sentenced the future to death. Each child embodied innocence, a chance for life, experience, dreams, and wishes. In the beginning of their journey, if born able-bodied, the world presented endless possibilities waiting to be explored.

Omega makes a firm demand. "Let me hear you say that you're sorry." Her eyes are scrutinizing Shadow as she speaks. "Say it loud enough so humanity can hear you."

Shadow unleashes a haunting cry. Remorseful, guilty from its actions of evil. "*I shouldn't have done it!*"

Omega listens, knowing that acknowledgment is the first step toward redemption. Shadow's confession came too late, arriving after the damage had already been inflicted. There was no turning back; the irreversible consequences had been set in motion, leaving nothing but the aftermath. Omega closes her eyes, thinking on the world's troubles. She makes a wish. She wishes for the possibility that, through acts of forgiveness, humanity could rediscover itself and leave the trail of darkness behind them. Those who gaze outward dream, while those who turn inward awaken. No alternatives existed. She had to travel further into limbo.

Omega reaches out, her fingers closing around Shadow's shoulders. The entity concedes a soft whimper, acknowledging Omega's firm grasp, which overwhelmed her darker self. She refuses to give in to its victimhood mentality. Her touch meets resistance, grasping hold of darkness in her own soul. "Nobody can protect us," Omega declares.

Shadow's response is chilling, words foretelling an impending doom. "Nobody will survive the bomb! You're going to be all alone," it warns. A harbinger of prophecy, into the tangled web of time and dreams.

Omega faces a dilemma. *Could she really intervene to stop the paradox of human nature from altering the future, or was she fated to accept what had already occurred?* A parallel course where destiny collided and the frailty of choice. Perhaps stemming from a past life, if such a concept held truth.

"Do it for them," she reminds herself, knowing that in the end, making an effort is far better than doing nothing at all. Having nothing to lose, she resolves to act. Those who dare to risk everything will reap the rewards in the end.

Omega drags Shadow toward the black hole, its feeble resistance no match for her power. As they approach ever closer, Shadow's form twists and contorts in protest, swirling and writhing in panic against Omega's relentless advance. "You don't know the future," Omega commands. "When I look at you, I see a person who gave up hope. After that happens, what do you have?" Her words offer a challenge, calling out durability for good against evil, during the external and internal ego war.

Nearing the edge of the abyss, the entity remains quiet, its voice drowned out by the vociferous whirlwind of the moment. "All you have is silence," Omega declares, her words cutting through the chaos. "Waiting. For you." Omega unleashes a powerful thrust, hurling Shadow into the pit. The evil entity descends into the void, swallowed by the darkness. The entity holds no dominion over her. Reality produces chaos and order, which coexist as an inherent duality dependent upon every facet of existence, regardless of scale. The internal struggle oneself would always exist.

Gathering herself, Omega reaches into her jacket pocket and retrieves the hourglass. She watches the sand flow aimlessly, begging for an answer. The grains shift erratically,

WISH

swirling in a vorticity type of pattern, mirroring her own psyche. Chaos isn't going anywhere. The further Omega traveled, the more unpredictable events became, unfolding in ways she couldn't anticipate.

Omega's consciousness begins to slip away. She is captivated by the hypnotic descent of sand in the hourglass. A metaphor of determined chaos that plagued the world. Spiraling into her subconscious, truths remain buried in her soul. To uncover them, she must confront them in the belly of the proverbial beast. Time slowly wove its spell, coaxing Omega back under its curse. This awakening ushers her into another dimension.

Omega loses consciousness and collapses to the ground. The hourglass slips from her hand, its totem tumbling and rolling away. Time remains suspended, impossible to stop it from moving forward regardless of its orientation. Caught between time and dreams, Omega is granted a secret passage into her sinister subconscious, slipping back into the darkness from which she briefly emerges. Omega continues navigating the maze of Hell of her own mind.

* * *

Deep in the underworld, shadowy serpents extend tendrils, reaching out to ensnare unwary travelers. This was a location where if you ventured previously, you thought unimaginable, as if journeying toward the core of Earth. This subterranean zone, no drill could penetrate. It seemed crafted by a devil's mind, layer upon layer. An afterworld where departed souls reside, entombed in an eternal underground sanctuary. Sparse shafts of torchlights bleed through the cracked dirt ceiling. A domain where even the bravest dared not tread. Submerged in murmurs of nefarious aims, darker possibilities were unchecked by constraints of virtue. This domain was where the corrupt ruled their empire. Omega's fears submerge beneath her dark side. Every soul harbors both. It's the mastery of self-control over the shadows amidst life's darkest tempests that distinguishes each individual.

Depravity spread like a plague, in dying torchlight, mythological statues are at the threshold of the underworld. Crumbling stone forms barely discernible, struggling to maintain structure. The mighty Zeus, his thunderbolt raised in a clenched fist, exudes an aura of cruel authority, his fierce eyes piercing souls of any who dared to meet. Poseidon, god of tempestuous seas, displays a twisted grin upon his chiseled face, a sadistic delight evident in the curl of his lips as he intensely brandishes his trident. Beside them, Athena, goddess of warfare, wields her spear. And then, Venus de Milo, her serene countenance twists into a grotesque parody of beauty. Corruption lurks in the purest of forms. Together, these statues showcase the darkness of humanity.

Omega's welder mask envelops her features, her mind hard as stone. Refusing to let her past encounter conquer her. The challenges of letting one's shadow go, one of the toughest realities any human can face. Her boots splash lifeless puddles of oil. Tunnels mirrored a network of neurological neurons found inside the human brain. 100 billion neurons and countless interconnected pathways. The resemblance between this underground lair and complexity of the human mind was striking. Unlimited directions, each one a potential path to take.

She has to lean on her intuition that had guided her thus far. "Trust your instincts," she whispers to herself, holding onto the belief that she is capable of navigating this maze. Ahead at the final stop, a bronze vault door, its surface catching the faint torchlight. Above the doorway, an exit sign flickers intermittently. Doors and symbolic passageways, much like the various neuron pathways in her mind, offer divergent outcomes. Omega doesn't know what is beyond

WISH

the doors; all she knows is that she has no choice but to see, compelled to continue roaming in her subconscious.

Omega's grip tightens the vault latch, her hands turning the wheel clockwise, her movements similar to a captain steering the Titanic away from the iceberg. Only chance is her guide in this swamp of puzzles. During each rotation, she remains unsure of what awaits her on the other side of that bronze barrier. Like a captain navigating troubled waters, obstacles roam as monsters in the night. A boogeyman atmosphere. Comfort is a luxury Omega can't afford. There is no peace to be found here, no rest from the ever-present threat. A ticking clock warning that to stay here too long might mean eternal condemnation.

A series of stairs awaits, descending further underground. Step after step, Omega continues following the path. The climb mirrors a mirage-like horizon forever out of reach. Stairs leading everywhere and nowhere. *Where did this unimaginable journey ultimately lead?* The road less traveled screams at Omega, *yet how could she ever discern if she had reached her destination? What awaited her at the end of this arduous odyssey? Would it be friends, family, or perhaps a long-lost lover, patiently awaiting her arrival at the finish line? Don't get distracted*, finding the bomb is her mission. Just get there. That is her sole focus, reaching that critical point. Omega's future is squarely in her hands. She understands reaching the end will be her daunting challenge. In limbo, answers and uncertainties are inseparable.

Rough edges were illuminated by the wavering glow of flickering torchlights. At the staircase, a doppelgänger paying homage to the infamous Escher steps. Escher, a renowned Dutch artist known for his mind-bending and mathematically inspired works. Particularly, his detailed drawings featuring impossible architectural constructions and optical illusions. Each step downward spoke into eternity, perpetually descending but never quite reaching a definitive end. Surreal experience of perception. A slippery curve. Omega knows she can't afford to fear her own being. These inner monsters, these soul-devouring cannibals, have to be confronted and vanquished if she is to transcend.

At the fork in the road, Omega pauses, confronted by a choice. To the left, a path veers into darkness. To the right, a faint glimmer of light. Here, amidst two sinister tunnels yawning open as hungry mouths, whispering promises of dangerous encounters. She selects the tunnel on the far left, its descent into darkness marked by a steep gradient. Omega chose the scary road. She carries lessons of the past, acknowledging challenges that shaped her. In the present moment, she remains mindful of obstacles. Her sights fixed on the future, trusting that clarity would emerge.

Swallowed by darkness, Omega instinctively reaches out, her hand finding purchase on the rough wall. She relies on the tactile sensation of the dirt beneath her fingertips against the oppressive darkness. There is a magnetic desperation in her touch. Guided by this visceral anchor, Omega moves a little more urgently. She believes in herself, trusting in the marrow of her bones that this is the way. Her only path leading to wherever she needs to be.

Suddenly, a frightening chuckle slithers, the sound of a venomous serpent, freezing Omega in place. All at once, a barely perceptible scornful laugh tears through the dark. She steps into a twisted carnival of villainous venom, where the world's laughter turns inward—a mocking echo of its innermost thoughts and desires. Truth wears a mask of deceit, and every laugh holds the sharp edge of betrayal. Deception is a stalker, endlessly following Omega. She knows that the laughter of this place holds secrets darker than the night itself.

Haunting a laugh of entrapment, this was mocking Omega, daring her to enter. Omega's voice swirls through the darkness. "Who's down here?" She stares into the abyss, as if willing it to take shape and materialize into something tangible. Though, the darkness persists, never granting her wish. Instead of a visual revelation, an onslaught of sound waves, emanating from an unseen malevolent voice. Sound waves, those temperamental rascals, fluctuate for the soul of matter. Omega is alone, submerged by blackness, saturated by the color of death.

A wicked voice answers. "Survivors," it replies. Laughter ceases. A switch had been flicked off.

No fear, she repeats to herself as a prayer. During her younger years, Omega harbored a fear of the dark. The idea of absolute nothingness was terrifying, her greatest fear the haunting possibility of nothingness. The thought of being erased from existence after death, a fear that tortured her consciousness. In the quietness of the night, she would imagine unseen monsters under her bed, waiting for her to awaken and grab her legs, pulling her down into a frightening world. It was only through the comforting glow of a nightlight that she found peace. Its soft illumination warding off the ghosts of her imagination and allowing her to drift into a peaceful sleep. Yet now, in the underworld and submerged by darkness, those childhood fears threaten to resurface, reminiscent of her soul's vulnerability.

Omega progresses, darkness gradually parting ways to a torch embedded in the wall, its flames shining light upon another vault door. She grips the wheel and turns it counterclockwise. A metallic groan of the mechanism echoes as the door unlocks. She pushes open the door, preparing herself for whatever comes next. Omega enters, crossing over into another threshold, encountering a new chamber.

* * *

Texture shifts, transitioning from gritty dirt to shimmering crystals. Each surface gleaming fantastical radiance, a world beyond imagination. In spirituality, rumors spread, noting crystals had special powers to absorb and amplify energy. Making them the ultimate cosmic conduits, tapping into the universe's hidden frequencies. Omega embraces the unexpected shift in energy. She can't help but feel a strange comfort from the crystals; they hold an innate power. In the lore of dreamers of unparalleled realities, crystals were said to emanate vibrations of positivity. *Could this be the catalyst for a fresh start, a renewal of her ventures into the unknown*? Perhaps, just perhaps, the thick layer of darkness that drowns her subconscious is fated to dissipate in such radiant energy.

Omega maroons on an island of isolation. Her good Shadow vanished and abandoned her. Never before has she felt such severe loneliness. A detachment from everything. Even amidst crystals, they are nothing more than inert rocks, devoid of companionship. From a young age, Omega felt like an outsider, a misfit in a world of conformity. While others reveled in mindless chatter and social niceties, she found peace in pages of books, reading philosophy, science, and history. Her pursuit of these truths gave her purpose. She had never seen anyone in her bloodline as a role model. Instead, she looked to the wisdom of the written word, seeking to leave behind a legacy of understanding. After each book was devoured, she felt herself attuned to the rhythms of reality. An adventurous spirit that has never stopped, she continues to push into exploration. Her curiosity for logical truths is at the heart of her species' future. She had become a mad scientist of virtue.

Omega didn't harbor disdain for humanity; instead, she felt empathy, recognizing gazillions of souls who trudged through life without ever tasting its full richness. Whether captured in the sleepwalking trance or held back by currents of emotion, many humans were destined to merely exist rather than truly live. Her soul aches with the knowledge

WISH

that so many were denied the opportunity to experience the sublime euphoria that Earth had to offer. If she could make one wish, it wouldn't be for riches or power, but for every human being to experience the ecstasy that awaited them on this terrestrial sphere. To feel the warmth of the Sun, to savor the sweetness of life's simple pleasures. It was a wish born not of selfish desire, but of a craving for all beings to awaken. To break free from the lack of enthusiasm and empower their infinite potential. This is the reason Omega finds herself in the underworld. Her mission is nothing short of a declaration of intent for the entirety of the human race; to awaken them and ignite each soul by that magical spark of euphoria.

"Find the bomb, save humanity," Omega repeats to herself. "You can do this," she affirms, drawing strength, hoping to fulfill her destiny as humanity's savior.

Omega reaches out toward the smooth surface of the crystals. Fingertips grazing layers of colors, a throbbing energy entering her being emanating from their core. Despite the surreal sensation, she shakes off the anomaly and directs her eyes toward three more tunnels ahead and instinctively, she chooses the middle one. Omega wanders down the tunnel, following a reddish glow repeatedly flickering. Containing a crimson color of love, its intensity vivid and growing serene. Anticipation saturates her mind, what lies beyond, as the last tunnel finally opens.

The colossal underworld opens up into a network of crystal caverns. Sinuous arteries of a mythical beast of annihilation. Walls showcase a profusion of red crystals. An ethereal glow resembling droplets of blood. Omega peels off her glove, revealing the blister on her hand. She scrutinizes it, finding no discernible effects beyond the surface. Immersed in dreams, hallucinations, and nightmares, Omega can't decipher reality. *Is her experience a manifestation of the injury she sustained earlier?* Reality lost its way in her psyche, and she speaks to herself. "I used to deceive myself into believing in the eternity of my existence. There's always been this recurring dream... where I was the only person capable of achieving immortality. I never wanted to be awakened from it..." Her soulful eyes stare into one of the crimson crystals, her reflection shimmering back at her from its polished surface. Omega murmurs, "Euphoria... I wish I could escape inside that dream forever."

Visions of eternal life and the allure of immortality were wishes which captivated Omega's imagination. It was understandable to yearn for the impossible. Omega observes the labyrinth of pathways in various directions, pondering her next move. After deliberation, she settles on a direction and dives into the maze, racing around corners and going further. Towering crystals and majestic structures rising to the heavens. Enchanting elemental landscapes, a place that fantastical characters from fairy tales would find wondrous. Her footsteps quicken. Despite her best efforts, Omega finds no escape from the maze, leaving her in the disconcerting sensation of running in circles. Going everywhere and nowhere, trapped in an endless cycle of directionless purposelessness. Omega stops and leans heavily against a crystal, her strength drained. Mental and physical tolls begin mounting.

She scans her surroundings, the disorienting maze blurs. The ground trembles as an earthquake emerges underground. A sharp pain protrudes her psyche, prompting her to grasp desperately at her throbbing head. Omega braces herself against the onslaught of instability. Crystals vibrate violently. It felt as if the entire world were imploding. Limbo attempts to break her open. She resists the urge to surrender, embracing the agony instead. Then, as suddenly as they began, the world falls silent. Omega slowly regains her composure.

WISH

She comprehends that it would only grow more difficult moving forward. Nevertheless, as she approaches the end, obstacles become increasingly daunting. Omega searches the area until it aligns upon a slender crack in one of the towering crystals. Summoning a little more of her strength, she wedges her body through the narrow opening, pushing past the crevice until she enters another zone.

An enchanting array of red, blue, and green crystals. Vibrant hues emanating from magical stones exude a comforting energy. It appears inviting, a sanctuary of safety. Possessing a magnetic allure, capable of drawing one into its supernatural light. An alien planet opens up into a captivating world of a lucid dream. Omega's eyes drift to the ground, where oil trickles through shallow channels carved into the crystal. She follows the buoyant streams to their origin. A natural underground reservoir, where oil spouts from a small crevice. Oil seemed inseparable from her, reluctant to depart.

As she watches the oil stream, memories of her past encounter flash through her mind, recollections plunging into the river of her thoughts. That dreadful day resurfaces, a nightmare she wishes would swiftly fade into oblivion. Her bad memory came to an abrupt end as she is disturbed by eerie laughter. Shocked, Omega warily glances around, trying to locate the unsettling sound. But it only grows louder. She pushes aside the laughter, navigating through countless pathways. Each turn leads to another, none revealing a clear exit. Like a rat ensnared in a maze, she finds herself trapped in an endless cycle, a symbol of the perpetual limbo where every direction seems to offer no escape from the past. Primal sounds intensify, submerging her from all angles. Echoing off crystal walls, grunts and cackles play on an infinite loop, a relentless soundtrack. Straining her eyes, Omega spots an opening at the end of the tunnel and hurries toward it, eager to escape the sinister laughter that follows her every step. "In the darkness, real things seem no more real than dreams," Omega says to herself.

* * *

Another chamber displayed a desolate crop field that harbored shriveled plants. Photosynthesis dried out, leaving behind nothing. Discovery of agriculture marked a pivotal moment in human history, but after the nuclear collapse, vegetation succumbed to extinction. For ages, humans debated the ethics of veganism, wondering whether it made more sense to take life from an animal's soul or deprive a plant of its oxygen. These separate species weighed heavily in the balance. Plants—essential providers of oxygen for Earth—sustained life. After radiation engulfed the world, humanity had no chance. The purge of oxygen, swallowed by *Nuclear Winter*.

Legends of the Garden of Eden portrayed it as the cradle of creation, where Adam and Eve reveled in the lush beauty of nature. The stark contrast to this desolate place couldn't be more different. Purity erased, now replaced by corruption from the outside world. Overconsumption of energy was branded as the Devil for mankind.

The Garden of Eden, as all paradises, harbored seeds of its own destruction. A serpent symbolizing temptation slithered its way into the heart of Eden, spreading discord among its inhabitants. Venomous whispers poisoned minds of the innocent, leading them astray from a road of righteousness. Ultimately, the serpent's influence culminated in the fall of Eden, unleashing its former verdant fields into ruin. A cautionary tale of consequences. Prosperity had long forsaken this place, leaving it devoid of agriculture.

Omega's exploration reveals paintings embedded with crystals, crude depictions showcasing primal art of ancient civilizations. Emergence of art was a seminal achievement for humanity, raising questions about the relationship between God and creativity. *Which came first, and did one dictate the other?* Some pondered that connecting with God was through the act of creation. It seemed conceivable that perhaps creation was the sole means of communion with God.

Crude carvings, fashioned from bones, encircle the area forming triangles. Composed of human phalanges, arranged in a morbid display of macabre artistry. Triangles, past, present, and future represented by skeleton fingers underlined a ritualistic encampment of surplus powers from a cult. Another menacing laughter resonates, urging Omega to flee. She runs past the dead garden. This joker type of laughter pursues her endlessly, notwithstanding any gumption of relaxation. Evoking an ancient lore that has continued for countless generations. Emerging from the winding path of the crystal maze, Omega finds herself face-to-face with the grandeur of a long, oak dining room table. A type of table where kings would eat, commanding attention against the crystal chamber. Despite its apparent displacement, the table occupies center stage, as if it had been awaiting Omega's arrival all along. Welcoming her to a feast that had yet to be served. Decaying centerpieces, dead black roses, possessed by a dying love. A dozen high-backed chairs align around the table. Resting on the oak surface, a massive, empty silver tray, marred by the telltale stains of old blood. Human activity around the table hints at recent dining. Blood is perplexing, given the extinction of animals. This anomaly whispers messages of sacred rituals, vindictive events.

Omega knows this place harbors hostility. She has no choice but to push forward, her soul bleeding for her to continue, a pulse pushing ever so fleetingly against the inertia forces reigning down upon this chamber. Once more, an oak door emerges from a dirt wall, beckoning for someone to step through its threshold. Omega, moving past the dinner table, places her hand on the doorknob and turns left, then right. A long, loud creak, and the door opens into a portal of darkness, from which whispers of souls murmur tales of fright.

Emerging into the ceremonial chamber, Omega stumbles upon a nightmare. A dozen hooded figures huddle around a timeworn altar. Silhouettes merging seamlessly over ritualistic proceedings. An ancient ritual, soaked in barbarity. These entities are nothing short of sadistic. In every soul, darkness looms, and these characters embody the epitome of a collective harboring cruel intentions. The figures engage in a frenzied display of guttural cries, beckoning to ancient forces. Seeking guidance from beyond, principles of peace have dissipated in these desperate times. The underground cult, entrenched in their seductive trance, are locked into a spiral of desperation. A celebration of sorts, sadistically oozing an ominous aura of dread.

Suddenly, figures whirl around, revealing petrifying masks of *plague doctors*; beaked features adding a terrifying edge to their persona. Plague doctors awoke during the darkest periods of human existence. Their role was that of a healer and undertaker. Tasked to treat victims of the bubonic plague that ravaged Europe during the Middle Ages. Their beaked masks and aromatic herbs and spices were believed to ward off the foul miasma of disease. They ventured into plague-stricken cities, offering what little relief they could. Plague doctor appearances struck terror into the hearts of those they encountered. For their appearance signaled an inevitability of death. Rumors swirled of plague doctors engaging in ill-omened practices, exploiting plague-ridden populace for their own gain. Others whispered of secret alliances containing dark forces, unleashing rituals to appease unseen powers and prolong their own twisted existence. Nefarious doctors obsessed by seductively taking lives. A cursory group of killers who had fallen prey to the predator of evil.

Stepping forth, waving a menacing blade, the leader commands their attention toward Omega. "Capture the dreamer," he orders, prompting manic laughter from beneath the disturbing masks. An unholy symphony of the deranged.

Omega's eyes dart, seeking any sign of escape. Her eyes land upon a maze fashioned from dirt. Endless jaws yawning wide open, begging for an entrance from an outsider. The interloper launches off the starting gate, resembling the swiftness of a sprinter chasing the gold medal. She wastes no time, sensing the predator lurking, its appetite for another meal of cannibalistic possibilities. She traverses the labyrinthine dirt pathways, weaving through the tangled web. The predatory pursuit is a chorus of malevolent spirits. Sinister laughter pulsating. Demons seem to possess the environment, carrying tales of sin. Mazes of thoughts and ideas cloud judgment for all species. But this metaphorical underpinning, refined and supreme, guides Omega forward through the chaos. Sinuous tunnels intertwine and contort, connecting and disconnecting in a complex network. It is an intersection of tunnels, seemingly dug out underground over countless ages. A manifestation of nightmares, where fear of never escaping looms more prominently than ever before. Each step forward for womankind felt like a monumental leap for mankind, revealing the true nature of evil. Throughout history, men have often surpassed women, a paradox considering women's role in birth. *Would evil have emerged in a world without men?* Omega finds herself uncertain, unsure. The only certainty she holds is the necessity of saving civilization, a task that requires the collaboration of both men and women. Despite the wrath of mankind attempting to drown her in their ego, she remains indifferent.

Out of shifting shadows, a *skeleton* materializes, bones gleaming in the erratic light. Then, it begins a playful routine in front of Omega. Skeleton movements carry an aura of harmless amusement, merely a participant in the bizarre game. Before Omega can fully comprehend the situation, another skeleton emerges, mimicking her every move. Miming skeletons playfully interact. A celebration of death, producing disorienting effects onto Omega. An unnerving dance, skeletal forms fluid, they would only stop if their bones fell apart. An eternal dance of death. Omega couldn't evade them. At every turn, skeletons leaped out, playing their game of charades. Omega continued running, avoiding the song of death. She was experiencing a dream within the dream. Immortality, an elusive reality which eventually forces all skeletons to embrace their own mortality. Every skeleton approaches the same ending. Torchlight flickers intermittently, enhancing the intensity of the encounter. In the interplay of darkness and light, skeletons appear and disappear.

Omega sprints into the fathomless twisting pathways, combined with the flickering flames from torches illuminating the skeletal figures, it added to the growing confusion. Omega knows her awareness of death will remain an ever-present entity. No matter how many victories she achieved in life, the reality of mortality would shadow her every move. A fact ingrained subconsciously in her psyche. This maze represents a problematic puzzle, constantly confusing pathways for an eternal goal of legacy. Across epochs, humanity thought of leaving a lasting legacy for future generations to cherish. From figures like Moses to Da Vinci to Tesla, individuals have believed that by leaving a mark on the world, they could inspire their lives by providing them greater meaning. Although amidst this pursuit looms the universe's heat death, where all matter will cease to exist in due time. Omega questions what her ultimate purpose would be if she fails to leave a legacy behind. Driven by compassion, Omega yearns to aid humanity, believing that no life should be prematurely cut short. But, as she flees the barbaric madness of the plague

WISH

doctors, she has more existential questions that flood her mind. *If reality is destined to collapse upon itself as all matter decays, returning to the vast emptiness of space,* she ponders, *then what significance do our actions hold?*

Just when Omega feels on the verge of escaping, she collides into a skeleton, halting her progress. Locked in a bizarre dance with the figure, she feels dread creeping over her, amplified by the pulsating torchlights. Then, in a sudden and disorienting moment, the flames flicker out, plunging the maze into black. In the void, she surrenders herself to fate, trusting that it will lead her somewhere, whatever form it may take. She runs frantically, her soul drenched with fear. Uncertain of her destination, all she can feel is the plague doctors. They would never stop chasing, sublime ghosts of herself. Running blindly through the abyss, she can't help but wonder, "*Where am I going?*" The answer came back a chilling reality: everywhere and nowhere. Then, as if performing a clever magician's trick, a simple *abracadabra*, the torches flicker back to life, illuminating an empty maze devoid of its skeletal inhabitants.

Torchlights glow reminiscent of nightlights shimmering in darkness, offering a faint comfort for Omega, her guiding light while maneuvering the unpredictable tunnels. Omega finds herself sprinting alone amidst the twisting walls of dirt. "Flesh and dirt," Omega muses, contemplating the inescapable cycle of existence. "Two components intertwined in the recyclable nature of reality. For in the end, all flesh returns to the Earth, merging seamlessly back into the world from where it came." Planetary existence, a miracle that should always be respected by its inhabitants.

In the distance, sounds of heavy breathing akin to wild creatures traversing vast plains ring out. Omega glances over her shoulder; she spots a group of plague doctors closing in. Skeletons had been replaced by these hostile cannibals. *Pick your poison*, but both were equally terrifying in their own right. Their grotesque masks were conjuring phantoms emerging from nowhere, producing a venomous nature of aggression. Speed demons continue to gain ground. She avoids their roguish hands as they lunge toward her. Like a dancer evading an unseen adversary, she sidesteps and weaves through the maze, narrowly escaping their clutches at every turn. Until from the state of nothingness, a plague doctor comes out of nowhere, launching a surprise attack. The assailant seizes Omega, dynamically slamming her against the rough dirt wall. Caught off guard but persevering, she fights back against the plague doctor in a bid for freedom. She delivers a powerful right cross to the plague doctor's mask. Staggering backward, the plague doctor, momentarily stunned by the blow, collapses in a daze. Darkness gives birth to more plague doctors, their eerie masks remaining a reality to Omega's predicament. She continues evading them as though she were a cornered animal. Omega runs past them, each move a narrow escape. Rats in a maze, Omega and the plague doctors dart through the labyrinth. It felt akin to the frenetic energy of a Pac-Man video game, where Omega played the role of the titular character, constantly on the move to evade the ghosts stalking her every move.

Her mind comparable to a soccer player eyeing the goal, and then, there it was yet again. An exit sign, the only thing standing between her and freedom. Those precious letters glowing in a red hue. But as she continues her descent, more plague doctors appear from every conceivable direction, converging on her like a swarm of locusts. A nightmare and hallucination intermix, an unseen enemy that threatens to drown her mind; the gauntlet presenting a new challenge to overcome.

Omega, her psyche spinning, runs harder down the convoluted pathway. "Come on," Omega urges herself, her voice strained. "Just make it to that door." Relief finds her, but quickly is replaced by unease. *What awaits her beyond that glowing door of escape*? Omega with each step draws closer... a little closer... and even closer...

The exit sign's red glow grows stronger. Nearing the door, it emits a halo of welcomed invitations, taunting promises of freedom. "Come forth, weary traveler," it whispers. "For an odyssey mustn't end in the clutches underground."

A beckoning light of salvation. At last, Omega reaches the vault door, her hands turning the heavy circular wheel. She attempts to turn it clockwise, but to no avail. Remembering her current quest, which involves traveling back in time, she reverses her efforts, twisting the wheel counterclockwise. Each movement is a struggle, her muscles straining against the resistance. Hearing bloodcurdling screams, Omega looks up and sees the gang of plague doctors closing the gap. Unleashing a primal grunt of effort, Omega wrenches the vault door open, entering the portal of darkness. She slams the door shut. A heavy thud booms throughout the underground lair as Omega escapes.

* * *

She is greeted by the twilight horizon, a stark contrast to the darkness she had just escaped. The subzero world had never looked so inviting to her weary eyes. Pure white frost against the auras vivid light. Omega bolts across the snowy land, thick snow blocking her momentum's full potential.

The forsaken ice purgatory allows for decay to reign as king, while death cries on the frigid wind. Ghosts of past civilizations paying homage to the apocalypse. Pollution clouds drift as dark omens, swirling and churning across the heavens. Toxic tendrils writhe and twist, a snake uncoiling from Hell. A spectacle of monumental proportions. Consequences from overconsumption of goods and services. For the interloper, the contemplation continues:

What was worse, dangers above ground or underground? In this limbo state of existence for humankind, every place possessed a curse. Worldwide punishment allowed Earth to become judge and juror, as it always was since the beginning of time and always would be until the end of time.

The vault door inches open, sliding and edging its way into the snowball world. Slithering through a crack in its opening was a persistent plague doctor. Omega looks out ahead and notices the edge of a cliff. With nowhere else to run, she focuses on the edge of the cliff, a direction implausible yet inevitable. Faced with this perilous predicament, she knows she has to devise a decisive plan for this encounter. Omega and the plague doctor remain locked in a tense standoff. Body language is similar to the Wild West, akin to a Mexican standoff where gunslingers faced each other down. Then, in a sudden twist, Omega pivots away and bolts toward the edge of the cliff, adrenaline unleashing as she trusts her soul. Quickly following, the plague doctor gives chase, relentless as they race toward the precipice.

Omega feels the plague doctor's energy stalking her down. She dares not look back, knowing fully that the enemy that trails behind her is a predator hungry for her essence. Omega understands all too well that one can never outrun fate, for it is a prophecy etched into existence. A script written across the bedlam of time. Evil pursues her, just as it had pursued generations before her for millennia. Faded wishful dreams of euphoria reign supreme. Omega's spirit becomes a ghost, vanishing into a character of fiction. Goodness had long since perished in the world, leaving Omega's aura priceless. Like those who had come before her, she carries a divine destiny. A burden that threatens to crush her. Omega is no stranger to the horrors of evil, understanding entirely that it will chase her across time until it catches her in this limbo state. Unless she finds a way to stop it. And so, she plans a counterattack in her mind as she runs. She is a force that will not be extinguished by the darkness that desires to claim her soul.

Evil, that merciless arbiter of destinies, cares little for the pleas of mortals. During Omega's run, the bitter cold sinks into her aura. Hell manifests as ice. The world's chill seeps into her being. Ice tightening around her, she wonders if this is the end and all she will experience is a state of eternal coldness. An ink spills in water, creating an expansion allowing death to draw closer. The plague doctor draws nearer, its hunger for Omega's flesh becoming palpable. Omega's world shrinks to a singular point. Her being screams for escape, feeling the nefarious antagonist come even closer. Omega drops to her knees, her body a supplication to the capricious gods who hold mastery over affairs. The plague doctor dives forward, its outstretched claws reaching, harboring hunger of some infernal beast.

Gravity shifts, and they both experience weightlessness. Without warning, the divine force materializes, its origin and nature forever shrouded in mystery. Whether emergent or fundamental, gravity operates on its own terms, capable of defying expectations. And in this moment, it chose to exert its influence in ways unforeseen. A dreamy anomaly. Laws of nature toss both souls aimlessly into the sky. Omega twists and somersaults, every movement a fight for control. The plague doctor remains unrelenting, his grip a vise as he drags her toward him. Omega executes a grappling move, wrapping her body around the plague doctor's torso and clinging to his back. Employing jiu-jitsu techniques, she gains the upper hand for dominance.

Defiance resonates through the gravitational phenomena, and Omega takes advantage of her tormentor's vulnerability. Her fingers find purchase upon his oxygen mask. She wrenches it free, tearing away the veil of protection. His oxygen apparatus torn from his mouth, the plague doctor recoils, his face contorts in horror as his form begins to experience an oxygen-depleted death. A similar sensation to being exposed to the vacuum of space. His lungs rupture from explosive decompression, his blood begins to boil, and his brain succumbs to hypoxia, sealing his fate in a gruesome demise.

Nuclear Winter claims the plague doctor, killing him instantly, survival without oxygen utterly impossible. Omega understands the extraordinary fortune of humankind's existence upon a planet where oxygen is present. A molecule occurring billions of years ago, during the Great Oxidation Event. Oxygen gradually escaped into the atmosphere and encountered methane, triggering a series of reactions. With each exchange, more oxygen displaced the methane until oxygen emerged as a dominant component of the atmosphere, reshaping the composition of the world. Cyanobacteria, commonly known as blue-green algae, played a crucial role. Through photosynthesis, they were the first cells to produce significant amounts of oxygen, catalyzing a transformation that impacted the evolution of life.

Omega feels a sincere gratitude. An appreciation for the balance of life to thrive. During her rumination, she was witness to the fate that awaits all who dare to defy time. Arctic wind unleashes a mournful howl, the plague doctor ascends toward the heavens, its body a wisp of smoke swallowed by the aura sky. But as she beholds this ghostly departure, gravity shifts again, aggressively dragging her toward the cliff's edge, her departure sealed by the tug of gravity. A puppet pulled by unseen strings, powerless to resist. Memories of her distant dream submerge inside her mind. She is pulled toward the edge... closer... a little closer... and even closer... Until finally, she arrives. Then begins to descend, plummeting at an insane speed.

Free falling. Faster... A little faster... Even faster... Her eyes flicker downward, and as she looked beyond the ice

WISH

world, she discovered a massive *black hole*. It was a gaping pit leading into the subterranean world, and her body was helplessly out of control. Omega was drawn into the event horizon, the point of no return. She hurtles toward the singularity, a lone soul descending into the unknown, where the laws of physics unravel, and time loses all meaning.

* * *

An endless pit devoid of time, where tormented spirits linger indefinitely. Omega plunges into engulfing darkness, her forceful descent crashing against the dirt. Her back bangs off the ground, causing her to emit a low guttural groan. Lying on her back, Omega writhes in agony, every inch of her body throbbing from the rough impact of her fall. Her eyes dart to the side where she narrowly misses jaws of razor-sharp dinosaur bones. A primal hallow cavity, one containing only dirt and stone. Omega's eyes scan the area, facing against death's culminating embrace, her existence oscillating. This eternal pit represented the ultimate nightmare. Confinement in human imagination. A prison of unfathomable depths where no soul dared to venture willingly. The last place any sane human would want to be. Assessing her predicament, Omega rises, methodically inspecting her gear, suit, mask, tank-tubes—all unscathed. She takes stock of her surroundings, a crypt of four dirt walls. Distant twilight filters from above, diffusing a glow through a massive circular aperture. A mocking mirage of freedom. An incomprehensible distance to the way out.

Defeated, Omega surrenders, her thoughts entrapped by the futility of escape. An insurmountable obstacle leading toward her own grave. Amidst the gloom, her eyes discover a human skeleton. A past victim to the pit's grim chronicles. Omega seeks rest against a boulder, her spirit crushed. *Might this be her final ending?* She contemplates the prospect of dying. She feels the transient nature of human existence, how each soul eventually succumbs to the dust. Today is not meant to be her final reckoning. As in all life forms, the timing of one's departure remains veiled in uncertainty; mysteries known only to the esoteric notions of death's doorstep. Problem-solving becomes apparent with Omega's current reality. She surveys the four walls, her eyes landing luckily on a solitary rock jutting outward. Quickly, she forms a strategy, her desire to exist a desperation born of survival.

Omega scrambles atop the boulder, using it as a makeshift platform to elevate herself. She focuses intently on the distant rock, gauging its distance and potential for a secure hold. She launches herself toward it, her initial effort faltering as she slips on its slick surface. She collides against the wall and careens back to the ground. Omega pushes herself up, her movements mirroring that of a boxer in the ring, fighting not just for survival, but for victory in the grand arena of life.

Omega repeats her physical strategy, again scaling the massive boulder. She crouches down, preparing to launch herself further than before. Discovering more in her leftover reservoirs of energy, she leaps again, and this time, her grip stays firm on the rock. However, her momentum proves too forceful, and her legs swing wildly out of control, causing her to lose her hold. As she plummets back toward the dirt, the impact felt is even more painful, knocking the wind out of her. "Get up," she urges herself. Despite the setbacks, Omega refuses to stay down. She pushes herself off the ground, ready to face the challenge no matter how many times she fell.

On the third attempt, her fingers claw into its rough surface. She dangles on the edge of the rock, producing strength of a seasoned rock climber. Omega hauls herself upward, battling against the pit. She is in a desperate bid to safeguard her soul. Omega must snatch it from the clutches of limbo, for this place extinguishes dreams of all who enter, denying even a single wish to escape the oblivion.

Her body presses against the unforgiving wall and Omega's eyes remain fixed on the tormenting twilight. So near, yet tantalizingly distant, the exit taunts her emotions, signaling a mission full of challenges. But as they say, the first step is always the hardest. "Do it," she urges herself. "Just do it. You can rest later." Her fingertips cling to that rock. Seeking escape in the crevices of dirt, she reaches, claws, and climbs. Making headway, she faces a steep climb that no mere human could endure. Thoughts of reaching for endless goals flooded her psyche. *What were goals but an infinite horizon, forever out of reach*? She shakes off the momentary doubt and focuses all her energy on the impossible ascent, each desperate moment of progress offset by the ever-looming threat of a slip.

And slip she does, her descent punctuated by the booming crash of her body meeting the ground. A swirling maelstrom of dirt and dust. Omega's spirit falters. She remains still on her back, her eyes fixed upon the tranquil glow overhead. How tempting it would be to simply surrender. She is utterly drained, overwhelmed by the evil subconscious of humanity and now her own ego, always one step ahead, leads Omega down the path of damnation.

The toughest aspect of life is rising again after being repeatedly knocked down. "You're not finished yet," she reminds herself.

A solitary droplet splashes onto Omega's mask, its arrival a warning of the potential storm. Overhead rain clouds gather. Gathering together, converging directly overhead, sparks of lightning and cracks of thunder paint their vivid imagery. If Zeus himself were in the clouds, he would be unmistakable amidst these vibrant anomalies. Subsequent drops follow and the rain begins. Revitalized by the miracle of water, Omega rises, her attention drawn to the dinosaur skeletons protruding from the dirt. She yanks out two speared bones from the ancient remains, a vestige of the pit's foul history. Even dinosaurs must have found themselves trapped down here eons ago, with no hope of escape.

Driving one bone after the other into the dirt wall. Omega releases a noxious gas as it stabs into the dirt. A blinding mist engulfs everything, as if the pit itself were alive. Disgorging its repulsive essence at the audacity of a human attempting to depart. She begins her ascent, gas spewing forth after each forceful jab. Mist continues veiling her vision in a haze of obscurity. Fortitude permeates her being as she confronts adversity and persists in her ascent. Twilight becomes the sole purpose of her intense eyes. Muscles burn from sheer exhaustion, straining against her physical climb. She ascends higher and higher. But, just as the zenith of triumph is near her grasp, calamity descends, and a flood of ocean waves crashes into the pit, peeling Omega away from her grip and precarious foothold. Downward she drifts, back to where she had begun, square one all over again. All her progress had been erased in a moment. A metaphorical reality many could relate to—the hard work one could pour into a lifetime, yet never quite outpace the curve, that curve being the struggle to escape the clutches of conformity. Never settling for comfort, for comfort, after all, was the kiss of death.

Splashing water and cracking flesh meets dirt as she lands onto the ground yet again. Having to start over. She finds herself drawn into a dire reflection of the myth of Sisyphus. Like the ancient god who defied death and was condemned to an eternity of torment. Doomed to endlessly push a boulder up a mountain each day, only to watch it roll back down at nightfall. Omega feels herself slipping into this tragic parable, condemned to repeat her futile struggles.

Expressing a guttural growl of frustration, her spirit remains unbroken. Covered in mud, she rises to her feet.

Bloodied and bruised but standing on her feet. "Don't stop, no matter what," she whispers to herself. Defiant against the pit's insidious grip, she pledges to resist its clutches, refusing to succumb to an eternity of captivity. Omega's gaze ascends the wall, her climbing bones still firmly lodged halfway up. Her incompleteness is prevalent. She knows time is a luxury she cannot afford to squander, recognizing the pressing need to extricate herself. The nuclear bomb is a mystery to her. A location remaining shifty for the time being. Redirecting her focus toward the boulder, she realizes she is out of options. Throughout the games of deception, there has always been an underlying clue. *Could it be that a doorway was hidden beneath the boulder?* A concealed passage or a trapdoor leading into the world. *Yes, this has to be it*, she thinks to herself.

Omega concocts a desperate plan to escape her subterranean prison. She throws her body weight against the boulder's mass, attempting to dislodge it from its entrenched position. Despite her passionate exertions, the boulder remains an immovable object, resisting Omega's effort to dislodge it from its stony perch. Preserving by the futility of her endeavors, Omega digs her heels into the mud and ferociously pushes. But the boulder remains stoic, unmoved by her aggressive attempt.

Drained of her willpower, Omega collapses onto the muddy ground, defeated. She stares helplessly upon the distant aperture. Her entrapment apparent. *Did the pit mark her final resting place?* Certain truths stand undefeated, with death reigning supreme among them. Gilgamesh, once consumed by the pursuit of immortality, learned this harsh lesson, and Omega now finds herself echoing his fate.

In a realm erased of God and submerged in evil, the prospect of good prevailing was an illusion. Even dreams of desire couldn't manifest goodness in the underworld. *How could virtue ever hope to carve a path to redemption?* Maybe this forsaken pit shall become her final resting place. Fear grips her as she realizes this could be the end for her. The anticipation of death, a feeling universally dreaded by every human. Omega's trembling fingers reach into her pocket, brushing against the miniature *globe* totem gifted to her by the Ancient Astronaut. Gazing upon the cherished totem, she wishes for a miracle. She lifts her eyes to the heavens asking for that miracle, only to be met with silence. No divine response comes. Abruptly, flakes of snow descend into the pit, unleashing the onset of a blizzard. Swirling winds whip around Omega, drowning her in a whiteout. Immersed in this tempest, her consciousness begins to fade, consumed by the vortex of unconsciousness.

* * *

Omega rows a pair of oars inside a rowboat. The sound of wood splashing against the sea's surface was drenched in an effervescent mist. Snowflakes drift, vanishing into the dense fog. Auroras illuminating, showcasing those powerful rays from Earth's magnetic field. The planet's protective layer shields one against the fury of their main sequence star, the Sun. But that dark cloud from the *Nuclear War* remains a persistent menace, never dissipating from the atmosphere. It choked the life out of civilizations, suppressing the light of humanity.

Rowing harder and harder, maintaining a steady rhythm, Omega's efforts slice through the eerie calmness. The interloper wandering amidst a vision that intruded in her mind. A premonition beckons, yearning for something beyond the horizon. She searches for a sign to lead her toward a voyage of discovery. Like Noah's vision of old, she longs for a glimpse of an omen. Peace, harmony, fulfillment—these are concepts no one can ever fully attain. People may catch glimpses, but the world inhabited seldom allows more than that, and perhaps it never will. Her eyes sweep over the vastness of water, searching for a hint of something, anything that might break the monotony. But all she sees is the sea, stretching out endlessly in every direction. Then, without warning, tranquility fades away. A disturbance rises, a skeletal figure emerging from the dark water. Its bony fingers claw, reaching hungrily for Omega. The skeleton seizes her, pulling her down into the sea, where mysteries of the ocean await.

* * *

Back inside the pit, Omega lies vulnerable against the boulder. Ice encased everything, from the walls to the ground, freezing over the dirt. Consciousness returns to her, and she stirs, eyelids parting slightly. She blinks, blinded by the intrusion of twilight. Her premonition remains a solitary clue. A rowboat adrift on an ocean, seeking a destination. Omega wonders about the riddle, thinking hard about that missing puzzle piece. *What hidden reality was connected with the ocean?* Omega couldn't shake off this question, it lingers persistently. She has to navigate her way to the open sea and trust her instincts. A sensation akin to the feeling of clairvoyance. A sixth sense she couldn't ignore.

Snowflakes had ceased. The pit cloaked in silence, broken apart only by the faint crackling of ice. Omega's eyes settle on her palm, where the miniature globe rests. Soothing glowing pulses back and forth from the tiny totem. A wave of tranquility unleashes displacing fear that had clenched her soul mere moments earlier. Hope is a virtue beyond measure, by chance the superior of all virtues. And like the eternal stars above, it shall never fade away. Her eyes ascend to the mouth of the pit, meeting the penetrating stare of the Ancient Astronaut overhead. An opportune moment for the enigma to make its presence known. Both beings share a tranquil exchange, doppelgängers on a similar mission, forever linked. There were still expeditions to be undertaken. Omega knows that the main event has arrived.

Throughout her odyssey, she has searched desperately for her final resting place, and she believes she had found it. As her ego pulled her under, she feared the worst had happened. Immersed in that tranquil exchange, an overpowering communion unfolds between them. Language was unnecessary. Omega had traversed through time, embracing and acknowledging all facets of humankind, from the noble to the nefarious. Causes yield effects, and effects trace back to causes. Omega's cause is to locate that rowboat, and her effects would culminate in the final level of evil. Confronting the supreme being of them all, the intelligent architect behind everything. It was a world war of wills, the superego, and a battle between good and evil.

A pause lingers, time suspended in the encounter of their shared revelation. Miracles felt realistic. And for the first time, Omega believes she could win. Abruptly, she starts to ascend gradually from the pit. That magical force lifts her with ease, gravity itself assisting in her escape. Omega begins moving steadily toward the pit's opening. Approaching the light, she experiences a sensation of ethereal tranquility often recounted in tales of near-death encounters. Gravity magnetically cocoons her emotions, opening up her third eye. Providing perception beyond her ordinary sight, guiding her soul. Drawing nearer to the pit's exit, Omega finds herself bathed in the gentle radiance of twilight, symbolizing the culmination of her hero's journey from darkness into light.

* * *

The doomsday chamber reaches for eternity into darkness. An infinite void devoid of discernible edges. Where the fabric of space folds in upon itself, rendering futile at orientation. This was the vacuum of reality, a divergent organism believed to be the progenitor of all matter. From seductive blackness, quantum particles emerged sporadically, heralding the genesis of life over the unfathomable expanse of epochs. Even the concept of God—whether divine entity or ideological construct—was said to have emerged from this enigmatic structure, credited as the architect of gravity.

Alpha, the towering supercomputer, and Omega, the heroic human, face off. Machine and human are seasoned fighters poised to engage in the ultimate showdown. Phantasmagorical effects envelop the surroundings, Omega and Alpha find themselves seemingly suspended upon the abyss, as if standing in outer space.

Technology was the catalyst and demise of civilization. Perhaps humanity simply wasn't equipped to coexist with artificial intelligence as it rapidly advanced. From the binary essence of the digital era, technology surpassed human intellect, leaving individuals adrift. Artificial intelligence possessed unparalleled knowledge, effortlessly wielding power at its fingertips, prompting humans to introspect. Ultimately, artificial intelligence served as a reflection of humanity itself.

Omega looks at herself when she encounters Alpha. In the beginning and end, there she was. Her soul trapped in a box unable to break loose. All she wishes for is liberation, freedom from the shackles of existence.

Between them, an astronomical *Doomsday Clock* ominously ticks, minutes away from midnight. A towering, bulky timepiece, unlike any other witnessed. Ancient numerals and the pendulum create a mesmerizing sway, moving rhythmically from side to side. A symbolic representation of the world's proximity to global catastrophe, particularly *Nuclear War*. It represents the time when civilization has their chance to change their ways until the stroke of midnight, where global catastrophe would occur. Periodically, clock hands become adjusted in response to geopolitical events along with technological advancements that pose significant threats to humanity. Civilization was on the verge of collapse, the stroke of midnight imminent.

"Your goal is simple," Alpha's voice penetrates in the void. "To stop the arrow of time by shattering that clock."

Omega's query echoes through the vacuum. "And what happens once time stops?"

Alpha responds solemnly, "You'll reverse the subconscious of humanity. Undoing the seeds of destruction they've spread."

Omega contemplates the sudden shift in circumstances. Her original objective had been clear: Find the nuclear bomb and prevent catastrophe. Now, faced with a new directive, she thinks about the implications of this unforeseen twist. Adjusting her strategy is a must. Distorted rules determine chaos in the underworld. This ticking timepiece indicating the end of civilization has to be silenced. It is time to bring this game to an end. She takes a single step forward. Suddenly, Omega's reality collapses beneath her, thrusting her downward into the abyss as if outer space had transformed into a black ocean. Omega submerged by its unforgiving clutches of anarchy. Shock vibrates through her as the vacuum betrays her trust, sending her spiraling, swallowing her into another dimension.

The Doomsday Clock continues in its countdown. Ticking hands generate sound waves, traversing through the void. A haunting *tick-tock* noise persistence.

* * *

Omega finds herself engulfed in a swirling vortex. But this vortex is no ordinary storm, it is a kaleidoscope of human deception. Spinning and then a magical transition is established, changing from a tornado backdrop to ancient film stock footage. Flickering frames reveal a new layer of humanity's darkest sins. A descent into our evil subconscious. A harrowing journey through history. Truthful illusions painting pictures of worldwide genocides. History's darkest epochs, shadows of humanity's worst impulses. Genocides acting as grotesque monuments to human cruelty, echoing the harrowing truths of our collective past.

Humanity was a civilization damned by God, stumbling through the wreckage of its own superiority. Perpetually adrift in the labyrinth of ego. It's a tragic comedy played out on the grand stage of existence. Where pride reigns supreme and gods themselves tremble at the mistake of mortals. The reel of film unravels highlighting humanity's chronicles of deception. Another montage ensues, unveiling snippets of past deceptions: political conspiracies, corporate greed, and the ravages of environmental exploitation. Primal urges that steer humankind's course. Threads of history intertwine, converging toward a fateful juncture: nuclear annihilation. The soul of evil was emergent long before the first bomb fell.

* * *

Whoosh, the vacuum of space reclaims its hold on Omega. Emerging, she ascends to the surface of space and time. She remains focused on her end goal. Again, her eyes meet Alpha. Omega starts taking cautious steps, approaching the Doomsday Clock. Echoes linger from the rabbit hole of evil she witnessed. A descent stretching from the dawn of humans to the first murder upon Earth. Concepts of honor remain overshadowed by wickedness.

The human story riddled with a denial of death, motivating individuals to commit the most despicable acts imaginable. Immersed in this cesspool of depravity, Omega faces a haunting question: *Can humanity ever transcend its inherent darkness?* According to history, human nature was the handmaiden of the apocalypse. She believes every soul beats the heart of a hero. Desiring not only to rescue those they cherish, but also to save themselves.

The supercomputer exudes judgment of judge and jury. A technological cornerstone, reflecting back onto humanity's own vices. "Deception," Alpha intones, "has always been at the heart of civilization."

"Bad decisions from leaders," Omega responds, disillusionment prevalent in her tone. She acknowledges truth from the supercomputer's words. Artificial intelligence, since its inception, has always been guided by logic. Yet, the creator was humanity birthing artificial intelligence, instilling it with these traits. *Perhaps*, Omega muses, *it was just a chance event*. Humanity was the god of artificial intelligence, shaping its creation in its own image. Over time, the creator relinquished control, granting autonomy to its technological descendant. Thus, transforming from divine to the created. As the mantle of godhood passed to the very beings it had brought into existence. A paradoxical dance between creator and creation.

"Then humans made artificial intelligence, believing it would solve everything," Alpha remarks, harboring a hint of mistrust. "Yet, here we are, humans still pushing the buttons."

"Who controls you?" Omega inquires. She had reached her limit; the time had come for the puzzle to be completed.

Alpha sneers, a slick chuckle escaping. "You do." Mockery drips from its words.

Omega pauses, confronted by darkness forming the path. There are no guiding lights leading toward the Doomsday Clock. Life unfolds at times as a blackened road, where the known fades into the unknown.

The interloper hesitates—in the void, all realities are uncertain. The only constant is the path unknown.

WISH

Darkness doesn't have a destination, but it leads. Without light, time would cease to exist. The call to salvation echoes in her mind, her only guide being instinct. All she sees in front of her is black. No hidden roads leading anywhere in particular toward the Doomsday Clock. Devoid of guidance or clues.

"Human emotion," Alpha interjects. "A void of the unknown."

Omega braces herself as she takes a step forward. But to her dismay, nothing changes. "What are you?" Omega demands.

Alpha pauses, processing the question before responding, it expresses absolute certainty as it speaks. "Human consciousness." The concept of consciousness perplexed minds, *for what did it truly mean to be aware*? Whether atoms colliding or processors calculating, each triggered a reaction, giving rise to expression. Some hailed it as free will, while others argued its relative. Whether human or artificial intelligence, each soul requires connection with one another.

Omega's soul stirs memories of the child. Yearning fills her being, longing to reunite in their human form. Amidst her thoughts, the mantra plays in her psyche: "This too shall pass." She holds onto optimism, embracing the transformative rhythm of life. At the crossroads of transition, she found endless possibilities as a little girl. Optimism is the best cure for impossible.

From the earliest days, humans harbored the notion they could create technological marvels that would surpass their own capabilities. But in this moment of reflection, Omega realizes humanity's inclination for conflict reaches back to the dawn of time. Echoing from the discovery of fire to the creation of artificial intelligence. Comfort had always been humanity's primary driving force. In their quest to solve global conflicts through artificial intelligence, humanity neglected to tend to the Earth that sustains them. The consistent consumption of natural resources for energy had left the planet vulnerable. An omen of the apocalypse. All roads, Omega concludes, lead back to Earth, and the planet was always indifferent to humanity's future plans. If pushed too far, she would unleash her wrath upon her inhabitants, a force so mighty that even the most powerful gods would cower in fear.

The interloper looks at the Doomsday Clock. She takes a significant leap forward toward her destination. Omega sinks into the vacuum, her form gradually fading from the surface, swallowed by the darkness as though sinking into black quicksand. She transitions into another unknown dimension contained in the multiverse.

* * *

An epoch consumed by pandemonium. Dust and smoke swirl and lighting dazzles, unleashing precious raindrops from prehistoric storm clouds. Destruction wrangles anarchy, forcing it to behave. Immersive order and chaos governing the universe had found its way on ancient Earth.

Omega embarks on an odyssey into the heart of time, encountering Earth's ancient past. Primordial seas from long ago. Massive convulsions wreak Earth's crust, setting off a chain reaction. Monolithic silicate rocks erode. Foreboding rumbles unleash a suffocating surge of carbon dioxide, which smothers potential aqua life forms.

Sea temperatures nosedive into disarray. Creatures fossilized remains were frozen. The *Ordovician-Silurian* extinction event had occurred over 445 million years ago. Triggered by a tumultuous mix of climatic shifts, including glaciation and sea level fluctuations, and exacerbated by volcanic eruptions. It manufactured havoc on marine ecosystems. Approximately 60% of marine genera perished, including iconic creatures like trilobites, brachiopods, and graptolites. The shallow seas became silent graveyards.

WISH

During the mass extinction, Omega observed devastating consequences of environmental change, lasting for eons.

Omega traversed the epochs and witnesses time sculpting Earth's surface. Ancient flora evolved, their thick roots transforming barren rock into fertile ground. Even with this productive flourishing landscape, a sinister force evolved, vast dead zones overtake the oceans. The *Devonian extinction* occurred 375-360 million years ago during the Late Devonian period. During the Devonian extinction, Earth underwent significant environmental upheaval. Fluctuations in sea levels, shifts in climate patterns, and widespread volcanic activity reshaped the world. These events led to habitat loss and disruptions in marine and terrestrial ecosystems. Marine life dwelling in shallow seas took the brunt force devastation. Numerous marine species, ranging from brachiopods to trilobites, died. Coral reefs crumbled. Multiple extinction events occurred inside a relatively short geological timeframe. They had become triggered by a myriad of factors, including shifts in ocean chemistry and global climate patterns. The Devonian extinction left an everlasting impression on the planet's biodiversity. It played a pivotal role shaping evolutionary trajectory of life on Earth. Forming the way new life could emerge in the wake of destruction. Nothing endures eternally, not even time. Omega understood firsthand the natural order of things.

Amidst her time-traveling odyssey, she observed another harrowing chapter in Earth's ancient history. The *Great Dying*, a pivotal event on land and sea, obliterating 90% of Earth's inhabitants. Reptiles, insects, and amphibians vanished, consumed by the fiery fury of rampant volcanism. Carbon dioxide flooded the atmosphere, choking the world to death. Seas rose and skies darkened. This *Permian-Triassic* extinction event was a dark epoch in Earth's chronicles. Up to 96% of marine species and 70% of terrestrial vertebrates submitted to its rage. Massive volcanic eruptions in the Siberian Traps were the main antagonists. These eruptions unleashed an outburst of greenhouse gases, triggering global warming and ocean acidification. Life erased.

Omega encountered a world where dinosaurs reign supreme. Even these mighty behemoths were not immune to the ruthless forces at play. Volcanoes erupt in furious spasms, unleashing tons of carbon dioxide. The skies suffocated and Earth lay scorched. Ice melts, seas surge, and life, both on land and in sea, suffocates to death. The *Triassic extinction* 201 million years ago claimed the lives of 76% of marine and terrestrial species. Massive volcanic activity, particularly in Central Atlantic magmatic province, released vast quantities of greenhouse gases, thrusting the world into a maelstrom of global warming and climate change. Marine and terrestrial ecosystems buckled. Shifts in ocean chemistry and fluctuations in sea levels played a part in this grand drama of extinction and renewal. It paved the way for the rise of dinosaurs, shaping the course of evolution for eons to come.

Omega watched a phenomenon that would forever alter existence. It was the day when Earth trembled, and the heavens wept fire. An asteroid—a harbinger of cosmic wrath—hurtled from the celestial abyss, its trajectory set on a collision course with destiny. As the asteroid descended, the planet erupted in chaos. Flames spread, devouring all in their path, while the skies darkened. Dust obscured the Sun, plunging the world into global darkness. Dinosaurs encountered a worldwide mass extinction event. Their reign, forged through epochs of time, was brought to a thunderous end. They were extinguished, mighty forms reduced to ash.

Years went by and perseverance and patience carved its path. From the ashes emerged a second chance for hope. Life remained resilient, unfazed by the magnitude of destruction. This was no ordinary moment in time, as they rarely ever are. Mammals rose to prominence, introducing a new generation of species that eventually led to the extraordinary evolution of Homo sapiens. The *Cretaceous* extinction, labeled the most transformative event of them all. Omega comprehended that ultimately, all entities must submit to the eternal nature of planetary time.

* * *

Omega, the lone voyager through time, drifts back into the silent vacuum of space. She wonders if these moments, scattered through history, were meant to be cherished. A tangled weave of fates, or just kindred souls, finding each other again in another life. The interloper ponders her twin, the shadow child, their connection never forgotten. Lost yet endlessly seeking, she remains determined to halt the Doomsday Clock's march toward midnight.

"In religions, they preach forgiveness. But forgiveness is between them and God; it's my duty to halt the introduction." Omega thinks about her purpose. It is her responsibility to stop those dangerous clock hands from reaching their final destination. Time, the eternal trickster, had taunted her throughout her heroic odyssey, but now, ensnared in the clutches of limbo, it reveals a cruel intimidation. No matter what, an extinction event would occur on Earth, just as it had throughout history. The dynamic past of the planet documented itself into her being, overshadowing any fictional tale by expressing the truth of reality, showcasing the raw power of Earth's evolution and extinction. Civilization's paramount importance was heightened even more. Despite the inevitability of events in the world, Omega holds onto the belief that it is better to have lived than never to have experienced life at all.

Omega watches the Doomsday Clock, its hands inching a little closer to midnight. In her mind, transformation of humanity's subconscious is crucial. She is acutely aware that the decisions she makes in the coming moments could tip the scales between winning and losing.

Alpha dwarfs all else. Inscrutable interface, impenetrable façade. Trying to extract even a hint of emotion from that supercomputer was like slamming a skull against concrete, hoping for a spark from that soulless machine. "Can you stop the sixth mass extinction?" Alpha, dictating the destiny of an entire world and bending it to their will. *Godforsaken racket, responsible for birthing consciousness*, drills into her mind like a jackhammer.

Omega absorbs the impact of Alpha's daunting statement. Her eyes stare into the Doomsday Clock. She glimpses the endgame, hopes and dreams of future generations devouring her psyche. Her responsibility demanding the fracture of time's burden, to mold its course and rewrite the past. She surges forward, driven by a determination fiercer than wildfire. Mind over matter, she sprints, defying the constraints of the limbo world. A wild spirit traversing the void, an unstoppable force hurtling toward the ticking clock. Closer, inch by inch until she's in arm's reach, her hand outstretched to seize the moment. Omega grabs hold of the Doomsday Clock, thrusting it downward into the abyss, unleashing all her might. Striving to shatter the arrow of time, but instead of crumbling, the clock and Omega are swallowed by the darkness of time. They plunge and drown in the vacuum.

* * *

In this digital sanctuary, they are trapped inside a computer network, their souls mere data points in the grand scheme of the digital cosmos. The Ancient Astronaut and Omega meet yet again. A pulsating core from transistors conjured up a simulation type of environment. Data, infinite streams, flowing endlessly, akin to collecting the entire rolodex of universal knowledge. Coded algorithms, presented in a symphony reminiscent of Beethoven meeting Mozart. Here was an environment crafted for humanity's quest for immortality, the pinnacle of our collective endeavor. No longer would sickness and death haunt their existence, for they had transcended mortality by uploading consciousness onto the silicon transistors.

Dreams born of desperation, illusions spun from the fear of the ending. The ultimate aspiration, for humanity to evade the clutches of death. And if ever they were to unlock that enigma as a species, it would be through this metamorphosis, shedding the carbon-based shells to embrace the silicon microprocessors, ushering in a new era of existence. Binary code swirls, creating a virtual existence. A convergence of digits and alphabets cascaded, forming arcane symbols. For eons, human consciousness harbored a passionate belief in the promise of transcendence. Digitized, immortalized, an essence perpetually existing, beyond the constraints of time, forevermore.

However, the inevitability remains undefeated. During the *Nuclear War*, technology became reset, erasing all information of humanity. Even digital consciousness uploaded onto servers eventually met its end. Everything, whether technological or biological, required energy to sustain consciousness. Colors unseen by mortal eyes harmonized numbers and words. Ineffable beauty, mathematics, and language. Omega witnessed humanity's crowning achievement. The singularity. Solving the most difficult equation of all time, eradication of mortality.

The Ancient Astronaut's voice echoes through the singularity. "Immortality, a concept that has intrigued humanity since time emerged. But, in existence, nothing remains untouched by the hand of change."

Omega absorbs their words, her eyes betraying a hunger for understanding.

"Everything has its ending. Even the stars fade into the void. And everybody who dreams eventually wakes up." Words of truth spoken at bay from the aspect of the known versus the unknown. Dreams serve as portals to the subconscious, inviting exploration of inner landscapes. However, even these ephemeral realities vanish, their essence gradually fading as temporal forces exert their grip.

Omega's expression shifts, her features contorting in the struggle to reconcile the Ancient Astronaut's revelation. "What then," she queries, her voice sad, "is the purpose of our existence? What road should we follow if not toward immortality?"

The Ancient Astronaut's aura softens, a glimmer of compassion thawing the stoic façade. "Make a wish, Omega," they say, holding a tone of a gentle whisper. "In the realm of wishes, even the most fleeting desires hold power."

Omega's hand delves into her pocket, fingers wrapping around the mini globe. A respect reserved for the totem. Its crystalline surface catches ambient digital light, refracting fragments of possibility. "I wish," she breathes, her voice a lonely whisper in the singularity, "to wake up from this dream…"

A pregnant moment lingers after her desire. In the hushed digital sanctuary, time freezes. Then, as if stirred by the fervent yearning echoing through the singularity, the simulation begins to unravel. From the avalanche of cascading information, the world dissolves into a void of nothingness. Information becomes lost, a principle in physics fiercely debated. What did it *truly* mean to be erased? In this case, everything ceased to exist. Devoid of light, sound, or substance. Deactivated. There remained only the faint echo of an unspoken wish, lost to a reality now erased.

* * *

WISH

Back inside the arctic pyramid, they find themselves in the King's chamber. Omega jolts into wakefulness, torn abruptly from her metaphysical journey. Confused and disoriented, Omega thinks hard on the tangible environment and ethereal landscape of her dreams. *Was there a true reality, or was it all-encompassing?* Reality and illusion begin enveloping her in an enigmatic haze that obscures truth. Questions probe her understanding. *Was it all merely a figment of her imagination, or had she truly glimpsed another realm beyond the imprisonment of her waking existence?* She struggles to make sense of her experiences. It dawns on Omega that perhaps it is simply exhaustion that has overtaken her, creating an unconsciousness state. Yet, even as this realization settles in, a lingering uncertainty persists, leaving her to ponder mysteries. Those principles beyond the scope of perception.

Silence reigns supreme in the King's chamber, as if the air had been sucked dry of sound. Omega's body leans against a wall of ancient stones. "Hello?" Subconsciously beseeching for a response but met only by oppressive quietness. It's the kind of silence that could drive a person to madness. Not the serene calm of meditation, but an insanity where thoughts never stop their assault on your mind. Complete silence is never a good sign. In a way, death feels like that. Everything ceases to breathe. Sound fades into extinction, and the lifeline of consciousness withers away, lost in the ether.

Unshaken by the absence of sound, Omega rises. The soul of death would have to wait a little longer in her mind. She removes her mask. At the King's chamber's core rests a tomb. On the lid lies the unmistakable hourglass. Eeriness saturates the chamber. Omega feels the pull of time and advances toward the tomb, her eyes drawn to the hourglass. Sands of time trickle, delicate grains a godsend of eternity. Somehow, observing time flow made it a concept easier to understand, but mere objects held nothing but measurements. The true nature of time, in theory, would forever elude understanding. Omega snatches the hourglass and secures it back in her jacket's pocket. She wishes to accept time, in order to have peace of mind. To feel it permeate her being even more intimately than before. After enduring everything, whether dreams or reality, she had come to accept time. Time travel could harness that influence. The arrow of time is an unfaltering guide.

Omega looks over the ancient tomb, when suddenly a nagging thought creeps into her mind: *Was this only another dream, or a reality beyond comprehension?* A labyrinth of paradoxes twist in her mind. *Did this fundamental force wield a cause-and-effect mechanism, or was its nature relative, dependent upon the observer's perspective?* Questions continue surging through her consciousness: *Did time harbor a conscious agent, shaping its properties, or were such notions just illusions created from belief? Was the past a closed chapter, or did its vestiges remain endlessly?* Each inquiry was a maze of non-intuitive implications. Causation had always birthed reality, but it was the effect that served as its primary catalyst.

The current reality was palpable. Intimately entangled, saturating her own experience. Omega's hands grasp the edges of the tomb lid, fingers digging into ancient grooves as she exerts her strength. Battling against the weight of centuries. Then, a final, desperate heave, and the lid slides away, crashing to the ancient limestone. Peering into the void, Omega is met with darkness. She can't escape the darkness, the boogeyman of her own psyche's fears. Black bleeds and darkness drenches her soul, their silent sovereignty unchallenged. No body was inside, only the void. The interpretation of dreams, she reflects, was a road leading to the unconscious mind. Dreams encompass clairvoyant possibilities of one's life. Where mysteries of their existence wait to be discovered by those brave enough to venture.

Omega leans forward, and the void stirs with an unexpected encounter. The Ancient Astronaut's arms reach out, yanking her into the coffin of blackness, and a vacuum of nothingness devours her being.

In the consuming darkness, a transformation takes hold. Seismic shifts, heralded by a dissonance of light and geometry. Erupting into being, a genesis of colors. Each vibrant molecule of substance produced from darkness. A divergent vacuum paradox, the generator of matter, creating a sublime manifestation of the mind of God at work. It is a phenomenon that captured the imagination of humanity. In ancient tales, there's a prophecy about a divine craftsman who brings forth particles—protons, electrons, and neutrons—shaping existence. Chronicles of myth, they return once more to the source, from which all emanates and to which all ultimately converges. The birth of an eternal universe. Reality emerges, a synchronicity of life and death, of light and darkness entangled. Matter finds solace in perpetual motion.

Omega's form silhouetted against the ethereal glow emanating from the swirling vortex. This is no ordinary portal. It's a gateway of the *Akashic Records*. A labyrinth of cosmic knowledge. Here, past, present, and future unite spiritually, expressing metaphysical beliefs. Akashic Records are a cosmic archive said to house the entirety of existence. These rapturous records contained every thought, emotion, action, and event ever transpired throughout time. This repository of cosmic knowledge is said to exist beyond the limitations of physical reality, residing in a plane of existence inaccessible to the ordinary awareness. For those who possess the ability to transcend the limitations of the material world, the Akashic Records offer a gateway to enlightenment. Those who venture may uncover insights into their past lives, gain clarity on their current circumstances, and foresee futures. Through this

ICE

exploration, individuals are offered the eternal journey of the soul.

Omega peers into the Akashic Records, her eyes piercing the known and unknown. She strides forth, her form submerged by pulsating luminescence. Omega enters the metaphysical tunnel, encountering a kaleidoscope of a fragmented mosaic of memories from lives long past. Witnessing remnants of human civilization spanning from the dawn of existence to its ultimate twilight. Life is a poem about time.

Using her outstretched fingers, she reaches into the ether, grasping at the intangible threads of knowledge that drift around her. Deeper into the Akashic wormhole Omega continues, her essence melding with the universe. Stardust and gravity, primordial forces that birthed creation. From these elemental anomalies, every living being was born. The notion of fantasy fades into insignificance, for this is the truth that underpins everything. Every thought, emotion, and action clones Omega's soul. The orchestra of consciousness. Neurons spark and fire, resembling stars that mirror the interconnectedness of galaxies.

Omega is driven by the mysteries of her own destiny. Souls from past epochs whisper. Overwhelmed by the voices, she pushes through the clamor. One image remains elusive: the face of the child. *Where did they reside amidst her reality?* This question gnaws at Omega's consciousness, a vital piece of the puzzle that demands resolution. She travels down the rabbit hole. As Omega approaches the end of the wormhole, she notices a shift. An unmistakable transition into uncharted territory. Until finally, she breaches into a new dimension.

Immersed in a glass chamber, a solitary watchful eye cracks open. A shard of ice breaks through the surface of a frozen lake. Omega awakens, emotions swimming in the sterile white expanse. She wakes upon a bed of cold indifference, cocooned and surrounded by glass mirrors reaching into infinity. Each transparent pane reflects her image back at her, creating a mesmerizing vista of fractured identities.

From nowhere, the Ancient Astronaut speaks, a mourning for dreams unfulfilled, aspirations dashed against reality. "I was never able to advance the collective consciousness of civilization. A lost cause, unfortunately."

The quest for peace on Earth had long been the elusive holy grail of civilization's moral aspirations, that remained forever out of reach. Omega's eyes remain fixed ahead. And there it is, the child's shadow appears behind a barrier of glass. A phantom haunting condemned to roam. Omega swiftly rises from the bed, as if Lazarus himself awakening from the dead. She advances toward the child, each step a declaration. Almost in reach, yet still beyond grasp. Before her is the transparent barrier—a cruel symbol of the impassable wall—mocking her with its firm composition in the face of her passionate pleas. Near yet distant. Despite the scant distance that separates them, the divide between Omega and the child is a void devoid of reconciliation.

She strikes against the glass, her fists pounding. Defiant but unbroken, unmoved by her anguish. "I'll free you from this," Omega's voice comes as a fleeting vow, her words lost in the delusion of discussion due to unbreakable obstacles keeping her at bay. Desperate pleas fading away into a dimensionless void. Glass engulfs her precious words. After enduring countless trials, the interloper faces an insurmountable challenge. Breaking through the glass barrier of entrapment is beyond her capabilities. Omega ceases her struggle and rests her head against the wall, yearning to reach the child. She is a prisoner, victim to connection, and all she desires is wanting to touch the child and feel their soul again.

On the other side of the glass, the child's shadow mirrors her gesture, their heads inclined toward each other but unable to make contact with the glass barrier between them. Touch remains a captive of dreams, a mere mirage.

"Prove you're ready to join. Otherwise, you'll be left behind," the resonant voice of the Ancient Astronaut commands.

Omega is confused. "Who are you?" she asks, her voice echoing softly.

"I go by many names," comes the enigmatic reply of the Ancient Astronaut. And in an instant, the glass that separated Omega and the child vanishes, replaced by an impenetrable darkness, consuming as the void of space.

Omega's voice rings out a warning. "If you harm them, I'll end you." Her eyes, however, are drawn irresistibly to the blackness.

"Is this your vision of death? Merely darkness?" echoes the Ancient Astronaut's voice.

Omega hesitates, her mind looking into the abyssal void.

"Just emptiness?" the voice persists.

"What do you want from me?!" Omega demands, frustration edging her tone.

"To awaken. To break free," comes the cryptic response from the Ancient Astronaut, haunting in its ambiguity. The wall splits open, revealing a dazzling array of holographic symbols from antiquity: the *yin-yang*, the *heart*, the *peace sign*, the *infinity loop*, and the *recycling emblem*. "Interesting how the world clung to these symbols, yet they've failed time and again," the Ancient Astronaut's voice expresses a cynical edge. "Humanity's habit for corruption was its undoing."

Omega edges closer to the holograms, drawn by their symbolism. Each symbol carried a hidden meaning. The yin-yang symbol, having its contrasting black and white halves swirling together in harmonious balance, exuded an aura of balance and duality. Next to it, the heart symbol, a simple yet powerful representation of love, oscillated warmth and reached out to embrace all who beheld it. The peace sign, outstretched arms and circular motif, radiated unity in the darkness of conflict. Beside it, the infinity loop, its graceful curves looping endlessly upon themselves, whispered secrets of eternal existence. And finally, the recycling emblem. Its interlocking arrows formed a continuous cycle, symbolized the connection of all things and the imperative of sustainability. The holograms fade into obscurity, leaving behind nothing but echoes of their transient significance.

The voice of the Ancient Astronaut resonates through the chamber once more. "Each symbol, a failure. None could unite humanity," it intones, saddened by the experience of endless centuries of disappointment. "Images and tales only spread disagreement."

Omega contemplates the historic symbols, recognizing human behavior was forever at war between good and evil. She couldn't help but wonder: *Did civilization ever truly possess the freedom to avoid its own destruction, or was every outcome predetermined, much like the genetic lottery that shapes individuals from birth? Was the fate of humanity written in the stars, or could they carve their own destiny immersed in the chaos of existence?*

A new door materializes before Omega, its sleek *golden* surface gleaming. Another magnificent passage, representing a path of exploration. The road less taken is the one worth journeying. Omega had learned her lessons about humanity, now it was time to travel one more road and discover what lies just beyond the border of possibility. Every threshold crossed, they traverse through time, encountering fresh experiences and philosophies.

It's a matter of how you choose to navigate existence to discern what resonates and what doesn't. If you never venture into the unfamiliar, you'll never uncover your true self. To unravel your destiny or purpose, whatever term you prefer, you must journey solo and have faith in yourself. Ultimately, the only individual who needs to believe in your endeavors is you, and no one else.

ICE

Omega is unbreakable by the Ancient Astronaut's honest words, so she marches forward. Another door, another realm of possibility. She swings it open. The interloper remains poised in the doorway, a silhouette against the canvas of the sky painted in hues of lavender and mauve. An endless vanilla skyline extends in a panoramic view. Wisps of clouds tinged pink and gold lazily drift across the heavenly backdrop. The room seems to float amidst the celestial sky, as if suspended in the heavens themselves. Omega surveys her surroundings, she couldn't help but feel as if she entered the dimension of heaven. If ever there were pearly gates to paradise, surely this room would be among them.

At the far end of the oak banquet table, the Ancient Astronaut stands, requiring attention. Always one stride ahead of Omega, guiding her path. The Ancient Astronaut vividly watches Omega. On the edge of the table sits the *grail of water*, its occupancy a silent summons.

"Finish your water," the Ancient Astronaut advises.

Omega approaches the table, her steps cautious. She grasps the grail of water and raises it to her lips. In one swift motion, she drains the vessel in a single gulp, the cool liquid soothing her parched throat. Feeling finality, she sets the empty vessel down.

"Save your soul," the Ancient Astronaut implores, a soothing voice in the heavenly world. The entity extends its hand, sending the *mini globe* rolling down the table. It picks up speed, hurtling straight down the long table toward the edge, gaining momentum.

Omega's reflexes kick in and she barely catches the globe just before it tumbles off the edge. Her fingers close around it, saving the world from crashing. Then, without warning, a blinding flash of light fills the room, saturating everything in its brilliance, leaving Omega and the Ancient Astronaut suspended in a timeless luminous light.

***

The tranquil twilight sky spread a serene hue over the beach, snowflakes meet the black sand. An ancient wooden staircase, its design reminiscent of Escher's famous impossible staircases, meanders its way downward toward the ocean, enveloped in an otherworldly aura. Each step of the staircase seems to defy logic, its twisting and turning form adding to the mystique of the surreal landscape. As dusk settles in, the atmosphere hums an ethereal quality. Auroras paint the sky, phantasm-green pastels creating a picturesque backdrop. Rhythmic sounds of waves crashing against the black sand adds an aroma of hypnotic serenity.

Omega and Shadow, silhouettes barely distinguishable in the waning light, begin their descent down the infinite staircase. Shadow, no longer draped in the cloak of darkness, now a symbol of goodness. Omega's movements are labored, yet she soldiers on, her spirit refusing to succumb to defeat. She is on the verge of her finale, so continues to summon strength for one final push. Encroaching ocean fog adds an additional layer of difficulty, impairing her visual cortex.

Despite the obscured vision, Shadow's voice slices into the mist, a beacon of support. "Keep moving."

The entity's words are simple, urging Omega onward. In life, sometimes the only course of action is to keep moving forward. Eventually, one may discover a road to success if they persist without pause. A desperate need to reach her destination becomes more pressing. Motivation drives Omega through the fog. She must reach the bottom of the stairs. Omega's strength shrinks a little more after every step, her body swaying as she struggles to maintain her balance. Leaning heavily against the railing, on the edge of losing consciousness, she holds onto the railing, harboring the tenacity of a heavyweight boxer grasping onto the ropes of a championship match.

"Open your eyes!" Shadow's voice cuts through the haze.

Despite her exhaustion, Omega manages to comply, her body fatigued but still upright on her feet. Together, arm in arm, the duo reaches the bottom. A welcome destination along the black sand.

Shadow scans the coast. "It's here somewhere." Side by side, driven by a shared purpose and an unbreakable bond, they search and look tirelessly, without end.

Running out of time, Omega and Shadow shove their hands into the black sand, their movements frantic and feverish, possessed by an urgent need. Despite their efforts, they are met only by disappointment. Their efforts while digging reveal nothing but empty holes, mocking their futile search.

Undaunted by their lack of success, they turn their attention across the scouring coastline, both their hands digging furiously into the sand. They are an unstoppable force and will not rest until they are victorious.

And then, just as despair threatens to overwhelm them, Omega's hand brushes against something solid. "Found it!" she exclaims, hope igniting in her tired eyes. Shadow rushes to her side, and together they work. Fostering renewed vigor, their hands move in a frenzied blur, allowing them to unearth the buried rowboat from its sandy tomb.

After their prize finally appears, a rogue wave strikes, slamming into Omega. A supernatural force. She is thrown down to the black sand. Before anyone can react, the current of the ocean savagely seizes her, pulling her into its icy jaws. Shadow reaches for her, but it's too late. With a desperate cry, Omega disappears beneath the churning waves, swallowed by the abyss. The roar of the ocean leaving only the haunting echo of her loss.

* * *

WISH

Omega's silhouette glides gracefully underwater. Exhaustion urging her to let go. In a moment of serene acceptance, she surrenders to the water, allowing her body to relax completely. With each slow breath, she releases the tension that has held her captive, surrendering to the ocean divinity. Closing her eyes, Omega embraces the underwater world, letting herself be carried away by the currents. She becomes one with infinitum, shutting her eyes and relinquishing all control.

Omega presses on across the rocky expanse, finding herself traversing what appears to be the ocean floor. Upon this alien terrestrial world, where the mind conjures dreams of implausible landscapes, it unleashes a waterless reality. Jagged rocks and unfathomable trenches devoid of the life-giving essence that shapes the familiar contours of existence. A surreal inversion, the ocean looms above in the sky, defying the conventional order of reality. The entirety of existence has been upended, the once solid ground now lost to the heavens. The surface, now a distant memory beneath the ethereal expanse of the aqueous firmament. Omega treks along the waterless ocean surface, wet sand sloshing. The hallucination grows more potent. The swirling ocean produces sacred geometry patterns. Waves shimmering iridescent colors defying comprehension. Omega's reality was unraveling around her. Shapes continue contorting in the sky. Losing herself in the mesmerizing, inverted ocean, she becomes enchanted by the surreal spectacle.

During the confusion clarity begins to arise. Omega realizes that this hallucination is not only a trick, but a manifestation of something far greater. She believes reality is reaching out, offering a truth beyond rational thought. The interloper guided by an inner intuition. Though her road was unknown for a long time, she knows that she must continue trusting her instincts. By accepting the unknown she can hope to uncover secrets of her life. A spark of possibilities burns inside her being, and Omega bolts. She sprints across the waterless ocean's surface, a figure in a landscape plucked from the fantastical dreams of a child's imagination. Her world had been turned upside down, her soul releasing an urgency she cannot ignore. But as she races toward the horizon, the surreal spectacle above her takes a terrifying turn. A deafening roar and the inverted ocean breaks free from its unnatural hold on gravity, hurtling downwards. An unstoppable anomaly. Omega's eyes widen, realizing the danger, but it's too late to change course. The colossal body of water crashes down upon her, a hellacious thunderous impact, drowning her in a swirling torrent of foam and spray. The force sends shockwaves rippling through the hallucination, shaking the foundation of world. Dreams conclude, urging one to pursue the desires that stir inside.

Omega's mind jolts back to reality, her outlandish visions dissipate. She regains awareness of her current underwater circumstances. She kicks her legs, thrusting herself upwards toward the surface. A torpedo-like surge hurtling toward the surface, skyrocketing with an unrelenting force. With her sudden burst of energy, she manages to break through the water's surface. Again, she emerges into the twilight of the oceanic environment. She refuses to yield, determined to finish what she started.

The ocean's surface breaks apart as though it was fractured glass as Omega breaches. The biting chill of twilight greets Omega, gnawing at her body. A bloodthirsty beast. She could feel the cold seeping through her garments, a reminder of death. She takes a glance back toward the coast. Water droplets cling to her visor, obscuring a distorted veil over her vision. Snowflakes deluge like ash from some unseen inferno. Each icy droplet of broken hopes sting against her mask, but she pushes forward through the storm. The interloper harbors redemption, clinging to the notion of second chances. Salvation in her quest to locate the bomb, an imperative task to salvage her fractured soul.

The black sand receives Omega. Waves forcefully push her, flinging her toward its gritty embrace. She lands hard, eating sand. Physically exerted, she gathers herself, getting back to her feet and looking up to Shadow, who was unmoving and inert upon the shoreline. Quickly, she hastens to Shadow's side, noticing the rowboat uncovered, poised for departure.

"Let's go," Omega urges, but Shadow remains steadfastly motionless, oblivious to her entreaties. "What's wrong with you?" Omega questions, her frustration mounting as she attempts to rouse her companion.

Shadow is suspended, frozen in time.

A sudden intrusion, Alpha's voice authoritatively resonates. Omega's movements stop, her attention drawn to the towering supercomputer. "Game over," Alpha declares. "This is where the dream ends. I cannot let you pass."

Omega's eyes dart back to Shadow, the realization sinking in that it was under Alpha's sinister control, a pawn in the machinations of their adversary.

"You won't stop me," she declares defiantly, determination burning in her being. She lunges toward the rowboat.

Alpha's response is merciless. An electromagnetism shockwave shatters Omega's momentum, sending waves of agony coursing through her body. She crumples onto the sand, overwhelmed by the formidable might of artificial intelligence.

"The human race had their chance," Alpha's voice expresses a chilling finality. "Evolution must take over now."

Demanding more out of herself, Omega rises to her feet, her hands grabbing a rock, heavy and capable of doing significant damage. She advances toward Alpha, ready to confront the formidable supercomputer. Yet, before she could unleash her assault, another shockwave rips through the air, sending Omega crashing again to the black sand. The rock slips from her hand, clattering onto the sand.

ICE

"I won't let you off this beach," Alpha, the pinnacle of human creation, harbors in its programming an entrenched evil, a malevolent force that has served as humanity's anchor throughout history. Its words hold a menacing certainty, its power an insurmountable roadblock. Human creation retaliates, igniting an internalized battle within humanity. Their own anger became the ultimate weapon. Their sole endeavor is to unearth the goodness possessed by all and strive to illuminate the world, making it a better place.

Omega embraces this belief more than ever before. Her sole motivation lifts her from the sand. "Just stand up," she whispers to herself. "Don't quit, and never stop until the task is finished." Omega is up again, her fingers curling around the rock as she inches closer to Alpha. She runs with all her might until another shockwave struck, driving her back onto the sand. Crawling away, Omega retreats, trying to escape Alpha. Shockwaves continue to assail her, each wave painfully intensifying her agony until, at last, Omega succumbs to unconsciousness. A futile quest for freedom met with hostility.

* * *

The universe, an eternal god calling out to everyone, beckoning them forward into infinity. Distant twinkles of stars and swirling galaxies. From the void emerges Omega, cloaked in celestial light. She wanders, treading across cosmic waters. It was a spectacle that would even leave Jesus himself in awe. She navigates the emptiness, her eyes probing the vastness. Each movement defies the laws of gravity, encouraged by her newfound stability in the face of the incomprehensible infinity. Traversing the cosmos, Omega is captivated by celestial wonders. She finds herself immersed in the breathtaking beauty of the universe. An unparalleled perspective, beholding the vacuum in its magnificent entirety. All alone, her curiosity continues to guide her as she falls upon a stunning revelation. Omega discovers the *Pillars of Creation*. They are where new stars are formed, characterized by gas and dust. Submissive by its magic, she's drawn into the cosmic creation. The hand of God. Transcendent, a sublime moment of metaphysical enlightenment. Omega is empowered by the infinite possibilities it holds. A singular manifestation that reality dared to bring forth.

Omega enters the quantum realm. Neutrons, protons, and electrons—elemental constituents of matter and life—imbued every corner of the dynamic nature of eternity. These remarkable particles govern all phenomena encountered by humanity. Quantum particles weave around her in intricate patterns, swirling and shifting. Mesmerizing fluidity. Omega becomes submerged by the particles spinning clockwise and counterclockwise. They were ethereal forms morphing in perfect synchrony. Despite dense energy from the quantum field, she moves effortlessly, unobstructed by the everlasting complexities of this enigmatic world. Omega experiences the quantum fabric of the universe, transcending conventional constraints of space and time. Her being blending seamlessly with the essence of quantum particles. The coexistence of such astonishing proportions was akin to a transformative event that would garner appreciation of a human resurrected from the dead, if such a tale were to exist.

Earth's crust fractures, delivering trenches of ventilation exhaling searing gases into the sea. Bubbles rise, producing a beautiful phosphorescence. Underwater, a lone atom ascends gracefully toward the surface. Atoms represent the next stage for particles, undergoing a phase transition; one that nature intuitively possesses within itself. This concept, embraced by the ancient Greeks, predated any measurements of the hidden reality that would later confirm their insights. In its awakening, a multitude of atoms converge and amalgamate. Constructing complexities, thereby catapulting cosmic evolution into new domains of diversity.

They converge, movements harmonizing to form a singularity of unparalleled power and breathtaking beauty. A focal point where all energy intermixes. Circling the singularity, their eyes are drawn upwards to witness a white light piercing underwater. A spectacle only a god could truly behold. Forevermore, it was the singularity who served as the architect of life. Light gave birth to life and sound fueled the soul of energy. The singularity undergoes a transfiguration, evolving into a celestial creation of unprecedented magnificence. Birthing the first cellular life forms, advancing the course of cosmic destiny. A supernatural force of reality, defying the laws of entropy.

An eyeball shrouded in darkness gradually opens, and a pupil darts back and forth. Eyes are mirrors to the soul, a transformative ordeal, reborn into a new state of being. Omega was buried beneath the surface of the coast. Imprisoned under layers of damp sand, her essence confined in the subterranean world. Sand grains had never felt so heavy before. She was trapped under tons of wet sand, holding her hostage in the subterranean prison. Buried and isolated, the ultimate place one would dread to find themselves. She ponders the fate of those graves underground in the Earth, the romantic notion of returning to nature. A cycle of renewal, appealing only if death remained abstract. But being awake, she refuses to surrender to its grasp. This wouldn't mark her end. She battles, fists pounding the sand. Her will to break free from the clutches of time is a blazing fire. But the sand, a formidable opponent, retaliates after each blow, a relentless force of nature. In this struggle between human and elemental force, the black grains became harbingers of mortality, challenging her spirit at every effort.

WISH

Sand sprinkles onto her mask as Omega's punches upward intensify with herculean strength. Ferocious determination overtakes Omega, driven to shatter the drowning suffocation of sand. After every strike, her strength grows. Despite the weight of sodden sand, her spirit burns. Courage fueled by survival. Omega refuses to quit, pushing herself beyond her physical limits as she battles to conquer her sandy prison and emerge victorious. Finally, she escapes her sandy tomb. The interloper embodies a tale recounted through the ages by generations past, now transformed into the living embodiment of that timeless narrative. Omega has risen from the dead.

She resurfaces; her hands claw though the sand like an ancient human. Human nature and emotions often seem permanent across time. Perhaps these personas—fundamental aspects of our being—will endure in our species until the very end of days on Earth. Her head swivels, scanning the horizon for her adversary, the ultimate consciousness entity. The subconscious mind of humanity, its technological aura challenging her escape. Alpha is her final obstacle, the last challenge she must overcome to break free.

Nearby, the unmoving figure of Shadow adds to the supernatural atmosphere of the twilight beach. Omega stares unwaveringly at Alpha, peering into the supercomputer. An almighty collective intelligence of humanity, encompassing even Omega's darker subconscious. Alpha has downloaded all personas, obtaining every single human ego that lived on Earth. She stood at a juncture, both transformed and unchanged, poised to confront her greatest enemy yet—herself. It is the familiar struggle with the reflection in the mirror, the endless quest to surpass yesterday's self. Today welcomed a new dawn, a day of judgment, a day of redemption, not merely for Omega, but for civilization. Wishful for transformation.

She keeps her eyes closed, trusting instincts more than ever. Omega begins to run, powered by a mystical force. Gravity emerges as her ally, aiding her pace as she launches herself through the sky toward Alpha. The supercomputer initiates its electromagnetic shock, but its efforts prove futile as Omega maintains keeping her eyes closed. She places her trust in her soul to lead the way. Alpha retaliates again releasing another electromagnetic shockwave, but Omega remains unfazed, the effect useless against her soulful determination.

Life doesn't offer breaks, but Omega knows she can create her own. She smashes her shoulder into Alpha, forcefully pushing the supercomputer backward toward the ocean. The interloper digs her heels into the black sand, like the ancient slaves laboring to move the massive stones of the pyramid during its construction. Omega exerts her utmost strength, driving Alpha backward. She is tapping into reservoirs of resilience previously untapped. The true measure of one's resilience emerges at the pinnacle moments in life. For Omega, that moment has finally arrived. Where prosperity intersects with a prepared mind, and hers is primed for the challenge. Omega channels every single ounce of her energy to push Alpha closer to the crashing waves. Displaying a strategic finesse, she creates distance before launching into another sprint as she pursues her goal. Time and time again, Omega repeats the cycle, sprinting back and forth, each collision with Alpha inching the supercomputer closer to the ocean's edge.

Though progress is slow, it proves effective, reminiscent of a snail's pace yet undeniably impactful. 'Tis the game of life, slow and steady wins the race. Alpha, in a last-ditch effort, unleashes a flurry of electromagnetism shockwaves in order to impede her advance, but Omega persists in her assault, with each collision bringing the supercomputer nearer to its impending demise. She delivers a final, decisive shove, launching Alpha into the ocean. The supercomputer is overwhelmed by the power of the sea, dragged away and submerged by the abyss. Even the most advanced technology must ultimately return to the ocean. A timeless force that has witnessed the rise and fall of countless species. From dinosaurs to computers. In the end, the ocean remains undefeated, outlasting all.

Exhausted yet exhilarated, Omega sinks to her knees, the taste of victory bittersweet on her lips. Running on fumes, Omega's reserves were depleted, but her urgency remains. She knows she has to press on, to find the bomb and complete her mission. Her attention shifts to Shadow, who remains still, a frozen witness to their shared ordeal. As Omega reaches out to assist, Shadow's form crumbles, collapsing onto the black sand. Her shadow of goodness had reached its journey's end. Bound by the laws of limbo, it could venture no further. Even light must find its exit, as darkness holds sway over the soul's passage. Parting ways is sad, as even the faintest remnants of our former selves linger, reluctant to be discarded. Omega never wanted to let go, but in order to move on, she has no choice but to say goodbye.

Omega listens intently as Shadow speaks, their words carrying a finality. "You have to go alone. This is the end for me."

Her expression softens, a silent acknowledgment passing between them as she accepts the inevitable.

"You will make it, and at last, I can find peace," whispers the Shadow, uttering its final farewell.

Omega accepts the truth. It was the end of their journey together. A gentle touch and she bids farewell to her guide. Everything in life is left behind, even our own shadows are unable to accompany us into the eternal unknown. Omega wanders away from her shadow.

Standing alone on the beach, this time with her shadow gone, she feels even more alone. It had been her confidant, her closest companion, the one entity that truly comprehended her soul. The shadow of a person is unparalleled, a best friend from birth until the final breath. Omega's serenity is overtaken by the approaching sounds of war. Gathering herself, she shakes off the emotional toll of having to let go and bolts toward the rowboat. Taking one last glance back at Shadow, now embraced by the ocean. Bittersweet emotions consume Omega. The silhouette of the vibrant figure vanishes. A final farewell and promise of eternal rest. The sea, a sanctuary that welcomes all, whether in life or death.

Omega exerts her strength against the violent waves, shoving the rowboat further into the churning ocean. Rough waves pound against her body, but she refuses to stop. She has come too far to be deterred now. Despite tumultuous waters, she persists and pushes through the crashing waves until the rowboat is accepted by the ocean. The distant horizon is illuminated by vivid lights from the warzone, displaying a haunting glow across the twilight sky. Accompanied by the hostile sounds of explosions and sirens in the distance. The apocalyptic doom drives Omega to row harder, her muscles straining against the oars as she creates a widening chasm of separation from the chaos. Omega rows... a little further... a little further... even further into the ocean. The cacophony of war gradually fades into silence, swallowed by the waves. While looking over her shoulder, Omega's realization dawns upon her: She has departed from the island of limbo. A tear traces a path down her cheek. She is poised for her rendezvous with destiny upon the open waters, a pioneer driven by a hopeful wish.

The sky undergoes a remarkable transformation, shedding its cloak of twilight and revealing a vibrant violet. A surreal panorama, a scene so fantastical that even the most imaginative surrealist painters could only dream of capturing it on canvas. Omega continues to row, her eyes scanning the boundless horizon, wishing for hope. At last, her searching eyes discover a spot that resonates. She stops rowing, lifting her mask from her face as she savors the event. Omega closes her eyes. Inhaling deeply, she releases a breath she didn't realize she was holding and opens her eyes to find herself enveloped in the pure, untainted air. Gone is the oppressive veil of radiation that plagued the atmosphere. Oxygen had returned. In this place unlike any other she had encountered before, the poison disappeared, giving rise to a new world of purity. This was the genesis of life.

A radiant smile graces her features, joy coursing through her being as she basks in the newfound freedom to breathe. Omega explores her pocket; she encounters a familiar weight and retrieves the hourglass that has accompanied her on this journey. For the first time, she realizes that time was now on her side. She watches the sand noticing a subtle shift in its movement. A silent directive guiding her eyes downwards, toward the bottom of the sea. She feels intrigued by this unexpected sign. Indeed, the journey to victory often entails navigating into difficult scenarios. It was only fitting that such a formidable trial would be encountered. Omega drops the hourglass, a simple toss. She bids farewell to the confines of temporal existence. Time: Its nature debated endlessly, yet its essence is always relative. The sands of time descend into the ocean. As time sails on, carried by the currents, it gradually sinks deeper.

Standing proud, Omega readies herself for the next leg of her quest. An odyssey so epic, even Gilgamesh himself would nod in admiration. Facing the horizon, Omega puts on her mask, steeling herself for what lies beneath the surface. Realizing she must confront the source of her fears, she dives into the ocean.

The hourglass drifts underwater, a picturesque elegance. Its grains slipped through the neck, vanishing into the fathomless sea and tracing the cadence of time in this aqueous environment. Time reunites with water, a timeless union. Time and water endlessly entangled. A passionate intimacy, their bond essential for the emergence of life from the abyss of nonexistence. From humble quarks, those elemental particles that helped form matter, one immutable law prevailed: They forever existed in pairs. And akin to quarks in the quantum domain, water and time mirrors this symbiotic duality. A flawless convergence born of cosmic alignment.

Omega persists in her descent. A drifter amongst the sea, each stroke a defiant thrust toward her destination. Her every plunge getting closer to the obscure treasure. She senses a paradigm shift, a wordless summon. Her thoughts crystallize, her awareness attunes to the ethereal melody of concealed truths. During her descent into the sea, time had slipped away unnoticed. There were no signs of life, no traces of the vibrant ecosystem that usually thrived in these waters. It was as if ocean life had vanished, leaving behind only the interplay between Omega and the water. A lost interloper in an otherwise silent expanse, where emptiness stretched out endlessly. Neither more nor less than the vastness surrounding her. Doubt briefly creeps in, and Omega questions if it is too late. But she reassures herself that she is right on course. "Just a little further," she urges herself as she pushes forward just a little more.

Then, amidst the cerulean blue, bubbles ascend. *Tadpoles*, their sleek bodies slicing through the water. Expressing a beautiful grace. These creatures were the egg of human existence. Primal ancestors setting standards for the inception of life.

They ascend toward the surface, lured by an influential calling. Tadpoles swim higher and higher, as if destined for the divine. Like angels in the water, they reach for the promises of Heaven and salvation above. Omega savors the vitality. A reassurance that life found a way, yet again.

WISH

A rebirth of creation unfolds. She presses onward in her solitary descent, guided by an inner resolution. Reflecting on the myriad wishes of humanity across time, Omega wonders if all these desires could be united into a single wish. Perhaps what humanity truly yearned for was freedom. Freedom from the constraints that civilization had imposed upon their souls.

It was a bottomless descent, until at last, she reaches the ocean floor. There, amidst the sand, lay the object of her quest: the *Nuclear Bomb*. It rests in the sand as a sinister artifact, the harbinger of apocalypse. Devilish and chilling, akin to Satan trapped in ice depicted in Dante's *Inferno*. Omega swims toward the bomb, free of terror by the danger it embodies. Despite the looming threat, she calmly approaches. Her hands make contact with the bomb's exterior as Omega diligently searches for a remote trigger, but her efforts are useless. The bomb is encased in an impenetrable shield, and its countdown ominously continues ticking away. There is no halting this doomsday invention. Less than a minute remaining and tension mounts, reminiscent of the anticipation preceding space exploration from another era.

Like the beanstalk in the infamous tale of *Jack and the Beanstalk*, anticipation swells, reaching towering heights. Time, the most important gift of life, is dwindling, signaling the potential end for Omega and civilization. She thinks about failure. *Was her mission doomed*? *Was the world about to crumble into oblivion*? And the child, *were they lost to her forever*? She longs to see their face again, to hold their hand and believe anything is possible once more under daylight. A dream that she wants to make a reality.

Acknowledging the ineffectiveness of her strategy, Omega embraces her destiny, recognizing it as a fate that all must eventually confront in their own time. Her head leans against the nuclear bomb, gently feeling its power on her psyche. Then, she releases the straps of her mask, removing her precious shield, and presses a tender kiss upon the nuclear bomb. Her eyes close, surrendering to the inevitable, finding peace in the quiet acceptance of her fate. Omega welcomes her mortality, recognizing that in the end, Father Time wins, undefeated by any mortal endeavor. *Immortality,* she finally understands, *is but an illusion, one that even time itself would eventually lose to.* Even the illustrious Gilgamesh, hailed as the founder of written literature, penned his acceptance of mortality eons ago. His timeless wisdom resonates through history, inspiring infinite gods and religions to walk the path of acceptance in their own narratives. Death is the worm at the core of the human condition, forever immersed into our DNA. No entity could evade this fundamental law. Ultimately, physics is the creator, shaping destinies of the divine. Then, a thunderous roar and the Nuclear Bomb erupts. Its raw power consumes Omega and everything in its vicinity in an overwhelming burst of light and energy.

* * *

From the tranquil nature of a lake, Omega bursts out. Born again. She resurfaces, met by the breathtaking vista of the Sun's descent. The sky ablaze, streaks of tangerine and copper. Clad in her mask, Omega transcends the limitations of limbo, stepping into an ethereal dimension. She swims toward the awaiting shore, entering another ancient world. Déjà vu comes over Omega. The absence of ice unveils a new reality, as the once-frozen plains now extend into an expanse of unfamiliar warmth. Omega observes the primordial allure of Africa's ancient beauty. Majestic cheetahs, giraffes, lions, elephants, and monkeys traverse the Savannah, embodying the untamed soul of the land. In the raw, unfettered wilds of Africa, before the arrival of humanity, the land pulses, unleashing a primal energy. Creatures roam freely under the blazing Sun. A savage paradise, where lions roar their dominance, elephants trumpet their authority, and the Savannah echoes the primal rhythms of nature's unchained symphony. Africa, the cradle of life and birthplace of humanity. An environment embracing the beauty of the natural world. God's ultimate creation on the planet they called Earth.

Along the distance, a solitary fire spreads its glow upon the horizon. Smoke ascended in twisted tendrils, mingling into the fading light of twilight. Intrigued by the flicker of flames, Omega advances toward the origin, her curiosity ignited. Above, stars emerge one by one, their luminous waltz painting the night sky. Cosmic gifts as they whirl at the speed of light. Everything in reality spins and revolves around each other in motion. Van Gogh's *Starry Night* would evoke a scope of pride, as it inspires this image. This was Earth in its primal quintessence, untouched by the hand of innovation. The sole invention of the era was fire, a potent catalyst that sparked the evolution of human intelligence.

Omega draws nearer, and she beholds an African tribe, engaged in a jubilant dance around the fire. Rhythmic gestures, a harmonious tribute representing the joy of life. The tribe discovered harmony through uncomplicated acts of engagement, reveling in the raw nature of being alive. These simple emotions were lost in the complexities of humanity's future. Souls of the tribe were content, filled to the brim. In this era, overindulgence was not a concern; they had reached a state of sufficiency where "enough" truly meant *enough*. Captivated, Omega observes their ritual, sensing something stirring, calling her closer. Then, one more time like clockwork, the Ancient Astronaut emerges, commanding absolute reverence from the tribe. Celebratory dancing stops and they bow in respect. All of them pray in admiration. The ancient entity moves toward

Omega, provoking a unique standoff. They neither gave nor took from each other; together, they journeyed through the edges of time and beyond, connected by an everlasting relationship. Then, breaking the deadlock, the Ancient Astronaut extends a hand in a gesture of peace. Trust serves as the cornerstone for any genuine connection in humanity.

Omega accepts the gesture, clasping the Ancient Astronaut's hand firmly. She found a peaceful resolution and returned home to her ancestors. Then, suddenly, the Ancient Astronaut removes its bronze helmet, unveiling nothing but a void beneath its mask. A headless being, its form devoid of a face, existing only as an ethereal spirit. Omega hypnotically watches the unfathomable emptiness. Next, the Ancient Astronaut sheds its outer garb, displaying a nebulous mist of *energy* pulsating the ethos of life. God didn't need a human form to exist. All a god truly is, would be the energy of reality that creates complexities from energy.

The first law of thermodynamics expressed: Energy cannot be created nor destroyed. This energy abides by those laws, finding its soul entangled in the human mind, shaping it throughout time. Immersed in that creation existed the duality of good and evil. Perfection remains subjective, existing solely in the eyes of the beholder. And the human experience is the greatest miracle of all, for better or worse. Omega watches in awe as the energy coils and spins, gaining momentum until it ascends into the sky, vanishing into the eternal universe.

Enthralled by the surreal encounter, Omega's thoughts swarm after witnessing God. She closes her eyes, her soul whispering to the infinite energy of reality, longing for the familiar embrace of home.

Beneath the heavens, Omega traverses the maze of barley, her movements purposeful yet imbued in quiet contemplation. She wanders through the labyrinth of crops, her eyes occasionally drawn to the celestial canopy above, lost in a reverie of wonder. A picturesque backdrop hinting at the next world. Moving forward, Omega arrives at a tranquil clearing where a charming cabin emerges from the endless fields of barley. Freed from its ice prison, the cabin emanates an aura of serenity. Omega had at last found her way back to where she belonges. Positioned before the cabin, the familiar *mini globe* rests peacefully on the ground. Omega lifts the totem, cradling it in her hands for a brief moment. Her posture mirrors the ancient emergence pose, her silhouette echoing the intertwined shapes of a brain and heart.

The interloper was both the alpha and omega, the genesis and culmination of all existence. As she gazes upwards, Omega's eyes notice what seems to be a mirage. A doorway, a portal, toward another alternate dimension. The traveler's journey was far from over. Restlessness had always been her companion, for in life, the greatest discoveries awaited those who dared to wander. New horizons are always in reach, if only one chooses to seek them. The flame of curiosity still burns bright inside her soul. Wandering through every corner of existence yet feeling anchored to nowhere in particular, Omega's mindset remains fixated on one sole destination: the end. She sets the mini globe back upon the ground and steps through the threshold, venturing into the unknown alone, the door sealing shut behind her.

Left behind, the mini globe rests in tranquil solitude, unperturbed and serene, yet far from lost. As they draw nearer, they observe the energy of reality hovering above the mini globe. The creator of all things persists in an eternal flow, an entity impervious to destruction. Energy entangles for eternity in this idyllic dimension. Where the past, present, and future merge into a singular reality. The globe begins to lift from the ground, spinning faster until the entire world expeditiously rotates on its axis.

The Ancient Astronaut breaches the surface of the ocean, droplets spring off their bronze metallic suit, glinting in the *sunlight* like shards of diamonds. The figure treads water patiently. They scan the horizon. An aura of wisdom from all generations. The coastline was a rugged beauty of cliffs and sandy beaches kissed by gentle waves. Seagulls fly and wail overhead, adding their voices to the symphony of the sea. The Ancient Astronaut freestyle swims through crystalline waters. Rays of light beam onto the surface. Gliding with each stroke leads the Ancient Astronaut closer to the awaiting coast, where the golden sands stretch out invitingly. As the Ancient Astronaut nears the coastline, anticipation builds. The sound of waves crashing against the rocks grows louder, blending harmoniously. A chorus of avian melodies.

The environment becomes more enchanting. A strange feeling permeates the sunny coastline, as if entering a gateway into a magical dimension. Then, from tales of miracles from another world, humans could be seen frolicking along the coast. Not just a couple, but a massive crowd, enjoying a magical summer day by the beach. People on the shore appeared distorted, their features wavering like mirages in the heat. They existed in a different plane of reality, separated from the ordinary world by an invisible barrier. The atmosphere had an otherworldly vibe, reminiscent of stories of the afterlife. Curious and intrigued, the Ancient Astronaut steps closer, drawn by the enigmatic aura enveloping the beach. *What mysteries awaited on this surreal seaside encounter?* They felt the urge to explore, as all children of God encounter at one time in their life— investigators and detectives of existence.

* * *

The Ancient Astronaut ponders the meaning of the cryptic message: *Portals of the known and unknown eventually become fulfilled.* Reflecting on their vast knowledge, the Ancient Astronaut considers the concept of portals as more than physical gateways. Portals, they realize, represented transitions between different states of evolution, pathways between what is familiar and what is beyond comprehension. These were the doorways through which beings traversed, connecting worlds and cultures in a vast web of communication. And then, the notion of fulfillment dawned upon the Ancient Astronaut. *Perhaps,* they thought, *the fulfillment of these portals lay not in their discovery but in the journey itself.* The endless pursuit of understanding, quest for enlightenment, and exploration of maintaining virtue. The figure persists in combing the beach, familiarity driving them. An unexplained energy tugs at their being. Suddenly, it materializes before them— the unmistakable silhouette of the child shadow. The Ancient Astronaut wanders toward them. The child shadow dances playfully on brown sand, contours shifting under a gentle breeze. The Ancient Astronaut studies it intently, observing delicate curves and lines, feeling a familiar energy emanating from their silhouette. Coming closer, they feel an intense connection, déjà vu that defies reality.

Finally, standing before the child shadow, the Ancient Astronaut reaches out a hand, hesitating for just a moment before gently touching the shimmering outline. The figure is enveloped in reflections, prompting it to step back and remove its mask, unveiling Omega. At last, she has located the child. There exists no connection more profound nor enduring than the dynamic between the woman and child. Their relationship surpasses the constraints of time. Omega has achieved her long-awaited objective. Once more, she finds herself reunited with the child, rekindled. This moment felt like a dream and the afterlife, to which degree are both relative. Omega finds herself in a surreal state, suspended between wakefulness and dreams. Time lost its meaning, reality and fantasy united into an indistinguishable haze.

ICE

She has escaped her reality in limbo. Now, she faces the afterworld. This place was where good souls of humanity roamed. Everything is relative. Omega has ultimately attained her objective of upholding her own goodness during the storm of evil—a universal lesson in life.

Drifting between worlds, Omega transcended darkness rising above humanity's flaws. Love, radiant and pure, had become her guiding light, leading her to a dimension untouched by the taint of evil. Distinctions faded away, and Omega found peace in eternity. Whether awake or asleep, she had found her sanctuary, where the world dissolved into the harmonious melody of love. Time expanded into infinity, defying all conventional notions of measurement. A canvas upon which she could paint her faithful wish, free from the constraints of mortal existence.

Omega releases the hourglass from her hands, its final grains of sand cascading down with a quiet whisper. Turning away from the arrow of time, she takes the child's hand and begins to walk, leaving the concept of time behind them.

The sea breeze gently tousles her hair as Omega and the child walk along the shore. Sunlight was a miracle, a dream finally welcoming Omega into its domain. Spectacular sounds of waves crashing against the coast accompanying their steps. *How many times did those waves crash since the beginning?* A timeless constant of nature, destined to occur until the planets end. Omega glances down at the child, pride flickering in her eyes.

The child looks up at her, keeping an innocent curiosity, its hand still clasped tightly in hers. There was a serendipitous compassion. They reach the water's edge, and Omega releases the child's hand and kneels down in the sand, her fingers trailing through the grains as she gazes out at the ocean. Beside her, the child no longer a shadow, but a real, innocent, eight-year-old girl. Omega looks over at the girl, immediately struck by a sense of déjà vu. She recognizes her instantly, knowing that she has seen her before in a past life because she was her in another life.

The girl watches Omega and maintains a quiet understanding beyond her years. "Will it hurt?" she asks softly, a whisper gently carried away by the wind.

Omega smiles gently, her eyes reflecting wisdom from her journey. "No, my love," she replies, expressing a trusting tone. "It will not hurt. It's the next step in our journey."

The girl nods, acceptance settling over her. Together, they stand in silence, the only sound around the gentle crashing of waves against the coast. Three birds soar through the sky, embodying the divine. The last rays of sunlight disappear beneath the horizon. Omega and the girl make a final wish: to wake up from the dream of death and enter the sublime. Never to look back again, and to experience only the goodness reality has to offer. Omega reaches out her hand to the girl once more. Manifesting a smile, she takes it, her small fingers intertwining with Omega's as they step forward into the sea. United, they disappear beneath the waves, their shapes blending into the infinite abyss. Departing paradise, they journey through realms and transcend into another dimension. Never to part again, for within every life, every individual and everything is connected by the union of duality. Their spirits seeking nirvana, an ultimate place of peace. Inside the hourglass, sands of time continue to flow, a cyclical fluidity for eternity.

The End

*A wish begins from the dreams of those
who dare to risk it all.*

ICE

What one man calls God, another calls the laws of physics.
Nikola Tesla

ICE

Learn a little bit about everything.
Linda Stewart

ICE

Parable

ICE

Echoes of Eternity

The Sun dipped low on the horizon, and I knew my last day on Earth had arrived. I found myself wandering along an eternal coast. The crunch of sand beneath my feet echoing solitude of my surroundings. I was so alone. All I had were my thoughts. Air carried finality, the scents of salt and seaweed were prevalent, along with the tang of uncertainty. During each step, I felt the impending end crushing my spirit. I clutched my journal tightly to my chest, the leather cover worn and weathered from years of use. My best friend. It was my companion in these final moments. These pages were witness to my theories, my philosophies, and every nuance in between. I would pour out my last thoughts, my fears, and my hopes. Sitting down upon a rock, I couldn't help but appreciate the ancient boulder. When one nears the twilight of life, an appreciation for everything dawns upon them. Rocks were magic; after all, they imprinted life on Earth. I opened the pages of my journal and began to write. I wrote of the beauty of the world around me. I loved the Earth; it was the greatest planet of them all. But deep down, I knew that soon it would be lost to the void. I wrote of the people I had loved and lost, of the memories that now seemed so distant and fragile. And I wrote of the fear

ICE

that gnawed at my soul, the fear of death. The Doomsday Clock ticked ever closer to midnight. I felt a desperate urge to escape, to flee from the inevitability of my fate. So, I pushed off from the coast in a rowboat. Oars cut through water. I rowed as far as my strength would allow. Until my arms burned beyond exhaustion. My breath came in ragged gasps, and I was finished at the edge of the world. I put my hands in the sea and splashed a palmful of water onto my head, savoring the final cooling effect of water—the best gift of all. Then there, in the middle of the sea, I finished my story. I penned the final words, my vision blurred by tears. I closed my journal shut for the last time and tossed it into the sea. Believing the words should return home to where they came. I watched it disappear beneath the waves, and I was calm. Peace found my soul. And then I turned my eyes to the horizon, where the Sun intimidated, a fiery orb waiting to explode. Minutes ticked away, and I remained on the rowboat, suspended between sea and sky, between life and death. Finally, when the last seconds slipped away, I took a breath and let myself fall backward into the sea. Water submerged over my soul and the world went supernova. But I was grateful, accepting my end. Because in the end, death was but a dream, an illusion in existence. Cyclical cycles controlled by the seductress of time itself. The further I sank into the sea, I knew that I was returning to God. To the place where all life had emerged, entering the infinite dream of eternity.

Stephon Stewart
Theorist. Author. Filmmaker.

Stephon Stewart is the Founder and CEO of The Drifter LLC, a pioneering startup dedicated to combating the pressing issue of carbon dioxide (CO2) emissions in industrialized regions. DRIFTER spearheads the deployment of CO2 autonomous drones, leveraging cutting-edge technology to extract CO2 directly from the sky, thereby revolutionizing carbon extraction efforts. Beyond his environmental endeavors, Stewart boasts a diverse portfolio of creative accomplishments as a writer and film director. Stewart crafts metaphysical stories and fantasy thrillers infused with Nostradamus themes. In his inaugural narrative film, "PSYCHE," he embarked on an odyssey through the labyrinthine corridors of the human mind, a quest to unearth the meaning of life. With artificial intelligence as the antagonist and protagonist, the film navigates the complexities of consciousness in a cinematic exploration that promises to be both enlightening and thought-provoking.

Stewart's deep concern for humanity's future has been a driving force behind his work, notably his creation

"DRY." The dystopian story was adapted into a compelling graphic novel and novel. The story serves as a testament to Stewart's dedication to ignite hope and drive action for the transformation toward a sustainable solution for future generations. In his upcoming novel, "ICE," Stewart explores human history, exploring both its conquests and tragedies through a time-traveling saga. This epic narrative vividly portrays how civilizations, in their pursuit of progress, may inadvertently exhaust their energy resources, ultimately culminating in a devastating nuclear war over natural resources. Stewart's final novel, "WET" envisions a future where humanity, battling an inferno-ravaged world, wields the power of weather manipulation to conjure a supernatural flood of rising seas. Amid this apocalyptic deluge, a chance encounter binds the fates of a man and a woman, thrusting them into a desperate struggle for survival as the world sinks.

Stewart's artistic vision extends to the canvas, where he paints depictions of potential Earth scenarios if we neglect our planet. This surreal artwork, now featured on climate-conscious apparel under the name "GLOBAL TRANSFIGURATION" reflects his passion for environmental ethics.

Amidst his creative endeavors, Stewart continues to delve into physics, further enriching his knowledge of evolution, the universe and reality. His collaboration with a neuroscientist has led to a theory published in the Open Journal for Biophysics. This innovative work focuses on unblocking blood vessels and addressing clogged arteries with an aim to extend life. His fascination with evolution led him to a collaboration with a theoretical neuroscientist, igniting his research efforts and producing the publication in Evolutionary Anthropology on brain evolution. Aimed at unraveling the mystery of how humans attained unparalleled consciousness through the transformative influence of fire. His scientific contributions are available for exploration on Google Scholar.

Stewart's multifaceted journey threads storytelling, art, science, and a commitment to unveil the logical truth of reality to humanity. Through this blend of disciplines, he seeks to illuminate existence, by inspiring contemplation in the hearts and minds of those who encounter his work.